Seeking Osiris

By Hilary Cawston

Text copyright © Hilary Wilson 2014
Cover image © Hilary Wilson 2014

All Rights Reserved

To the little girl whose birth announcement inspired this story.
Thank you for lending me your name.

Table of Contents

Chapter 1: What's in a Name?
Chapter 2: The Luck of the Draw
Chapter 3: First Impressions
Chapter 4: A Change of Plan
Chapter 5: Arrivals and Departures
Chapter 6: Friends and Allies
Chapter 7: Council of War
Chapter 8: Turning Points
Chapter 9: A Meeting of Minds
Chapter 10: Damage Limitation
Chapter 11: Moments of Doubt
Chapter 12: A Change of Minds
Chapter 13: Questions of Integrity
Chapter 14: The Beginning of the End
Chapter 15: Revelations
Chapter 16: Loose Ends
Afterword

Chapter 1: What's in a Name?

Perhaps he should have taken his mother's advice and paid a visit to the barber, Simon thought, pushing the reddish-brown hair back from his forehead. She had been dropping hints for ages but, much as he wanted this research post, he drew the line at cutting his hair. As if exchanging his habitual jeans and sweatshirt for a suit were not bad enough, although Dr Beaumont's reputation suggested that the temporary discomfort was the least sacrifice required to make a good impression. He straightened his tie, wondering if it was too gaudy and regretting, for a moment, his refusal of Dad's offer of a grey one. But no, he was not a grey-tie sort of person, and his mother's Samsonian remedy would have made him feel a complete fraud.

He had tried to read Beaumont's most recent paper on the train but had given it up in favour of the latest Terry Pratchett. He put the churning of his stomach down to guilt over his lack of preparation, although it probably had more to do with his skipping breakfast, and the short walk from the station had only the mildest calming effect. Once through the university gates he inspected the white-on-navy signs with the oak-tree logo to discover that Main Reception was located in the St. George's Building, where he would also find the Buckminster Library, the Registry, and Theatre A. A stroll along a tree-lined path brought him before the imposing grey façade of the oldest building on the site.

Huge pillars, the full three storeys in height, supported a classical pediment. Rows of identical sash windows were regularly placed to left and right. Tired tendrils of ivy clung to the far end masking the junction with a more recent concrete block, added at right angles. In the cornice he saw, deeply carved in Roman capitals, ST GEORGE'S HOSPITAL MDCCCLXXII. Out of habit, Simon converted the numerals in his head; fifty years after Champollion, and fifty years before Tutankhamun. He guessed that the exterior of the building was protected by listed status but inside the designers had been given a free hand. Beyond automatic sliding glass panels the original heavy wooden doors stood open admitting him to a light and modern foyer, a dream in brushed aluminium and pale oak, with the corporate blue of the carpet just a tone or two warmer than the grey stone of the window surrounds. He gave his name to the smiling receptionist who checked her computer screen.

'Ah, yes, Mr Evers-Goodhill. You are a little early but I believe Dr Beaumont has sent someone to meet you.'

She indicated a tall stick-insect of a young man who had been trying to blend in with the foliage of a potted plant display. He had heard Simon's name and was already moving to greet him with outstretched hand. 'Hi, I'm Peter French. I'm one of Dr Beaumont's MSc students. The Doc asked me to find you. As your appointment isn't 'til eleven, do you want to go for coffee or would you like a whirlwind tour of the sights?'

'Coffee sounds great, thanks – er – Peter?'

'Call me Pete, everybody does. We go this way. I've been told to take you to Theatre A,' he raised his eyebrows suggesting that this was some kind of honour. The symbols of a coffee cup and crossed cutlery on the sign indicating 'Theatre A' informed Simon that they were not heading for a lecture theatre.

'Did you have a good journey?'

'Not too bad. The worst thing was getting up at the crack of dawn.'

'Yeah, we students don't do mornings.' Pete grinned, a spark of mischief in his brown eyes lighting up his narrow face.

'You mean, you're not outside the library every morning waiting for it to open?' Simon was a couple of years older than Pete so he could speak with some authority. 'What's the collection here like?'

'Pretty good, apart from its location. Biological sciences are in the sub-basement – bilge in the bilges,' Pete grinned at the in joke.

'And archaeology in the attic?' Simon suggested.

'You got it!'

Theatre A was fronted by double swing-doors with porthole windows and a chalk board to one side. 'Today's Specials', Simon read, included thick vegetable soup, lasagne and spicy chicken wraps. He wondered if the catering here would attain the same mediocre heights as his previous institution, where reality always fell short of the menu descriptions. Inside, the café's décor was in stark contrast to what he had seen so far. The walls were half-tiled in dark green, the floor was grey-green linoleum, or its modern equivalent, and displayed in glass cases above the servery were shiny metal tools that Simon, at first, took for kitchen equipment. Waiting as Pete ordered their coffee, he identified the 'tools' as surgical instruments and seeing the girl behind the hatch dressed in green hospital scrubs, he realised that this must have been an operating theatre, hence the café's name. Now, judging by the clientele, it was a venue favoured by university staff and mature students. The prices seemed a little steep for undergraduate budgets. Even assuming he was lucky enough to get the job Simon doubted that he would be eating here often.

Pete carried their cups to a shelf-like counter along one wall where they perched on old-fashioned wooden laboratory stools. 'Makes you feel at home, doesn't it?' the student said, 'It's mostly medics and science bods you find in here. The sensitive souls from Arts and Humanities don't like to think of what went on in here in the olden days.'

'Not too macabre for you, though?'

'Nah! When you've excavated plague pits without losing your squeam there's not a lot you can't face. Besides, I don't suppose even the tiles are original. Health and Safety will've seen to that. Anyway, what about you? What made you apply for this job?'

Pushing back his hair Simon answered with barely a moment's hesitation, 'Dr Beaumont, of course. In the field of archaeobotany there really is only one expert. The chance to work with H.P. Beaumont was too good to pass up.'

Pete nodded, then said, 'If you don't mind me asking, that double-barrelled name of yours, the Evers part I mean. You wouldn't be related to Eric Evers by any chance?'

Simon's heart sank. Was there nowhere he could escape from the charismatic malignity he knew as Uncle Eric? Affecting the nonchalant tone he used for such occasions, he said, 'Unfortunately, yes. He's my mother's brother.'

Pete almost dropped his cup. 'No shit! Well, I wouldn't let Doc Beaumont know that if you want to impress her. Eric Evers is not her favourite person and that's about the understatement of the millennium.'

'Really?' This was not the reaction that his Evers connection usually evoked. 'Is there something I should know?' Then Simon's brain replayed what Pete had just said. 'I'm sorry, but did you say "her"? Dr Beaumont is a woman?'

Pete's anxious frown gave way to an impish lop-sided smirk. 'You didn't know? Oh, this is going to be interesting! Can I be a fly on the wall?'

Simon was conscious of sweat beading on his brow and his hands were clammy. He had not yet had enough caffeine to explain his quickened pulse. Two things now dominated his thoughts. How could he have been so crass as to assume that H.P. Beaumont was male, and why did it matter to him so much that she wasn't? And another thing, was Uncle Eric going to blight his career before it had even started? If Pete had recognised the name then surely Dr Beaumont, with her apparent antipathy towards his relative, would have picked it up from his application forms. His secret was out before he had known it ought to be kept a secret. Why were names so important?

*

Names matter. Hermione was a name she could live with. Hermiones were rare in the days before Harry Potter but then the name became fashionable, and now they were two a penny – in primary schools. Of course, when she was born thirty-something years ago Miss Granger was not even a twinkle in J.K.'s eye. She had become accustomed to having her name mangled by people whose tongues were unfamiliar with its Greek cadences. She readily answered to even the most approximate of pronunciations, as long as she did not have to explain her second initial. In fact, H.P. Beaumont would go to such lengths to ensure that people understood about Hermione that they never thought to ask about her other name.

Hermione's grandmother had called her skinny and suggested she was not eating properly, but Nonna's concept of the ideal female figure was from another age, another culture. Hermione's short, dark hair framed an oval face dominated, in her own opinion, by a long straight nose. Her thick eyebrows had never been plucked into shape because she could not bear the thought of the pain involved. Her grey eyes, speckled with brown, had been described by her optician as being the colour of a gull's eggs. Knowing that she was not pretty, Hermione tried to emphasise her intelligence, by the plain cut of her hair, the sober frames of her spectacles, the discreet stud earrings and the sensible shoes. She had cultivated a studious air that was, somehow, the archetypal Hermione as later envisaged by Rowling.

At school, a private all-girls establishment, where nicknames were more often used than given names, she had been known as Saucy, which had been so inappropriate to her character that it had been considered one of the better soubriquets of her generation. She bore this indignity because it helped to conceal the dreadful truth behind the P. She told everyone that she had a godmother called Patricia, who had been her mother's bridesmaid. She let it be assumed that she had been named after Auntie Pat. That was good enough for most school friends.

The true potential for humiliation had been brought home to her when she had attended her older brother's graduation. As each graduand was called to the stage, his or her full name, unabridged, warts and all, had been announced to the assembly. Every unusual name, every long combination of names, every foreign name that caused the Beadle to stumble over its pronunciation, drew raucous applause from the crowd. It was easier for a man to carry off an outlandish name. Her brother had always introduced himself by his initials in such a confident manner that no one thought to ask what they stood for, but it was different for a girl. When T.C.'s moment arrived and the audience cheered his name to the rafters, Hermione realised the horror in store for her when she stepped on to that stage in her own right, under the full glare of the auditorium spotlights.

By the end of her third year at university, the Potter effect had begun to take hold and Hermione was in fashion at last, but as Graduation Day approached the anxiety mounted. She had considered feigning illness. She even toyed with the idea of breaking something but winced at the mere thought. The truth was that Hermione could not find it in her heart to deprive her parents of their pride in her achievement. For days before the ceremony she had suffered insomnia, indigestion and borderline panic as she steeled herself to face the moment when she would hear her own name, pronounced in sonorous tones that no one could ignore. The memory of that momentous occasion was still raw, the damage to her self confidence still unhealed.

Since then the use of her initials had become her defence and it was as H.P. Beaumont that her reputation had been made. After all, she reasoned, this device had proved successful and lucrative for A.S. Byatt and J.K. Rowling, neither of whom had such an embarrassing name as hers to hide. People set such store by names. Certain names led to preconceptions about personality which were hard to shake off. Who could take seriously an astrophysicist named Chardonnay? Who would have confidence in the artistic flair of an interior designer called Ethel? Who could trust the objectivity of a Research Assistant with the surname Evers?

Whatever her personal misgivings, Simon had answered all her questions well, although he was clearly nervous. The way he kept pushing back that wayward fringe would soon have her reaching for the scissors. The tie had been a mistake, too, but his credentials fitted her requirements perfectly and among the many applicants for the post there was no other half as well qualified. Forcing herself to overlook the unfortunate part of his name she took comfort in the fact that Goodhill was the English version of her own surname. She must take this as a favourable omen. Hermione closed the file and leaned back in her chair. 'I think that's all I need to know. I'm happy to be able to offer you the post, Mr er-Evers-Goodhill.'

Stunned by his good fortune Simon hardly noticed her hesitation over the 'Evers'. As they shook hands across the desk he stammered his gratitude.

'You'll need to go to Human Resources and they'll tell you about the post-grad accommodation options. Later we'll sort out the registration for your PhD. I'm sure Peter is loitering about somewhere. I'll get him to show you around properly.'

Simon was still in a daze. He could not remember a thing about the interview. From the moment he had walked into the room and seen his idol for the first time he had been too stunned to think clearly. H.P. Beaumont was hardly in her thirties and behind the dark-rimmed spectacles lurked a passably attractive face. That would have been disconcerting enough had not Pete told him, on the way to her office, that Dr Beaumont believed Simon's Uncle Eric had plagiarised and corrupted the findings of some of her most important work. The fact that Eric Evers had made a great deal of money out of his 'did-aliens-colonise-the-Earth' brand of sensationalism had made matters worse. But H.P. Beaumont would not lower herself to contest the matter because that would have given academic credence to theories she considered ridiculous. People around her knew better than to speak *his* name in her presence.

Pete escorted him to the Administration block, glad of the chance to hear how things had gone. 'Did she ask you about Eric Evers?'

'No, he was never mentioned. Do you think I ought to have told her?'

'No way! Get stuck into the job first. Make yourself indispensable then it won't matter who you're related to.'

'You're probably right. No sense in looking for trouble.'

*

Wsir took Ast's hand as they stood together at the viewing port. 'The Bau who surveyed this planet were right about its potential. The scanners show that the inhabitants in several zones are already on the brink of civilization.'

'When will the lottery be drawn?'

'Soon. Before the end of the next planetary rotation we will know the location of our new home and who our companions are to be.'

'I can hardly believe it. At last the chance to start anew, to live the simple life we have always dreamt of.'

'You are not a little apprehensive that we are giving up so much?'

'A little. There has been plenty of time to think on the journey. I am sure it will be harder than any of us anticipates, but now this new world is closer than the old. We have arrived. There is no turning back.'

'No,' he squeezed her hand, 'No going back.'

Chapter 2: The Luck of the Draw

The Bau gathered in the eating hall, the only space on the ship big enough to hold them all at one time. Even so, Wsir found himself perched on a ledge against the rear wall with the mass of his shipmates between him and the small platform which was the focus of all their attention.

A map of the planet beneath them was projected on the wall behind the raised area and the potential settlers were studying it as closely as if they were seeing it for the first time. The sites identified for Experimental settlements were all close to water, either in one of the broad river valleys, or beside a substantial inland lake, or on a well-drained coastal plain. The crucial factor in the selection of these sites was the existence of agricultural communities, however primitive, into which the settlers hoped to merge. The original survey team had dismissed certain regions of the planet which were environmentally inhospitable, or where the native society was not sufficiently developed, or where the physical appearance of the inhabitants was too different from that of the Bau, but that did not stop the potential settlers speculating on what might be found in the featureless areas of the map. Wsir smiled in amusement at the constant murmur of discussion accompanied by pointing and some more expansive hand gestures, suggesting where they would like to go if they had any choice in the matter. Everyone knew that the order of the allocation of the sites for settlement would be decided by the drawing of lots. The lottery bowls had been arranged on a bench. Filtered by the deep tinted semi-translucent glass, the ballot rings were just visible while their colours remained unidentifiable.

Ast entered the hall through a side door. She had been working late into the night, studying the files on the biology of the indigenous beings of the planet, and she had overslept. She looked around the crowded room, searching for her mate. He waved his arms above his head to catch her attention and was rewarded by the brilliant smile that thrilled his heart still, after all their time together. While Ast wriggled through the throng, Wsir moved farther into the corner to allow her to sit beside him. As she took her seat, he said, 'You have not missed anything.'

Ast stretched her neck to peer over the crowd. 'They seem very excited.'

'And you are not?'

She gave a little snort, followed by a giggle. She sounded so like a youngling that he reached out a hand to ruffle her blue-black hair. She leaned into the paternal gesture and yawned. 'You stayed up too late,' he admonished her.

'I could not have settled. I needed to work.'

A ripple of noise, quashed almost as soon as it started, marked the arrival of the ship's commander. The senior Ba present, she was not to be included amongst the settlers, and so was deemed impartial enough to draw the ballots for the disposition of the settlement groups. During their long voyage from Perbau, Wsir had developed a great deal of respect for this elderly Ba, a respect that had been justified the previous evening when the Commander had entertained all the settlement leader candidates to what she had humorously described as their last proper meal. When he and his fellow leaders were assembled, she had surprised them with an unwelcome announcement.

'You must know that you are either very brave or very idealistic to believe that this Experiment can succeed,' she had said, 'but I cannot challenge your right to attempt it and I wish you every success. No one doubts your sincerity nor the dedication and perseverance you have all displayed during our time together on this ship. I know that you are as prepared as you could ever be for this venture and, though I am aware that my good wishes will be of little practical help, be assured that you have them.

'However, I have to tell you that a reassessment of the sites chosen for your settlement has shown that there are fewer areas than previously thought where the Bau can easily blend in with the native sentients. I have a duty to my species not to allow settlements that have no prospect of success, so I have arranged this evening to give you a last opportunity to reconsider. I will give you a final taste of what you are about to foreswear, the best of Ba food and drink, the best of Ba entertainment. If, when the evening is over, you feel that you cannot give up all that Ba culture has to offer, no one will think the worse of you for opting out of the Experiment. If, after everything, you are all

determined to continue, I have to say that yellow of you will be disappointed.'

As stewards brought in the first dishes there was a subdued air about the party. The Commander signalled the start of the meal by raising a morsel of bread in the age-old custom of greeting. 'With this bread I welcome you to your new home with the wish that there should always be bread upon your table.'

Her cook had prepared delicacies from all the home regions of the leader candidates. Wsir savoured the braised fowl flavoured with herbs from his beloved Dwat and a dessert topped with moonberries that was almost as good as the mooncake that Ast had cooked on their last day on Perbau. While they ate, Ba music played over the sound loop. The Commander's choice was subtle. Poignant words reminded them of the families and friends they had left behind. Evocative themes painted sound pictures of the Ba planet. The would-be settlers experienced a torrent of emotions as the flavours, scents and sounds of their home world, the world they had agreed to leave, possibly forever, assaulted their senses. Wsir saw tears in many eyes through the blear in his own. He was not surprised that this reminder of what they were giving up should have had the effect the Commander desired. By the end of the evening, red of his fellow leader potentials had chosen to withdraw their names from the ballot. Wsir had not the heart to tell Ast that there was very real chance that they would be returning to Perbau.

The Commander was speaking but, without the benefit of a voice projector, her words were indistinct. The crowd in the hall fell silent and all ears strained to hear her. A tech hurried forward to pin an amp bead to the Commander's tunic and suddenly her voice rang out across the hushed company. '...the crimson ballot.'

'What did she say?' Ast asked.

'I think she was saying that the first thing to do is to identify the survey sites. Then they will be matched to their leaders.'

The Commander lowered her hand into the crimson bowl and brought out a ring which she held up so that everyone could see. It was tawny. At once a tawny light appeared on the map. The first decision had been made, the theoretical Experiment was about to become reality.

The Commander's hand hovered over the red bowl. 'If she takes too long there will be people fainting,' Ast muttered.

Wsir found that he too had been holding his breath and forced himself to inhale deeply and slowly to steady his quickened pulse. When the Commander revealed the next ring as yellow, Ywti raised his arms in triumph, showing the yellow bands about his wrists. His mate was jumping up and down at his side. Wsir wondered if Ywti also had not been able to bring himself to tell his companions about the Commander's revelation the previous evening. Conscious of the anxious anticipation of the remaining candidates, the Commander called for quiet and returned to the crimson bowl to withdraw another ring. It was blue and when the red ring was drawn from the red bowl, Frya and her mate celebrated.

Every ring revealed reduced their chances of completing the mission for which they had prepared. Wsir closed his eyes and forced himself to breathe steadily preparing for the worst. In doing so, he missed the next couple of draws. He only opened his eyes again when Ast's elbow dug into his ribs. A cobalt light was shining in the corner of the continental mass which Wsir had always thought of as being shaped like a femi pear. This was the area he had secretly hoped would be his. He shut his eyes again, not bearing to see the Commander take the ring from the red bowl. Ast's sudden fierce embrace told him that it was green. He slid from his narrow seat and lifted one arm to show the green band. The other arm was immobilised by Ast's proprietorial grasp.

But the lottery was not yet completed. By the time leaders had been allocated to the red, amethyst and white sites, the sense of anticipation in the hall was almost tangible. Someone had noticed that only a pair of rings remained in each bowl. The Bau clustered around the leader candidates were talking in urgent whispers, their brows furrowed. What had happened?

The Commander recognised the reason for the restlessness and again appealed for quiet. 'It is clear that not all of you are aware of the necessary changes in our plans.' Wsir's conscience squirmed at the reprimand in her voice. He could not look at Ast, knowing that she too would be frowning in puzzlement. The Commander continued, 'Only red sites remain that are suitable for your settlement and, since yellow leader candidates have chosen to withdraw...' a communal intake of breath made the Commander pause. The silence was now almost overwhelming. All eyes turned to the remaining leader candidates, attempting to discover who could be guilty of such weakness at the very last moment.

The Commander swept the assembly with her shrewd gaze before resuming her speech. 'Yes, it is true. By withdrawing before the ballot, those brave Bau have entrusted the rest of you with achieving their dreams. However, this implies that the teams of the leader candidates who have stepped down will also be dropped from the Experiment. This would be most unfair to those who have dedicated so much time to preparation for this venture. Consequently we have decided that the teams should be reorganised. No potential deputy should be excluded from the Experiment simply because his or her leader has chosen to withdraw, so all of them will be included in the tawny ballot to be matched to settlements in the order in which the sites were picked. This means that they will not necessarily be partnered with the leaders with whom they trained, but we think this is the fairest way for everyone. That being so, no one will think badly of any candidate who now chooses to step down. The other members of each group will be allocated from the remaining pool of specialists, with priority being given to those Bau who have already developed good working relationships with their leaders. Of course, even at this late stage, some of you may still decide to follow the example of your leaders and remove your names from the list, but anyone who wishes to continue with the Experiment will be found a place on one of the settlement teams. I will allow you all green parcycles to make your decision before the final ballot.'

The assembly broke up into groups surrounding the declared Leader candidates as the potential settlers tried to understand the implications of the Commander's announcement. During the ensuing discussions, some animated to the point of shouting, Ast became aware of a trickle of Bau leaving the hall. She would have drawn the exodus to Wsir's notice but he was in earnest conversation with Dna, the physician who had been expecting to be his Deputy. All the while other Bau who had hoped to join his team were clamouring for his attention. The time allowed for discussion passed all too quickly.

The Commander reappeared and called the assembly to order. 'The ballot for the deputies will now commence...'

Ast moved to her mate's side and laced fingers with him, saying, 'Dna will be so disappointed if she is not to join us.'

Wsir whispered, 'I will be more than disappointed if I have to put up with Swty as my deputy.'

The instant this thought had crossed his mind, he regretted it. The capricious spirit of the lottery did not take kindly to pre-emptive criticism and he had tested its nature once already by wishing for the cobalt site, so he was not surprised by the shout of triumph as the cobalt light shone out on the map and the Commander was holding up the purple ring that matched the shoulder tabs on Swty's uniform.

'Oh dear,' Ast sighed.

'Indeed,' her mate agreed.

*

The allocation of specialists to the different groups was more complicated than anticipated because of the last moment changes in their plans. It was several planetary cycles later before all the team lists were completed and their members had undergone the final medical examinations and vaccinations. Their last days on the ship were spent familiarising themselves with the most recent environmental and cultural information about their intended homes. Intensive sleep-learning gave them some basic language skills though the records compiled by the survey team were sparse. The linguists had been unprepared for the wide variation in grammatical structure and level of language development they had encountered across the planet. They hoped that an acute sense of hearing and natural empathic ability would enable the settlers to bridge any communication barriers. Each group was provided with the clothing and cosmetic camouflage to allow them to blend in with the native populations of their settlement area. In particular, they were all fitted with long-life polarising contact lenses. Ba eyes, finely attuned to the wavelengths of their home star, would suffer irreparable damage from the brilliance of their new sun's light, enhanced by the oxygen-rich atmosphere of the settlement planet. Each almost black lens disguised the typical Ba eye colouration by covering the entire iris, and also hid the distinctive slit pupil which would immediately identify a Ba as alien. All the settlers found the lenses disorientating. Their usual sharp-sightedness was noticeably reduced and their acute colour-sense was diminished so that they no longer saw the upper and lower bands of their spectrum. Several settlers found this so disturbing that they gave up their places to others.

Wsir, as the agriculturalist of his team, spent some time in the plant banks and hydroponics laboratories selecting the seeds suitable for his projects, as suggested by the original planetary surveys. Now he knew which area he would be working in, he could be more precise about his requirements such as environmental tolerance and resistance to disease. Ba scientists had realised that their settlers would not be able to survive without certain vitamins, minerals and trace elements in their diet and, since the initiation of this project, they had genetically modified botanical and zoological specimens from the planet to be compatible with Ba physiology, while retaining the appearance of the original plants and animals. Wsir would introduce the new plant stock to provide essential nutrients for his people and, at the same time, improve the quality of the crops for the natives.

In one laboratory he found Nyayt, his textiles specialist, poring over the botanical records. 'Our new countrymen,' Nyayt explained, 'make most of their cloth and cordage from plant fibres. They already cultivate a plant very similar to our own flegyss, albeit on a very small scale. The botanical survey was quite extensive and several hybrids of the fibre-bearing species grew well at home so I know which will produce the best quality fibres but I do not know enough about the growing conditions of our site, so would you help me choose the right seed?'

Wsir was grateful to have something to keep his mind occupied. Ast and their veterinary specialist, Hwthr, were conducting similar searches in the zoological laboratories, alongside Nebt, the nutritionist of the team, and her mate Swty, the hunter. Wsir had no complaints about Hwthr, and he felt very sorry for Nebt who had not expected to be attached to this group and was quite upset about being separated from her training partners, but Swty was another matter. Wsir's concentration on Nyayt's problem helped to divert his thoughts from what his deputy might be doing to stir up trouble within the team even before they had set foot upon the new planet.

The time flew by. Everyone was regretting not making better use of the long journey and there were few who felt themselves ready for what the future held. But an air of excitement had flooded the ship and even the crew were eager to help the settlers with their final preparations.

At last, the day designated for their disembarkation was upon them. Each party would be transported to the planet's surface just before local dawn. The whole ship's company was assembled on the hangar deck to see them off and to hear the Commander's briefest speech yet.

'Once the shuttle has left you, there will be no further contact between you and the home world for green cycles of the new planet. After that time, a scout ship will return to the same spot where today you will be dropped. It will wait for green planetary rotations only. If, by that time, you have not appeared, or no message of any sort has been found, then the scout will return to the mother ship and no further contact will be attempted. We wish you every success in your enterprise.'

As Wsir led his team aboard their shuttle, Ast murmured, 'It is strange. I have this sense of something ending when I should be thinking about something starting. Are we at the beginning or the end? I cannot tell.'

Swty, overhearing her, said, 'It is the beginning of the end, pretty one. Nothing will ever be the same again.'

Wsir flinched at Swty's familiarity but refused to rise to it. He squeezed Ast's hand and said, 'Everything is a beginning, my love. This is the beginning of our new life. We will remember this day and celebrate it.'

'Pompous pertjak,' Swty muttered.

Wsir had endured enough of Swty's taunts and jibes over the years to be able to ignore his brother now. There was much more to think about than sibling rivalry.

*

Pete looked up in time to see the unruly flop of red hair appearing round the door in advance of its owner. 'Come in, Si,' he called, 'You must have heard the kettle.'

Before Simon crossed the threshold he glanced to each end of the lab, checking that Pete was alone. 'What's up?' Pete asked, spooning instant coffee into two mugs, 'You seem a bit edgy.'

Simon gave a huge sigh as he hitched himself up onto one of the benches and accepted the steaming cup. 'Uncle Eric has found out where I am.'

'Oh bollocks!' Pete swore as milk slopped over his shaking hand. 'How did that happen?'

'My mother has a very big mouth,' Simon said with vehemence. He loved his mother dearly but she had a blind spot about her brother which allowed her to see only the successful, popular, television personality while ignoring the controversial, unscrupulous pseudo-scientist. When she had told him about Simon's success in gaining a research post, Eric Evers had recognised the name of the University at once and put two and two together. For three years he had been trying to make contact with H.P. Beaumont, to lure her into public debate about his theories, but all his advances by letter, telephone, fax and e-mail had failed to elicit a single word in response. Now, with his own nephew accepted into Beaumont's inner circle, he saw a golden opportunity to achieve his aim through personal introduction. That Simon would be unwilling to help him had never entered Eric Evers' mind.

'He wants me to arrange a meeting with the Doc,' Simon said, 'and I know he won't take "no" for an answer. He's not used to people refusing him. He seems to think that Doc Beaumont ought to be as eager to speak to him as he is to her. If I don't do anything, he's just as likely to turn up here uninvited and say that I asked him to come.'

'The Doc won't be too impressed by that,' Pete said. 'How are we going to head him off?'

'I haven't a clue,' Simon said with another enormous sigh.

Pete thought for a moment as they sipped their coffee, then he said, 'I take it your Uncle Eric is just as egotistical as his TV persona suggests?'

'Oh, yes,' Simon said, with feeling.

'Then how about this. Contact one of the University clubs, like the Historical Society or the Archaeology Forum. Say that you think you can get them Eric Evers as a speaker and they'll love you forever. Could you persuade him to lower his usual lecture fee, or even speak for free?'

'If he thought he might get to meet the Doc that way, he'd probably pay them.'

'Well, there's you answer. It gets him out of your hair and by the time the Doc hears about his visit you can blame it all on the organisers of the meeting. She wouldn't even have to know that you suggested the idea to them.'

'I suppose she could still choose not to meet him,' Simon mused.

'Sure. If she has any sense she'll find some reason to be a long way away from here. There's bound to be a seminar or a conference she can use as an excuse.'

'And why would I need an excuse?'

The two conspirators turned in guilty haste to find Dr Beaumont standing in the doorway.

'How much did she hear?' Pete mouthed at Simon.

'And I'm a pretty good lip-reader too,' Hermione said, her voice closer to a snarl than Pete had ever heard it before. 'In answer to your question, I heard more than enough of what you were saying. I was coming to check on the set-up for this afternoon's lab class and I heard you, Peter, say that man's name, so I stopped just outside to listen.'

Pete mentally rewound their conversation, trying to remember at what point he had actually spoken the dreaded name. As far as he knew, Dr Beaumont was still unaware of the family connection between Simon and the hated Evers. Simon had dropped that part of his name on his appointment and always introduced himself as Simon Goodhill. After three months in the post he had relaxed into the comfortable belief that his secret was safe.

Hermione advanced into the room, a dominant presence despite her slim build and somewhat diffident stance. Pete backed away until his gawky elbows made contact with the sink unit. Simon had slid from the bench and sidled in the same direction, dodging stools. Hermione stood between them, drumming her fingers on the laminate worktop, her short nails clicking out her annoyance. She looked from one face to the other. Pete's eyes were wide and his mouth was tight-lipped. Simon's naturally pale complexion had drained to an alabaster white. They gulped in unison.

'Do you have something to tell me Simon?'

Chapter 3: First Impressions

Simon jabbed the ENTER key to submit his request to Inter-Library Loans and pushed his chair back from the computer. A sharp intake of breath and the sudden resistance to the chair's motion told him he should have been less hasty. An apology forming on his lips, he looked up into a pair of startling blue eyes and he was lost. The pure fury evident in the girl's glare rendered any words he might have composed – given a few hours warning – inadequate. She hissed, 'Some people have no manners,' before tossing her honey coloured hair over her shoulder and striding away towards the exit turnstile.

Simon was frozen to the spot, as immobile as one of Medusa's victims. He could do no more than stare after the golden-haired vision and watch the sliding doors part to allow her through. Momentarily she stood silhouetted against the wintry light, hunching her shoulders in the cold morning air, then she stepped out and the spell was broken. Driven by instincts as old as humankind, Simon gathered up his books and papers in frantic haste and hurried after her only to be stopped by the insistent beeping of the security gate. The uniformed library attendant leapt from his seat to challenge him. 'I know, I know,' Simon said, and he took the books back to the loans desk to have them checked out.

The librarian gave him a sympathetic smile. 'Don't worry,' she said, 'It happens all the time.'

Simon ran his fingers through his hair. 'I suppose so, this being a library.'

'Not the books, silly,' she said, 'the collision.'

'You saw?' Simon tipped his head in the direction of the computer terminals.

The librarian nodded. 'If people will use the computer aisle as a shortcut they have to expect to get their toes crushed occasionally.'

'Are they always so devastatingly polite?' Simon asked.

The librarian laughed. 'No. The language is usually much worse, heavy on the single syllables.'

He grinned and packed the books into his knapsack. 'Thanks Sylvia.'

'Bye Simon,' she said.

Having negotiated the security system without further incident, he paused in the foyer to double his scarf about his neck and zip up his jacket. His eye was drawn to a garish poster on the information wall, an A3 sheet bordered in vivid day-glow green. As he approached the notice board the poster came into sharp focus and he stopped dead in his tracks. The Archaeology Forum was thrilled to announce the forthcoming visit of the renowned TV personality Eric Evers, who would be giving a lecture entitled 'Beyond the Mists of Time'. The poster was illustrated. There, smiling through his badger-stripe beard, was Uncle Eric, in his trademark safari waistcoat and bowtie. Though Simon had known it was going to happen he had tried his best to put it to the back of his mind but the lurid poster was hard to ignore. He pulled up his collar against the cold and headed off towards his office.

Out of the shelter of the St George's Building, the icy wind caused him to put his head down and increase his pace so that, rounding a corner, he barged into a figure studying the glass-fronted notice board outside the Archaeology Building. 'So sorry,' he said, struggling to stop the books tumbling from his knapsack, which had been knocked from his shoulder.

'Are you naturally clumsy or have you been practising?' The voice was as frosty as the grass. The cornflower eyes sparkled with indignation.

Simon's natural reticence was overcome by recognition of what she had been reading. Another bright green poster had taken up the central position on the board. 'I'm not daft enough to be taken in by him,' he said, pointing at Evers' disturbing image.

'And you think I am?' she seemed to grow taller, or perhaps he was shrinking under her withering gaze.

His temporary boldness deserted him. 'I said I'm sorry,' he muttered. Was it his imagination, or did she nod an acceptance of his apology? He tried a smile though it was a bit forced as he gritted his teeth against the wind.

'Perhaps you need to cut your hair then you'd see where you were going,' she said before turning on her heel and walking up the slope to the entrance of the Garstang Building, his building, where his office was. He was reluctant to follow her lest she should think he was stalking her, so he stood stamping his feet to rid them of the chill and allowed a decent interval to elapse before he, too, hurried into the building. And all the while he could feel Uncle Eric's beady eyes drilling the back of his neck from that ghastly poster.

On entering the warmth of familiar surroundings, Simon's first thought was that a cup of coffee would be very welcome, and his second thought was that Pete was sitting an exam in the Sports Hall so he would have to fend for himself. That meant braving the coffee machine. He dumped his coat and bag inside the door of his office before making his way to the temperamental apparatus situated in a dark corner of the ground floor corridor. He rummaged through his pockets to find the necessary coins. The machine brew might be a third of the price of a Theatre A coffee but it was hardly comparable. The only similarities were that it was hot and wet and coffee-coloured. The thin plastic cup was no insulation against the heat and he had to hold it by the rim while being careful not to squash it. Concentrating on this tricky business he failed to anticipate people coming out of Dr Beaumont's office directly in his path. He cursed as hot liquid sloshed over his hand and he dropped the cup. There was a yelp as what passed for coffee splashed at the feet of…it was her!

The girl jumped back, avoiding the worst. Her boot-cut jeans protected her from the hot liquid thought the carpet was not so lucky. Simon raised his eyes, unsurprised to meet incandescent rage.

'I don't believe it!' she said, turning to Hermione who had followed her through the door. 'This is the idiot I was telling you about, Doctor.' The blonde almost spat out the words in her fury. 'Not content with breaking my foot and knocking me to the ground, now he's tried to scald me.'

Simon's automatic defence system clicked into action. 'I hardly think that's fair,' he said. 'You came out of the door without looking, and I didn't actually knock you over, and you seem to be walking all right for someone with a broken foot.'

Hermione was having great difficulty keeping a straight face. 'Simon, we were just coming to find you.' She glanced at the floor and said, 'Perhaps you'd better get some paper towels and mop that up as best you can. Then come back here so that I can smooth some ruffled feathers.'

'Yes, Doc,' Simon said, hardly daring to look at the girl again.

As he turned to fetch the towels he heard her say, 'That's Simon?' in a tone that started a blush rising up his neck. At least he had ceased to feel cold.

A short while later, in Dr Beaumont's office, Simon and the girl sat like naughty schoolchildren called before the Headmistress, or, Hermione fleetingly thought, like an estranged couple seeking advice from a marriage guidance counsellor. She tried to remain serious but the expressions on the two faces were so comical in their determination not to look at each other that she had to laugh. 'Can we pretend that this morning hasn't happened, please?' she begged. 'I really need you two to get along.'

The girl unfolded her arms and Simon relaxed his shoulders. 'That's better,' Hermione said. 'Now I can introduce you properly. Sally Rowe, meet Simon Goodhill, my research assistant as I was telling you earlier. Simon, this is Sally. She's an archaeological artist who has worked with me in the past, providing illustrations for my publications. I've asked her to help us with the drawings of samples from the Nagada dig, both my cereals and your fibres. Sally has the best eye for detail that I know and she can often pick out things that don't show up even in microscope photos. I need you to be friends.'

Simon dared a glance at Sally, but the smug look on her face only made him resentful of Hermione's glowing praise.

'Well?' Hermione's black eyebrows were raised in question.

'What do you want us to do?' Simon asked, his voice sullen and choking on 'us'.

'That's better. First I want you to show Sally the most significant of the botanical finds so she can get an idea of what we need.'

'Will I be using the same lab as last time?' Sally asked, still not looking at Simon. 'The light is pretty good there.'

'That is my plan,' Hermione said, 'though you'll have to share it with a human remains investigation this time. We're a bit pushed for space to accommodate all our MSc projects this semester.'

Sally's face registered the slightest frown of annoyance before she smiled her acceptance of the arrangements. 'Fine,' Dr Beaumont went on, 'then we're all set. Sally will be starting next week, Simon, so I would like you to sort out a work area for her in the laboratory before then. I know what sort of a state it gets into when Peter starts spreading out.'

Simon rose to his friend's defence. 'Skeletal remains take up a lot more space than botanical specimens, and it is for his dissertation.'

'I know that,' the Doctor said, with mild reproof, 'but the exercise in organisation will do him good.'

For the first time Sally turned to look him in the eye, her fixed smile holding nothing of warmth only smug superiority. Simon wondered what Pete's reaction would be to the news he was going to be sharing his lab with the Ice Maiden.

The meeting was over. Simon stood up and politely stepped aside to let Sally leave the room ahead of him. As he was about to follow her, Hermione said, 'I've seen the posters, Simon.'

'Er, yes, sorry!'

'You can't be held responsible for your relatives,' she said. 'I'm only glad I've had enough notice to prepare myself.'

Simon nodded. Up until the Christmas vacation he had successfully evaded all Eric Evers' attempts at communication, no matter how devious, but the annual family get-together was one event he could not avoid. His mother had issued him with a three-line whip to make sure he was there when Uncle Eric came to visit. After the communal meal Simon had sought comfort in a bottle of vintage port but that had only given him a headache and weakened his resistance to Evers' blandishments. He had a vague memory of agreeing to 'speak to someone' about inviting Uncle Eric to the University in the New Year. Despite his woolly-headed state and his uncle's persistence, he was careful not to make any promises in the matter of an introduction to Dr Beaumont herself, but his mother would not let the matter lie. The last thing she said to him when the holiday was over, was, 'I'll be very cross with you if you don't get that invitation for Eric. He so wants to meet your Dr Beaumont and share his ideas with her. It might be very useful to some of her students.'

Simon asked Hermione, 'Are you going to go to the lecture?'

'I hadn't planned to. I had thought to take Peter's advice and be as far away as possible when it happens, but I've had time to think. I've avoided the issue for too long. Perhaps now is the time to face up to it. I need to know just how that man is using my work. I might sit at the back of the lecture theatre but I'm not sure I want to meet him face to face, so don't you dare tell him that I'm there and don't even think about introducing him to me unless I ask you to.'

'Fair enough, Doc, as long as you understand what a devious so-and-so he is. I can't guarantee that you'll be able to steer clear of him if he really gets the bit between his teeth.'

'I understand, Simon. Just do your best.'

All this time a bemused Sally had been listening to their conversation. She fell in beside him on their way to the laboratory, and although she had determined not to start up a conversation with Simple Simon, her curiosity got the better of her. 'Who was Dr Beaumont talking about back there?'

'Someone you don't want to know,' Simon replied.

'But...' she started, not used to being thwarted in this way.

Simon stopped and turned, looking directly into her face. 'No, really, you don't want to know. And if you value your friendship with the Doc, you won't ask.'

For a fleeting moment doubt registered in those impossibly blue eyes. Then Sally's composure returned and she stalked past him in the direction of the laboratory, treating him to a disdainful toss of her hair and a mutter of, 'Idiot!'

Simon suppressed an unmanly giggle. The Ice Maiden had very nearly cracked. There was hope for him yet.

But after an hour in her company, poring over botanical specimens in Perspex boxes and plastic bags, listening to Sally's caustic comments about their state of preservation, which she implied was wholly Simon's responsibility, he was wondering why he was bothered about what she thought of him. Abruptly, Sally glanced at the clock and said, 'I have a train to catch. I'll be back on Monday, as Dr Beaumont said. I expect everything to be ready for me to start work then.'

Simon's sense of injustice was tempered by the realisation that he was soon to be rid of her. He bit back a tart response about being her colleague not her servant and instead said, 'I'll let the lab technician know.'

'Huh,' she said and without a backward glance, she took her coat from the hook by the door and left. Simon heaved a sigh of relief, then sighed again when he realised he had to put all the specimens they had been examining back into the storage facility. He was closing the last drawer when the door crashed open and Pete stomped in, sat down on a stool and proclaimed, 'I failed!'

'It can't have been that bad,' Simon commiserated. 'Wasn't it Prof Jameson's paper? You've always said he's pretty fair.'

'Normally. But that was a bastard of a paper, and it's a core unit.'

'I still don't believe you've failed. You did enough work for it.'

'Probably not enough,' Pete said, leaning forward to rest his head on the bench.

Before his friend could think about knocking himself out, Simon said, 'Well, I've had a pretty traumatic morning, too.'

Pete raised his head. 'Yeah?'

'Yeah. I've been roped in as gopher for the Ice Maiden.'

'Oh, so you've met Super-Sallius.'

Simon blinked at the nickname. 'You know Sally Rowe?'

'Everyone knows our Ms Rowe,' Pete said. 'Ice Maiden, eh? That's pretty good for a first encounter. What did you do to annoy her? Not that it takes much.'

Simon recounted his experiences from library to laboratory and by the end of his tale Pete was hooting with laughter, his exam forgotten.

'So you never did get a cup of coffee?'

'No, though the stain of the one I nearly had remains to haunt me.'

'Well, I think we deserve some cheering up. I noticed they're serving treacle pud at Theatre A. What d'you think?'

'Great idea.'

The frost had long been burnt off the grass by the watery winter sunshine and the wind had dropped. A few hardy students were sitting on the benches beside the lawn outside the St George's Building, but Simon and Pete hurried past; the cosiness of Theatre A beckoned. They found the café almost full and worried, for a moment, that the famous syrup sponge with custard would have sold out, but they were lucky. As they stood, with their trays bearing large lattés and puddings, Simon noticed someone waving at them.

'Look, Sylvia's got seats at her table,' he said, and made his way, with care, across the crowded space.

The librarian took off her glasses and closed her book as they sat down.

'Really, Sylv, don't you ever feel the need to get away from books?' Pete said, screwing his neck round in an attempt to read the title of the paperback.

'No dear,' Sylvia smiled, turning the book over. 'Some of my very best friends are books.'

'You should get out more,' Pete said, tucking into his dessert.

'And you should eat a more balanced diet.'

'This is comfort food, and we're both in need of a little comforting at the moment.'

'Tell Auntie Sylvia,' she said, and between them, Simon and Pete related the tragedies of their day.

'Well, what a sorry tale!' Sylvia said, trying not to smile.

Pete groaned, 'I'm done for.'

'You realise,' Simon said, 'that he hasn't really failed his exam.'

'Of course not. He'll probably get a distinction.'

'And he's fallen for Super-Sallius,' Pete retaliated.

'Naturally. She's a beautiful girl, and she's showing interest in him.'

Both Pete and Simon stared at the librarian with open-mouthed amazement.

'Wha...?'

'How...?'

'She dropped into the library again, just long enough to request a copy of your MSc dissertation, Simon.'

'Checking your academic credentials! You are honoured!' Pete smirked.

'I'm not sure I want to be. I think she's pretty high maintenance and I'm not looking forward to working with her.'

'Eat your pudding, dear,' Sylvia said. 'You'll feel better with a good dose of carbohydrate inside you.'

'So how come he doesn't get the balanced diet advice?' Pete asked in an aggrieved voice. 'I bet it's the hair,' he persisted, with a pout. 'You women just can't resist that little boy lost look. He'll probably have her eating out of his hand within the week.'

Simon spluttered into his coffee. Dabbing his chin with a paper napkin, he said, 'Remember, you'll be sharing the lab with her.'

'Oh, bugger!'

Sylvia laughed, 'You two are a real tonic. Thanks for brightening up my lunch break. I look forward to the next instalment.' With that, she collected her book and spectacles and stood up. 'Have a nice day, boys.'

*

Hermione spotted them through her window as they were returning from Theatre A, and waved them to come to her office. Pete noticed the coffee stain in the corridor as they passed, commenting, 'What's it worth not to grass you up to the cleaners?'

Simon snorted, 'I've got enough to worry about without having them on my back, too. What can I offer?'

'An intro to Uncle Eric?'

Simon elbowed Pete in the stomach before knocking on Hermione's door. Pete was still gasping when they entered.

'I'll get straight to the point,' Hermione said, speaking to Simon. 'I've just had an e-mail from Ian Masterson in Egypt. He's found out about the lecture. Apparently your uncle has posted details on his website and there could be a lot more interest in it than we anticipated. Ian is worried about how this might be perceived by the Antiquities Authority in Egypt. You know how sensitive they are and how little excuse they need to interfere. As co-sponsors of Ian's dig, the University cannot afford to annoy the powers that be. They could withdraw the license to dig on any minor pretence.'

Simon was stunned by the implications. 'I'm so sorry. Do you want me to see if I can get him to call it off?'

'No, no,' Hermione said, 'that would only create more trouble for everyone. Can you imagine the publicity? I can see the headlines now –"University pulls plug on TV personality".'

Pete, recovered from his breathlessness, said, 'And Evers would make a meal of it too. He has a big following. His website will be buzzing with indignation if he's asked to cancel, and the speculation about the reasons for a cancellation – well it doesn't bear thinking about.'

'Exactly,' Hermione said, her mouth set in a prim expression. 'And how much of that speculation do you think will centre on our work here?'

'Oh sh...sugar!' Pete said.

Dr Beaumont glared at him over her glasses. 'Indeed, Peter.'

Simon's mind was in turmoil. How could matters have deteriorated so far, so quickly? He had been in the post for barely six months and now it seemed he was to be the cause of, at the very least, severe embarrassment for his department, and, at the worst, the suspension of a prestigious archaeological expedition that was beginning to show some astonishing results. The Egyptian authorities were notoriously jealous of the success of any foreign excavation on their soil. Anything that promised to be newsworthy was routinely taken out of the dig director's hands so that the Egyptians could put their own spin on it. The only thing that had saved Dr Masterson's dig from unwanted attention last season was that it was an early Predynastic settlement site where the archaeologists were not expected to find anything like the spectacular jewellery, sculpture or gilded grave goods that attracted international media attention.

Eric Evers had, in the past, made some highly inflammatory comments about the intellectual abilities of Egypt's most famous archaeologists. If he was publicising the forthcoming lecture as an opportunity to legitimise his ideas in association with bona fide non-Egyptian academic interests, this would certainly draw the gaze of the Antiquities Authority towards Masterson's work. Simon was appalled at how much trouble he could have caused and yet how little control he had over events. He could find no words to say. His only consolation was that Dr Beaumont looked sympathetic rather than angry.

Hermione knew she should have predicted the escalation of the situation. She had resigned herself to the inevitability of a confrontation with Evers, even before Simon had come into the picture. He could not have imagined how his unfortunate family connections could impinge on so many interests, but the snowball of coincidence was rolling, gathering speed as well as mass. There was no stopping it now.

*

When Wsir brought his people out of the desert they were greeted with awe by the natives of his new home, but not with as much surprise as they might have expected. The humans marvelled at the height of these beautiful folk, a full two digits taller than the tallest man of the Black Land. They longed to stroke the golden skin, smooth and devoid of hair. They were amazed by the delicate hands, with fingers so long that they appeared almost to have an extra joint. They wondered at the bald pates of the males compared with the luxuriant blue-black hair of the females. They puzzled over the strangely accented voices that nevertheless seemed to speak directly to their hearts. But they also remembered stories of such magical beings, stories told by their grandfathers about a previous visit heralded by a falling star.

When the shuttle had landed with a flash of light and the high-pitched squeal of its anti-grav drive, the natives had been less frightened than excited about the return of the sky folk. Everything about the newcomers was wonderful, from the even weave of their soft linen garments to the sleekness of the cattle that they brought with them. The humans opened their arms to the golden ones, embracing them in friendship, welcoming them to their settlements, encouraging them to stay, for surely the presence of such beings could only bring prosperity and good fortune to their communities. In return for this acceptance, Wsir, the leader of the Bau, as they called themselves, presented their farmers with seed corn of such quality that a bumper yield was expected of the first harvest after their arrival. The seven beautiful pregnant heifers, under Hwthr's care, promised equally wondrous offspring. The hunter, Swty, astounded the humans with his ability to throw a spear with unerring straightness and reed-shafted arrows flew far and fast from his bow. Every one of Wsir's folk, from the potter Khnm to the artificer Pth, took an almost childlike delight in acquiring the simplest of manual skills and the humans were so touched by their eagerness to learn that in return they were generous with their practical knowledge. It never occurred to the natives that the Bau might be possessed of even greater gifts, knowledge that the barely civilized people of the land they called Kem, were incapable of comprehending and which would be dangerous in ignorant hands.

Their gentleness and courtesy endeared the Bau to the people of the Black Land, reinforcing the idea that these beings were divine. The Kemites believed that they had been blessed when the Bau chose to live amongst them. They built fine dwellings for the Bau, with woven wall panels of intricate designs, and gateways marked with symbolic emblems and flags. Men and women considered it an honour and a privilege to serve the Bau, to keep their houses clean and comfortable, to feed and clothe them using the very best produce of their land, to entertain them with music and dance and the telling of tales. Above all the people wanted to ensure that the Bau, now they had settled, would not leave because that would assuredly bring disaster. The Kemites seemed to think that as long as the Bau were content then the land would prosper. There was no doubt in the minds of the humans that the Bau were the children of the gods, sent by Ra himself to live amongst them. The presence of these golden beings was a blessing and a protection. May it continue for millions of years.

Chapter 4: A Change of Plan

Adjusting to their new planet was more difficult than the Bau had expected. At first they relished their enhanced physical strength, resulting from a gravity three-quarters of that on Perbau. Their superhuman abilities in running, jumping and throwing, combined with their exotic appearance, served to confirm their status as gods.

But other differences between the planet the indigenes called Geb and the Ba home-world had less welcome consequences. The planetary day was two-thirds the length of a rotation of Perbau and from the moment they arrived their sleep cycles were severely disrupted. Wsir asked Skhmt, the physician of the group, if this problem had been foreseen by the Experiment Directors. 'Yes,' she said, 'we should have spent the latter part of the journey in acclimatisation. The ship's day-night sequence should have been altered gradually until it matched this planet's cycle. But then the crew would have had to go through the process in reverse before their return to Perbau. There were fewer of them than us, but their needs were considered above ours. Even now, I could help if I had the right light sources, but we have no such technology.'

'Then we will have to bear it as best we can,' Wsir said. 'We always knew we were unlikely to have prepared for every eventuality, though it is disappointing to encounter such a problem so soon, especially since it should have been predicted. But we cannot let this setback alter our resolve.'

The settlers were those very rare beings, Bau who were willing to test themselves against, and be tested by a totally new, technology-free environment, ready to give up all the conveniences and comforts of their civilised life to experience the hardships, challenges and triumphs of living by their own resourcefulness and fortitude. Most Bau had, at some time, dreamed this back-to-basics dream. In Wsir's youth there had been a planet-wide obsession with home-grown food and domestic power generation, but this fad was as short-lived as it was short-sighted. The Bau, in general, were too reliant on the products of their technological heritage to do without them for very long. However, the temporary fashion for self-reliance had been the seed-corn from which the Experiment had grown. Wsir and his companions were the embodiment of their planet's hopes and the focus of the expectations of all their fellow Bau, whose vicarious experience of their successes and disasters would enrich their lives for generations to come.

The more serious purpose of the Experiment was to explore how well Bau could adapt to the primitive lifestyle of a colony planet. In spite of birth control measures, the need for which was well understood and generally accepted, the rate at which the population was growing would inevitably lead to pressure on resources and overcrowding. The Bau had already built domed colonies on a second planet and three moons before the development of hyper-drive engines had allowed them to explore beyond their own solar system. The Experiment planet had been found by a mission sent to identify and survey worlds suitable for colonisation. There was no question of the Bau colonising a planet where sentient life was already established but then they discovered one inhabited by a bipedal mammalian species so similar in appearance to the Bau that some had suggested they might be genetically related. That theory had quickly been disproved after a more detailed survey was ordered and samples of suitable animal and plant species were returned to Perbau for analysis. Experiments on the most promising specimens had shown that they could be genetically enhanced to provide certain essential nutrients and serve as an agricultural foundation for a possible colony. The level of sophistication of the indigenous population on Geb had been deemed low enough for the planet to serve as a testing ground without compromising the natives' natural development. Few Bau appreciated the urgency of finding new planets and those that did knew the rarity of planets supporting a Ba-friendly environment. Geb was a lucky discovery. None of the planets surveyed so far had come as close to matching the Bau's requirements. It was hoped that more might be discovered during the course of the Experiment so that the lessons learned from Geb could be applied to a real colonial mission. The experiences of Wsir and all his comrades would be instrumental in planning that enterprise.

More problems became manifest earlier than expected. The visual discomfort caused by differences in the visible spectrum of Geb's sun was not completely alleviated by the contact lenses. Even with their eyes closed, the effects were appreciable. Skhmt developed a barrier ointment of finely ground charcoal or mineral powder mixed with animal fat to paint over the eyelids and under the eyes in an attempt to reduce the uncomfortable glare, but this remedy was inadequate.

Within days of their landing, all the Bau were complaining of headaches which, in combination with the disturbed sleep patterns, caused violent mood swings and outbreaks of bad temper. As the headaches became more debilitating, Skhmt started administering analgesics from her limited drug supplies. She was reluctant to do this because it went against the guiding principles of the Experiment. The small store of medicines allowed to each settlement group was supposed to be used in the case of real emergency and then only if the Bau had been unable to find local substitute remedies.

'It cannot be helped,' Ast reassured her. 'This must count as real need since we have not been here long enough to find alternative medicines and we certainly cannot go on biting each other's heads off or the Experiment will be over before it has even begun. We can only hope that the natives already have pain-killing drugs, however primitive, that they will be willing to share with us.'

The slightly higher proportion of oxygen in the air caused a mild euphoria, which helped to mitigate the effects of the light-induced problems by keeping the Bau permanently on the edge of inebriation. Once their body chemistry had adjusted to the new atmosphere, they found the physical discomforts easier to bear, but then they became aware of the silence. The Bau had failed to appreciate how quiet a primitive, non-industrial world could be. Despite their advances in crystal and opti-sonic technologies, Perbau hummed with the power supplying all the machinery, communication devices and transporters without which most of its inhabitants would be lost. They had become so accustomed to this background noise that it was hardly noticeable, and that was not all. Since most were, to a greater or lesser degree, telepathic, the mechanical and electronic ambient noise of their home world was augmented by the mental whisper of billions of Bau. From birth they had learned to deal with this cacophony by following a strict etiquette. Thoughts were private property and a Ba knew better than to listen in to thoughts that were being transmitted to another person. They were able to close their minds to the constant non-verbal babble of irrelevant, irrepressible and irrational thoughts which formed an audible backdrop to every Ba's life.

The settlers had been chosen from amongst the most powerful telepaths, Bau who as often communicated mind to mind as by vocalising their thoughts. Given that they were to be deprived of all artificial means of communication, it was felt that they should at least be able to hear *one another over distance. The Experiment organisers failed to realise that, not only was the population of Geb much smaller than that of Perbau, but also that the sentients of that planet had not yet developed even minimal telepathic abilities. The Bau settlers found themselves capable of hearing other minds but, at the same time, having very few minds to hear. To them, Geb was a disconcertingly silent planet and there was nothing they could do to change that.*

Of Wsir's group, Swty was the only Ba who seemed not to sense the isolation and loneliness that all his fellows experienced through noise deprivation. He relished his hunting trips, seeking out the game that inhabited the secret gullies and thorn-brush hollows of the desert fringes. His excursions to explore the region became more frequent and longer of duration and his extended absences from the group during the crucial settlement phase increased the pressure on Wsir. Despite the fragile nature of their relationship, Wsir had hoped that Swty's belief in the Experiment would overcome his antipathy towards his brother. It was so important for the leader to have a reliable and, above all, supportive Deputy. Swty was proving to be neither, and wherever he went, Nebt went too, depriving Ast of her principal assistant.

'I need Nebt here,' Ast complained to her mate. 'She is our nutritionist and, much as we need Swty's contributions to our food supplies, we cannot rely on his hunting for much longer. We must look to the domesticates and we have to find the best means of food processing to meet our dietary needs. That is Nebt's speciality.'

'You know what I think about Swty's behaviour,' Wsir said. 'Dna would have been so much more reliable.'

Up to that moment, Wsir had not voiced his annoyance at having his brother nominated as his second in command, but his feelings had always been clear to Ast. She insinuated herself under his arm, clasping his waist and leaning her face against his shoulder. 'I do not mean to add to your worries,' she said. 'Skhmt and Nyayt have been enormously helpful, so I can cope without Nebt on occasions, as long as we can still hear *each other. I would just like to know when she is going to be available in person so we can make plans.'*

Wsir kissed the top of her head. 'You are so amenable. I know it is not entirely Nebt's fault but she should be less quick to jump to her mate's every whim.'

'They are in love,' Ast said, as if that explained everything.

'So are we, but we still know our duty.'

'Swty was right about one thing,' Ast said, with mischief in her eyes.

'What?'

'You can be a pompous pertjak sometimes.'

To Ast's relief, Wsir smiled and then ruffled her hair. 'And you are almost as incorrigible as my brother.'

'I think I will have to take that as a compliment,' Ast said, with a sigh.

*

The settlement sites were all in the same hemisphere of the planet so that the landings could be timed to match the local planting season and Wsir was pleased with the condition of the soil he saw being prepared for the cereal crops. His instincts about this place had been good. The land was rich and fertile. He could not resist plunging his hands into the dark loam, crumbling it between his fingers and taking a deep breath to savour the wholesome smell. As far as the Bau had been able to ascertain from the natives, the history of settled agriculture in this region was measured in a few generations. Long stretches of the banks of the great river were still untamed. Seen from above, as in the images from the original Ba survey, the irregular patchwork of tiny fields and garden plots surrounding the small communities looked like little islands of order in a broad strip of green chaos.

Language had proved to be less of a problem than had been predicted. Djhwty, the group's communications expert and archivist, had spent much of his time with the local sentients just listening to them talking. Their language was simple, its vocabulary limited to everyday matters and life in general, but Djhwty had heard them refer to themselves by several different names, which he said was a sign of sophistication of thought. One evening, as several of the settlers sat watching the sunset, he explained these nuances of language. 'I find that, most often, they refer to themselves as remetch *which simply means 'people', but they are happy to be called Blacklanders in reference to the colour of this remarkable soil.'*

'*It is clear they recognise that they owe everything to this glorious fertile earth,*' *Wsir said. He was dragging his long fingers through the fine tilth of the vegetable plot which the Kemites had provided for the Bau beside the grand house that was being built for them.* '*They are sensible of what it can give them if they treat it with respect.*'

'*They are a very pragmatic species,*' *Djhwty said.* '*They find methods that work and stick to them. Their principal philosophy is very much the same. They believe there can be no success, no progress, no growth without equilibrium. They know there has to be what they call* maat, *balance; balance between male and female, dark and light, good and evil. The Black cannot exist without the Red, which is their description of the desert. Only by contrast with the infertile and inhospitable sandy wastes can they fully appreciate how remarkable their Kem is.*'

Imn-Min, the group's geologist and energy specialist, was also fascinated by the composition of the soil. With the simple tests available to him he had identified several unusual components. '*I knew the basic geology of this region was sedimentary – limestones and sandstones – but the soil is enriched by sediments and minerals from areas of igneous formations – granites and basalts. Those rocks are not found within white-by-white arur of here. I cannot account for it.*'

Khnm, the hydraulic engineering expert, was also a skilled ceramicist. He was often to be found searching the boundaries of the cultivated land and the banks of the river for clays suitable for his pots. He was equally at a loss to explain the condition of the earth. '*There is little or no prolonged rainfall and these small communities have only a rudimentary grasp of irrigation, but the soil is perfect. The harvest should be good.*'

Whatever the explanation, the growing conditions were ideal and Wsir was so confident of the potential harvest that he contributed half of his treasured enhanced seed to be mixed in with that saved by the natives from the previous season. The cereal grew tall and strong with some plants outstripping their fellows by a full handspan in height.

Their healthy blue-green colour identified them as the modified Ba wheat and the size of the grains in the developing ears gave Wsir great hope for the season's yield. At harvest time, with some difficulty and initial misunderstanding, Wsir directed the reapers to cut these plants first, to keep the augmented crop separate from the rest. Eventually he demonstrated what he wanted them to do by working through one of the small fields himself, grasping the heads of the taller plants and cutting them just below the ears. That the leader of the Bau should work the land in this way, with his own hands, reaffirmed his godlike status which, in the opinion of the natives, must be higher than that of his companions, the other Golden Ones. Wsir was, without knowing it, well on his way to becoming a god-king, whose every action, every word was revered by his human followers.

When all the fields were cleared, Wsir's simple visual analysis of the harvest revealed that the proportions of grain from the taller and shorter plants matched the ratio of new to old seed corn. He had no way of analysing the grain to assess the degree of cross-pollination which he hoped had occurred. The stronger plants might still represent no more than the pure strain of the modified cereal. The smaller plants might be infertile cross-breeds. But until the next planting he would not know if the old and new wheats had produced a viable hybrid that would continue to grow true.

He was not too disheartened. Hybridisation took time and he would have considered himself very lucky to achieve his aim so quickly, but he regretted his rash decision to use half of his special grain in such a small area. Now he had to decide how long his reserved seed would remain viable and how much he could afford to commit to the next planting. With nothing more than his physical senses to guide him, he had no reliable way to test the fertility of the remaining seed, nor that of the newly garnered grain. He reckoned he had about a third of Geb's year to make up his mind before the time of planting.

Meanwhile, Ast and Nebt conducted a series of experiments using the old and new grain in varying proportions to make bread. Nebt had been surprised to find that, as well as producing a basic leavened bread with a somewhat unpredictable sourdough based on wild yeasts, the locals had also refined a liquid barm which gave much more palatable results. Even with their primitive methods of processing, the new grain ground finer and produced a whiter flour than the unmodified wheat. Combined with the yeasty liquid the resultant bread was paler of crust than anything the locals had seen before. They viewed this marvellous food with a superstitious reverence, especially since the Bau reserved it for their sole consumption.

'I feel bad that we cannot share this bread with the humans who have contributed so much to its production,' Nebt said, 'but we are in sore need of the minerals it can provide. There is little enough of the crop as it is.'

By agreeing Ast felt a twinge of guilt at the implied criticism of Wsir's agricultural experiment. After setting aside a portion of the meagre harvest for next season's planting there was, as Nebt and others had recognised, hardly enough grain to feed the Bau for more than a quarter of a year. Since the means of its production had been taught to them by the gods themselves, the humans came to believe that the white bread was the only sort that their gods would want to eat. Wsir had to guard his stores against well-meaning pilferage to prevent all of his precious seed migrating to the Bau's food tables by way of the village ovens. Despite his diligence a significant part of the reserved modified grain was lost.

Ast tried to comfort her mate by saying, 'At least by eating it we have benefited from the additional nutrients in your grain.'

Wsir sighed, 'But that is a short term solution. There is not enough to feed us through a full planetary rotation and the amount of seed corn remaining will produce only a fraction of this year's harvest so our rations will be even shorter next time. We cannot rely on the rest of the harvest having been improved to meet our needs. I have no way of analysing it.'

'Are there no other vegetable sources of the minerals we need?' Ast asked.

'Some of the pulses looked promising but our scientists at home found them difficult to modify. I begin to think that they did not really try. I'm sure no one realised just how significant a problem mineral deficiency would prove to be. The reports they produced on the diversity of food plants from all over this planet were rather dismissive of anything other than the mass cereal crops. That is why they chose settlement sites in regions where cereals were at least being cultivated and preferably where they had already been domesticated.'

'The whole survey of this planet seems to have been conducted with a great deal of complacency and very little imagination,' Ast said.

'I cannot disagree,' Wsir admitted. 'It is most disappointing.'

'Disappointing?' Ast snapped. 'It was a dangerous miscalculation. If this was the only error of judgement made by the Directors it might be excused, but look at all the other problems we have encountered. The fact is we are woefully unprepared for life on this planet, and the fault is not ours.'

*

Hwthr was doing her best to augment the Bau's food supplies by way of the vitamin-rich milk produced by her beloved cows and she sought the nutritionist's help in finding ways of preserving it. 'I begin to realise how much we took for granted as far as food storage is concerned,' she told Nebt. 'It will not go to waste entirely because I can always give the milk away. The humans who help me care for the animals, and those who have chosen to serve us here are so embarrassingly grateful for anything I give them that I sometimes have trouble persuading them to accept it, but I want us to benefit too.'

Nebt agreed, 'We were expecting the milk to make a significant contribution to our nutrition by now so we cannot afford to lose it. Cooling, freezing, irradiation – all are denied to us here. Drying, salting and smoking are our best options, but in this heat I cannot make the sort of hard cheese that would keep longest. Fermentation must be the solution, but even cultured milk turns within a day and a night under normal conditions. I do not want to waste the bounty your animals are producing, Hwthr, especially as it provides many of the nutrients we cannot find elsewhere. I have not identified another equivalent source of the calcium we must have to maintain bone density and we need the zinc too to support metabolic function.'

Ast nodded. 'Skhmt is already concerned about mineral deficiencies, particularly in conjunction with the effects of the reduced gravity.'

'The dietary changes are having more of an effect than we might have expected at this stage,' Nebt confirmed. 'Ba physiology requires more protein from animal sources than the humans understand, but the balance of trace elements in the native species is so different from what we are used to that no matter how much meat they provide for us it will not satisfy our needs. Some of the pulses and legumes are good alternatives but there are limits to the sheer volume of food we can consume. If only Wsir's next experiments with the augmented cereal are successful.'

Hwthr's fascination with milk fermentation led her to follow the grain experiments with interest. She helped Ast and Nebt in their attempts to brew the cereal-based drink that the locals called beer. Mostly this was made from the barley grain that the Ba scientists had been unable to modify, but the village brewmaster was eager to discover whether a stronger beverage could be produced from the superior wheat which seemed to be the preoccupation of the Bau. The results were of widely differing palatability but Ast had to admit that Hwthr's brews were the most successful. While the humans preferred beer made from the sweetest malted barley and flavoured with fruit, the Bau enjoyed the more subtle tastes of wheat and bitter herbs. Wsir, glad to serve as a taster in these experiments, said, 'I do not believe you could ever produce a beer sophisticated enough in flavour to match even the roughest wine, but some of these drinks are highly acceptable.'

Skhmt's opinion was more fulsome. 'Well done, Hwthr. You have found the first local analgesic remedy. If you can produce a brew with a higher alcohol content I believe I could even use it as an anaesthetic.'

Wsir congratulated his veterinarian then added, 'Of course, when my vines reach maturity, I might be able to give you something better.'

Skhmt shook her head. 'That day is a long way off and I do not believe you will be able to distil the wine to any greater potency than Hwthr has already achieved with her strongest beers. I will be happy to be proved wrong but, for now, we must make the most of what we already have.'

Hwthr's generosity in giving them alcohol of such quality endeared her to the local people. They had had more contact with her than with any other Ba as she supervised the servicing of their cows by the mighty black bull and helped in the birthing of his offspring. She had an intimate knowledge of village households and farmsteads where she had spent days and nights observing and advising on their animal *husbandry practices. She never shirked from hard physical labour and yet always maintained a calmness and elegance that were the envy of every human female. The people said that her presence brightened their lives and when she left to move on to her next assignment, it was as if a cloud had passed in front of the sun. Her image, distinguished by cow's horns and ears, was to be found everywhere, carved on the lintel of a cattle shed or painted on a pottery milking vessel, even on the palettes and pots used for mixing and storing the eye-paint that had become so popular since the arrival of the Bau. If Wsir was gaining a reputation as a protector of the land, Hwthr had become the patron of the home.*

Ast had continued to assess the health of the indigenous population as a species, and while they were working together, she compared her observations with Hwthr's experiences. 'They are well suited to their environment and they have shown considerable ingenuity in domesticating plants and animals, though I think their success is based, for a large part, on pure luck and the congenial climate.'

Hwthr was stirring a vat of barley mash over a simple hearth. 'I think it is more than luck. I have found them to have a quick, native intelligence and a respect for life that is quite touching. Every birth is cause for celebration.'

'Oh, yes,' Ast agreed, 'they cherish their young and no surprise there, given the difficulties they have in reproducing. Conception is not a problem but the way in which their younglings are born puts so much stress on mother and child that both are as likely to die as to survive.'

'I, too, have found that one of the most distressing aspects of my contact with them,' Hwthr said. 'For all that they have essentially the same mammalian physiology as the animals, they are much more susceptible to injury and illness. It is as if their intelligence has been won at the expense of a more robust constitution.'

'The report of the Ba surveyors made the whole process of human reproduction sound so simple, but I believe they cannot have observed a single birth at first hand or they would have known better. I think they were extrapolating from their zoological studies, with a lot of not very educated guesswork.'

Hwthr gave the pot an extra vigorous stir, causing some liquid to splash over the rim and hiss on the hearthstone. 'I think that the surveyors must all have been male!'

Skhmt's mate, Pth, was the least satisfied with his role. As metallurgist and artificer he had been disappointed to find how meagre were the land's mineral resources. He and Imn-Min had confirmed the presence of several ores of copper and they knew, from the original survey maps, that gold was to be found in streams and quartz veins to sunrise and upstream of their settlement. But there was barely a trace of the ores that could give them iron, aluminium or zinc. In his report to Wsir, Pth found he could not hide his frustration. 'I am sure we will find tin, and silver is out there too, but at this stage in our explorations we can do no better than follow the example of the locals and use stone tools and flint blades for everyday purposes. Swty has found volcanic glass in the desert and Skhmt has already shown that it can produce surgical knives every bit as sharp as steel, but for larger, sturdier cutting implements we would have to make do with copper, though the ores of this area are not blessed with the right combination of impurities that will harden the metal. I fear I will have to look elsewhere.'

'Introducing metallurgical skills at this stage in the Kemites' development would be seen as interference. Unless we can find a community where the essential processes are already understood I think we must be very wary of teaching them before their time,' Wsir cautioned.

'That is exactly what we were promised by the surveyors. We were assured that copper-working, at the very least, was established in this region,' Pth's tone expressed his exasperation.

Djhwty said, 'If we had a more efficient way of communicating with other settlements along the river we might be able to find those more advanced communities. Unfortunately, our attempts to get the natives to hear us have failed. When we try to send they become agitated and confused because they have no concept of telepathic transfer and they do not understand what they are experiencing.'

'How else can we contact other villages?' Wsir asked, 'when writing is out of the question?'

'The length of the Experiment is insufficient for any real progress to be made there,' Djhwty said primly. 'The humans see little reason to acquire what they consider to be unproductive skills. I would think it a great achievement if I could get them to use a few pictorial *symbols for labelling and quantification of their trade goods. It will be many years, if not generations, before they are capable of writing continuous text.'*

Pth raised his brows in surprise. 'Trade goods? What do they have to trade?'

For a moment Djhwty looked at his colleague in bewilderment, then he said, 'Nothing special. Boats are going up and down stream all the time, you must have seen them. They exchange their surpluses and the local specialities with other villages, things like pottery, stonewares, animal skins and worked bone. There is quite a demand for the hides and teeth of those ugly river beasts that Swty likes so much.'

'And what do they get in return?'

'Wood is their principal need. You must have noticed how tree-poor this region is. That is why most structures are built from reeds or mudbrick or a combination of the two. Palm trunks may serve for building purposes but only once the trees have outlived their use as food sources. The size of their buildings is limited by the wood available locally for roof beams and supports. Have you never thought why the rooms are so small?'

Wsir looked around and ran a hand over one of the slender wooden uprights forming the frame of the wall, noticing for the first time that it was composed of three tree limbs spliced together, the joins strengthened by tight bindings of vegetable fibres. The jambs flanking the entrance were more solid-looking but, on inspection, he discovered them to be fashioned from sheaves of reeds bound around a timber core, the outer surface smothered with a mud plaster. 'They are so ingenious,' he said, 'to make such substantial structures from inferior materials. Coniferous trees would provide timbers of suitable length and straightness but there are no such forests within our region. As I recall, the nearest would be in Astrt's zone.'

'Just imagine what they might do if they had access to those resources,' said Pth, excitement raising the pitch of his voice.

'It is possible that the people downstream already know of such materials,' Djhwty said. 'From what we have heard from the traders who make the journey this far, several of the downstream settlements are larger and more sophisticated that those of our friends locally.

They frequently barter with exotic materials like seashells and decorative minerals, which they must have acquired as the result of a chain of exchanges. If their boats were big enough I am sure that they would make a good living importing timber.'

'They would also know where to find the ores we are seeking,' Pth's voice had lost all trace of his earlier despondency. 'We could trace their lines of communication.'

'I suppose we could,' Wsir sighed. He had always suspected that the shuttle had landed them in the wrong place, since the small village in which they had settled was not as big or as sophisticated as those recorded by the Ba surveyors. If Djhwty's information was correct, they should have been sent to one of the downstream settlements where resources were more readily available and the arrival of their large group would not have been such an imposition on the local population. He knew that, sooner or later, if they were to give themselves the best chance of surviving the Experiment, his group would have to split up, but he had hoped that their little community would remain intact for some while longer yet. The close friendships and productive working relationships that had been formed during their time on Geb were bound to be tested by the departure of some of the most reliable members of the group. Wsir looked from one excited face to the other. He could not deny them the opportunity to satisfy their personal and professional curiosity. 'Make your plans,' he said, 'but please, delay your expedition until we have seen all that a full planetary rotation has to throw at us.'

Djhwty smiled. 'Of course. I want to finish drawing up my calendar so I have to have a full year's worth of astronomical observations from the same viewpoint. Our time-sense is already disrupted by the change in day-length and we must have some means of keeping track of the passage of time. I do not want to give up when I have just acquired a group of admirers.'

'What do you mean?' Wsir asked.

'In recent days, at my pre-dawn observations, I have had the company of some of the village elders, including the chief religious officials. They have been most interested in what I am doing, and they seem to have a pretty fair knowledge of the sky, at least as far as this time of year is concerned.'

'Why is that, do you think?'

'I am not certain but I believe we must be nearing some stellar event that they consider important. They keep count of lunar cycles and they seem to have a rough idea of the length of the solar year, probably by noting the growth of plants since there is very little in the way of meteorological variation to go by. They do not comprehend that Geb is in orbit about the sun, and I cannot convince them that the stars do not move around the planet, but my recent conversations have shown that they recognise seasonal constellations. They seem to be waiting for a significant astronomical marker, by their reckoning, to tell them that a new solar cycle is about to begin.'

'I cannot understand what they might be anticipating. As far as agriculture is concerned we are well into the hottest season. Little will be done in the fields for yellow-by-white days or more, by my estimation. Then we will see how the natives begin to prepare for planting. Khnm is particularly eager to see how they irrigate the land to achieve the soil condition we found on our arrival.'

Djhwty said, *'I am enjoying our new association. I will try to find out what it is that they are so eager to see.'*

The object of interest to Djhwty's fellow star-watchers became apparent a few days later, when the brightest star in Geb's sky cleared the horizon at dawn moments ahead of the sun. The Bau were at a loss to explain the excitement shown by the humans, which was out of all proportion to the event. At the next day's dawn Djhwty found himself surrounded by most of the local population, males, females and younglings alike, all intent on seeing for themselves this wondrous sight. As the sun's light overwhelmed the shining star the people made a joyous procession down to the river bank, singing songs as they went. At the water's edge, they gathered to chant verses so ancient that their words were nothing but noise and rhythm, and yet the sincerity of their voices was more expressive than meaningful words. The Bau, mere spectators, were moved almost to tears by the simplicity of the ritual, for ritual it surely was, as offerings of flowers and fruits were thrown into the water, but the Golden Ones returned to their mansion none the wiser.

It was an announcement from Khnm that both explained and changed everything. *'I was not convinced until now, because it goes against all sense, but I cannot deny the evidence of my own observations. The river is rising!'*

*

'At last,' Simon muttered as he read the e-mail from the Library. He glanced out of his tiny office window to see if the rain had stopped, but it opened on to a dingy concrete enclosure that pretended to be a light-well and gave him no sight of the sky. The persistent dripping sound might just be the overflowing of a blocked gutter. To be safe he grabbed his umbrella, and headed for the St George's Building.

The heavy rain of the morning had given way to a fitful drizzle which, nevertheless, soaked everything it touched, and most sensible people were staying indoors. At three thirty on a Tuesday afternoon there were few students about anyway. Arts students would have already finished for the day, if not the week, science students would be involved in practical classes, and the geeks in IT would be, as ever, huddled over their keyboards.

His bright yellow and red golfing umbrella put up a stubborn resistance to being folded and while struggling with it he wondered why he had bothered to bring it at all. Careful not to incur the wrath of the library attendant, he remembered to put the brolly in the stand by the entrance. It was so horrible that no one would want to steal it and easily recognisable when he came to collect it, as he knew he would, despite the occasional temptation to abandon it. He had a strange sentimental attachment to that umbrella, which had been his companion on several digs. He had once thought that, when he became a world-famous archaeologist, it would become his signature like Evans's walking stick or Carter's Homburg hat. Now it was more of an embarrassment, far too garish for its owner to be considered serious. Leaning at a sorry angle amidst an odd assortment of student compacts and the traditional cane-handled black umbrellas favoured by academics, it looked rather pathetic. Simon nodded to the scowling officer and pushed through the turnstile.

He was glad to see Sylvia at the Loans desk. 'Hi, Sylv. I've just got the message that the book is in at last.'

The librarian looked at him over her glasses. 'It must be a good one. I only sent the e-mail a few minutes ago.'

'Well, you know how long I've been waiting for it. I thought Inter Library Loans would be quicker than this.'

'Normally it would,' she said with an apologetic smile, 'but there was a mix-up to start with because, according to our records, there was a copy here already, so the loan request bounced back immediately.'

'But I ordered it because it wasn't here,' Simon sighed in exasperation.

'Yes, I know, dear. Some light-fingered so-and-so has obviously taken a fancy to it and we no longer have a copy that we can lend you.'

'Yeah, well, I couldn't understand why the Library didn't have such a basic reference text. Trouble is it's so expensive that I can't afford to buy it for myself. I used the department's copy in my last place.'

'Well, it's here now, so cheer up,' Sylvia said with the voice of reason. She took his library card and ran it through the scanner. 'At least you haven't any outstanding loans to complicate matters, but remember, it could be recalled at any time if someone else requests it.'

'Thanks.'

Simon tucked the book into his knapsack and was about to leave when Sylvia said, 'Oh, Simon, I meant to ask you. Do you know if Dr Beaumont has read your uncle's latest book?'

Simon had not known that Sylvia was aware of his family disgrace. He looked at her in silent amazement.

'Don't leave your mouth open like that or you'll catch a fly,' she laughed. 'I read, Simon, it's what librarians do. I've known for ages about Dr Beaumont's bête noire. And your full surname is on your library card. It doesn't take a genius to make the connection. You look a bit like him too.'

'Now you've really spoilt my day,' he said in the petulant tone brought out by any mention of Eric Evers.

'Anyway, back to my question. Has Dr Beaumont read Evers' latest book *"The Dawn of History"*?'

'I don't suppose so for a moment. Hell, even I haven't read it!'

'Well perhaps you should. You and the Doctor need to be fully informed before the lecture. I'd hate her to be ambushed by that smug, self-opinionated egomaniac.'

Simon's face broke into a broad grin, 'Sylvia! You know my uncle?'

'I don't need to. His character comes across loud and clear in his writing.'

'So what do I need to warn the Doc about?'

'You have to see for yourself, Simon. Here,' she reached below the counter and brought out the paperback she had been reading in Theatre A, 'you can borrow mine.'

'You paid good money for this?'

'No, of course not! That's a cheap Book Club edition. Tell Dr Beaumont she needs to know her enemy and she needs all the allies she can muster. I suggest she calls on her brother.'

'Her brother?'

'Read the book, Simon, and you'll see what I mean. But do it quickly. Dr Beaumont will need time to get her ammunition together and the lecture is only a couple of weeks away.'

Chapter 5: Arrivals and Departures

Since Sylvia's advice was usually sound Simon swallowed his pride and began to read the book that evening. Much as it hurt to admit it, he found Eric Evers' writing compelling. On principle, Simon had read none of his uncle's best-selling publications, a fact he had never confessed to his mother, though he had been forced to sit through family viewing sessions of the associated television programmes, which had been broadcast under the loose heading of 'documentary'. He could see why Uncle Eric was so popular. He oozed self-confidence, self-belief and self-satisfaction, but he also had a way with words. His knack of putting complex ideas into simple phrases without appearing to patronise his audience was a gift that some of Simon's lecturers had lacked. Evers' writing was well-crafted and he was a natural story-teller. Despite his misgivings, Simon found himself engrossed in the text from the beginning, though some passages caused him to wonder whether he had inadvertently slipped into one of his science fiction novels.

There was little in *'The Dawn of History'* that seemed relevant to the Doc's dispute with its author. He finished reading it over his lunchtime sandwich the next day and as he munched on a banana Simon forced himself to step back from the bewitching prose and the beguiling artistic photographs in an attempt at dispassionate analysis. What was it that Sylvia had seen? He needed a second opinion.

Later that afternoon, Simon wandered along to the laboratory where he found the usual state of armed neutrality between Pete and Sally. His friend was sorting through a collection of small bones, putting together what remained of the hands and feet of a skeleton from a Roman Christian burial. Simon was impressed by Pete's skill at this task which looked, to him, like doing a three-dimensional jigsaw puzzle with missing pieces and no picture on the box.

Sally, as always, had her back to Pete as she moved between a binocular microscope and her drawing board. Two angle-poise lamps flooded her work area with the nearest possible artificial equivalent of natural sunlight, but Sally was not happy because the daylight coming through the window was fading as the slate-grey sky threatened a spring thunderstorm. She looked over her shoulder at the noise of Simon's arrival. 'Oh, it's you.'

'Hallo yourself,' he said.

'Well, now I've lost the light,' Sally said, implying it was Simon's fault. 'I'll have to call it a day.' She tidied her table and gathered her belongings with cool, silent efficiency and left without another word.

'Thanks for the rescue,' Pete said. 'The atmosphere was becoming poisonous. What can I do to show my appreciation?'

'Just listen,' said Simon, and he recounted his conversation with Sylvia and its aftermath.

'And you've actually read the book now?' Pete asked. 'I thought you'd vowed never to sully your eyeballs with such trash!'

'Yeah, well,' Simon felt his cheeks burning. 'Sylv seemed to think it was important but I honestly can't see why. Have you read it?'

Now it was Pete's turn to feel embarrassed. 'Yeah, my guilty secret. I'll admit to reading the first one, too, the one that got the Doc in such a lather.'

'So, between us we should be able to work out what Sylv was on about.'

'You've read it more recently than me,' Pete said. 'Tell me what you remember that might have any connection with the Doc's work.'

'That's the trouble. There's only one casual mention of grain in a chapter that's otherwise just a re-hash of the old Thera eruption theory.'

'Thera! You mean Santorini? Well, that's it.'

'Huh?'

'A volcanic eruption! You really don't know?'

'Know what? I'm the new boy here, remember. I don't know anything.'

'You must know the name Theo Beaumont.'

Simon's eyes bulged, 'The vulcanologist? T.C. Beaumont is HPB's brother?'

'Yep.'

'We really need to talk to the Doc.'

*

Hermione answered the phone in her usual defensive manner. 'H.P. Beaumont speaking.'

'T.C. Beaumont calling,' came the amused reply.

'Theo! What a surprise. Where are you?'

'Heathrow. I've just flown in from Vancouver. Have you got room for a houseguest for a few days?'

'Of course! But have you told Mum and Dad? They'll be disappointed if you don't check in with them on one of your flying visits.'

'I've spoken to Dad and he agrees you need my company more than they do.'

'What are you talking about? I'm not in any sort of trouble, am I?'

'The Evers' lecture is plastered all over the Internet. I couldn't let my kid sister face the dragon on her own. We think you need to rally the troops.'

Hermione felt the suspicion of a tear forming in the corner of her eye. 'Thank you, Theo. When will you arrive? Do you want to go out for a meal?'

'I'll be there by about eight, but put the meal on hold. I'm pretty whacked from the journey and I think I'll need to crash out for twelve hours or so. Hey, my battery's going. See you later H.P.'

The knock at the door came the moment after Hermione had replaced the receiver. 'Come in,' she called with a cheery voice.

Simon poked his head around the door. 'Can we have a few words, Dr Beaumont?'

'We?'

Pete's face, sporting a silly grin, appeared above Simon's. 'Me too.'

'I might have known. You two seem to be joined at the hip lately. But if it's another petulant complaint about Sally, I don't want to hear it.' Hermione's light-hearted tone suggested they might expect a friendly reception so Simon almost fell into the room in his eagerness to get to the point before the Doc's mood changed.

Once they were settled in chairs pulled up in front of her desk, Hermione leaned back and said, 'Well? You seem to have something on your collective mind. Who wants to start?'

Simon took the plunge. 'It's about the lecture. I've been feeling so guilty about putting you into this position and we've been trying to come up with some sort of defence strategy.'

'You think I need defending?'

'No, not really, bad choice of words, but – well, I don't want to be responsible for sending you into an ambush. I know my uncle and he's a devious bastard.' Simon looked into her face, expecting the famous HPB scowl that registered her distaste for bad language, but all he saw was a calm, slightly amused expression, so he persisted. 'We think you need to gather together some ammunition in case of a showdown.'

Hermione's eyes opened at Simon's metaphor which was so similar to that used by her brother only a few minutes before. 'You make it sound as if I'm going to war. It's only a public lecture, Simon, and by a not very distinguished speaker at that, at least in academic terms. I think, if necessary, I can stand my ground on my home turf.'

Pete spoke for the first time, 'The trouble is, Doc, you don't think like him so you can't see where he's likely to set his traps. We don't want you to be hijacked by a pillock like Evers – sorry Simon!'

'Don't mind me. I've called him worse.'

'What makes you think I can't give as good as I get?' Dr Beaumont asked.

Hermione's remarkable calmness made Simon bolder. 'It's like Pete said. Evers is different from anyone you've ever met. He's never happier than when he can score points off a proper academic. He has this enormous chip on his shoulder about not having any qualifications in his own right and he tries to hide it by pouring scorn on the scholarship of others. His favourite saying is, "I've learned more in the University of Life than all the tweed-jacket brigade in their ivory towers." He got to be where he is today on sheer force of personality and knowing a few people in media circles who recognised a bandwagon when they saw it. He has tunnel vision when it comes to archaeology. All his studies have been exclusively aimed at proving his pet theories, theories he formed as a teenager when he first read Von Daniken, theories that've been discarded long ago by most sane people. But he's become the world's expert at selective research and a past master at ignoring inconvenient truths. His skill is in synthesis, putting things together in a way that makes even the most fantastic ideas believable, and delivering those ideas with such sincerity that absolute drivel appears like the soundest of common sense. He's a showman, a professional con-man, peddling fairy tales to the gullible who love him for fuelling their over-active imaginations, and he's come to believe in his own fantasies. He's made a good living out of them, after all, and he's not going to give them up easily. He's as protective of them as any proud father of his child and he won't hear a bad word said about them. He rushes to their defence armed with little more than words and the results of other people's hard work, adapted and contorted to his own ends. To call what he does 'plagiarism' doesn't come close. He's so far beyond that now, he genuinely doesn't see the problem. If any academic is brave enough to speak out they have to contend with Evers' intimidating public persona and the support of his devoted fans – all the conspiracy theorists, the Roswell believers, the legion of alien abductees. They'll greet any word of contradiction with choruses of "sour grapes" and "professional envy", shouted so loud that the courageous opponent is forced to retreat before their fury. And if any serious scientist persists in demanding satisfaction, they'll come up against the really big guns, the publishers. With the threat of never getting their own research into print, in the public domain where the real money is, most would-be authors back down.

'You've survived so far, Doc, because you've avoided any confrontation. You've denied him the opportunity for public debate, by which he means public humiliation. He sees you as the ultimate challenge, someone who hasn't succumbed to his magic but who hasn't yet nailed their colours to another mast. He doesn't know where you stand and it irks him beyond belief. He wants to have you on his side, to give legitimacy to his hair-brained ideas, but as he can't have that he wants to neutralise the threat, to eliminate your potential to demolish his theories. You have to understand, Doc. My uncle's brain functions in a different way from any ordinary mortal's and he won't play fair. It's my fault that he's got the chance to attack you and I want to do all I can to help.'

Hermione was stunned. This was the longest speech she had ever heard from Simon. He had always struck her as shy, often to the point of clumsiness, as when he first encountered Sally. His tendency to blush at the slightest thing may have been endearing when he was an undergraduate but now, when he wanted to be thought of as a serious research scientist, she knew he found the trait an embarrassment. But he had managed the whole of his monologue without a hint of pink appearing in his cheeks, and without once raising a hand to his hair. His expression of loyalty to her at the expense of his own family was touching. She was lost for words.

Pete broke the silence, 'It's not all Simon's fault. I suggested the invitation but we honestly thought you'd want to be far away from here when the time comes.'

Hermione rose to the implied criticism, 'So that man would be able to call me a coward? I think not. I am made of sterner stuff. But I do recognise your dilemma, Simon, and I am grateful for your support.'

'You're welcome,' Simon muttered.

'Moral support isn't going to be enough,' Pete said, now desperate for Hermione to realise the real danger Evers posed to her reputation and her career. 'Proper academic support and expert opinions have failed against Evers' brand of populism because they're too nice. They don't obey the same rules. Hell, he doesn't recognise their rules. He's a shit!'

'Peter!' Hermione scolded, leaning forward over her desk to make her displeasure clear. 'I know you are concerned, but I can speak for myself. It's just that, in the past, I have chosen not to.'

'But now you're going to be forced to,' Simon said, 'and all because of me. You can't face Evers on your own, Dr Beaumont, he'll tear you to shreds and I couldn't bear to be the cause of that.'

'Sylvia gave us an idea,' Pete interrupted.

'Sylvia? Librarian Sylvia?'

'Yes. She said you should ask your brother for help.'

Hermione sat up in amazement, a smile twitching at the corners of her mouth. 'And did she say why?'

'She told me to read the book,' Simon explained, 'so I did, but it wasn't until Pete told me who your brother was that I got the message.'

'You mean, use one media star to catch another,' Hermione's smile became broader as she surveyed their bemused faces. 'Well, it seems that my family have had much the same idea as you. Theo is arriving this evening and I think he's planning a council of war. Would you care to join us?'

*

Hermione tried to reach the door before Theo rang the bell. She failed. Her hand was on the latch when Miss Phillips appeared from her downstairs flat. 'Visitors?' the elderly woman said, the prim set of her mouth indicating disapproval. But Hermione knew her neighbour better than to be fooled by the indignant spinster act that she had cultivated over the years. She smiled and opened the door.

Theo entered, dropped his bags on the threshold and greeted his sister with an exuberant hug.

'Oh, it's you!' Miss Phillips said.

'Hi there, Adeline. How are you?'

'I'm fine, thank you for asking. It's about time you showed your face,' she said. 'Hermione could do with some family support.'

Hermione's eyebrows rose above her glasses in astonishment. 'Does everyone know my business?'

'I may be retired, dear, but my brain still functions. I keep an eye on the Internet and there's been a lot of talk recently about that Evers person, and I've seen the posters advertising his lecture.'

'Our Adeline's the queen of the chat-room, didn't you know?' Theo laughed.

'Less of the cheek, young Theo,' Miss Phillips said, but her admonition was softened by the slight upwards turn of her mouth.

Hermione never ceased to be amazed at the effect her brother had on people. Adeline Phillips occupied the ground floor of the house where Hermione had lived since her appointment to the University. Miss Phillips had been a mathematics teacher for her entire working life, having retired fifteen years ago. Since then, she had indulged her passion for science, astronomy in particular, by completing an Open University degree. She and Theo had enjoyed many a lively debate over afternoon tea. Just as she had taken it upon herself to watch out for Hermione, so she had also followed Theo's volcano-chasing activities across the media. She had appointed herself their unofficial godmother.

For his part, Theo had told his sister, on many occasions, how much he valued Adeline Phillips' opinion. His highest praise of her was, 'She has her feet firmly on the ground.'

Theo picked up his bags and said, 'Love to talk, Adeline, but I've just flown in from Canada and I'm pretty near collapse. I'll drop in tomorrow some time.'

'I'd better make some scones then. Good night, dears.'

As Miss Phillips closed her door, Hermione took Theo's holdall and said, 'Come on up. Tea or brandy?'

'Both I think.'

While Hermione made the tea, Theo rummaged through his bags, tossing his belongings around making the spare room his own within minutes. When his sister brought the tea into the sitting room she found him stretched out on the settee, his eyelids fluttering with fatigue. 'I see it's caught up with you at last,' she said, setting the tea down on the glass-topped table. 'What's this?' She indicated the flat rectangular package that she had moved to make way for the tray.

Theo shook himself upright and accepted the proffered cup. 'Oh, that's a little something I found for you in Vancouver. Open it.'

Watching Hermione carefully peel back the sticky tape and unfold one end of the plain blue wrapper, Theo said, 'Most people would just rip it open.'

She stuck her tongue out at him and slid the present out of its paper sleeve. Within a double layer of tissue paper was a framed photograph, a theatrical signature scrawled across one corner. Hermione gasped, 'How did you get this?'

'There was a *Stargate* convention on in the hotel where I was staying. I know you're a fan so I sneaked in under the wire and got that.'

'He wasn't there?'

'No, but it is a genuine autograph, I made sure of that. I thought you could keep it by your bed.'

'I'm not that besotted,' she said, though her lingering gaze on the photograph might have suggested otherwise. 'This will go in my office.' She looked up, surprised that Theo had not retorted. He was fast asleep.

*

Over his years of globe-trotting Theo had developed a certain immunity to jet lag. Hermione envied his ability to adjust his sleep patterns to counter the changes of time zone so that, within twenty-four hours of even the longest journey, he could appear almost human. She knew that caffeine was an essential element in his recovery process so she had a pot of strong coffee ready when he appeared in the kitchen at nine o'clock.

In silence Theo poured a mugful of the black brew and stirred in two large spoonsful of sugar while his sister made scrambled eggs. Hermione usually made do with a brioche roll or a banana in the morning but Theo's visits were excuses to indulge in the luxury of a more substantial breakfast. Her brother made short work of both the glass of orange juice and the fruit yoghurt that she set before him. 'Eggs won't be long,' she said, as Theo smothered a croissant with Miss Phillips' strawberry jam. 'Keep an eye on the toast.'

Theo nodded. He would be incapable of coherent conversation until at least halfway through his second mug of coffee. A loud ping caused him to frown but he deftly caught the toast as it was expelled from the toaster, juggling the hot slices onto the plates. Hermione spooned out the egg, put the pan to soak and sat down to eat. Theo ate greedily. Once he had sufficient carbohydrate under his belt he said. 'What's the plan for today?'

'The MSc lab classes have finished for this term and I don't have undergraduate lectures on a Wednesday so I'm pretty much free all day. I've asked Simon and Peter to meet us at eleven. Is that too early?'

'These are your student devotees?'

'Yes.' If Theo had been in a less fragile state she would have challenged his choice of words.

'What suggestions have they offered?'

'They both say I need to prepare my ammunition.'

'They're right. Tell me, honestly H.P., have you read Evers' books?'

She looked a little sheepish. 'Not completely, and certainly not recently,' she admitted.

'Then that's your first task. It shouldn't take more than an hour to read the relevant passages. Here.'

Hermione had not noticed the paperbacks Theo had placed on the counter by the toaster. He passed them across the table. 'I've marked the key chapters. You read them while I have a shower. Then we'll go and meet your co-conspirators.' He pushed back his chair and stood up. 'Oh, and resist the temptation to throw the books in the bin. Treat this as serious research.'

Hermione made a rude noise, though admitting Theo's advice was good. She had to know her enemy. She cleared a space on the table and opened *'The Makers of Mankind'* at the first of Theo's post-its. When her brother returned, rubbing his hair with a towel, he found her muttering to herself and marking the pages of the book with angry strokes of an orange hilighter pen, which told Theo, more than any words, that she was anxious. In normal circumstances Hermione would have considered the defacement of any book as sacrilege. Adeline had been right. Hermione needed her family around her. She would never have asked for help. She would have continued ignoring the Evers problem, becoming less and less communicative, more and more bad tempered, until her work began to suffer. Taking out her frustration on a paperback book was the first step in her catharsis.

*

Simon's first impression of T.C. Beaumont was that he was taller than he appeared on television. Otherwise, with his dark hair and aquiline nose he was so obviously a masculine version of his sister that Simon was amazed he had not made the connection before. It was all a matter of context and context was everything, as Simon had learned from his lecturers over the years. A talent that distinguished a good archaeologist from a great one was the instinct to recognise when things were out of context and then provide an explanation. Everyday existence relied on context. Objects or people encountered in the wrong place or at the wrong time failed to register against the stored images that constituted the human memory. In Simon's mind, Theo Beaumont was visualised against a backdrop of smoking mountains, flows of glowing lava or bubbling pools of steaming mud. In that sort of setting he was immediately recognisable for what he was. But in spite of the shared surname, Simon had no contextual clues to link T.C. Beaumont, vulcanologist, with H.P. Beaumont, archaeobotanist.

As he shook Theo's hand Simon was treated to the famous easy smile that was reputed to melt any female heart. 'Hi there, Simon. Glad to know someone else is looking out for H.P.'

'Theo, you'll make him blush,' the Doc said, her smile a carbon copy of her brother's.

'And I'm Peter French,' Pete said, reaching across Simon's shoulder to press palms.

'Glad to meet you, Pete,' Theo said. 'So, is this the full complement?'

'I've only involved this pair so far, or rather, they involved themselves. Do you think we'll need more?' There was a hint of anxiety in Hermione's voice, but apart from that, both Pete and Simon were struck by how relaxed she looked. Theo's charming presence was already having its effects.

'Let's see how we get on today before we send for reinforcements. Sit down, fellers. I want to hear what you think first, 'specially you Si, as you know the nature of the beast we're up against. Can you think of any weaknesses we can exploit?'

'Not personal weaknesses, no,' Simon said. 'My uncle has an ego the size of a planet and a skin as thick as the planetary crust. Any attempt at hurting his pride will bounce right off, and with such force that you have to duck the ricochet. He plays on the knowledge that his opponents have to be more protective of their own reputations. No one has dared to challenge the central premise of his theory for fear of seeming to endorse his ideas. He has everything to gain from the debate and they have everything to lose. He's also media-savvy. No proper scientist can afford to be publicly ridiculed by a sensationalist TV presenter.'

'Much as I thought,' Theo mused, 'but if we can't dent his personality perhaps we can cast doubt on his material.'

'You mean, come up with alternative theories?' Hermione asked.

'Yes, exactly. But Evers' overarching theory, that aliens somehow kick-started human civilization, is far too vague and we'd get nowhere trying to break his fans' belief in their prophet. We need to address more specific points. We have to target our attack on areas where we're on safe ground, scientifically speaking. So, you guys,' he turned to face Simon and Pete, 'I take it you've both been genning up on this stuff. What struck you about it?'

Pete answered first. 'He's plausible, that's the real problem. For someone who doesn't know much about archaeology, it's all very enticing. You want to believe him. F'rinstance, I don't know much about Mesopotamia or China and I could have been easily convinced by what he said about them, but I do know about bones and whenever Evers mentions something about human remains, it grates. To the ordinary punter it probably sounds perfectly reasonable and he uses just enough scientific vocabulary to make it sound legit. It's hard to put a finger on it, but that's the only area where I feel I might be able to help, bones I mean.'

'You are being too modest, Peter,' the Doc smiled. 'I've seen your exam results and I have high expectations of your dissertation. There's potential there for a PhD.'

'There, you see, Pete,' Theo said, 'H.P. has faith in you. And if bones are your bag, that's what you have to go for. I want you to sieve through Evers' writing and try to sort out the truth from the twaddle as it relates to your area of expertise. I bet you've been doing that anyway, haven't you?'

Pete nodded. Theo Beaumont was as perceptive as he was decisive, the ideal opponent to set up against Eric Evers.

'And what about you, Si?' Theo asked.

'Well, plants are my thing, fibres to be specific.'

'So, that's your job, if you're up for it. H.P.'s told me about your moral dilemma so we'll understand if you want to keep your head down. I know I wouldn't want to annoy my Auntie Aspasia.'

Dr Beaumont giggled, which Simon found rather disconcerting.

'And don't think I've forgotten you,' Theo said, rounding on his sister. 'After all, we're only here because of you.'

'And I'm very grateful,' Hermione said. 'Of course, cereals are my speciality and since my work overlaps, to a certain extent, with Simon's, I think we'd better combine our efforts.'

'Fine. And I'm i/c seismology and geology in general. I think we have a lot covered, unless there's anyone else you think we could use?'

Pete and Simon looked at each other, both mouthing, 'Sally?' Hermione caught their wordless exchange and said, 'I'd like to keep Sally out of this, at least for the moment. There's still work to be done and I don't want her distracted.'

'So, there's no one else?' Theo asked again.

Simon had been thinking about Theo's proposed strategy, and realised that if they were to prepare a defence against only a small part of his uncle's extraordinary theories, they needed to have mastery of all pertinent facts. Evers had developed opinions on almost every ancient civilization and yet he had never studied any one in depth. Because superficial speculation sold more books than sound academic debate, he had developed selectivity to a fine art. He could put together fragments of information from a range of unrelated sources and present it as a genuine, original theory. Anyone who had an equally superficial grasp of the subject could be fooled into believing his specious arguments. But, as Pete had shown, if they were to beat Evers at his own game they would have to concentrate on one specific area where they had the most expertise. Simon's and the Doc's work with plants, and Pete's interest in human remains, had most recently been focused on the analysis of finds from Dr. Masterson's Egyptian digs. But the narrowness of their specialisms gave them a limited view of the Egyptian scenario that Evers had exploited.

'We need an Egyptologist,' Simon said.

Theo looked surprised. 'Explain.'

'Obviously we have to concentrate on what we know if we're to be convincing, and that means Egypt. But we can only pick holes in Evers' theories, we can't tear them apart. We need someone who has a thorough knowledge of early Egyptian history and culture. We need to be able to see the big picture. We need someone who can spot immediately where things have been taken out of context, 'cos it all hinges on context. I don't think we have enough breadth of knowledge between us.'

'He's right,' Pete said. 'Evers can't be challenged one little point at a time. He'd laugh at us if we tried. We have to co-ordinate an attack on a broad front.'

'So, sis, what do you think?' The tone of Theo Beaumont's voice was not as confident as it had been. Simon's heart fell. They had given the Doc hope, for a while, but now it seemed that even her brother was having doubts. Simon looked up, prepared to meet disappointment in HPB's gaze, but to his surprise she was smiling.

Answering Theo's question, she said, 'I think it's lucky that Ian Masterson will be back at the University tomorrow. Can we reconvene then?'

*

After an hour of intense discussion, Simon and Pete decided they deserved a Theatre A coffee, especially as neither of them was ready to face the inevitable interrogation by Sally as to why they had been summoned to the Doc's office when she had not. On the way to the café, Simon said, 'Did you notice the new photo on the Doc's wall?'

'You mean the one beside her certificates?'

'Yeah, I couldn't see it very well from where I was sitting. It looked like a chap in uniform. Did you recognise him?'

'Not sure. There was something familiar about him but I couldn't really study it without looking as if I was staring at Theo Beaumont. What's your interest?'

'I was just wondering, d'you think the Doc has a bloke?'

Pete stopped dead in his tracks, 'Now there's an interesting thought.'

*

Miss Phillips poured tea from a glass *théiere* into plain white bone china cups while Theo helped himself to a scone with jam and thick clotted cream, saying, 'You spoil me Adeline.'

'I enjoy the civilized ritual of afternoon tea, but it has to be shared. Milk or lemon?'

'Milk of course. Taking tea with milk is what reminds me I'm British.'

'Do you need reminding?'

'From time to time, when I'm dashing from one side of the world to the other, I lose track of where I am and how I got there. Tea sort of grounds me.'

'You need roots, Theo.'

'If you're going to tell me that I need to find a nice girl and settle down…'

'As if I would!'

'You'd be surprised how often I hear that.'

'Not from your parents, surely.'

He laughed. 'No, not from them, at least not the settling down part. They can hardly preach when both H.P. and I were born in camp at the foot of a volcano.'

'How are they both?'

'Dad's still lecturing in London and Mum's taken up crochet.'

'I don't believe that for a moment.'

'It's true. It's a traditional Greek craft and she's good at it, too. Of course she still does some tutoring and she's still writing.'

'Hermione gave me a copy of her last novel – a bit too spicy for my taste.'

'I'm only glad she writes under her maiden name. I'm too old to suffer from embarrassing parents.'

Adeline chuckled. 'And what about young Hermione?'

'Oh, she's not embarrassing at all.'

'Theo!' Miss Phillips gave him a playful slap on the knee.

'Ow!'

'Don't be a baby. Now, what have you done to help your sister face her demon?'

Theo gave her a summary of the morning's meeting. When he mentioned Simon's suggestion of recruiting an Egyptologist to their cause, Miss Phillips said, 'He sounds a sensible boy. I think I'd like to meet him.'

'You'd frighten him half to death.'

'Oh dear! Am I that much of an ogre?'

'Of course not,' Theo's eyes sparkled with affection, 'but he's easily scared. He's Eric Evers' nephew.'

'So, you have found Hermione a mole.'

'Hardly, but he could prove very useful.'

'And have you got an Egyptologist lined up?'

'H.P. mentioned a colleague called Masterson. Does the name mean anything to you?'

'Indeed it does. Let me show you.'

Adeline moved to the computer desk in the corner of the room and logged on to the University's website. A little skilful navigation brought up the Archaeology pages with excavation reports and current dig diaries. Smiling from beneath the peak of a faded brown baseball cap was Dr Ian Masterson, director of the University's expedition to Nagada.

'Ooo…kay!' Theo said.

'What is that supposed to mean?'

He pointed at the computer monitor. 'Now I know why Hermione was so chirpy about him joining us.'

*

Wsir sat beneath the wild fig trees, watching the glinting of the water as the golden sunshine pierced the early morning mist. He had left the mansion at dawn, seeking the solitude of the little wooded rise overlooking the fields – or what had been fields a lunar cycle ago. Where he had so recently relished the success of his harvest, several younglings were splashing knee-deep in the floodwaters, chasing fish into the shallows. Where the feet of the Bau and humans had worn a broad path from the settlement down to the riverbank, farmers paddled reed skiffs across the floodplain. The river had risen so quickly and overflowed its banks so comprehensively that the landscape was now unrecognisable.

The inundation that had been so eagerly anticipated by the locals had been a devastating blow to the Bau. Not believing that the waters would rise more than a few hands-breadths, they had ignored the entreaties of the humans to move some of their stores and equipment away from danger. Djhwty's star observation hut had been washed away and with it his calendar records so painstakingly written on scraped skins. The clay pits worked by Khnm had turned into muddy hollows and the mudbrick walls that were to become his workshop had been undermined by the flood and disintegrated before they had been built above waist height. The rising waters had soaked Nyayt's store of fibres from the first harvest of augmented flax. The smell of the rotting and mildewed bundles had been as distasteful as it was distressing.

Wsir's grain was safe because he had heeded the human custom and kept his valuable stock close at hand where it could be easily guarded. Only now did he appreciate that the basket-lined pits dug within the enclosure of the Ba mansion were doubly safe, being on the higher ground, as were all the local habitations, and so out of the reach of the flood. His vines had not been so lucky. Planted on the dawn-facing side of a broad wadi that cut through the fertile region channelling a seasonal stream from the desert hills, the vines on the upper part of the slope had survived but, as the river spilled over, the water had undercut the sides of the gully, loosening the roots and tearing the young plants from the soil. The growing of vines had been Wsir's pet project, and its failure felt like a stab in the heart. Contrary to the Ba survey report, the Kemites in this region had no tradition of wine-making and they failed to appreciate just how much those unpromising twigs had meant to the Ba leader. No one could offer any consolation or provide any remedy. Wsir was so down-hearted by the experience that he gathered up the pitiful remains of his vines and burned them.

Looking out over the drowned land Wsir felt nothing but despondency. The event that the humans had clearly anticipated, and which they had received with unaccountable joy, had taken the Bau by such complete surprise that the Golden Ones were still in shock. They had not believed that the forces of nature could be so chaotic.

Wsir had much to think about. The Experiment was now in serious jeopardy. For almost a complete solar cycle they had survived their simple existence on Geb, celebrating every small achievement and proud of their adaptability. But it was one thing to indulge in a technology-free life on Perbau, where they knew that all the mechanised systems their kind depended on were still in place in case of emergency, and another thing entirely to choose to be stranded far from their home-world and all its sophistication, on a primitive planet where even the most basic of Ba technologies was beyond the imagination of the inhabitants. Wsir knew that, despite all the training and preparation, the Experiment had been an unattainable goal from the start.

The surveyors who were supposed to have provided all the data needed to inform the settlers about their new home had either cut corners or not understood how important the accuracy and scope of their reports would be. They had exaggerated the availability of natural resources and underestimated the effects of Geb's environment on Ba minds and bodies. But the biggest fault of the surveyors was their narrow view. They had concentrated on areas of promising resources where the indigenous population had already demonstrated that a minimum level of civilization was achievable. However, by considering only limited areas within the few target regions the surveyors had failed to consider the wider implications of geography, climate and weather. For all their scientific knowledge, they had declared Geb to be as near a perfect match for Perbau as they had ever found and so they ignored, wilfully or otherwise, the signs that should have told them a different story.

Wsir and his fellow settlers were not space explorers or planetary scientists, though each was a scientist of some sort, but such was the advance of technology on Perbau that there had been no teachers to hand on the craft knowledge that they needed. The skills required for survival on Geb, the ability to observe, to improvise and to adapt, had been acquired through personal research and experimentation. They had had to rediscover or re-invent the most fundamental skills, working with their hands at tasks that, for generations beyond counting, had been done by machines. They had, perhaps, become over proud of their new-gained dexterity and complacent about their level of expertise. When they encountered the people of Geb, the Bau soon realised that they were mere amateurs by comparison, dabbling in crafts and activities at which humans had become adept long ago out of necessity. The Bau had learned more from the primitive indigenes in the first few lunar cycles of the Experiment than the humans had learned from their alien visitors. Yet the natives continued to revere the Bau as all-knowing and to think of them as their patrons, their protectors, their gods.

Even Khnm's training as a hydraulic engineer had not prepared him for the remarkable flood. His plans for improving the irrigation of the fields had been overtaken by the event. He could not imagine how such a force of water could be controlled with the primitive tools and materials available to him. However, he was prepared to try. He had said, 'I need to know more about this flood. Its secrets lie upstream so that is where I must go.'

Wsir understood. Khnm and his mate Stt had said their tearful goodbyes before loading their belongings on to the small wooden boat provided by local traders who knew the river. After they had experienced some difficulty conveying to their guides the nature of their journey, Wsir had intervened and for the first time had used his position as god-king to instruct the humans to carry out his wishes. The departure of Khnm and Stt had caused a cloud of depression to fall over the Bau and the sorry air spread to the villagers. Wsir and his fellows would, at least, remain in telepathic contact with their friends, but the humans saw Khnm's leaving as desertion. And now Pth and Djhwty were talking about starting on a quest to develop metal-working, and Imn-Min wanted to go with them to explore the geology of the valley.

Though, by Wsir's own observations, the waters were receding, and the people remained in buoyant mood, his instincts were to rail against the losses caused by the inundation and the subsequent break-up of his community. His serious doubts about the viability of the Experiment had been revived by this disaster and now all he could think of was how they were to survive until the scout ship came.

He turned at the sound of footsteps and frowned when he recognised Swty approaching. To Wsir's irritation his brother sat down without invitation.

'It is a fine morning,' Swty said. 'The day will be hot.'

'When is it not?' Wsir's tone was tetchy.

'The water is falling quickly now. I think I will make one last expedition up the wadi to see what game might still be trapped there.'

'We could certainly do with the meat,' Wsir said, begrudging the admission.

'Do not look so glum, brother. Your subjects still love you.'

Startled by this mocking statement, Wsir looked into his brother's eyes but the dark contact lenses rendered his gaze unreadable. The imminent departure of Pth and his group would be of some concern to the locals but, as Swty implied, Wsir's acquired kingly position placed him, personally, beyond rebuke. Swty's unspoken implication was more worrying. The break-up of the Ba community could be seen as a vote of no confidence by the Bau themselves in Wsir's leadership. Was Swty suggesting that Wsir's Bau followers were beginning to question his authority?

Chapter 6: Friends and Allies

'Why do they persist in bringing us fish?' Ast groaned as she lifted the lid of one of the provisions baskets.

Wsir's nose wrinkled at the wafted stink. Try as they might, the Bau could not bring themselves to eat this particular gift. The rivers and oceans on Perbau were populated with an abundance of aquatic mammals, reptiles and insects but the life in Geb's waters was of a different quality. Ba physiology could not cope with freshwater fish and barely tolerated the produce of Geb's saltwater seas. But the humans relied on fish as an easily accessible source of protein and they were making the most of the swarms of catfish left in the catch basins as the floodwaters receded. They could not understand that the Bau had no desire to share this bounty. Knowing that fish was a good source of some of the minerals they lacked, the Bau had all tried to eat it with some uncomfortable results. The smell alone was enough now to turn their stomachs. *'Pass it on to the servants before it goes off,'* Wsir said.

'That will not rid us of the smell,' Ast frowned. *'They will only hang it up to dry and the whole place will be surrounded by the stench for days.'*

'It cannot be helped,' Wsir said, *'but perhaps I could issue some sort of decree forbidding the bringing of fish into our presence.'*

'You are beginning to believe in your own divinity,' Ast chided him. The Bau had long ago outgrown the need for deities and to accuse someone of acting like a god was a serious insult, but Wsir knew that his mate's warning was well meant.

'I fear that becoming gods is the only way we will survive. We came here so full of our own superiority, so complacent in our own sophistication, so confident that our very presence would enhance the lives of the primitive folk of this place, and what has happened? If it had not been for what we have learned from these people we would not have survived that first flood. Had they been less welcoming and more suspicious of us, we would have had a very hard time of it. But they interpret our unworldliness as divinity, they excuse our lack of practicality by calling us lords and ladies who should not have to work with their hands. They recognise our weaknesses, but choose to celebrate our strengths, and all that makes us different from them, by

revering us as gods. We are totally dependent on their goodwill. We cannot betray their trust by becoming the sort of capricious, dictatorial, vengeful deities that the ancient Bau once worshipped. We have moved so far away from the principles of the Experiment that I fear we have already abandoned it. All we can hope is that these people will not abandon us.'

Ast sat down at Wsir's feet, clasping her knees to her chin. 'I wonder whether, instead of becoming gods, we should be trying to become more like the humans,' she mused. Wsir's questioning look made Ast smile. She explained, 'They seem to be quite capable of looking after themselves. They do not need more gods. They had perfectly serviceable deities before we arrived. And what have we contributed to their society? We must face facts. We are not made for this planet so we must learn from those who are if we are to stand a chance of surviving the next four years.'

Wsir blinked in surprise. For a moment he wondered if he had heard her correctly, then, with the suddenness of a lightning strike, he realised how much like the humans they had already become. 'You have stopped counting by colour,' he said.

Ast sighed, 'Yes, and I am not the only one. Djhwty explains it as a matter of communication. The humans do not see colours as we do and we do not see them as well as we should with these.' She pointed to the contact lenses that made her irises appear as two black circles. 'Because they do not recognise the same colours in the spectrum as we do, they cannot associate a numerical order with spectral frequencies. If we have to accommodate our vocabulary then so be it.'

'It was inevitable, I suppose, that we should become more like them,' Wsir admitted. 'We could not expect to maintain the Ba lifestyle in isolation. Nor could we expect to change the humans. That was never the purpose of the Experiment.'

'Their influence on us is far more striking than anything we have done for them,' Ast agreed. 'We can learn so much from them. If only we had not considered ourselves so much wiser than them from the start, we might have been better prepared for the inundation.'

*

The fields were still sticky with the deposit of rich alluvium left by the flood and the local farmers were inspecting their land twice a day. Wsir listened to their discussions as they assessed the state of the soil and the best time for ploughing while making his own plans for a second Ba crop. He had planted up small samples of his precious seed grain in trays containing different mixtures of sand and loam. He suspected that the combination of trace elements and minerals needed by the Bau from their wheat could not be achieved naturally. In particular he believed that the precise balance of zinc, calcium and silicon was unattainable without manipulation of the soil but he could not convince the people of Kem to contaminate their rich earth with what they thought of as the barren desert sands. And why should they? Wsir was painfully aware of his selfish motives, putting the needs of the Bau before those of the humans. But the people of Kem were intrigued by his seed trays and watched them as eagerly as he did himself for signs of germination.

When the first hair-fine blue-green shoots appeared there was much excitement which became more animated as the tray was identified as that containing the local soil, unadulterated. Wsir could not explain the scientific significance of this result to his enthusiastic followers. They were convinced that this was some sort of omen, presaging another good harvest, and nothing he could say would persuade them that he had not personally influenced the corn's growth. They begged him to walk the fields so that his very footprints would confer this magical fertility on their land. He was handed a mattock and urged to turn the first clods of earth. The landowner held a basket to receive the soil dug by the hand of the god himself. When, later, the Bau heard that the villagers had shared out this divine gift to scatter on their vegetable plots, Swty snorted with scorn. 'You are becoming a legend it seems, brother. What will you do if the harvest fails to meet their expectations?'

Wsir deemed the question unworthy of response, though his silence made Swty laugh.

*

Imn-Min had sent a message to say that he had established himself in a settlement at the entrance to a broad wadi that stretched far into the dawn-side desert. He had high hopes of finding significant mineral resources there and had made some useful local contacts. 'I believe I may be able to gain knowledge of some of our fellow Bau. The wadi provides a natural line of communication between the river and the sea and there are traders here who come from Tiamt's zone. They speak a different language and it is difficult to make them understand what information I want but my appearance is of no surprise to them and I think I have heard them mention Mardk who is Tiamt's deputy. I am still not close enough to make direct contact but if I travelled as far as the coast I might come within telepathic range.'

Wsir and his companions celebrated this news with an impromptu party involving large quantities of Hwthr's strongest brew and the over-loud rendition of sentimental Bau folk songs, much to the wonderment of the humans. This led to aching heads and churning stomachs the next day but the knowledge that at least one other Bau settlement had, apparently, survived its first year was of great comfort to the group.

The news from Djhwty and Pth was also encouraging. Djhwty was thrilled to report that some traders were using rudimentary pictorial labels on their goods but this was of less interest to any of the Bau settlers than Pth's observations of the expertise of the downstreamers. 'They are producing pottery every bit as fine as Khnm's wares and their kilns are impressive,' he sent. 'They can achieve temperatures high enough to smelt copper at least.'

Wsir was in two minds about the implications of these discoveries, as he confided to Ast one evening while they sat watching the flocks of waterfowl returning to their roosts. 'I have always been uneasy about Djhwty's obsession with writing. The humans have a long way to go before they develop the abstract thinking required for symbolic representation of sounds. I do hope he will not press the matter. Influencing the natural evolution of the indigenous civilization in that way was never part of the Experiment.'

'What about Pth's metal-working?' Ast asked. 'Surely you would welcome metal tools.'

'Of course metal tools would save a great deal of time and effort – for us. But the locals are so proficient with what they have that I cannot see any benefit to them in advancing their technological development artificially. They did not need us to show them how to carve those wonderful vases and bowls and, though Pth may be unwilling to admit it, they are well on the way to acquiring metallurgical skills on their own.'

'I sense your frustration, Ast said, placing her hand on his arm, 'and your disappointment. The Bau are not as superior as we thought ourselves to be. Many of us would likely be dead by now if it had not been for these humans we so insultingly call "primitives".'

'And yet these "primitives" continue to revere us, to support us, to maintain our very existence amongst them. What have they to gain from this arrangement?'

'I can see nothing,' Ast said. 'We must just be grateful that they have chosen this path. I tremble at the thought of what might have happened if they had taken against us from the start.'

'And I fear for our fellows in other settlement zones. I cannot believe that all the inhabitants of Geb are as affable and amenable as the people of Kem.'

*

The fields were greening over with the new crop, the humans were planting peas and beans in their gardens and Nyayt was crying. She had sought solitude behind one of the store huts, hiding between clumps of reedy grass. But she could not conceal her misery for long. Ast heard her soft sobs and hurried to her side. 'What is it, sister?' she asked, putting an arm about Nyayt's shoulders.

For a long while Nyayt could not speak through her tears though her hands plucking at her simple linen shift gave Ast an idea of what the problem was. The loss of the augmented flax crop had been a heavy blow to Nyayt's self-esteem. She had already begun to doubt her position within the group as her skills at spinning and weaving were shown to be far inferior to those of the humans. The thread and cloth produced by the females were almost as fine as the materials of the costumes the Bau had provided for themselves at the start of the Experiment. While the little of Nyayt's flax that had been saved had been spun and woven by local women into fabric that demonstrated the promise of the new crop, she herself could take no credit for it. Indeed, she blamed her own envy of their handiwork for her obstinate refusal to take their advice and move the harvested flax fibres to dry storage. Seed had been saved only because one human had dared to steal some from

Nyayt's personal store. Far from being hailed as a hero, the man had been beaten and expelled from the village for this act of sacrilege, and Nyayt could not bear to think that she had been the cause of his disgrace.

Her sobs subsiding, Nyayt choked, 'I did not listen. I should have listened.'

Ast stroked her friend's hair. 'What would you have heard, dearest?'

Nyayt kept her gaze fixed on her hands. 'I would have heard wisdom,' she said.

Ast nodded. 'Yes, the humans are very wise, in their own way. We all do well to listen.'

Nyayt's shoulders shuddered with a final sob and she turned to look into Ast's eyes. 'But I have failed you all.'

'No, no! You must not think that. We have all met with setbacks but we have not failed. We are still here. What has made you so miserable at this particular time?'

'Have you seen today's delivery to the Mansion?'

Ast had noticed the file of offering bearers approaching from the village that morning. It had been Nyayt's turn to receive the gifts so generously given by the locals, gifts that were intended to make life so comfortable for the Bau that they would not want to leave. These offerings had become more elaborate since the departure of some of their party, as if the humans were trying to atone for a perceived lack of generosity that had caused the Golden Ones to desert their subjects. Where once the Bau had been provided with the raw ingredients for making their own food and drink, now the people brought them baked bread and cooked meats, pressed oils and cleaned vegetables. To provide every domestic comfort the humans gave reed matting and wooden furniture, pottery and stonewares, and most recently, as Ast guessed from Nyayt's reaction, woven cloth.

Ast had to acknowledge that it was needed. It had been assumed that, by this stage in the Experiment, the Bau settlers would have become self-sufficient in most things, including clothing. Like many assumptions made by the Experiment Directors, this had been *drastically over-optimistic. Acquiring and practising basic life skills while in a controlled environment on a sophisticated planet was very different from being able to demonstrate proficiency in those skills when there was no technological back-up. In spite of being a star pupil of the weaving masters on Perbau, Nyayt had soon realised how very limited her skills were in comparison with the women of Kem. They had not belittled or chided her when she had failed to replicate the soft, silky fabric of the clothing in which the Bau first appeared, but she had suffered acute embarrassment as her place at the loom was taken by an immature human female, who took to the task as naturally as a bird takes flight. Compounded by the disasters of the inundation, these experiences had dented Nyayt's confidence so badly that Ast doubted it would ever recover, and yet none of her comrades had criticised her. If the humans had noticed how threadbare and ragged the Bau clothing was becoming, it was natural that they should be concerned for the comfort of their gods. They had no concept of how their gifts would simply enhance Nyayt's sense of failure. In her own mind she had let her friends down and was contributing nothing to the success of the Experiment.*

'My dear Nyayt, what does it matter if the humans have given us cloth? They see our needs and respond. They do the same with our other requirements. Hwthr has not been allowed to make beer for some lunar cycles and her followers have even taken over her milk cultures. They do not think it fitting for the gods to do such menial work.'

'But we are not gods. I am not a god,' Nyayt said in a very small voice. 'How can they see what I have done, the mistakes I have made and still think of me as divine?'

'It is their nature. And do not think that you are the only one amongst us with doubts. I have watched mothers and babies die for no reason other than a cruel twist of evolution and still they beg me to attend their birthings to bring them good luck!'

Nyayt's eyes opened wide in astonishment. 'But...'

'No buts, Nyayt, this is the truth we must all face. The humans are, for all the deficiencies of their biology, better suited to this life than we are. They are more resourceful, more resilient, more patient than we can ever hope to be. We are, as their saying is, "like fish on a sandbar".'

'And yet they worship us.'

'Yes, and we must be thankful that they do or we would be in a very poor state.'

Nyayt sniffed. 'But I cannot face them, knowing that.'

'Then perhaps you should not have to for a while. Why not go to see Pth's new settlement? I am sure Skhmt would welcome you.'

'Are you sending me away?'

'No, dearest. I am suggesting that you need time and space to compose yourself. New surroundings, new people might be just the answer. Staying here to be daily confronted by those matters that have caused you such pain, can only do harm. You are no use to us or them if you are depressed.'

'How do you stand it, Ast?'

'I have Wsir.'

*

Hwthr ran her hand over the red cow's flank. She was concerned at the staring of the animal's coat. The flooding of her favourite grazing areas had come at just the wrong time. Now that the new growth had started, the cattle were regaining some of their condition but not as quickly as the native beasts which were better suited to Kem's environment. Hwthr's sleek creatures, nurtured in space, weaned on hydroponics, hand-fed and groomed into docility were a far cry from the semi-wild, lean animals of Kem's marshes and water meadows. In appearance Hwthr's pampered darlings were magnificent specimens of the breed but the veterinarian knew that they were not adapting wel to the planetary conditions. There had been successful cross-breeding, though the evidence was indisputable that the one calf resulting from an unplanned union between the red cow and a wild bull was proving to be of hardier constitution than the hybrids sired by Hwthr's black bull on the local cows. But still the village herdsmen sought to have their stock serviced by the Ba bull, and Hwthr could not persuade them otherwise.

As a more viable project, she was trying to encourage selective breeding amongst the native flocks of sheep and goats, but the humans thought her interest in what they called 'small cattle' was mere condescension. They made it clear to her that such lowly beasts were beneath the notice of a goddess of her stature. They continued to invite her to their homes and their farms but their attitude towards her had changed. She was kept at a distance, allowed to be a spectator only as the quick-learning humans followed the practices of animal husbandry and welfare that she had demonstrated. Hampered by their respect and care for her dignity, Hwthr felt trapped.

She held a bunch of sweet grass to the cow's muzzle and the animal greedily snuffled it up, her warm breath comforting on Hwthr's hand. We have done all we can here,' Hwthr murmured into the cow's ear. 'It is time we moved on.'

*

The meeting had begun in subdued mood but quickly developed into heated argument. Wsir had been astonished by Swty's attack on his leadership. His brother blamed him for the collapse of morale within the group that had, Swty asserted, driven both Nyayt and Hwthr to leave. Swty called Wsir arrogant, self-obsessed and uncaring. It was the last taunt that Wsir found most hurtful but he was too dejected to rise to his own defence. Perhaps Swty was right. Perhaps the worship accorded him by the humans had gone to his head and in responding to their respect he had ceased to care enough about his own people.

Ast, predictably, had leapt to her mate's support. 'You are wrong, Swty, so wrong. You have no right to say such things. Wsir cares deeply for all his...'

'Subjects?' Swty interjected with a sneer.

'We have heard you without interruption. Now, have the courtesy to let me speak.' Ast spat out her words with a sharpness no one had heard from her before. 'Wsir cares deeply for his friends...'

'Friends?' Swty laughed, his mocking tone challenging those around him to take sides. The result was not to his liking.

Khnsw, the youngest of the Bau, stood up and said, 'I am proud to call Wsir my leader and honoured to know that he thinks of me as his friend.'

Bst and Ndjty leapt to their feet, clapping and saying, 'Well spoken!'

Sbk, Srkt and Inhr were quick to follow their lead. Then, to Swty's confusion, dismay and anger, Nebt joined them. The general murmur of approval swelled to a chant of, 'Wsir! Wsir!'

Ast could not resist giving her mate a lingering kiss before turning to face Swty's scowl, her triumphant smile enough to make him back down. He pushed through the still chanting Bau and out into the gloom of twilight. Ast caught Nebt's hand to prevent her from following. 'You have made your choice as he has made his. You are better than him. Stay.'

Nebt's tears flowed freely but she remained at Ast's side, her fingers responding to her friend's tight grip.

Wsir shook his head and waved his comrades to silence.

'Much as I appreciate your support, my dear friends, this puts me in a very difficult situation. By the conventions of the Charter governing the Experiment, which have not, until now, been invoked, this meeting will be seen as a formal expression of dissatisfaction with my leadership.'

'Only if it is reported,' Khnsw said. 'We have more than three planetary rotations to live through before we will be in contact with the Bau authorities. If we are to survive that far we must make our own rules here to suit our circumstances.'

'He is right,' Srkt said. 'The conventions do not cover our situation because the authorities failed miserably in their predictions. It is no thanks to them that we are still alive, that every member of our party has survived.'

Sbk's deep voice carried over the chatter of agreement, 'We are all with you, Wsir. Your word is our law now. Whatever you decide, we will follow.'

*

Simon and Pete came to the mutual decision that old-fashioned methods were probably going to have the best results. Having taken over the largest study table in the library, they immersed themselves in defensive research until the bell sounded to announce the imminent closure of the St George's Building. They left a 'Do Not Disturb' notice on the pile of journals and books before adjourning to the Royal Oak for pasties and chips washed down with a potent pint of scrumpy. To the evident disbelief of the library attendant they were both waiting for the turnstiles to be unlocked at nine the next morning and waved to Sylvia on their way through. Soon they were spreading their papers out on the requisitioned table and repelling boarders, in the form of undergraduate students who were inconsiderately looking for a quiet place to work, with hard stares and the occasional muttered 'piss off!'

Simon kept an eye on the clock, a heavy mahogany-cased instrument with large Roman numerals, aware of its soft ticking marking off the time until their meeting. They had decided to call a halt to their efforts at eleven o'clock, allowing half an hour for a visit to Theatre A before they were due in the Doc's office. Simon felt a trifle guilty at leaving their reference materials on the table instead of putting them on the 'For Reshelving' trolley, but time was of the essence.

When they emerged from the stairwell into the atrium they were surprised to see Theo Beaumont at the Loans Desk, in cheerful conversation with Sylvia. As they approached, the librarian looked up and said, 'Hello boys. Theo's been telling me about your plans. Have you found what you needed?'

Their puzzled looks were met by Theo's brilliant smile. 'Sylvia tells me the café here does a mean cappuccino. My treat?'

'Thanks,' Pete said, with an uncertain frown in Sylvia's direction.

She laughed. 'I've known Theo for years,' she said, 'ever since he was researching for his PhD on Montserrat.'

'Sylvia's grandmother makes the best goat water I've ever tasted,' Theo said, leaning across the counter to plant a kiss on her cheek. 'See you later, Sylv. Lead on fellers.'

'Goat water?' Pete mouthed at Simon.

'I have no idea,' Simon muttered, shaking his head at the latest in a string of amazing coincidences.

With coffees and cranberry muffins claiming their attention, they had no time to consider the implications of Theo's Caribbean connections before he was pumping them for information. 'So what's this Masterson chap like? How old is he? Can we trust him?'

Simon answered, 'I've only met him a couple of times. He's been in Egypt since before Christmas.'

Pete, taken aback by the tone of Theo's questions, was wondering how much he ought to say. They were due to meet Ian Masterson in a matter of minutes and yet Theo seemed antagonistic towards him already. But Theo persisted, fixing Pete with a penetrating look. 'So, Pete, what do you know about him?'

'Like Si said, he hasn't been around much recently. There was a big Egyptological conference in Cairo back in November, and Dr Masterson stayed on for the dig season after that.' Theo's intimidating gaze suggested that Pete should say more. 'I took one of his modules in my second year. He's a great guy. Late thirties. Cricket mad.'

'And are you certain that he's the right person to have on our team?'

'Absolutely,' Pete said, rising to Masterson's defence with enthusiasm. 'He'll want to put distance between himself and anything to do with Evers' fantastical theories. If the Egyptian authorities get a hint of a connection they could pull the plug on the University's excavation. Mac'll be as keen as we are to put Evers in his place.'

'Mac? I thought his name was Ian,' Theo queried.

'Oh, it's an old joke, goes back years. Apparently he looks a lot like MacGyver.'

Theo's raised brow indicated his lack of understanding but Simon slapped his hand to his forehead saying, 'Of course! I knew he reminded me of someone.'

'If one of you doesn't put me in the picture soon, I'm going to get mildly annoyed,' Theo said.

'The American actor, Richard Dean Anderson,' Pete explained. 'He played this all-action CIA agent type character in a TV series, in the Eighties I think.

'And Jack O'Neill in *Stargate*,' Simon added.

'I thought that was Kurt Russell,' said Pete.

'That was the film. I'm talking about *SG-1*, the longest running SF series ever,' Simon was amazed at his friend's ignorance.

'Being an impoverished student I don't get to watch much TV,' Pete pouted.

'When you two geeks have finished,' Theo interrupted, trying unsuccessfully to conceal his amusement, 'I think I've got the message. Shall we go and meet the man himself?'

*

Dr Ian Masterson was standing in front of the photograph, his faded Surrey County cricket cap clasped in his hands behind his back. 'My hair's not as grey as his, is it?' he turned to Hermione.

'Not yet,' she said with a hint of mischief.

'You mean, in spite of the Antiquities Authority doing its best to drive me to an early dotage.'

'You're stronger than that.'

'I hope you're right. Evers sounds like a tough customer.'

'And you're every bit as tough. That's why we need you.'

'We?'

Hermione felt her cheeks burning. 'I need you. Oh, Ian, I am glad you're back!'

They were still in each other's arms when the door opened.

'I hope your intentions towards my sister are honourable,' Theo said, his tone not entirely unfriendly.

Surprised at her own composure, Hermione extricated herself from Ian's embrace and said, 'Hallo Theo. I'd like you to meet Ian Masterson.'

Her brother could not help but notice that Masterson had kept hold of one of Hermione's hands. The smile spreading across the archaeologist's face was confident as he extended his other hand in greeting. Theo realised he had met his match and immediately his attitude changed. He returned the smile and shook Ian's hand with genuine warmth.

Pete and Simon, stood in the doorway, jaws dropping in disbelief. Hermione took one look at them and burst out laughing.

Chapter 7: Council of War

'Well, who wants to start?' Theo asked, placing his hands palm down on the table as he surveyed the eager faces of his companions. They had appropriated a seminar room to give themselves more space. Chairs had been pulled up around two tables pushed together to accommodate their collection of books, papers and notes. Ian had set up his laptop connected to the room's data projector and was logging on to the internet.

Pete said, 'I probably have the least to say so shall I get my bit out of the way first?'

'Good man. Fire away.' Theo said with a beam of approval.

Pete took a deep breath and began, 'I've been trying to find where Evers got his Egyptian material from. We know he's never done any original research of his own – no academic institution worth its salt would touch him with a barge pole. So I started with the assumption that he synthesised his data from other sources.'

'Synthesis is a very generous way of describing his methods,' Hermione muttered.

'Sorry Doc,' Pete said, 'I'm trying to remain objective.'

Hermione smiled an apology and Pete continued. 'Anyway, it wasn't hard to find what those sources were. His principal theory is that the civilization was set in motion by some sort of superior beings and this theory isn't new.'

Theo looked surprised. 'You're telling us that it wasn't only H.P.'s work he plagiarised? This sounds good.'

Pete said, 'Exactly. The idea that the course of social and technological development in southern Egypt was influenced by incomers from the eastern desert regions was proposed as early as the end of the Nineteenth Century by Petrie himself. The theory was resurrected and revised by several well-respected Egyptologists over the years and most of them began to agree that the infiltration or, some even suggested, the full-scale invasion originated in Mesopotamia, hence the similarities in things like architecture and pottery styles.'

'But what has this got to do with your speciality, Pete?' Theo asked, with a hint of impatience. 'I thought you were our bones man.'

'I'm just coming to that,' Pete said, with a smug grin. 'One of the means of proving this theory was the analysis of Predynastic burials, particularly in the cemeteries at Nagada…'

Ian's head lifted at the mention of his site. He nodded. 'That's one of the main aims of the current project – to reassess Petrie's work. Here, I'll bring up some pics to show what we mean.' He tapped a few keys and the image of a desertscape appeared on the wall screen. 'Those little hummocks are all Predynastic graves.' He clicked through several views of the site. 'You can see how many there are. Petrie only managed to scratch the surface, so to speak. We're having to make choices between exploring new areas where we might find nothing, or go over the areas where we know Petrie made significant finds. His work is the basis for so much later study of the period that casting a modern eye over it was always going to be more cost effective than starting a dig on a virgin site. We decided to review the analysis of these graves in the light of the new techniques that've been developed since his time.'

'So what did this analysis show?' Theo asked, 'And, remember, I'm not an archaeologist or an anthropologist. I need answers in simple terms that even the average Evers fan would understand.'

'Well,' Pete said, 'you have to bear in mind that I'm talking about the work done in the late eighteen-hundreds and the first half of the Twentieth Century. It seemed to identify a separate race, a physical type distinct from the people of the north. Combined with different funerary practices and the hint of ritual cannibalism…'

A scornful 'Hah!' was expressed simultaneously by Ian and Hermione. They looked at each other across the table with embarrassed smiles.

'Oh, please!' Theo said. 'Go on, Pete. Don't mind them.'

'Well, in the fifties a study of the skulls from several cemeteries seemed to reaffirm the existence of these super beings. They were called the Dynastic Race and were credited with the foundation of Egyptian pharaonic civilization. We're talking anthropometrics here, measurement of cranial capacity to indicate intelligence.'

'Like in Nazi Germany?' Theo said with evident disbelief. Ian responded with another series of images showing paired skulls and long bones with measurement scales for comparison of their dimensions. Theo whistled through his teeth. 'And this was considered good science?'

'Precisely. And for a while this "scientific" approach was adopted by some very influential Egyptologists.'

'Like Emery,' Hermione said. At Theo's questioning look she added, 'He was the Edwards Professor of Egyptology at UCL, the post first held by Petrie.'

Ian's computer displayed a portrait of a tall bearded figure followed by a photograph of a bespectacled academic who was considerably less imposing.

Pete was now well into his stride. 'Yes, that's the bunny, and Emery's work at Saqqara and in Nubia was so significant that he was allowed to indulge in these extraordinary ideas without much opposition. It's those same ideas that Evers jumped on. Of course, his theory is that the Dynastic Race was of extra-terrestrial origin.'

'Please tell me that the theory has been debunked,' Theo begged.

'Well, yes and no,' Pete said. 'Most Egyptologists abandoned that point of view years ago but it keeps cropping up in the more popular sensational media offerings.'

'Like Uncle Eric's "documentaries",' Simon sighed.

'Yes, and because it's backed by names like Petrie and Emery it seems to have a pretty impeccable pedigree.'

'So what's our counter attack?' Theo asked.

Pete's expression became, if anything, smugger than ever. 'He's relying on well-known names who can't argue with him about the way he uses their work. There's no copyright on the interpretation of data. He's using fifty, sixty, ninety, a hundred year-old material that's long ago been superseded by other studies but, since the authors of the recent work are still around, he's careful not to tread on the toes of anyone who might fight back. That's his weakness. He has a reputation for putting down all opposition, but that's not because his position is unassailable, it's because he's shit-scared that someone will rumble him.'

'That's my Uncle Eric,' Simon agreed. 'He's got the pre-emptive strike down to a fine art. Sensible academics give him a wide berth. They can't afford to have their names dragged through his mud.'

Pete said, 'And it's their apathy that's created their problem. By steering clear of him, they've seemed to condone or at least not actively oppose his theories.'

'That's all very well, Pete,' Theo frowned, 'but if all we can accuse him of is using out of date material, I can't see that doing much to dent his ego.'

Now in full flow, Pete continued, 'But it's not only out of date. The sources are flawed...'

'That's more like it. Tell us more,' Theo said, leaning forward to rest his arms on the table.

'I'm sure he will, if you would only stop interrupting,' Hermione admonished him. 'Forgive my brother, Peter. He likes the sound of his own voice. Please continue.'

'We all know that sharing information by publishing, putting it in the public domain, is essential. Even Petrie knew that but he did so much work that a huge amount of it never got into print. He left his notes and papers to UCL, boxes and boxes of them, but there wasn't room to keep them. His successor, Margaret Murray, made the decision to chuck out everything that had already been published and that included all the Nagada stuff even though Petrie had written up only a tiny fraction of it. It turns out that the analysis of the Nagada skeletons covered only about six per cent of the burials that Petrie found and he found thousands.'

'And that's hardly a stratified sample,' Ian chipped in.

'So that means what?' asked Theo.

'It means Petrie probably published what he saw as the most interesting of his finds but they weren't necessarily representative of the whole site. So Evers' conclusions are based on a biased sample and some very iffy methods of analysis,' Ian explained.

'And, of course, if they know anything at all, Evers' fans won't see beyond the name Petrie. By claiming the Father of Egyptology as his authority, how can he be wrong?' Pete leaned back folding his arms in triumph.

'Let me get something straight,' Theo said. 'How did Evers get from your so-called Dynastic Race to invaders from outer space?'

'A vivid imagination?' Pete suggested.

'And people who want to believe him,' Simon added.

'Evers relies a lot on belief,' Ian agreed. 'He's not only turned the Dynastic Race into aliens, he's made them out to be gods or at least the descendants of human-alien interbreeding. He identifies the actions of his ETs with the mythologies of the civilizations they're supposed to have spawned. You can find legends of the gods interfering with human development in every culture. Myths are designed to satisfy our innate curiosity, to explain the inexplicable, to justify human behaviour. In the subjective realms of mythology it's easy to match up stories with reality. Mythologies give Evers material to fill in the gaps in the science or to replace the scientific results that he finds inconvenient to his theories.'

Theo nodded, 'We all know that fiction is much more appealing than fact. Evers' fiction is dressed up as fact because he saw there was far more money to be made by releasing it as non-fiction with lots of glossy pictures. And I suspect he's come to believe his own theories.'

'Just as myths had a powerful influence on the cultures that created them,' Hermione added, 'and they continue to be used as metaphors and models for the working of succeeding societies, even societies whose belief systems may have changed dramatically from those of ancient times. Look at how classical mythology is still embedded in our Western, predominantly Christian culture. Look at the number of authors who have exploited the Arthurian legends and Grail romances in so many different ways. Look at how the writers of popular historical fiction and even science fiction reach deep into the mythological well for inspiration.'

'Our mother for one,' Theo's comment was received by blank faces around the table. He turned to his sister saying, 'You haven't told them.'

'I had hoped to keep that quiet,' she said with resignation.

'I'll tell her you disown her,' he threatened, with a quick smile.

'Are you going to let the rest of us in on the secret?' Ian asked.

'Sorry,' Theo said. 'What my sister has omitted to tell you is that our mother is Xanthe Crowther.'

'Wow!' Pete and Simon said together.

At that moment there was a knock on the door which opened before anyone could respond and Sally entered. 'Ah, you are here. Someone's been looking for you, Dr Beaumont.' She stepped aside to let Sylvia pass into the room. Masterson hastily cut his laptop's connection to the projector and the screen went blue. Sally frowned as she realised that she was not to be included in the business of this distinguished assembly.

'Nice timing, Sylv,' Theo said, jumping up to relieve her of the large cardboard box she was carrying. 'Luncheon is served. You must be Sally,' he said as he placed the box on the table in the space hastily cleared by Pete and Simon. 'Would you like to join us?' Theo asked Sally. 'There's plenty here.'

Simon groaned inwardly catching Sylvia's eye. He got the message when she tipped her head towards the pile of chairs by the door and soon the librarian and the Ice Maiden were seated on either side of him, making their choices from the selection of sandwiches and soft drinks Theo had ordered from Theatre A. Simon and Pete soon found that Sylvia knew all about Mrs Beaumont's alter ego. Xanthe Crowther had made her reputation as a writer of historical fiction with a series of novels based on the last days of Pompeii. The stories played on the decadence and depravity of the city set against the looming natural disaster of Vesuvius. Despite a hefty dose of the seamy and the salacious, Xanthe Crowther's writing was famous for its historical and scientific accuracy. Her latest books were set in ancient Crete, in the period leading up to the Thera eruption and her devoted readers had sent them all to the top of the best-sellers list.

If Simon deliberately turned his attention to Sylvia, Sally failed to notice. She only had eyes for Theo. Their conversation over lunch was superficial and not related in any way to battle plans despite Sally's blatant attempts to find out what was going on. Simon was pleased to see that Theo diverted her more obvious approaches with a flash of his smile and a few anodyne phrases. The Doc had warned him that she did not want Sally distracted from her work, though Simon thought it would be more difficult to keep her out of things now she had had a glimpse of what, or rather who was involved in this conspiracy. He was surprised how easily Theo managed to persuade Sally to leave when the food supplies were exhausted, especially as Sylvia had quite obviously been asked to stay, but Sally left as meekly as a lamb taking the lunch debris away with her.

Theo was straight back to business as soon as the door closed on Sally's back. 'I think the mythological line is worth following up but I don't know much about the Egyptian gods. Do you want to give us a quick lesson, Ian?'

Masterson sat back and, after a brief pause to collect his thoughts, he said, 'I suppose the best place to begin is the story of how the gods came to earth to live among humans. That seems to be Evers' starting point when looking for evidence of his aliens. The Egyptians believed that Osiris, son of Geb, the god of the earth, and Nut, goddess of the sky, was allowed to settle in Egypt along with his sister-wife, Isis, and their brother and sister, Seth and Nephthys. Osiris took on the role of king and taught the people of Egypt how to make tools, work the land and grow crops. In particular he was a god of grain who was thought to have influence over the growth of the corn and the success of the harvest. He was also the god of wine, like Dionysus for the Greeks, who taught the Egyptians the art of viticulture. Isis and her sister Nephthys taught the women of Egypt how to turn the corn into bread and beer as well as how to care for children and all the other household arts. Their brother Seth, apart from being a hunter and warrior, had no such significant role in the civilizing of Egypt and felt he had been short-changed in the power stakes. He was especially aggrieved when Osiris, having taught the Egyptians everything he could, decided to spread his teaching further afield into the lands beyond Egypt's borders. While Osiris was on his travels, Seth had expected to be left as regent of Egypt in his brother's place, but Osiris nominated Isis to that position, which alienated Seth more than ever. When Osiris came back Seth held a big welcome home party and, to cut a long story short, tricked his brother into lying down in a big cedarwood chest which Seth slammed shut and had thrown into the river.

'Isis, accompanied by Nephthys, who had been horrified by what her husband had done, searched for the box to give Osiris a decent burial, but when they found it, Seth seized it back and had Osiris's body torn into many pieces, each to be buried in a different place. Not to be deterred, Isis and Nephthys searched the length and breadth of Egypt for all the body parts, and Nephthys's son, Anubis, bound them back together in the form of a mummy. The only part they couldn't find was the phallus, which had been eaten by a fish, but Isis was known as the Mistress of Magic, so she was able to revive her husband long enough to conceive a child...'

Theo could not resist an interruption. 'I've heard of posthumous births but a posthumous conception is stretching the imagination a bit, especially as the poor bloke had already lost his wedding tackle.'

Ian grinned. 'Remember, they were all gods. Osiris never really died despite all Seth's efforts. But he was so disillusioned with his treatment that he retreated to the Underworld to become King of the Dead. I suppose he thought the dead were better company than the living. Meanwhile, Isis had to hide herself away in the Delta marshes to escape Seth's jealousy. Her son, Horus, was born and raised there, indoctrinated by his mother and her supporters into believing his first adult duty was to avenge his father.'

'Sarah and John Connor,' Simon muttered.

'A good analogy, Simon,' Hermione beamed, 'perhaps with Schwartzenegger in the role of Seth.'

'Eh?' said a bemused Pete.

'*The Terminator*, even you must know that film?' Simon said in an exasperated tone before he registered the Doc's part in this conversation. He blinked his surprise at her and she laughed again.

'Only one of the best films ever made, though perhaps the sequel was even better,' Hermione said and Ian nodded his agreement.

'Order, order!' Theo called them back to the matter in hand. 'Can we stick to the Egyptians, please.'

Ian's look of amusement was so perfectly mirrored on Hermione's features that Simon was almost embarrassed to face either of them and he felt a blush rising up his neck. He was grateful when Masterson resumed his story.

'During Horus's childhood, Seth ruled in his brother's place and there's no record of any complaint about his reign. When Horus came of age, he challenged his uncle for the throne which he claimed as heir to Osiris. Of course, Seth dismissed Horus's claim and their argument became a series of battles fought on land and water, and in the sky. At one time Horus lost an eye which was restored by Isis, or by Hathor or Thoth depending on which version of the myth you believe. So the Eye of Horus became a powerful symbol of regeneration and renewal. In the end, the argument had to be decided by a tribunal of the gods who, after a lot of hoo-hah, declared for Horus. Every Pharaoh of Egypt claimed to hold his throne in direct descent from Horus and was called The Horus – a euphemism for King. At his death, Pharaoh became one with the god Osiris in the underworld, from where he continued to influence the growth of crops and the fertility of the land.'

'And what happened to Seth?' Theo asked.

'He was declared god of the desert lands and all foreign countries. He was also given a couple of foreign goddesses as wives to make up for his being deserted by Nephthys.'

'So, in the end, he got the better deal.'

'Not in the eyes of the Egyptians,' Ian smiled. 'To them, Egypt was the world and everywhere else was, by definition, inferior. Foreigners were to be pitied for not being Egyptian.'

'So, Evers is claiming that Osiris and his gang were aliens.'

'Yes. He'd have us believe that the original "gods" were extra-terrestrials who taught humans all the skills of civilization from farming to pottery, wine-making to weaving. He won't have it that human beings could possibly have developed all these good ideas on their own.'

'And what evidence does he use to back up these claims?'

'All sorts, from every conceivable source that might be useful. That includes literature and mythology as well as scientific analysis of finds.'

'Don't forget,' Hermione added with feeling, 'that Evers has done no scientific research of his own. His scientific analysis is based entirely on other people's work.'

'Before we get embroiled in that subject,' Sylvia said, 'may I say something?'

'Fire away,' Theo said, glad to postpone Hermione's contribution for a while.

'Evers makes a very common error which Dr Masterson has, without realising it, condoned.'

Everyone looked at Sylvia with open-mouthed astonishment.

She laughed. 'I'm sorry, Dr Masterson, but you know I'm right. Where does your story come from?'

'From Egyptian religious literature,' Ian replied with a frown.

'And when?'

'Aah!' Ian nodded, 'I catch your drift.'

'Exactly. The Osiris story was not written down in the coherent form you have just retold until very late in Egyptian history. In fact, that version, the one that all primary school teachers will tell their classes, was not circulated until Classical times. The influence of Greek and Roman authors still predominates. Why, we even know the Egyptian gods by the Greek forms of their names.'

'Sylvia's right,' Ian confirmed. 'Osiris is really Wsir, Isis would be Ist or Ast or something similar. But we've become so familiar with the Hellenised names that we can't change them now.'

'So, what you're saying is that Evers picks and chooses the mythology that suits his theories, just like he selects the archaeological evidence.'

'He has to,' Ian said, 'The Egyptians themselves didn't go in for mythology *á la Greque*. There are scraps of the Osiris story to be found in some of the oldest writings, like the Pyramid Texts, but they are only scraps, incomplete, inconsistent and incoherent. Some of the language is so antiquated that it's virtually impossible to make sense of it at all.'

'And that's what my uncle will play on,' Simon added. 'Wherever there's an element of fuzziness or uncertainty he'll quote just enough to make a text fit the point he's trying to make. He'll forget to say that, a few sentences on, there's a section that contradicts what he's claiming as absolute fact. His craftiness lies more in what he chooses to leave out than what he puts in.'

'Using mythology in the way that Evers does is like the interpretation of the Delphic Oracle,' Sylvia said. 'The utterances of the Pythia were so garbled, ambiguous and vague that they could usually be interpreted by the people who consulted her in whatever way best suited them. They heard what they wanted to hear and because it was supposedly the words of the god Apollo the message was thought to be the divine truth. Wars were sanctioned on the most spurious of oracular interpretations.'

'The voice of reason. I knew I was right to include you in our little conspiracy,' Theo said, his devastating smile directed at Sylvia.

'I'm glad my area of expertise has come in useful at last.' Sylvia looking around the table at the puzzled faces, felt compelled to elaborate. 'I may be just a librarian now but my MA dissertation was on mythological influences in English Literature.'

'You're not *just* a librarian,' Pete said, more loudly than he intended, 'Like Theo said, you're the voice of sanity in an insane world. I wouldn't have got this far without having you to listen to my moaning.'

'How sweet of you to say so.'

'Before we drown in sentimentality, can we get on,' Hermione said with a sigh. 'It's already three o'clock.'

'Quite right, H.P., so let's move on to your area, as that's mainly why we're here. How did you get on with your reading this morning?' Theo's commanding presence silenced the group and all attention was directed towards his sister.

'To tell the truth, I had not read Evers' work properly before. I first became aware of it when one of my students asked me what sort of person Evers was, as if I ought to know from personal experience. The student was surprised that I had never met the man because, and I will never forget what he said, "I thought you'd worked with Evers on the Fayyum material." It turned out that one of the cornerstones of Evers' theories about Egypt was what he called the "sudden" appearance of domesticated wheat in early Predynastic times. He suggested that its appearance owed nothing to natural selection or human agency but that it was introduced by his aliens in the form of a genetically modified grain. My doctoral thesis was a reassessment of the significance of grain found in some of the Predynastic sites around the Fayyum area in the early twentieth century. Evers quoted this, taking excerpts out of context in the way you have all been describing, as proof of the alien influence. He then took the ideas further, extrapolating far beyond what was credible, to justify his theories in other areas of Egypt and even in other countries where completely different conditions pertain and cultures developed along totally different paths.

'I know he has twisted the work of many other scholars to his own ends but, as you have pointed out, most of them are dead or so eminent that they are beyond caring. I want to know why he picked on me and my work, why he singled me out as his sole modern reference source.'

'I think I can answer that,' Simon said. 'At the time he wrote *The Makers of Mankind* the ink on your thesis was barely dry. I have no idea how my uncle got hold of it but he must have thought, "Here's an obscure little work that no one else will ever read," and felt free to use it to give an air of genuine scholarship to his book. He thought he could do that without challenge because he's got no understanding of how the academic world works. He reckoned without your thesis becoming a standard reference for archaeobotany.'

'Not to mention a huge contribution to the understanding of the development of cereal crops for arid conditions.' The surprised silence which greeted Sylvia's interruption caused her a moment's confusion, but she passed it off by adding, 'Am I the only one who knows that Dr Beaumont's principal funding comes from Global Food and Famine Research?'

Simon slapped his forehead, saying, 'You're right Sylv! Of course we all know that but Uncle Eric won't know the Doc's work well enough to make the connection with GFFR. Like so many others he has no idea of how archaeological research can be applied to modern problems.'

'Ignorance is no excuse,' Theo snorted. 'He must be shown that he can't make free with other people's serious and valuable research.

Just what is it, exactly, that Evers has taken from your work?' he asked his sister.

Hermione took a deep breath. She always felt uncomfortable defending her work. In spite of her academic reputation, diffidence still dominated her personality. When presenting a paper at a conference she became more and more nervous as question time loomed, anticipating confrontation. The fact that her work had been, until now, received with universal approval had not prevented the butterflies. The main reason for her refusal to deal with the Evers problem was the inevitability of a stand-up argument which she could not be sure that she would win. Examining the evidence then writing about her theories, taking time over her choice of words, editing and rephrasing the paragraphs, checking her references, was what she did best. Extempore response to questions was not her strong point, and if questioners were as stubbornly attached to their theories as Evers clearly was to his, Hermione's natural politeness would prevent her from reacting in a similarly belligerent fashion.

But she was amongst friends here. She had heard how hard they had worked to support her and the least she could do was show them how their efforts had emboldened her. 'Well, the first major point of contention is the way he deliberately misinterprets my identification of the different forms of wheat that show the development from the cultivation of wild grasses to a fully domesticated crop. I was able to demonstrate that the emmer, that came to be the principal wheat type grown in Egypt, was a natural hybrid of two wild species. I also made some progress in tracing the evolution of those species from primitive grasses towards the eventual hybrid, which was chosen for its strong rachis and naked grains that separate readily from the glumes...'

'Whoa there! Jargon alert!' Theo waved his hands in a 'time out' gesture.

'Sorry,' Hermione said, 'I forgot. The rachis is the central stem of the ear of wheat. If it's brittle it will break during harvesting and the grain will be shed and wasted. Wild species depend on this feature to self-seed – the grains will be easily scattered if they break away from the stem on contact, say, with animals or if blown by the wind. But for farmers, who want to store the grain, it's much better if they can cut the ear and keep it whole. The glumes are the casings that surround the grains and they are tough, almost pure cellulose, so they have to be removed before the grain can be processed. This is done by threshing, which is hard work, so the easier it is to separate the grain from the glumes the better. The fact that emmer shows both these traits is pretty sound evidence that it was selectively bred from naturally occurring hybrids for precisely those reasons.'

'So it's evolution by human selection rather than natural selection,' Theo nodded wisely.

'That's very well put, though whether the selection was accidental or deliberate, and just how long the process took, are matters still open for debate,' Hermione said. 'He claims this supports his theory that parties of these aliens "seeded" civilization in different centres over a period of centuries if not millennia. What he doesn't say, or doesn't understand, is that successful cereal hybrids are usually self-pollinators, which is nature's way of ensuring they breed true and don't acquire unwanted traits through further interbreeding with other wild species. It is highly unlikely that cross-pollination with a supposed enhanced strain would be possible because the selfing property prevents this from happening. It's what we call reproductive isolation. Anyway, Evers also plays on the fact that similar hybrids had occurred at different times in different areas, so that emmer became the most widespread wheat type of the ancient Near East. Evers ignored the evidence for intermediate forms of wheat and claimed that the new, improved type resulted from interbreeding with a genetically modified grain introduced by his alien gods.'

'Is that all?' Theo sounded disappointed.

'I would have thought that was quite enough rubbish for anyone to be expected to swallow, but he goes further. He revives the old chestnut of mummy wheat.'

'Hah!' Ian exclaimed. 'I never cease to be amazed at people's gullibility.'

'That's what Uncle Eric relies on, his readers' gullibility, or rather, their willingness to have the wool pulled over their eyes. They so desperately want to believe him,' Simon contributed.

'Is someone going to tell me the significance of this mother wheat?' Theo's question was greeted with howls of laughter from all sides.

'Not that sort of mummy, silly!' Hermione said, eventually, having searched her pockets for a tissue to wipe the tears of amusement from her eyes. 'Mummy as in embalmed body.'

Theo seemed none the wiser so Ian came to his rescue. 'There was a tradition of burying foodstuffs in Egyptian tombs, provisions for the afterlife. Sometimes they made models of granaries with the grain bins full of real barley or wheat. But there was also a custom of including a shallow tray filled with a mixture of soil and seed grain, the idea being that the germination of the corn was symbolic of rebirth and resurrection. It seems these trays also formed part of the annual rituals associated with the planting season – sort of a token gift to the gods and also a sign of their blessing on the harvest to come. If the grain in the tray germinated successfully, the corn in the fields would grow well. Some of these trays, especially the ones in tombs, were cut into the silhouette of Osiris himself, shown as a mummified king.'

'What capital can Evers make out of that?' Theo was still puzzled.

Hermione took up the explanation, 'There have been many stories, for instance one concerning Tutankhamen's tomb, of wheat from Egyptian graves germinating as soon as archaeologists exposed it to the air. This is, of course, nonsense. Where such things are witnessed it usually turns out to be a scam practised on tourists by local entrepreneurs, but the myth is perpetuated that Egyptian wheat can still germinate even after thousands of years in the dark.'

'And it can't?' Theo queried.

'No, of course not. The grain survives in recognisable form because of the speed of desiccation in Egypt's incredibly hot, dry climate. But that very process destroys all hope of the grain remaining viable. Only seeds with a really tough outer coating can survive a long period of dormancy, perhaps centuries in extreme cases, but not millennia. And, anyway, wheat isn't tough enough.'

'So I ask again,' Theo said, a hint of exasperation creeping into his voice, 'What use does Evers make of this?'

'He claims that the miraculous viability of mummy wheat is due to its otherworldly qualities, being of alien origin. It's just another example of his taking an outdated or discredited theory and moulding it to his own design.'

'He does the same with linen,' Simon said, sensing it was his turn to add to the weight of evidence piling up against his uncle.

'Go ahead,' Theo encouraged him.

'Well, the few scraps of linen fabric from Predynastic Egyptian sites show that the people were spinning and weaving quite successfully at a very early period. The fineness of spun thread and the number of threads per centimetre in the weave were almost unbelievable. In fact, carbon dating had to be applied to convince people that these remains weren't the result of site contamination – more modern specimens brought in from somewhere else, by accident or design. But Uncle Eric says that the fine fabric is the result of another alien genetic modification, this time an adaptation of flax to provide the necessary quality of fibres. He won't accept that the Egyptians were an amazingly resourceful and practical people. He insists that they can't have had any of their good ideas or developed any of their fantastic skills, without help from a superior culture.'

'Busy little bodies these aliens,' Theo mused. 'Now tell me, what's the significance of carbonisation?'

'Theo!' Hermione gasped, 'You've been playing us along. You knew all this already, didn't you?'

'In outline, yes,' Theo admitted, 'but I needed you all to sort it out in your own minds, to be able to explain it as if to an idiot, because that's the only language Evers' readers will understand.'

'Absolutely right,' Sylvia agreed. 'He'll dismiss proper scientific language as a smokescreen, put up by academics who want to maintain some mystery about their subject. He'll say you are contemptuous of the ordinary people, that you are deliberately trying to make them look small, questioning their intelligence. Language is so important, and to give Evers his due, he uses language very well.'

'You wanted to know about carbonisation?' Pete asked.

'Yes I did, didn't I,' Theo gave his sister a hard stare.

'Yes. Well, carbonisation,' she said, suppressing the urge to giggle, 'is the best way for the original plant structure to be preserved.

Most of the grains we study have been carbonised. There was a theory that this was a natural result of aging but even Evers has to admit that, if that were the case, we'd be up to our ears in carbonised plant remains, accumulated over many thousands of years. No. Plant materials rot, or desiccate, or get eaten, or, when subjected to intense pressure underground, they turn into oil and coal. The carbonised grain we study is usually the result of charring, either through cooking or by deliberate or accidental burning.'

'That might be true for grain but linen fibres are not easy to work with,' Simon chipped in. 'They're so fine that charring destroys crucial surface features. Sometimes all we can see are their imprints in other materials, like pottery or plaster or human skin, so precise botanical identification is often impossible.'

Ian added, 'Most of the grains that Sally's been looking at are carbonised. They came from a grain pit that had been cleaned out by burning, to get rid of insect pests, probably. But why do you need to know?'

Theo leaned back and folded his hands behind his head. 'Because this brings me to my little contribution. My hackles started to rise when I saw how casually Evers cites volcanic eruptions whenever he wants to cover up a notable lack of evidence. He says that much of the proof for the existence of his aliens was destroyed by the fall-out from Vesuvius, or Etna, or Thera, or Stromboli, whichever happens to fit his timeline. His explanation for the destruction and carbonisation of organic remains is that they suffered from the searing heat of volcanic ash or lava. He quotes the discovery of layers of ash or pumice in northern Egypt as proof.'

'And you're saying that's not true?' Pete asked.

'That volcanic debris has been found in Egypt? Oh, that's true, to an extent. The Santorini eruption of around 1600 BC was gigantic, but the sort of fall-out that Evers suggests is like what you think of at Pompeii – metres of compacted ash or solidified lava – and that wouldn't have reached as far as Egypt. The eruption did generate large amounts of pumice that were carried by the prevailing winds and marine currents to the shorelines of the eastern Med, and some lumps of this so-called Minoan pumice have turned up in Egyptian Delta sites.

But that's a hell of a long way from proving that Egypt was covered in layers of super-heated ash or red-hot lava.'

'If you're talking Thera,' Ian said, 'the date's wrong too. We've been assuming, as Evers does, that these alien influences were active in the Predynastic age. Thera is New Kingdom.'

'Ah, that's where he's muddied the waters,' Theo said. 'We know that Santorini has erupted on many occasions, more or less violently than the Minoan event. There's a sort of pattern to these eruptions but without eye-witness evidence, like Pliny at Pompeii, we've no way of pinning down the events to a particular date, or even century. Also, the further back in history we go, the fewer humans there were to witness it and the impact on human culture is almost unnoticeable, especially the farther away from the actual volcano you look. But that just gives Evers license to mess around with dates to fit his own theories. We come back to this theme of his playing on his readers' ignorance. If you say something loudly enough, convincingly enough and often enough, people will start to believe you. To Evers, volcanoes are convenient disasters that he can call on to cover up truths which he finds unpalatable, just like the ash of Vesuvius covered Pompeii.'

'Yes,' said Sylvia, 'He relies on his readers being so engrossed in his narrative that they won't stop to question his facts. When he mentions a volcano, they all conjure up a mental image of Vesuvius, or Mount St Helens, or as it would be for me, Montserrat, and they nod wisely as they recognise the awesome power of nature. The fact that he takes these events completely out of their true context is obscured by the vividness of the description. In a way you have to admire him, if only for his ability to tell such convincing lies.'

'So, are we going to call his bluff?' Pete asked, a suspicion of concern in his voice, 'because he's got some pretty single-minded supporters who'll rush to his defence at the first hint of trouble.'

'Pete's right,' Ian said. 'Evers' camp followers don't care about the truth. To them he's a symbol of free-thinking, almost a spiritual leader, and you know how hard it is to confront blind belief. They're not interested in the facts, only the way Evers interprets them.'

'But what about the waves he's causing in Egypt?' Simon asked. 'The damage he's already done is bad enough. If he's allowed to go on promoting this rubbish without Egyptologists standing up to be counted, there won't be any sort of future for archaeology in Egypt.'

'Simon is right,' Hermione said, the quietness of her voice bringing silence to the room as they all remembered that she was the focal point of their discussion. 'We must confront him now while we have him at a disadvantage. Since the invitation to speak came only because of Simon, Evers will be thinking he's amongst friends. He may even be expecting to have me endorse his theories. But we must not go in all guns blazing. We must pick away at his ideas one at a time, just as we've been doing here. It will do no good to get angry no matter how aggravating the man is. We must stay calm and focused, keeping to the facts that we can defend and not straying into areas of conjecture. We must show Evers what true academic research is all about. We must show him up for what he is, a charlatan.'

'Way to go, sis!' Theo said, clapping. 'I knew there was a fighting spirit hidden somewhere under that mild-mannered exterior. You're too much like Mum to sit back and just let things happen.' He looked around at the faces of his sister's friends, smiling at their amazement. 'I think this council or war is concluded. Go forth, my children, and prepare for victory.'

*

Wsir looked at the ears of wheat which were just forming at the tops of the stems, and he smiled, but as his glance swept over the field his smile became a frown. Apart from some patches having a darker colour, there was little appreciable difference between the plants though the area had been sown with a mixture of the two types of seed reserved from his first harvest. The few plants which had retained the distinctive blue-green colour indicating Ba origins, were reduced in height and their ears were less weighty. The rest of the crop looked no different from the native wheat growing in the field on the other side of the narrow irrigation channel. He feared the modified stock was already reverting to type and after only one season that was a huge disappointment.

At least he did not have to suffer Swty's scorn at this notable lack of success. His brother had taken himself off into the hills on an extended hunting expedition taking several other Bau with him. Tfnt and Shw, he could understand. The meteorologist and her mate, the atmospheric scientist, had always preferred the freedom of the wild lands to the responsibilities of an ordered world. From the very first moment he had been allocated to his team, Wsir had also experienced doubts about the oil research scientist, Shzmw. He had a lust for blood that was unnatural in a Ba and even Swty had expressed surprise at Shzmw's boldness in the hunt. Since they had been amongst the first to declare their loyalty to him, it was to Wsir's dismay, that Inhr and Wsrt, together with Srkt, had also joined Swty's expedition. The splitting of the Bau community into two distinct factions was the most worrying aspect of this whole, unnecessary disagreement.

The avian expert, Skr, had a great love of the desert oases and marshlands, which reminded him of the landscape of his native Rstaw, but he had declined Swty's offer to join the hunting group. When he had informed Wsir of his decision he said, 'I told Swty the truth, that I am too old to keep up with the enthusiasm of his followers. He said he understood but I did not like his tone. Pth tells *me there is abundant avian life in the north. I think I should join him there.' When he remembered that Pth also hailed from Rstaw, Wsir could not disagree. Skr would be happier and safer far away from Swty's irrational behaviour.*

Wsir sensed rather than heard Ast approaching. He schooled his features into a welcoming look but she was not to be fooled by his exaggerated smile. 'What is wrong, dear one?' she said.

Not trusting his feelings to words, he spread his arms wide indicating the farmlands. Ast knew at once what he meant. His thoughts were so dark that he was sending *them quite clearly. That, above all, told Ast how troubled he was. For a Ba to lose control over his thoughts in this way was a sure sign of distress.*

'They will come back,' she sent.

Wsir, startled at the form of her response to his unasked question, looked dejected. His shoulders fell and his head bowed. Ast felt his shudder of emotion as she took him in her arms and Wsir, who had always been so strong, so certain, the rock on which her life was founded, wept on her shoulder.

Chapter 8: Turning Points

Ast was beginning to think that she would never see a Ba smile again. Since Swty had taken his companions into the desert the remaining members of Wsir's party had been thrown into each other's company more and more and tensions were rising. The Bau had always valued their personal space. A place where one could be truly alone had been a rarity on Perbau and so all the more to be relished. On Geb there was so much space and it was so silent that the Golden Ones had chosen to stay together rather than experience the uncomfortable solitude of the empty planet. Ast had been surprised by Swty's quick adjustment to the conditions of their new home and even more amazed that so many of their friends had chosen to follow him.

To keep their bodies exercised and their minds occupied the Bau has assumed regular daily tasks despite the disapproval of the people of Geb, who thought such mundane matters beneath the dignity of gods. Nebt, having taken over Hwthr's role in supervising the dairy, had become immersed in experimental cookery but Ast worried that Nebt's intense enthusiasm was covering up a deep unhappiness after the acrimonious leave-taking between her and her mate. It was difficult to imagine how painfully she must be feeling the physical separation from her life-partner. Ast suspected that Swty was still sending *to Nebt but she had no way of knowing if his mate was responding to his thoughts.*

The news from downstream continued to be encouraging. Pth and Skhmt had established themselves in a settlement on the sunset bank of the river, where the broader floodplain allowed greater scope for agriculture. Skr had joined them and in honour of his and Pth's shared home they had called their settlement Rstaw. Nyayt had also moved there and seemed much happier to be in a place where no one knew of her failure. The humans of Rstaw were not as awestruck by the Bau as their compatriots upstream. Nyayt had sent *news of how she was being re-taught the skills of spinning and weaving by some old women. 'They treat me like a youngling and are most forgiving of my clumsiness. It is so refreshing to be in the company of people who do not judge me and who have no expectations of me.'*

Hwthr had visited Pth's new home in her exploration of potential grazing areas. She had sent *such a glowing description of the settlement that the others had become even more disconsolate and only* the news that Hwthr had decided not to stay there had prevented more Bau from moving downstream. Hwthr had left her beloved cattle at a village called Iwnt on the opposite bank of the river to Qbt, where Imn-Min had settled. She had found a native herdsman who had shown an empathy with the beasts that encouraged Hwthr to think they would thrive under his care even if she herself were absent. Already she was preparing for the day when the Bau would leave Geb and the animals would be left behind, but for the while she would not be parted from them for long. She confirmed her safe arrival after the long river voyage by a sending to Skhmt. 'It is so good to be back. Forgive me, my dear friends, but I find I miss the company of my cattle more than that of my own people. When I reached the village and saw the red cow in the shade of the big sycomore tree I knew I was home.'

The news of Hwthr's new-found contentment had a strange effect on Wsir's companions. The Bau had difficulty in accepting that their absent fellows were happy when the members of their own community were so dejected. While they should have been celebrating these little successes instead they were becoming morose and self-pitying.

Ast had just returned from another unsuccessful birthing. One of the mansion servants had called her to attend the labour of his daughter. Arriving at the house, a primitive hut made from mud-daubed woven panels supported on a fragile withy framework, she was horrified to find the mother-to-be was no more than a child herself. Ast had been unable to dissuade the natives from their custom of pairing off their younglings as soon as a female showed the first signs of adulthood. The slim, almost emaciated figure lying on a straw-filled pallet was already near death when Ast arrived. Evidence of the girl's pregnancy was barely apparent and yet her father swore she was near term and the pains had started the previous day. Ast knew there was no point in saying that the girl had exhausted all her strength in trying to expel a child too big for her narrow hips. Without help the baby was bound to die along with its mother. Skhmt might have been able to do something had she been close enough to attend and had the natives accepted the idea of surgical intervention. Ast had bathed the girl's fevered body while softly singing a Ba lullaby which the distraught parents and bewildered husband took to be magical words of healing. When the frail body shuddered its last Ast closed the child's eyes and *murmured the Ba words of passing before leaving the family to their grief.*

Nebt recognised the look of helplessness on Ast's face and ran to embrace her sister. It was only after some while that Ast realised that it was Nebt who was crying.

'What is wrong, dearest?' she asked, holding Nebt by her shoulders, which were heaving with sobs that had been suppressed for too long.

'I am carrying,' Nebt said at last, her tear-swollen eyes downcast.

This was the last thing that Ast had expected. A principal criterion in the choice of the settlers had been that they should not have young children. The Bau believed that, since their younglings matured quickly, the length of time proposed for the Experiment would mean parents missing the most crucial period of their offspring's development and no Ba would want to delegate the responsibility for their children's upbringing to others. Since the Bau would not contemplate a separation that would make them strangers to their own young, it was considered inappropriate for younglings to be included in the Experiment. The survey scientists had ascertained that the differences in their reproductive systems prevented Bau and humans from interbreeding so there was no question of any unexpected mixed-race pregnancies. But because of the uncertainties of life on the Experiment planet all potential settlers had agreed to abide by the Charter which decreed that no Ba younglings should be hatched into the alien environment. The Experiment Directors believed that children born on the primitive world would find readjustment to conditions on Perbau too difficult. Only a few of the oldest Bau settlers had left offspring on the home-world and those were already adult, often with families of their own.

'How?' Ast asked, keeping her voice as neutral as possible, fearing the reply.

'The last time the hunters returned,' Nebt said, 'I kept my distance, though it was hard, but Swty must have empouched me while I slept.'

Ast's eyes strayed to her friend's abdomen. The slightest bulge, unnoticeable to anyone who did not know to look, showed that Nebt's breeding pouch was indeed full. 'How long?'

'I'm not sure how the planetary rhythm might have affected my cycle and I am out of practice at calculating in Ba time units but I think the egg will be air-viable in a matter of days – if I do nothing about it.'

Ast's gasp of horror made Nebt toss her head in defiance. 'He did not seek my permission. I did not ask for a child. You know we all agreed. What sort of life can I offer a youngling on this planet with an absent father?'

'Perhaps Swty will...'

'No, Ast. I will not have him back. This is the ultimate betrayal.'

Ast knew she was right. When Bau paired for life it was a matter of great commitment after sometimes years of deepening acquaintance and mutual respect. Before the announcement of the pairing, the couple would have discussed their future in detail, including the decision as to when they would start their family. By fertilising one of Nebt's ova without her consent, Swty had broken one of the most solemn vows of their life-partnership. Such situations were almost unheard of on Perbau, though Ast knew of one pair-break, and, in a case like this, Nebt was within her rights to abort the egg. But, in spite of the fierce determination in Nebt's eyes, she still loved Swty for what he had been and, since Bau did not take second partners, this was probably her only chance to be a mother.

Ast said, 'You will not have Swty back, but you will have his child. We will support you. Wsir is still leader and he is Swty's older brother. He will stand as the child's father. I suppose, as this is your first pregnancy, you have no sense of whether it is male or female?'

'No. I will have to wait until the air fixes the membrane.'

'Whatever the circumstances of his or her conception, the youngling is not to blame. We will tell Wsir tonight, then you can decide when and what to tell the others. Let us make this a matter of joy not sorrow.'

But the news of Nebt's carrying was overshadowed by a sending from Djhwty. 'Imn-Min is split! There was a rock fall in the quarry where he was working. Min was trapped, both legs broken. Imn is barely scratched but traumatised.'

The broadcast sending *brought an instant response from Skhmt.* 'I am on my way,' *but all the Bau knew that it would be days before she could reach him.*

'I am closer,' *Ast sent, her message coinciding with Hwthr's,* 'I can be there before nightfall.' *With their resources stretched so thinly, the veterinarian was Imn-Min's best hope.*

Imn-Min had been born one of the rarest of Bau, a double embryo hatched from the one egg. Though not anatomically joined, the two halves were inseparable. The physical discomfort a double experienced when out of each other's sight was so intense that the Bau used the term 'double agony' to describe any severe pain. The mental connection of a double was such that they thought and spoke in unison, two bodies considered as one person, speaking with a single voice. But one half of a double could suffer injury individually if an accident occurred while the two were far enough apart. This had happened to Imn-Min and the damage to the Min half was so serious that the mental shock had severed the pair-bond. Imn's body was unscathed but psychologically he was a wreck. Hwthr would try to set the bones of Min's legs but no one had the skill to repair the damage to the double Ba. The split was irreparable and, should Min not recover from his injuries, the best that could be hoped was that Imn would die of grief because descent into madness was the only alternative.

The settlers were suddenly united in their concern for their friend. The sendings *were broadcast generally to reach whoever wanted to listen. The hunting group returned to the mansion and disagreements were set aside. Imn's chaotic thoughts were difficult to block out and all Bau felt something of his distress. Hwthr's report on Min's condition was also pessimistic.* 'The thigh bones in both legs are shattered and one has pierced the flesh. I have no way of repairing the bone. At home we would use a bone grafter and regenerative therapy but the best I can do is to straighten them as far as possible and bind them tight.'

Skhmt, consulting with her colleague even as she journeyed upstream, advised, 'Remove any fragments of bone that you can see in the wound. Even a tiny splinter carried by the bloodstream to the heart or lungs could prove fatal.'

When the doctor arrived she found Ast and Djhwty caring for Imn while Hwthr tended Min's injuries, aided by a wise woman from the human village of Qbt where the double Ba had settled. The open wound was as clean as they could make it with astringent lotions and the last of Hwthr's small stock of antibiotics. The wise woman had been struck dumb at the silvery sheen of the exposed bones but Skhmt was concerned that the bone surface was not metallic enough. 'The low gravity and the diet have already taken their toll,' she said. 'All our skeletons must have been weakened like this. The breaks are far more serious than they should have been. On Perbau the same accident would have resulted in no more than heavy bruising. We must be careful.'

As Min lay in an alcohol-induced stupor, Imn's mental screams echoed the pain that his double was not feeling. The village woman had called in her son, a priest in the local shrine where Imn-Min was already revered as a divine patron. The man had tried to prevent Hwthr and Skhmt stitching the edges of the wound because he considered it an act of sacrilege and when they ignored his protests he began an animated conversation with his mother. The Ba doctors, distracted by the rambling thoughts of their friend, did not catch the significance of the humans' discussion until the woman darted forward and dragged aside the sheet covering Min's body. The priest's tirade was silenced as he gazed for the first time upon the naked body of his god. The hairless golden skin was unremarkable compared with the absence of any external sexual characteristics.

Ast noticed the humans' reaction and sent to Skhmt and Hwthr, 'Cover him, quickly. They have seen.'

The doctor twitched the sheet from the woman's hands, saying, 'This is needed. We must bind his legs together, the one to splint the other.'

Hwthr eased herself closer to the bedside, forcing mother and son to move back. 'What can we use for a catheter?' she sent.

With a movement of her eyes, Skhmt indicated her bag. 'That contains all the basic medical supplies I have. You will find a tube in there.'

Ast had to use all her mental power to calm Imn as her colleagues worked on his other half. When she next had a chance to look across the room the humans had gone. Later she recognised this as the moment when Min's godhood had been assured. When she first saw the white-swathed image of Min set up in his shrine, with only his hands and, in place of the necessary tube, a very human sexual organ emerging from his bindings, she understood how the artist who created this image had interpreted the description given to him by the priest. The emblem set up beside the shrine's entrance was a broken rod, the two parts separated by the circle of oneness. She wept at this eloquent display of human understanding.

*

Nebt, deprived of her sister's support, had to make her own decisions about revealing her condition, but when Swty reappeared she knew she could no longer hide it. He had known exactly what he was doing and he knew, almost to the day, when the egg would be ready to leave the pouch. After the initial shock of Imn-Min's plight had subsided, Swty sought out his mate.

'You have prepared the nest chamber?' he asked.

'Did you think I would do otherwise?'

'And it will be tomorrow?'

'Yes, I think so. But, in the circumstances, I am asking you to stay away.'

'It is my child. You cannot deny me...'

'Oh, but I can. You denied me the choice of time and place, you denied me the joy of that moment. You broke every promise that we made to each other and to our people. You are no longer in a position to say what I can and cannot do. This youngling will be mine, not yours, not ever!'

For a moment the anger in Swty's eyes made Nebt fearful, but she held her chin up and fixed him with such a ferocious stare that he knew he had lost her.

By the time Ast returned, the egg, its toughening membrane glowing with the deep tawny-red of the male Ba, was nearly full size. Swty and some of his party had left the settlement and Wsir had taken responsibility for Nebt, seeing that she ate properly and took regular rest. Ast examined the egg and declared it healthy.

'We must make the arrival of the youngling a cause for celebration,' she told her mate. 'He must be made welcome. You know how sensitive newborns are to their first surroundings. If we are all gloomy and thinking negative thoughts he will be disturbed from the start.'

Wsir agreed, 'I have told Nebt I am honoured to stand as his father and I will be beside her at the hatching. I have already sensed a bond forming between us.'

'He is a strong one,' Ast said, 'I only hope his birth on this planet will not make his return to Perbau too terrible. We have found the differences uncomfortable enough, but the reverse will be more difficult and, for a youngling with no experience of Perbau's light and the higher gravity, the transition might be too much.'

'We will have to deal with that when the time comes. For now, planned or not, his birth must be treated as normally as possible.'

'And has Swty spoken to you?'

'He has accused me of stealing Nebt's affections and coercing her into letting me usurp his position as the child's father. It is all bluster. He knows he has done wrong and his supporters have been shocked by his breah of Ba conventions. He is feeling isolated and so he lashes out at me. I am strong enough to take it. He will be back in time for the hatching'

The egg hatched as predicted and, when the first Ba to be born off the home-world uncurled and shook off the ruptured membrane, the mental cry announcing his birth was heard as far away as Pth's settlement in the north and Khnm's island home in the south.

'I am Inbw!' the youngling sent and all his fellow Bau sent thoughts of welcome to their newest companion.

Nebt took the child in her arms and kissed the top of his head. Still with closed eyes, Inbw's nose and mouth snuffled and twitched until they found Nebt's breast. As he took his first gulp of milk his mental sigh of contentment washed over all the Bau like a soothing balm.

While Wsir spoke the traditional words of paternal recognition, each Ba came forward with a gift for the newborn. Wsir's voice faltered when he saw Swty trying to push his way into the nest chamber, but Inhr and Shw held his brother back and Nebt's scowl kept her mate silent. Having taken his fill, Inbw pulled away from the breast and his eyelids fluttered open. Everyone present heard and felt his pain as the light of Geb fell on his unprotected eyes.

Before anyone else could react, Swty tossed a package at Wsir's feet, saying, 'Take it, quickly. Give it to my son.'

It was traditional for a Ba father to provide the first clothing for a child, as the mother provided the first food. Wsir had a smooth wrap of Ba cloth, taken from one of his own kilts, ready to hand and was put out by what he saw as Swty's attempt to exert his authority but his brother's tone was urgent, insistent, concerned. Wsir picked up the bundle and shook it out to reveal the fur of a young jackal. He was at first bemused by the oddity of Swty's choice, then he saw that the skin had been cured to a fine softness, and the mask had been fashioned into a hood with the eye-holes filled with discs of smoky rock crystal. Wsir could not imagine how many days of work it had taken nor how many pieces of quartz had been ruined before Swty had produced a matched pair of lenses. He nodded his appreciation and, with Ast's help and in spite of Inbw's frantic struggling, he slipped the protective mask over the youngling's head and wrapped the dark fur about his shoulders. The effect was immediate. Inbw relaxed in his mother's arms and began to twist his head this way and that to accustom his eyes to their new-found vision.

In a conciliatory tone, Swty said, 'It will not protect him from the fiercest sun but it should allow him to go out at dawn and dusk. That is why I chose the jackal,' and, before anyone thought to thank him, he turned and left. Afterwards, Skhmt consoled Nebt with the thought that the dimness of the nest chamber had saved the youngling from immediate damage but it was Swty's gift that would prevent permanent blindness and even make Inbw's life bearable.

To the satisfaction of the Bau and the astonishment of their human followers, Inbw grew quickly. The chubbiness of the egg soon left his features and his body acquired the proportions of an adult far earlier than a human child. Since his scalp was constantly covered by the jackal mask only Nbt knew how long his downy hatchling hair had grown before it disappeared. His speech developed with equal rapidity and he was as easy with the Ba tongue as with the language of Kem. When he became fully mobile and had been weaned he began to kick against the constraints of his life in the mansion. This became a cause for many heart-searching conversations between his mother and his adoptive father.

'I must find a suitable home for him,' Nebt said. 'I think a cave in the cliffs would be best but I do not want to take him anywhere near Swty.'

Wsir had been thinking along similar lines. Much as he hated to give up the settlement where they had made themselves so comfortable, it was time to move on. 'We will go downstream,' he said, 'Hwthr has identified a site which sounds ideal for our purposes.'

The decision to abandon his agricultural experiments, which once he would not have contemplated, had been made easier by the disappointment of the second harvest. Only a few baskets of the modified grain had been collected with which to start a new crop and that could be done anywhere, though his expectations of success were now miniscule.

Ast reminded him, 'If we are to move it must be soon. Khnm sends word that the river has reached its lowest level and Djhwty says the stars are close to flood alignment.'

'Yes,' Wsir agreed. 'We will tell the servants today. They deserve to know.'

When the villagers heard the announcement their reaction was not quite as dismayed as Wsir had expected. Then he remembered that not all the Bau would move with him. He had little doubt that the moment he and his followers had left, Swty and his companions would take possession of the mansion. Where once Wsir had been their beloved god-king, his brother would soon replace him in the people's affections. The humans had no interest in the disagreements between their gods and as long as there were still Golden Ones to protect their community it mattered little which of the Bau remained and which departed.

The boats were half a day's journey from their destination when they received their first direct *sending from another Experimental zone.*

Faint because of the distance and frantic because of the content, the message had to be relayed up and downstream where few of the Bau could bear to believe what they heard.

'*Mardk has killed Tiamt!*'

*

The huge black four-by-four drew up at the University's main entrance and the driver's window slid down with a mere whisper. Evers leaned out and looked around. There was no one in the security booth and no evidence of any official who might be asked for information. The red and white barrier was raised and had every appearance of being permanently fixed in that position. Evers peered at the sign, headed with the omnipresent oak tree, which gave dire warnings of the penalties for parking without displaying a valid permit. A second, smaller notice announced the existence of 'Guest Parking' with an arrow pointing to the right and an unreadable table of charges.

A car horn sounding behind him made Evers swear, then he stalled the engine in his haste to get moving. The impatient motorist hooted again and received a two-finger gesture for his trouble. Evers muttered to himself as he negotiated an ornamental mini-roundabout, still following the 'Guest Parking' signs with their discreet arrows. 'Anyone would think they don't want guests to find the bloody place! Well, Simon, where the hell are you?'

He had tried the mobile number given to him by his sister, Simon's mother, but the stupid boy had either switched the damn thing off or had forgotten to charge the battery. At first Evers had been surprised by his nephew's lukewarm enthusiasm for his visit. Now he was more than annoyed at Simon's failure to respond to every effort at communication. Evers could not understand Simon at all. Any other boy of his age would be bragging of the connection with his media-star relative, eager to bask in the reflected glory of his uncle's achievements. But it was as if the boy was trying to avoid making contact, almost as if he was embarrassed... Yes, that was it, Evers thought, Simon was so overawed by his uncle's success that he was ashamed to admit how little headway he had made in his own career. All credit to the boy, Evers grudgingly admitted, if he was determined to make it on his own rather than cash in on his uncle's fame. He would take Simon aside after the lecture, and see if he could do something for the lad, pull a few strings, perhaps get him involved in his next television project. Yes, Simon would like that. But that was assuming that he could find the wretched boy in the first place.

The late afternoon light was fading and the car park signs seemed to have evaporated in the gloom. Still on the look-out for a vacant bay, Evers was edging his overbearing vehicle around a corner when he became aware of a girl waving at him from the path. He stopped, lowered the passenger window and leaned across to ask, 'Is there anywhere to park around here?'

The girl was more smartly dressed than he would have expected of a student, in linen trousers rather than jeans, and a neat, white shirt under a round-necked sweater, though the effect was somewhat spoiled by the off-the-shoulder baby-pink padded jacket with its fur-edged hood and the straight fair-brown hair pulled back in a nondescript ponytail. Her grey-green eyes sparkled behind fashionable rimless spectacles as she said, 'Oh, Mr Evers, I'm so glad to meet you. I'm Holly Mitchell. I'm the Secretary of the Archaeology Forum and I've been sent to look out for you. We've reserved a parking space just around the corner.'

'Probably easier if you hop in and show me where,' Evers said, opening the passenger door.

The girl could hardly contain her excitement long enough to give directions. 'There's been such a response to our advertising that we've had to move the talk to a larger lecture theatre and even that's sold out. We've had enquiries for tickets from as far away as Bristol. Of course, the locals who know how awful the parking situation is will probably be getting here early.'

'Very gratifying,' Evers murmured. 'Will there be many University staff there?'

'Well, we gave out some complimentary tickets, as you suggested, and I know other members of staff have bought them, but I'm not sure who because I haven't seen the latest list.'

'Dr Beaumont?' Evers asked, trying to keep his tone casual.

'Oh yes, at least her name was first on the list as you specifically requested, but I don't know if we've had a reply from her. In fact... Oh, here we are.'

Another committee member, a prematurely balding young man who could have served as a model for a caricature archaeologist, right down to the shapeless tweed jacket and cord trousers, was standing in the middle of a parking bay. He gave the impression that he would gladly lie down in the path of anyone attempting to steal Evers' space.

With the two students wittering on either side, Evers was escorted to the lecture room where he was introduced to Chris Penney, the Forum's Chairman, and to far too many members of the committee. Simon was noticeable for his absence. A check on the audio-visual equipment and the loading of his presentation on to the laptop having been achieved without incident, he was taken to a seminar room where a buffet table had been set out with finger foods and a choice of fruit juices, but no wine. Chris promised a visit to the local pub after the talk.

'In my experience,' Evers said with condescension and a great deal of smugness, 'my audiences usually have so many questions that we finish way beyond last orders.'

'Oh dear,' said Holly, 'we only have the lecture theatre until nine thirty.'

Evers sighed. When he finally caught up with Simon he would have a few choice words to say about this amateur outfit. In his arrogance Evers had completely forgotten that he had all but invited himself. Thinking about Simon made him ask, 'Will my nephew be here soon?'

Questioning looks passed between his hosts. Holly broke the silence with, 'He was sent an invitation to this reception but we had no reply from him.'

'Typical. It seems I'm not the only one he's ignoring,' Evers said. His laugh had a hollow ring.

'It was very good of you to agree to this date at such short notice,' Holly said, anxious to fill the awkward silence. 'Your diary must fill up years in advance. We really are grateful, aren't we?' She looked around her friends for support and they all murmured agreement.

A load of sheep, Evers thought, biddable sheep, just how I like them.

Chapter 9: A Meeting of Minds

Perched on a bench in the laboratory, Simon looked at his watch again.

'It's about two minutes later than the last time you looked,' Pete said, before his friend could announce the time. 'You've got to get a grip.'

'How late do you think I can leave it?'

'Depends how easily your uncle gets pissed off. Has he called again?'

With a guilty frown Simon pulled his mobile from his pocket. Four missed calls were listed, all from Eric Evers. There was a text message too. 'WHERE THE HELL ARE YOU?'

'I think he's passed through pissed off into the realms of furious.'

'Don't worry. He'll soon forget you, basking in the glowing adulation of the Archaeology Forum. They'll be loving it.'

'But I was invited to the reception and he'll expect me to be there. That girl, Holly, made it clear that he specifically requested my presence and it's not fair to let her take the blame. I don't want her to fall foul of his withering sarcasm.'

'Well, it's too late now. They'll be moving to the theatre soon.'

'And that's just where we should be heading,' Theo said, appearing in the doorway with Hermione and Ian close behind. 'Come along, young Simon, you have to face the ogre sooner or later. We'll be with you.'

Simon could not believe his luck in having fallen in with such a prestigious crowd. With their support he could almost persuade himself that he could stand up to his domineering relative, and even win the odd point or two in an argument, something he had never done in the past. But as they left the comforting familiarity of the Garstang Building and crossed the car park, he spotted the black vehicular monstrosity with its brash registration plate and his new-found confidence collapsed. Unusually for a Thursday evening, the campus was teeming with people, appearing from all directions but moving with a common determination of purpose, their paths converging on the Courtney Theatre.

'I've never seen so many safari vests together in one place, even on a safari. Who do these people think they are?' Ian pondered.

'Hero-worshippers,' Simon muttered.

'Nutters!' Pete opined.

'It's quite pathetic,' Hermione said, with a touch of acidity.

'I had no idea we were up against this sort of lunacy,' Masterson sighed.

'I tried to tell you,' Simon said. 'If you want to cut and run now I'll understand.'

'Last to the Royal Oak buys the drinks?' Pete suggested.

'Don't you dare,' Hermione wagged a finger at him.

'Cheer up, chickens,' Theo ordered. 'We need to make an entrance.'

Holly Mitchell, hovering in the theatre foyer, almost squealed with relief when she spotted Simon. 'Oh, thank goodness you're here,' she said, having pushed her way through the throng to meet him. Tomorrow several sets of ribs would be suffering from the deceptive strength of those delicate elbows.

'Sorry,' Simon said, unable to think of even the feeblest excuse.

'Your uncle asked to be told whenever you arrived but it's too late now. He's gone to get changed.'

In answer to Theo's questioning eyebrow, Simon explained, 'The safari vest, the bowtie, the last-minute combing of the beard. He's a performer, remember.'

Holly was staring at his companions, looking from face to face with a worried expression. 'I'm sorry I have to ask but have you all got tickets? Because it's a complete sell-out.'

Hermione stepped forward from where she had been standing in her brother's shadow. 'Miss Mitchell, I think I can vouch for everyone here.'

'Oh, Dr Beaumont, of course. Mr Evers was most insistent that you were to be invited. I'm so glad you were able to be here. When you didn't come to the reception we were getting worried that you might have had….a prior engagement…and Dr Masterson too. This is splendid…and…' Holly faltered in the brilliance of Theo's smile.

'My guest,' Hermione said, her tone indicating that Holly should not enquire further.

'And Pete is my guest,' Simon added. 'I believe the invitation said I could bring someone.'

'Yes, yes, of course. This is…well…splendid.'

Holly was still puzzling over where she had seen Theo before when he asked, 'Do we sit just anywhere?' dazzling her with another grin.

Holly, startled out of her bemusement, said, 'The front two rows are reserved for special guests.'

'I think we'd prefer to find our own seats,' Hermione said.

'But…,' Holly started to panic again.

'No, really,' Hermione said firmly, 'I think our friends will be waiting for us,' and she moved forwards with a purposeful air that parted the crowd as effectively as a hot knife through butter.

'Who are these friends?' Theo hissed, following in his sister's wake.

'There,' she said as they passed through the open swing doors.

Adeline Phillips was standing guard over the back row in the central block of seats. 'You're cutting it a bit fine, aren't you?' she said as Theo leaned forward to plant a flamboyant kiss on her cheek.

'Nice to see you Adeline. Didn't know this was your sort of thing.'

'I wouldn't miss it for the world.'

'Who is she?' Pete mouthed at Simon.

'I've no idea, but she looks friendly and if Theo trusts her that's good enough for me. And, anyway, look who's at the other end of the row.'

Pete followed Simon's gaze and met Sylvia's smiling face, although the pleasure of seeing her was tempered by the presence of Sally at her side. 'Oh joy,' he said. 'The front row might have its attractions after all.'

The theatre was filling up and the rising hubbub of excited voices measured the height of the audience's anticipation. Simon sidled along the row of seats to greet Sylvia while others, who had clearly been in their places for some time, were looking around studying the faces of the late-comers.

'Celebrity-spotters,' Pete said, sitting down beside Simon. 'It's just as well we're at the back. We'll be able to make a quick exit.'

'What sort of celebrities are they expecting?' Hermione asked, taking the seat beside Pete. 'I don't recognise half these people, and the ones I do know are University staff or students.'

'I suppose someone might recognise your brother,' Ian said as he tucked his jacket under his seat.

'Price of fame,' Theo purred, casting a devastating smile over the entire company. His blatant grandstanding was rewarded with a few girlish squeaks and a more manly murmur of, 'It is him, isn't it?' He gave a theatrical bow before taking his seat.

'Do you have to draw attention to us like that?' his sister complained.

'It's all part of the fun, H.P. Don't take it so seriously.'

Holly was standing at the top of the aisle, looking for empty places where the latest arrivals could be shoe-horned in. She glanced to her left where there was a vacant seat at the end of the back row, but before she could find a body to sit in it, Adeline had filled it with her coat and bag. Holly said, 'I'm afraid we're going to need every chair.'

'Yes, dear,' Miss Phillips said in her firmest schoolteacher voice, 'my friend should be here soon.'

'Oh, I see…' Holly dared not contradict such a formidable woman in such elite company, though the exchange left her more bewildered than ever. She was still unable to place Theo and she found the fact that a lot of other people had recognised him instantly most disconcerting. She wandered down towards the stage to remove the superfluous reserved signs from the second row and was almost knocked over in the rush as some of Evers' devotees swarmed to claim the prime positions.

When Holly asked one of her fellow committee members to guard her seat, her friend asked, 'Well, what did he say to you?'

'What did who say?'

'You mean you didn't recognise him?'

'I haven't got time for games, Debs. Who are you talking about?'

'Theo Beaumont of course.'

The light dawned with a blinding flash. How could she have been so stupid? She could only put her temporary lapse of memory down to the overbearing presence of Eric Evers whom she had found to be quite obnoxious on closer acquaintance. 'He didn't say anything in particular,' she said, 'but I imagine he's here for a very specific reason. There's a whole gang of them together in the back row. Mr Evers' nephew, Pete French, Dr Beaumont and Dr Masterson as well as some people I don't recognise. I think we might be in for some fireworks.' She gave her friend a conspiratorial wink before making her way to the green room to tell Eric Evers that Simon had arrived. Her sense of mischief prevented her from telling him about Simon's supporters. She had the feeling that they were preparing some sort of surprise for Evers and she had no wish to spoil their fun.

'So, who are you saving that seat for?' Theo asked Adeline.

'Wait and see,' she replied.

Theo, who had thought that Adeline's 'friend' was a convenient fiction, was intrigued, but knew better than to ask her more. The seat was still unoccupied when a warning dimming of the lights heralded the start of the proceedings. As Holly and the other members of the committee took their places, the Chairman, Chris Penney, stepped up to the podium and gave the statutory and mercifully short welcoming address before announcing, 'And now I know you will all give a great reception to our speaker for this evening, Dr Eric Evers.'

Evers' chosen theme music began to play, reaching a crescendo accompanied by the whistles and clapping of his fans and rendering inaudible the indignant 'Doctor?' that exploded almost unanimously from at least six mouths in the back row.

Simon's uncle strode on to the stage, his arms spread wide as if to embrace the whole audience, his crew-cut head nodding in acknowledgement of their adoration. Ian put his hand over Hermione's, which was gripping the armrest with knuckle-whitening ferocity. 'Keep calm,' he advised. 'Focus on what he has to say then we'll see if there isn't more than one way to doctor the prat'

Hermione's snort of laughter was lost in the noise of the crowd as Evers milked it for all he was worth. Theo leaned towards her and said, 'Do you think I should get myself a theme tune?'

His sister laughed again, and felt an enormous release of the tension of the last few days. With such friends around her, she thought, she might be able, in some small measure, to enjoy the encounter she had feared for so long.

Evers turned his outstretched hands palms downward and patted the air a few times to encourage his fans to silence. The echoes of the last over-enthusiastic yelps were fading when the door at the back of the theatre opened allowing the bright fluorescent light of the foyer to spill down the aisle. A slender figure stood silhouetted in the doorway and the whole audience turned at the sound of the woman's voice. 'I'm so sorry I'm late. Traffic, you know,' and the late arrival slid into the seat so recently occupied by Adeline's belongings.

After what Evers considered to be an uncomfortable pause, but which went unnoticed by most people present, he regained his composure and launched into his well-rehearsed presentation. He had learned, long ago, the truth of the old maxim 'a picture paints a thousand words'. The images that flashed on to the huge screen were stills from his television programmes, artistically shot and artfully chosen to distract the viewer from the lack of substance in what Evers was saying. He knew that, once he had grabbed their attention with arresting images and peppered his script with those key words and phrases that his fans had come to hear, they would accept the truth of what he said and cheer his theories to the rafters. As long as he threw into the mix the occasional titbit of new material, hinting at further lines of enquiry being pursued, suggesting that another fantastic revelation was just over the horizon, it would not matter whether he was quoting Norse mythology or nursery rhymes.

Evers had perfected the art of surveying his audience as he talked, trying to spot sources of the inevitable questions. He made mental notes of those little quirks of body language that marked a potential challenge, relating them, in his memory, to the picture he was showing at the time so that he had at least a rough idea of the area of interest which would be the subject of the query. By the time he finished a talk he could usually identify the most vocal or opinionated questioners. But he soon realised that his customary strategy was being foiled by the lighting. In a normal lecture theatre where students were expected to be taking notes, there was usually a medium light setting. Since his popular appeal had made a larger hall necessary, the event had been moved to the Courtney Theatre, home to various university drama and musical groups as well as the local repertory company, and a regular concert venue. There were no desk benches and no more than the front four or five rows of seats were illuminated by the light reflected off the giant screen above the stage.

The only people that Evers could see were the earnest committee members and a few die-hard fans he recognised from previous encounters. He had not been able to pick out Simon before the lights went down and, despite Holly's assurances that his nephew had arrived and that Dr Beaumont was with him, Evers was still anxious that the meeting would turn out to be no different from any other. Each presentation had to be infused with the new blood of future plans and, although he was already in negotiation with the TV production company for the filming of another two-part series, he was running out of ideas that would satisfy his faithful followers, the buyers of his books. All his PR skills and the seemingly insatiable appetite for his brand of ancient mysteries seasoned with UFOs had not prevented the sales of his latest book failing to meet the publisher's expectations and now Eric Evers was facing the prospect of not being able to meet the expectations of his public.

His research for the next series was going far too slowly. Since he had plundered every available source in putting together his broad-brush theories, he knew he could not revisit those sources in closer detail without laying himself open to charges of plagiarism. His publisher had warned him of how close he had come to a legal challenge from one so-called expert, an anthropologist, with a particularly bad dog-in-the-manger attitude and, though things had turned out well in the end when the complainant had been persuaded that the attendant adverse publicity would only be to his personal disadvantage, they could not afford a repeat of that experience.

Evers' principal aim in agreeing to speak to this audience, in this sleepy shire town, was to gain access, through Simon's contacts, to an untapped well of material that could be adapted to his own needs. In his limited and poorly informed view, the University had not the international standing of Oxford or Cambridge, the only two academic institutions of which Evers was truly in awe, and he genuinely believed that the dons of what he thought of as a backwater of academe would be only too glad of the increased prestige to be gained from an association with a media star like him. He failed to see how anyone in this institution could object to giving him a few endorsements to blazon on the dust jacket of his next book, a few quotes, strategically edited, that would strengthen his credentials in the mainstream world of archaeology. Of course, his ultimate dream was to be invited on an archaeological dig and he knew from his background research into Simon's department that the University was involved in two or three projects that would suit his purposes.

Giving this lecture free of charge and allowing the students to benefit from the proceeds of ticket sales far greater than generated by their regular meetings, was his first line of attack. Selecting the people who would help him achieve his goals was next, but he was unable to see anyone who fitted his bill. He was acutely aware of a certain unrest, a whispering and fidgeting emanating from the back row. And then there was that woman who had made such an entrance. He had a bad feeling about her.

The last picture faded as Evers' theme was reprised, the house lights were raised, and the audience applauded. Simon felt the urge to sink into his seat, to make himself invisible before his uncle could embarrass him further. Hermione, temporarily speechless, was staring towards the late-comer sitting at the end of the row. At last she breathed, 'Mother?'

Theo turned to look in the same direction, his mouth curving into a benevolent smile. Xanthe Crowther paused in her earnest conversation with Miss Phillips and raised a hand in acknowledgement of her children.

'Did you know she was coming?' Hermione hissed at her brother.

'Not a clue,' he said, 'but I think she might be useful.'

'What do you mean?'

Before Theo could reply, Chris Penney had returned to the podium to a chorus of shushing so that he could deliver his speech of thanks.

'I think I speak for the Archaeology Forum and for everyone here when I say that we have shared a unique experience this evening. I must thank Mr Evers for his impressive and entertaining presentation. I am sure that many of you have questions which, I am pleased to say, Mr Evers has agreed to answer, but to keep things moving along, please don't just shout out. Raise your hand and if I choose you could you please identify yourself first before putting your question.'

Arms flew up like a stop-frame film of weeds growing. Penney surveyed the eager faces with amazement before finding someone he thought he could rely upon to ask a sensible question. 'Professor', he said, indicating a person in one of the front row VIP seats.

A short, portly gentleman in a dapper pin-stripe suit, stood up and said, 'I am Terence Jameson, Head of the Archaeology Division. I'd like to know, Mr Evers, who has helped you to acquire your archaeological expertise, as it seems to me that you are claiming knowledge of a vast range of archaeological disciplines as well as relying on the results of many sophisticated scientific techniques, more than I would imagine it is possible for one person to learn in a single lifetime. Who are your associates?'

The stunned silence of the Evers fan club made it clear that this was the last thing they had expected. Then a ripple of clapping began to spread, starting from the small claques of archaeology students scattered throughout the theatre. For a questioner to be given such a reception was a new and uncomfortable experience for Eric Evers. In the back row Pete joined in the clapping. 'Way to go, Prof! I didn't know the old bird had it in him,' he said, turning to Simon who now had his head buried in his hands. 'Don't worry, Si, Uncle Eric doesn't know what to do. The Prof's question has really caught him on the wrong foot.'

Theo asked Ian, 'Did you say anything about our plans to your colleague?'

'Not a word, I promise,' Masterson said, with an apologetic shrug, 'but I don't think it'll do us any harm.'

At least the applause, unwelcome as it was, gave Evers a short time to compose his reply. He was usually able to predict the sort of questions his presentation would elicit but this was one that he had hoped never to be asked. He could cope with a query about a specific point in his theories but a challenge to his own credentials from an academically credible source was his worst nightmare. He knew he would not be able to bluff his way out of this.

Chris Penney was looking in his direction with a worried frown. Though the Forum's Chairman was not a fan of Evers' work – what serious-minded archaeologist could be? – he was conscious that Eric Evers was a guest at this gathering and Chris's natural politeness made him uncomfortable on Evers' behalf. At last Evers signalled with a slight nod his readiness to answer the question and Penney sighed with relief.

In trying to appear unconcerned, Evers looked his questioner straight in the eye and then faltered, 'Professor – er…?'

'Jameson,' the Professor's tone was dismissive and Evers cursed his less than confident start.

'Professor Jameson, you must realise that all my researches are based on information that is in the public domain. I draw on as many sources as I can, cover every angle before forming my theories. The interpretation is my own, based on my experience of human nature and life in general, and solidly founded in common sense. I believe that too many academics have become precious about what, in modern parlance, they call intellectual property. Many of my lines of enquiry stem from published work that has not been followed up by the original authors who have become so blinkered to alternative interpretation that they cannot see the progress that could be made if only they were more imaginative. I have taken up many trails of evidence that have apparently been seen as stale or unproductive by their originators and I have given them a new lease of life. It takes a fresh mind, an outsider if you like, to see through the fog of narrow-mindedness, to cut through the bonds of professional self-interest, to free the truth by taking a truly holistic approach.'

Evers was proud of this impromptu speech, especially the use of the word 'holistic', and was heartened by a ripple of applause from his fans. But Professor Jameson was not so easily put off. 'So, sir, you are claiming to have seen to the heart of all the matters on which many of my colleagues have spent their entire professional lives. What is more, you are claiming to have made sensational – and I use the word advisedly – discoveries on the basis of other people's work. Is this not rather like exploitation? I believe you have made a good deal of money from these sensational theories. Have you never thought to publicly recognise your debt, perhaps by funding the work of some of those hard-working academics whose skills and expertise you have used without acknowledgement?'

The hush in the hall was palpable. In all his years of fielding awkward questions Evers had become expert at diverting attention away from his own intellectual deficiencies, usually aided by a degree of diffidence on the part of his interrogators. This was different. This was real. His followers had just witnessed the first major challenge to his credibility, the first chinks in the armour of his ego. Their idol could not be seen to have feet of clay, and yet…. Evers began to see a way out that might serve all interests, even if it ended up costing him personally a considerable sum of money.

'Indeed, Professor. I came to your university today with just such a plan in mind. I would very much like to be associated with some of the exciting research you are doing here, particularly the fieldwork, and I know archaeological projects are always short of funds. Perhaps we can arrange a meeting later to discuss this.'

The wind taken out of his sails, Professor Jameson resumed his seat without further comment. Simon groaned as Ian said, 'Oh no!' and Theo murmured, 'Clever bastard!'

Chris Penney seized his chance to cover Professor Jameson's lack of response. 'I am sure there are many more questions,' he said, casting his gaze over the audience until he found a candidate, complete with safari vest, who was burning with curiosity over the latest twist in

Evers' UFO saga. On familiar ground once more, Evers launched into the sort of reply calculated to feed the fire of his fans' enthusiasm.

Pete let out a soft whistle as Hermione leaned to whisper in Ian's ear and even Sylvia was muttering with restrained rage. Sally, who had been no more than an innocent bystander in the plotting of the previous few days, was intelligent enough to know that things were not going according to plan.

While the Evers Fan Club applauded their hero's response to a question from one of their own, Chris Penney prepared to call the next questioner. His choice fell upon a young man wearing the uniform blue jeans and sloppy sweatshirt of a student, who rose to his feet, clearing his throat, and identified himself. 'Dan Browne…with an e,' – the clarification was an automatic response to the inevitable ripple of amusement that his name usually seemed to generate – 'First Year Archaeology student. I'd like to thank Mr Evers for getting me started in archaeology.'

Evers' smile was benevolence personified. This was more like it.

Dan continued, 'I read your first book when I was at school and that's what made me think about taking up the subject at university because I wanted to be part of the exciting story you told.'

Evers' smile broadened to something rivalling Theo's.

'But,' Dan said, 'I soon found that it was just that, a story. My question is, how can you continue to mislead people in such a cynical manner when the truth is so much more fascinating than the fiction you peddle in your books?'

The collective gasp from the Evers supporters and the subsequent awkward silence made Simon sit up. For the first time he looked directly at his uncle to gauge his reaction to the surprise attack. To Simon's amazement Evers was speechless, his face contorted with indignation. As mutterings of discontent began in the audience, many of whom were subjecting Dan to looks of pure hatred, Ian said, 'I didn't know the lad could be so eloquent. I think I'll add a few marks to his next essay as a commendation for bravery.'

Much as Chris Penney enjoyed his speaker's discomfiture he realised that Evers should not be asked to reply to such a question. The

Chairman stood up and, speaking loudly to be heard over the incoherent murmuring of the crowd, said, 'I think we'll treat that as a rhetorical question, thank you, Dan. Are there any more questions?'

Dan Browne resumed his seat to be patted on the back by his friends. Chris surveyed the forest of waving arms, wondering how he could forestall a repeat of Dan's hijacking manoeuvre. Then he spotted Theo's raised hand. 'Yes, Dr Beaumont.'

Evers looked expectantly in the direction indicated by Penney's gaze and frowned when he saw that the questioner standing up in the back row was a man. This meeting was becoming more confusing by the moment and Evers was not enjoying it one little bit.

'T.C. Beaumont, vulcanologist,' Theo smarmed, smiling at the sea of faces, mainly female, which had turned in his direction at the sound of his name.

'How does he do that?' Pete whispered.

Theo stood like an actor bathed in an individual spotlight, ready to declaim a Shakespearean soliloquy, and after a suitable dramatic pause he said, 'Mr Evers, my particular interest, of course, is in your references to volcanic activity during the period you call – correct me if I'm wrong – the Age of the Gods.'

Evers nodded though he was wary. He had no idea what direction this was going to take. Theo was a totally unknown quantity, a random, unpredictable element in this apparently volatile audience.

Theo continued, 'You theorise that these alien deities jump-started civilization all around the Mediterranean some time in the late Neolithic or early Chalcolithic. You say that the absence of evidence for their existence can be explained, in part, by the devastation caused by volcanic eruptions.'

Evers leapt into a response before Theo's question took the turn he feared. 'Yes, yes. It is well documented, in the Med as well as other seismic regions of the world, that whole societies have been lost without a trace due to being overwhelmed by volcanic ash or lava or by the environmental changes caused by such calamitous events.'

Theo adopted a firm but patient tone, as if talking to a wilful child, 'Quite so, but my question is this, which specific eruptions are you claiming to have destroyed the evidence of your alien super-beings in, say, Egypt?'

Evers began to feel the firm ground, on which he thought his theories were founded, crumbling under the pressure of this antagonist who was, he grudgingly admitted, a media star of the same calibre as himself. Theo Beaumont's easy way with people, his facility for explaining complex scientific notions in accessible language without being patronising, were characteristics which Evers like to think that he also possessed. Evers was all too aware that he had cherry-picked a few of his facts from Theo's book *Volcanicity*, though he had hoped that he had disguised them well enough to avoid a charge of theft. Also, despite regular declarations of his eagerness to discuss his theories with 'the academic community', he had been quite grateful for the reluctance of real experts to engage in debate. Since his chance discovery of that obscure doctoral thesis Evers had considered H.P. Beaumont to be such a minor player in the world of archaeology, and a woman to boot, that she provided him with the ideal soft target, someone who would put up no serious contest if it came to arguing a point. Evers had seen the fortuitous appointment of his nephew to Beaumont's department as his chance to defend his case against the weakest possible opposition. He cursed Simon for not having told him about the woman's link with Theo Beaumont, who was an altogether different quality of opponent, and he cursed himself for not having made the name connection in the first place. How close was that connection? Was he facing her husband, her brother or a distant cousin?

A deathly hush fell as the whole audience, Evers supporters and otherwise, awaited his reply. 'Well – er – as I'm sure you all know, the greatest volcanic disaster in the Med was that of Thera or Santorini, which caused such widespread devastation that the Minoan civilization was completely obliterated…'

A loud 'Hah!' came from the back row in advance of Theo's interjection, 'But that was during what Egyptologists call the New Kingdom, about 1600 BC. I thought you said your aliens arrived a couple of millennia or more before that. Surely, no matter how dramatic the eruption, two thousand year's-worth of evidence would not be totally wiped out, especially in a society where written records were so important. And, anyway, the level of destruction depends on the direction of the winds and tides at the time and even so it diminishes exponentially with distance from the volcano. The effects of the Thera eruption on the Mediterranean coast of Egypt would have been minimal. In the south, which you claim to have been the main settlement area for your aliens, the population would probably have known nothing about it.'

Theo timed his pause to give Evers a chance to reply, but five seconds became ten without a word passing Evers' lips. Theo glanced at Simon, who shrugged his incomprehension. The silence was now more than uncomfortable.

Evers stood as if stunned, his eyes glazing over with a new experience for him which, if he had wanted to put a name to it, might have been called stage fright. The faithful fans began to whisper amongst themselves. Their shining idol was visibly losing some of his lustre, and the longer the silence the paler his light became.

Then it seemed as if Evers' salvation had arrived in the unlikely form of a female voice with a distinctive Greek lisp. 'I must say, Mr Evers, I think they are all being too hard on you. Speaking as one author to another I must congratulate you on your story-telling abilities. You have quite clearly acquired a loyal following which, more than anything, proves that you can harness the power of the imagination.'

Heads turned, necks craned and bodies swivelled in their seats as Evers' fans attempted to identify the woman who was brave enough to stand up for their beleaguered hero. The murmuring became louder as she was recognised by many including Holly, who darted forward to tell Chris Penney what was going on.

The Chairman took the initiative. 'Ah, thank you, Ms Crowther. Have you a question for Mr Evers?'

'Yes, Mr Chairman,' Xanthe Crowther's beaming smile captivated the audience at once. 'I too mix fact and fiction in my stories though I tend to stick to one area of the world and one period of history at a time. What I would like to know is how you manage to maintain so many very different story lines and yet link them together in a credible fashion. This is a skill that any novelist would envy. I really wish to know how you do it.'

Her words startled Evers from his fugue. He comprehended that the woman standing just two places away from that awful Beaumont man was an author, an author of fiction, and she was claiming that his work was of the same sort. His indignation reignited the flame of his ego.

'I hardly think, madam, that my books and yours come into the same category. They will be on different shelves in the bookshops for a start.' This quip earned Evers a little reassuring laughter.

'Oh, Mr Evers,' Xanthe Crowther cooed, 'you are teasing me. We are of a kind, you and I. Basing our stories on solid fact is what makes them so believable, so readable, and if our readers believe they will buy our books. And that is why we are in this business, no?'

'Madam,' Evers bristled, 'you cannot compare romantic fiction with scientific discussion…'

The gasp from the audience told Evers that he had gone too far. The Crowther woman's smile, which bore a disconcerting resemblance to that of Theo Beaumont, was now fixed and fearsome. 'Mr Evers,' she said wagging a finger at him, 'that is very naughty. I don't think you realise who you are talking to. I am not like you. I know my limitations. I write about what I have studied for myself. I do not rely on the work of research assistants and I do not scour the internet for obscure articles that I can cut and paste to my own requirements.' She glanced along the row and, catching Hermione's eye, winked.

Evers felt a sweat breaking out on his brow. Who did this woman think she was? He knew the name, of course. He had seen it often enough in the fiction half of the best-sellers lists, usually when checking his own entry in the non-fiction rankings. His arrogance would not allow him to admit that Xanthe Crowther titles had climbed those heights more often and stayed for longer than any of his. He could not guess at how many books she had sold but he was wondering now whether his pigeonholing of her work as pulp fiction might have been a bit rash. In an instant he decided to take a more conciliatory tone.

'Ms Crowther, your little stories have an impressive following, I don't doubt, but…'

'Excuse my interruption,' Dan Browne had leapt to his feet again, 'but I can't hear Ms Crowther's books dismissed as "little stories". I learned more about Pompeii from them, and in a more entertaining way, than from reading any number of dry as dust text books. And her facts are verifiable and accurate.'

Chris Penney had watched the discussion slipping out of his control almost as if he had been mesmerised by this collision of stellar bodies. Dan Browne's voice brought him back to reality. 'I'm so sorry, Mr Evers, we seem to have drifted away from Ms Crowther's question. Can you remember what it was or would you like her to ask it again?'

Evers' belligerence returned with full force as he said, 'I don't believe she had a real question.'

Xanthe Crowther tut-tutted loudly, forestalling the Chairman's intervention.

'Any intelligent reader will recognise that, while my stories depend on solid scientific and historical fact dressed up as fiction, yours are inventive fiction dressed up as scientific fact. But I want to know if *you* can tell the difference.'

'I must protest, Ms Crowther. I write non-fiction. The meagre scientific content of a mere novel cannot be compared with the breadth of evidence required by my readers. And though I concede that you may be better qualified than me to write about classical history, I suspect you have less claim to scientific expertise than I have.'

The roar of laughter that greeted this remark took Evers by surprise. The loudest reaction was from the back row but the pockets of mirth throughout the hall indicated that he had made a real gaffe. Scanning the faces with a defiant glare he spotted Simon at last, and was dismayed to see his nephew wiping tears of amusement from his eyes. Evers turned to Chris Penney and hissed, 'What did I say?'

'I believe, Mr Evers, that before Xanthe Crowther became an author she had an eminent academic career, as a geologist. She has at least two doctorates and numerous learned publications to her name, some in conjunction with her husband, the geophysicist Sir Anthony Beaumont.'

'Beaumont!'

'Yes, sir. She is Theo Beaumont's mother.'

'And H.P. Beaumont?'

'The Doc?' Penney seemed to make the connection for the first time. 'Of course, I suppose she must be one of the family too.'

By now, the audience was in uproar and the Chairman knew there would be no recovery. With relief he saw the computer clock was showing 21:23. Raising his voice Chris said, 'I'm sorry, but we've run out of time. I'd like to thank you all for coming and to remind you that Mr Evers has kindly agreed to sign books in the foyer…'

'You can forget that,' Evers snarled, unclipping the radio-microphone from his waistcoat and tossing the transmitter pack on to the desk. The last thing he saw as he stormed off the stage towards the green room was the movement of a substantial part of *his* audience seeking the autographs of the Beaumont mother and son.

*

Thirty minutes later, in the Royal Oak, Hermione said, 'Mother, how could you?'

'How could I what, dear?' Xanthe Crowther's Greek accent had miraculously disappeared.

'You know what I mean. You hijacked that meeting and turned it into a fiasco.'

'Isn't that what you wanted?'

'Well,…I,…no…I don't know what I expected but I didn't *want* that.'

'He deserved it.' Xanthe's tone was petulant.

'But we were ready, we had plans.'

Theo interrupted by placing a tray of drinks on the table. 'Yes, we had plans but they'd already been upset by your Prof Jameson and that Browne guy. Seems like a lot of people were on our side. Saved us a heap of trouble.'

'How's Simon?'

'Getting sloshed. He'll have a headache tomorrow. It's suddenly hit him that, though we don't have to face that man again, he can't avoid him, being related.'

'Who's looking after him?'

'Pete and Sally. Ian's delivering the next round.'

'What have we done Theo?'

Before her son could reply, Xanthe said, 'My dear Hermione, you have done nothing. Theo had his little say and I made my small contribution, with, I might add, your father's blessing. We realised that it would have done your reputation no good to have a public confrontation with Evers. This way your integrity and your dignity are intact.'

'Oh, I see. My integrity doesn't matter,' Theo pouted.

'You are quite capable of standing up for yourself,' his mother said, poking him in the chest with a well-manicured finger, 'and you are used to the limelight. Your sister is not.'

'I know, my sensible sis. H.P.'s always been your favourite, hasn't she?'

'Is he causing trouble again?' Ian asked, sliding into the seat beside Hermione.

'No more than usual,' she said, accepting the offer of his arm about her shoulders.

'Well, just tell me if he needs putting in his place,' Ian took a sup from his pint.

Xanthe's eyebrows rose in mild surprise and Theo chuckled.

'She's finally spread her wings, Mum.'

'Not before time.'

*

Passivity was such a dominant characteristic of the Bau that confrontation caused them mental pain, to the extent that they instinctively sought every possible way to avoid it. Potentially violent situations were quickly resolved but, when tempers finally flared, a minor disagreement could escalate out of control in moments. Following the last catastrophic intercontinental war on Perbau, and the lengthy negotiations culminating in the Peace Accords of Dwat, there had been generations of debate as to the wisdom of trying to eliminate violence from the planet altogether. In all their space wanderings the Bau had never encountered a hostile species with a level of technology that posed them a serious threat. But the cautious amongst the Ba leaders reminded their fellows that sooner or later such an encounter was inevitable. They could not afford to lose their capacity for self-defence. Violent crime was rare and becoming rarer. The war-games which had been developed as an outlet for aggression were declining in popularity and recruitment levels for the planetary defence forces were falling. It seemed as if militancy and pugnacity were being bred out of the Ba population.

Of course, there were still life phases when rebellion and conflict were part of a Ba's natural development and, for some, those phases lasted longer than others. A considerable number of Bau viewed the Experiment as one way of removing a few of the more independent and therefore unpredictable elements of their society to a safe distance from which their disruptive influence could be minimised if not neutralised. They considered that those who volunteered for such a mission, showed by their willingness to accept hazard that they were possible sources of disharmony better isolated from the peaceful majority to prevent the spread of their free-thinking.

The Ba settlers had accepted that they might not be welcomed by the natives of Geb and had undergone training with simple weapons in order to protect themselves. Some had taken to this activity with enthusiasm, becoming the hunters and security guards for the settlement groups. Others had found the whole idea of harming or taking sentient life so distasteful that they had refused to carry weapons of any sort. All the settlers had accepted that accidents could happen. It was highly improbable that they would have planned for every emergency, but no one had thought for an instant that one of their fellows could commit murder.

The thoughts transmitted from Tiamt's settlement were emotionally chaotic and confused by distance. When Wsir's companions compared the muddled images, a bare outline of their friends' experiences became apparent. Tiamt's group had not been as well received in the land the inhabitants called Sumer as had their compatriots in Kem. The Sumerian civilization was more advanced than that of the Kemites. The existence of several proto-cities with fairly efficient economic administrations and established religious elites had led to some serious resistance to their settlement. The only way to ensure their survival had been to adopt a dominatory stance, to impose *their authority on the region by explicitly calling themselves gods from the outset.*

Tiamt was a marine biologist by profession so naturally she directed her attention towards the coastal areas and the lower reaches of the two great rivers that passed through her zone. Her deputy, Mardk, had suggested that, in order to secure sufficient food supplies they should move further inland to one of the towns of the rich alluvial plains. Tiamt's mate, Apsw, a boat builder and the most aged of all the Bau involved in the Experiment, was torn between his loyalty to his partner and his desire to explore the waterways. The group's allegiances were split.

From what the medical specialists, Karrk and Gwla, had to report, the reactions of their fellows to their new environment had been more pronounced than those experienced by Wsir and his group. They had not successfully suppressed the mood swings and headaches. All the party had become edgy and quick to anger. Arguments tended to be settled, not with words, but with scrappy physical fights which became increasingly violent, even between the females. Gwla had long ago exhausted her supplies of antibiotics and quickheal on a succession of minor injuries, cuts and abrasions. To escape from these problems many Bau in Sumer had broken away from the principal settlement and in pairs or as individuals they had dispersed to all parts of the region with telepathic contact being their only means of communication. But the animosity and suspicion continued to grow. Skhmt described it as verging on mass paranoia.

In his self-absorbed exile Mardk chose to blame all the settlers' troubles on Tiamt's ineffective leadership and he set about persuading others that she should be removed. No one could have imagined the manner in which Mardk intended to achieve this removal. The end was so sudden that, apart from Mardk, none of the group would ever know the details. Karrk found the body so badly mutilated that she had been able to identify it as Tiamt's only by elimination, by checking the whereabouts of all the other Bau in Sumer.

As Tiamt's Deputy, Mardk had assumed the leadership of the group and was trying to bring the settlers back together, but few were prepared to trust him. Asswr proclaimed himself leader of the inland group while Nlil tried to regroup in the original coastal community. The Sumer settlement group was scattered and scared.

'And there is nothing we can do about it,' Wsir said, *'though I would counsel strongly against sending any sort of aid. Who knows how the conditions over there would affect us now.'*

'But we will welcome any of their number who can make their way here,' Ast added.

'Of course. But all we can hope is that we will continue to avoid those difficulties that have shattered their dreams.'

Chapter 10: Damage Limitation

Imn had received the first sending from Sumer and the horror of the news had put his own misfortunes into perspective. His double, Min, despite the damage to his legs, was still alive, and Imn himself was physically unharmed. Set against the death of Tiamt at the hands of another Ba any complaint would be petty. The shock that had temporarily stunned all Imn's companions seemed to have refocused his troubled mind. With Min's blessing, now that the pain of bodily separation was not an issue, Imn moved downstream, joining Djhwty in his new home on the sunset bank of the river. There he resumed his scientific research, drawing apart from his human followers who had no understanding at all of what he was doing. His Ba friends feared that he would relapse into depression but in discovering the true reclusive nature of his split self he had become content with his new life. His human companions were quick to accept his aloof behaviour because that was, they thought, the way a god should behave. Rather than losing their faith in him, he rose in their estimation as his absences became more frequent and prolonged. Djhwty reported that the local Kemites were already starting to refer to Imn as the 'Invisible One'. What Djhwty failed to relate was that those same humans had also started referring to Imn in the same way as the human inhabitants of the original settlement had referred to Wsir. Imn had unintentionally set himself up as a god-king.

Wsir had never felt easy under the imposed burden of his divinity but even he was beginning to see the necessity of maintaining the distance between Bau and humans. With the news from Sumer all the settlers had started to view the Experiment in a different way. Their long-term plans for gaining life experience by learning from the natives of the new planet had turned into a day to day struggle with the principal goal being one of survival until the return of the scout ship. Djhwty, who was doing his best to keep a record of their time on Geb, was bombarded with queries from his friends, who now eagerly anticipated the end of their exile. Of more immediate interest to Wsir was the flood.

The river continued to rise and there was no further sending from Sumer. Min was in the best position to receive any news but his attempts to reach out his mind to the settlers there were met by a dreadful silence. Even the speculative Sumerian traders who had occasionally braved the sea voyage and the journey through the desert, had ceased their activities. The Bau settlers in Kem were more alone than ever and the river continued to rise.

Khnm sent word that the human river-watchers were concerned. They predicted that the seasonal flood was going to be much higher than it had been for many years, and they were proved correct. Upstream, where the effects of the inundation were felt first and where the river plain was narrow, Khnm's experimental irrigation works were rapidly overwhelmed. Downstream, Wsir watched with dismay as his new fields were inundated and remained waterlogged well beyond the time when he had expected to be planting his next crop.

The Bau were plagued by biting and stinging insects hatching in huge numbers and appearing in dark clouds over the stagnant waters. Some, Wsir and Pth among them, seemed to be particularly attractive to these pests. Hairless scalps were especially susceptible and soon the male Bau were replacing the plain headcloths that protected them from the sun with a variety of closer-fitting head coverings. Pth chose a skull-hugging cap of kidskin while Wsir adopted a conical hat woven from reeds and grasses, of the sort that fieldworkers in Kem had been wearing for generations. With no chemical repellents available they resorted to plastering their exposed skin with a barrier concoction based on liquid mud which dried to a dark crust. The dehydrating effect of this treatment meant they could only use it for short periods at a time, usually when it was necessary for them to be out of doors. As soon as possible they washed off the unpleasant stuff and applied various lotions of oils or animal fat to moisturise and condition the golden skin that set the Bau apart from humans.

The great black bull, tormented by the biting flies, had broken his tether and escaped into the thorny wilderness on the edge of the flood plain. Hwthr knew that, even if he did not succumb to one of the infections carried by the pestilential insects, he was unlikely to find his way back home. His only hope was to seek out the company of some of the native wild cattle but, in spite of his size, Hwthr feared that the gently-reared beast would not survive a challenge by a dominant local male. One of her darling cows also developed a bad case of foot rot because the immune systems of the beasts reared in sterile conditions off-planet could not adapt to the extreme environment they were now *experiencing. The human stockmen, on whom she had come to rely, tried all the remedies they had, but to no avail. The cow was nursing a strong bull-calf and Hwthr was reluctant to give in to the inevitable before the youngster was weaned. To the disbelief of her human helpers, Hwthr took the drastic action of amputating the cow's foreleg though she knew this was a vain effort and the humans considered it a sacrilege to so mutilate the holy beast. The cow would not be able to stand without support and, since her supply of antibiotics had long been exhausted, Hwthr had no way of preventing the inevitable infection. The decline was swift but painful. When the cow's breathing became laboured and the calf's frantic bleating began to distress the other animals, Hwthr could no longer justify keeping the mother alive. She wept as the butcher drew his flint blade across the cow's throat and she cradled the animal's head as its life drained away, the blood soaking into her gown and spilling on to the ground, mingling with the black earth.*

Only one Ba demonstrated the excitement and wonder that all the settlers had shared when they first arrived on Geb. To Inbw everything was new and each sight, sound and smell was soaked up and stored away in his active mind. Though he could only venture out at night and in the twilight, he made the most of his freedom to roam. Nebt was worried that he would come to some harm but Ndjty offered to keep the excitable youngling company in his explorations of the desert hills. The older Ba went so far as to acquire a jackal skin and made himself a mask so that Inbw would not feel too different. The local humans took Inbw to their hearts, feeling blessed by the presence in their midst of the one and only Ba child, and they followed his progress with affection and pride They called him 'the Lad' and, for his role as guide and guardian, Ndjty became known as 'the Pathfinder'. Nebt was reassured that her son was probably better supervised and protected than any youngling on Perbau.

Wsir had delayed, for as long as he could bear, the planting of his grain, that pitiful quantity of seed which he had brought with him from the First Settlement. He wanted to resume the normality of the Experiment as soon as possible and he had assured the local farmers that the Ba grain would prosper. Watching him sow the seed in his small field, the humans had hesitated to caution a god against impatience but they were not confident enough of his wisdom to follow his example. All too soon Wsir had to admit his mistake when the grain became mildewed in the wet soil before it could germinate. This was final proof that the genetic modifications, which should have made the grain resistant to such predictable problems, had failed. There was no point in trying again since all that remained of the enhanced cereal were the small reference samples kept from each planting and harvest – all had proved less productive or less hardy than the native grains from which they had been modified.

While Ast was happy that her sister was more contented, she was increasingly concerned at her mate's depression. Seeking respite from the summer heat in the cool interior of their new mud-brick residence, she found Wsir sitting alone in the communal room. In front of him was the chest of koram wood that they had brought with them from Perbau as a receptacle for their few personal belongings, mementoes of the home-world such as all the settlers had, to remind them of where they had come from and the place to which they would return. Laid out along the flat lid were several small pouches. Wsir had cut squares of cloth from one of the garments provided for the settlers at the start of the Experiment. He had used these to create makeshift bags tied with twisted cords and labelled with wooden tags. Ast recognised them as the containers for his grain samples, some of seed corn and others collected and painstakingly separated after each harvest. He was resting his forearms on the chest, his fingers caging one of the pouches, his face wreathed in misery.

Though it hurt her to criticise her mate, Ast knew she had to say something to bring him out of his despondency. 'There is no point in dwelling on what might have been,' she said, with a touch of accusation in her voice. 'Let me put that away, then, perhaps, you will be able to concentrate on more important things.'

He looked up at her and in his blank, black-lensed eyes she saw the glint of tears. At that moment she could have taken him in her arms and murmured words of comfort as she had done for Nebt, but while Ast knew that it might be what Wsir wanted, it was not what he needed. She gently lifted his hands and removed the pouch from his unresisting grasp. The wooden tag identified the sample as the last of the 'pure' Bau grain gathered from the first harvest. She scooped up the other bundles and lifted the box lid. 'I shall pack these away now. I know you *want to find out what went wrong but there is nothing you can do about it until we return to the base ship.'*

Ast rearranged the contents of the box so that the grain samples were buried beneath their other meagre possessions. Wsir watched her concealing the evidence of his failure, then his head drooped to his chest and his sigh was almost a sob. Ast rounded on him.

'Wsir, you cannot give up. We have to survive for more than two solar cycles before the scout ship will reach us. We still have to eat. If we cannot use the augmented species that we brought with us, we must make do with what this land has to offer and we must take the advice of the Kemites who, after all, were not doing so badly before we arrived. We must swallow our pride and ask for their help.'

Wsir nodded, but he remained silent, not trusting his voice to conceal the depth of his emotion. Ast checked her instinct to place her hand against his cheek. Instead she made a fuss of knotting the ties fastening the grain pouches. 'I know the farmers would still welcome your agricultural advice. You should get out into the fields and help them.' With that Ast turned to remove some imaginary spider webs from a corner of the wall, hiding the tears in her own eyes. When she turned back, Wsir was gone. She breathed a sigh of relief when she saw, through the door, his tall figure striding towards the fields.

*

The grassy stems of the new crop had just become distinguishable from the persistent weeds when the boat from First arrived, though none of Wsir's group had received any telepathic warning of its coming. Wsir, hoeing the field, was first alerted to the arrival by the reaction of his human companions who downed tools and ran to meet the visitors as they pushed through the reeds at the edge of the cultivation. His puzzled frown gave way to a delighted smile as he recognised Inhr and Wsrt with Srkt. He sent a message to the others as he hurried to meet his friends, but his smile turned again to a frown when he saw their sombre expressions. This was not a social call.

In the light of the setting sun, the Bau gathered in the courtyard of the Residence. On their own initiative, the humans had put together a feast and were vying with each other for the honour of serving their guests with the best of everything – roasted wildfowl and toasted flat breads, stewed pulses and fresh fruit. The inevitable beer was of the strongest brew but the brewmaster had also provided a jar of a wine made from the native tree-fruit that proved to be quite drinkable. Wsir quashed memories of disappointment at the failure of his vines. Ast was right; there was little the Kemites could learn from the Golden Ones.

As the sun set and the humans left, Wsir surveyed the Bau faces, glowing even more golden in the light of the flaring torches, his gaze lighting on Inhr.

'Tell us,' he said.

Inhr glanced at Wsrt, who seemed reluctant to release her grip on his arm. She nodded her encouragement. 'I think Swty has gone mad,' he said. His fearful statement seemed to echo around the hushed company.

'Tell us,' Wsir repeated.

Inhr inhaled deeply, then the story came pouring out, as unstoppable as the river's flood.

When the dreadful news of Mardk's crime had reverberated through all Bau minds, Swty had reacted in a different way from his fellows. He wanted to know more. In particular he wanted to know every grisly detail of Tiamt's injuries.

'Of course,' Srkt added, 'he could find out no more than anyone else. The sendings from Sumer were so vague and disjointed.'

'But Swty would not let go,' Inhr continued. 'What he could not discover he began to imagine. He created a sort of litany describing the weapons and the blows that inflicted a series of ghastly wounds. He repeats it over and over and, as he does, his face twists into a mask of such fiendish pleasure that no one can bear to watch.'

'Worse,' Wsrt said, 'he is subconsciously sending when he is ranting and anyone within range receives such horrible images that we have all, at times, felt physically sick.'

Inhr pressed on with his account, 'He has taken to going hunting alone and when he returns he is bloodied but brings no game with him. We fear he is eating the meat raw but worse, we fear he is killing for pleasure.'

A gasp of horror whispered around the company. Most of the settlers had found killing to be the most difficult and distasteful aspect *of their training for the Experiment. It was one thing to kill, for food, a domestic animal which had been specifically bred for that purpose. To hunt and kill wild game, no matter how much the meat was needed, had proved too difficult for the more sensitive Bau. A readiness to kill indicated a side of their character that the Bau were reluctant to admit, that primal violence, that cruel streak which had been suppressed, hidden, denied for generations. But, of necessity, each settler group had been allocated a hunter, a Ba who had no qualms about this role and whose skills would be essential in the early phases of the settlement. Swty had taken to the role as naturally as a bird taking flight, and there was no question that his efforts, and those of the Bau who followed his lead, had kept the settlement from starving in those early days.*

From the start, Wsir had worried that, as the need for hunting diminished, Swty would have to find another outlet for those violent tendencies that he had always known his brother to possess. With every demonstration of anger or arrogance, Wsir had tried to convince himself that Swty was displaying the typical aggression of a resentful younger sibling, but Swty was too old, now, to have his behaviour excused so casually, especially since his treatment of Nebt had become known.

Wsir read the fear in Inhr's face. 'You think he might attack one of you?'

Inhr appeared to be relieved at Wsir's calm statement. 'Yes,' he breathed, his shoulders sagging with the admission. In the silence that followed a soft sob was heard. Ast thought it was Nebt.

'What about the others?' Wsir asked.

'They are as frightened as we are,' Wsrt replied. 'We volunteered on behalf of them all to come here to seek your advice.'

'If the matter was so urgent,' Ast asked, 'why did you not send*?'*

Wsir answered her question, 'Swty is a particularly strong telepath. If he is sending *at random he would have overheard any message and I, too, would be worried about his reaction to signs of what he would consider disloyalty or treachery. I had put his changed mood down to the combination of his natural character and the environmental problems we have all suffered. Perhaps I should have taken more notice but I could not see beyond his resentment of my* leadership, the same resentment I have experienced from him all my life.'

Inhr's mouth curved into an apologetic smile. 'We know that now, Wsir. We truly understand how difficult it must have been for you and we are sorry for being so hasty.'

Ndjty stood up with a grunt of disdain, shaking a fist in Inhr's direction. 'Is it not rather late for an apology? You must have known what Swty was capable of. You were in his company long enough.'

Wsir waved Ndjty back to his seat. 'Now is not the time for recriminations. We have to admit, on the basis of the news from Sumer, that any of us could have been affected in the same way as Mardk and any of us could have become a victim, as did Tiamt. It is a terrible way to be taught a lesson but we must learn from it and be on our guard against it happening again. What do you want of us, Inhr?'

'We want to rejoin you, if you will have us.'

'All of you?'

Srkt answered, 'Most of us. Shzmw will probably stay, and maybe Mafdt, and one or two others.'

'Of course,' Ast said with some asperity, 'the same type of character is likely to respond in a similar way to Geb's conditions. Have you noticed such changes in others?'

'I am afraid so,' Inhr nodded, 'though not as severe as in Swty's case.'

'And none in the females,' Wsrt was quick to add.

Ndjty snorted again. 'How can we be sure this sickness has not infected all who have been close to Swty? Why should we risk contamination? We have Inbw to think of.'

Wsir spoke sharply, 'That is enough! I know feelings are running high. Tiamt's death, and the manner of it, was a huge shock, but if we, for one instant, believe that the same fate is inevitable for us all then we might as well surrender to that base nature now. Understanding a problem is the largest part of solving it. We are Bau, we can overcome this. We must.'

*

In response to tight-focus one-word sendings *the fearful Bau of Swty's company started to leave First. Some made their way south to join Khnm, others decided to stop at Min's settlement, but the majority accepted Wsir's offer of refuge at the Ba Residence in the village the locals called Abdw. For a few days all they needed was a chance to talk through their fears and to exorcise their nightmares. Wsir presided over several community meetings where everyone had the opportunity to speak for as long as they felt necessary, to openly discuss their plans for the future – at least their immediate future. Never, since their landing on Geb, had the Bau thought so much about their leaving.*

Now that the period of the Experiment was more than half over, and the Bau recognised the failure of its main principle, they had to make the most of their remaining time on the planet, to rescue something from their experiences that they could take back to their home-world, something that would, in some small way, justify the huge investment and meet the high expectations of the people of Perbau. The settlers began to look to their specialities, the reasons for which they had been selected to join Wsir's group. Self-sufficiency was no longer a realistic goal. The Bau had proved, beyond all doubt, that they were incapable of living the simple life without substantial technological back-up, and that without help from those primitive humans, who knew their own planet so well, they could not survive. In accepting the support of the natives, the Bau also had to accept their worship. However uncomfortable they might be with their godly status they saw no other way to live out the duration of the Experiment.

The native inhabitants of Abdw, at first, were delighted to play hosts to more of the Golden Ones but, before long, the pressures on resources became apparent as stores were depleted and humans went hungry in order to feed the extra mouths. The Bau began to recognise their extreme good fortune in having been welcomed so wholeheartedly at First. The Kemites there had kept them in comfort, bordering on luxury by human standards, for almost two solar cycles, often depriving themselves and their families to keep the Golden Ones happy. Wsir could well imagine how other Experimental settlements might have fared worse, much worse. He tried not to think about the dangers and disasters his fellows in other zones might have suffered. For all he knew, the Kem settlement could be the only one to have survived relatively unscathed, but for how much longer would he be able to make that boast?

Inhr and Wsrt were the first to leave. They went downstream to Djhwty's town where they decided to stay to help Imn with his research. Srkt travelled furthest to join Pth and Skhmt, moving into Nyayt's little home on the outskirts of Rstaw in an area surrounded by reed-beds and flowering pastures. There, at last, she found a use for her skills as the entomologist of the group, devoting her attention to the domestication of bees and the production of honey, and, as Skhmt also reported, to making Nyayt happier than she had ever seen her.

Hwthr finally agreed to leave her precious cattle, acknowledging that the local herdsmen were more than capable of caring for them. She accepted Sbk's invitation to join him on an expedition to Kem's only lake of any size which he had long wanted to visit since he first identified it from the survey's aerial images. They had heard from Pth that the native settlements of the Lake region were quite advanced and likely to be welcoming. The zoologist, Sbk, hoped to use one of the villages as a base for his study of the wildlife in the area. Hwthr was interested to see how the more established communities dealt with their domesticated animals. Wsir was glad that both his friends had found a worthwhile project to occupy them at this troubling time. As had become their custom, all the remaining Bau in Abdu gathered at the riverside to watch the latest departure.

Ast said, as they waved the boat on its way, 'It is so nice to see smiling faces for a change. I feared, after the news from Sumer, that we would never know happiness again on this planet.'

Wsir put his arm around her shoulders, saying, 'Your optimism is one of your many endearing features.'

'But you do not share it?' her brow wrinkled with the query.

'I worry that this renewed enthusiasm for exploration and research is no more than displacement activity, taking our minds off the underlying problems.'

'Is that such a bad thing?'

'No. I agree that, since we cannot, in all honesty, say that the Experiment is still viable, we must salvage what we can from our experiences. But the difficulties that disrupted our plans have not gone *away, much as we try to deny the fact. We have to be wary, still. We must not allow ourselves to be lulled into a sense of contentment and purpose that could be shattered at any moment.'*

'I suppose you are right to be cautious. There seems to be no way of predicting when or whom the madness will strike.'

'You are calling it madness?'

'How else would you describe it?'

'Inhr said that the humans at First called Swty's behaviour an upset in maat. *That is the Kemite word for balance and order.'*

Ast pursed her lips and said, 'That is a very charitable way of explaining it. Since the Bau alone are subject to the madness, I would not have been surprised if the humans had made some attempt to excise the evil element in their midst, to prevent contagion.'

'That is what I fear may have happened in other settlement areas. If Bau exhibited such symptoms among a less well-disposed human population it could promote a violent reaction, perhaps even a massacre.'

'But surely we would have heard.'

'Perhaps the silence is the message.'

*

The corn was ready for harvesting when they received Skhmt's frantic sending, *'Pth has been poisoned!'*

Every Ba within range, hearing *the panic in her thoughts, knew that Pth's situation was grave for the calm and dependable Skhmt, the doctor, could not detach herself from the fears of Skhmt, Pth's mate.*

Srkt and Wadjt, who had made a study of Kem's venomous creatures, reported that the local Kemites declared Pth to be the victim of a cobra. Since one bite from this serpent brought certain death to humans, Pth was believed to be beyond help. Skhmt, of course, would not accept that. She interrogated every wise woman and priest in the area as to possible anti-venoms. When they had no relief to offer she became increasingly irrational, accusing them of holding back the cure. In fact, the humans were astounded at Pth's resilience. The poison coursing through his system would have killed a human male within a day but, despite almost total paralysis, he was still alive after four days, breathing with difficulty but still alive. In her moments of reasoned thought, Skhmt admitted that it was a neurotoxin which would have been beyond her powers to analyse even had she had all the facilities of the base ship at her command. Had such analysis been possible it would still have taken too long to be of any use to Pth. Skhmt could only hope that the snake's venom, evolved to deal with Geb's life-forms, would be less effective on Ba physiology, and Pth's continuing hold on life, when the local humans were already mourning him as dead, gave his companions hope.

But all Skhmt's fellows shared her pain and anguish, felt her sense of helplessness and anger, as her mate weakened and fell into a coma, and, in the darkest moment since their landing, Pth died.

The standard protocol for the death of a Ba off-world was that the body should be preserved by whatever method was available locally, and kept safe until rendition to Perbau was possible. Wsir insisted on the application of this protocol to remind everyone that all the Bau who had set foot on this planet would be going home. On a more technologically advanced world, the body would have been plasticised or, at the very least, frozen. While he had no wish to allow humans a closer knowledge of Ba anatomy, Wsir knew that he would have to make use of local expertise. The Kemites buried their naked dead in the hot desert sand, which desiccated the flesh and shrank the body to the form of a leather-coated skeleton. The burial specialists at Pth's settlement recommended haste but the grieving Skhmt could not bear to think of her life-partner becoming an unrecognisable shell and she refused to let the vultures, as she called them, come near Pth's body. Decomposition set in far more quickly than she expected but, in spite of the smell and the threat to her own health, still she refused to let him go. It was only with the arrival of Hwthr that Skhmt was tricked into drinking one of her own sleeping potions disguised in strong beer. When she roused after a full day's drugged sleep, her beloved was buried and no one would tell her where for fear she would try to exhume him.

Skhmt's pent up grief and fury, enhanced by the peculiar conditions of Geb's environment, were finally released. Overnight she disappeared from Rstaw. Rumours reached her friends of her roaming the desert fringes, in all the areas where the humans had established burial grounds. Recently dug graves were discovered to be disturbed, their contents scattered. Outlying farm settlements and villages were raided, with quantities of food taken and other stores destroyed or tainted. The settlers were appalled at such un-Balike behaviour, especially on the part of one of their most respected and trusted companions.

But Skhmt's madness caused some of the settlers to reconsider their allegiances. Shw, Skhmt's brother, came downstream from First with his mate Tfnt. They met with Inhr on their way and together planned a hunting expedition with the sole purpose of capturing Skhmt and saving her from herself. Beyond all expectation they succeeded in repeating the ruse adopted by Hwthr. By predicting Skhmt's movements, they planted some jars of drugged beer in an open store hut. When she woke up she found herself securely detained, with Ast and Nebt ready to offer the care and counselling that she needed. The third year of the Experiment was drawing to a close as Skhmt regained her senses and the Bau tried to convince themselves that, barring further disasters, they could last out until the arrival of the scout ship. It was the very unpredictability of those disasters that most worried the settlers. They had overcome or minimised the effects of the problems encountered so far, but many began to fear that next time they would not be so lucky.

*

Pete poked his head round Simon's door. 'What are you doing here? I thought you were staying with your Mum and Dad for a few days.'

Simon looked up from his perusal of a heavy reference tome. 'That was the plan but then Uncle Eric invited himself for Easter.'

'Oh shit!' Pete said as he sidled into the tiny room, trying not to dislodge anything from the piles of books and papers stacked on the floor inside of the door. Just in time he managed to prevent an avalanche of journals and perched on the edge of a chair, drawing up his long legs and tucking in his elbows. 'I can see how that would ruin things. What did he want?'

'What d'you think?' Simon leaned his arms on the desk.

'I guess he wasn't happy about the Forum meeting.'

'That's putting it mildly,' Simon sighed. 'He wanted to know why I didn't stand up for him and who'd invited that Crowther woman, as he called her.'

'But you had nothing to do with that. She came of her own accord.'

'Try persuading my uncle of that. There was an awful scene with him accusing me of disloyalty and Mum wringing her hands and saying "How could you, Simon?" over and over. I couldn't stand it any longer. I'd been planning to come back at the end of the week but I cut and ran on Tuesday as soon as I knew the University would be opened up after the Bank Holiday. Why are you here?'

'The dissertation calls. I can get so much more done when the place isn't cluttered up with undergrads.'

'I've been trying to check some references but my heart's not in it. I must have read this page at least three times and I'm still none the wiser.'

'Coffee?' Pete asked.

'Yeah, why not. Is Theatre A open? '

'For snacks and drinks but they won't get into hot meal mode until the students come back.'

'Still, that means they won't be crowded. Let's go.'

Theatre A was busier than they had expected but they found a table to themselves and lingered in silence over cappuccinos and giant cookies.

Their contemplative mood was broken by Sylvia's arrival. 'I thought I saw you two going in this direction,' she said taking a seat at their table. 'Why the long faces?'

'Same old, same old,' Pete said.

'Not that Evers man again?'

'Still,' Simon said with feeling. 'He's never going to forgive me and now my Mum's hardly speaking to me. It's horrible at home.'

Sylvia stifled a chuckle, with difficulty, saying, 'You poor dear. But I might have something to make you smile.' She pulled a copy of the local weekly newspaper from her bag.

'Yeah,' said Pete, '*The Gazette*'s always a barrel of laughs.'

'I think you'll be surprised when you read it. Page five, full-page spread. You can keep this paper. Perhaps you could send a copy to your uncle for his cuttings album – I'm sure he has one.' Sylvia patted Simon's hand where it lay on the table, 'Cheer up. It's all over now,' then she stood up and left.

The page in question was marred by the photograph of a grinning Eric Evers under the headline '*TV archaeologist fights his corner*', but, after reading a few lines of the article, Simon gave a snort of disbelief and Pete stifled a guffaw. A paragraph later they were almost helpless with giggles.

'Do you think Uncle Eric will want this in his collection?' Pete asked, wiping away tears of laughter.

'Oh yes,' Simon said. 'He's of the belief that no publicity is bad publicity, and this journalist...' he checked the by-line, '...Bruce Perkins, is clearly on his side.'

'It's a masterpiece of twisted logic,' Pete admitted. 'This Perkins guy is obviously a closet Evers fan, not an unbiased observer. It reads like he's trying to convince his readers of Evers' bona-fides in spite of all the evidence to the contrary. His memory of events is a tad different from mine. Do you think he was actually at the meeting?'

'Oh yes, there was a gaggle of press in the theatre foyer afterwards. Uncle Eric was very keen to get his side of the story across to them, having been put in his place by Prof Jameson and then being upstaged by the Doc's mother. She won't be forgiven for stealing a lot of Uncle Eric's press coverage. That was one of his major complaints at the weekend – why should that woman benefit from his publicity? But this is different, isn't it?'

'Way different! No need for accuracy when uninformed speculation will do instead. Find the sensational whether it's corruption in the Council or disagreement in the WI. Isn't the English local rag a great institution?'

'Perkins isn't very polite about Xanthe Crowther. I wonder if the Doc has seen this.'

'She's in her office now. Let's go and show it to her,' Pete's mischievous grin was irresistible.

'Why not?'

Pete's knock on the door was answered by a cheery, 'Come in.'

They found Hermione with the same edition of *The Gazette* open on her desk. The gentle smile on her face reassured them as to their welcome. 'So you've seen it too,' she said, indicating the paper in Simon's hand.

'You don't mind?' he asked.

'Of course not. I have no respect for the integrity of *Gazette* journalists. If this had been in a national I might have been a bit more concerned. But my mother has broad shoulders, metaphorically speaking, and so has Theo. Anyway, Mother is back in London and Theo has gone on volcano-watch in Chile. They will see the funny side of this, though it is a masterpiece of twisted logic…'

'Just what I said,' Pete interrupted.

Hermione reproved him with a frown over her glasses, 'Yes, well, I have no worries about *The Gazette*. Besides, I am not mentioned and neither is Ian's work in Egypt so no damage has been done. And on the subject of work, what are you two up to at the moment?'

Pete muttered something about beginning the write-up of his skeletal investigation and how he ought to be getting on with it. 'Quite,' Dr Beaumont said, and he took the hint. When Pete had closed the door behind him, Hermione continued, 'I have had the abstract of that paper accepted. We will be presenting it at the Cambridge conference in June.'

'We? Really?' Simon said, colouring and running a hand through his fringe..

Hermione smiled at his modest response. 'Of course. I employed you as my Research Assistant. You have shared the research so you must share the glory of presenting the paper.' She had been looking forward to the day when she could hand over that scary aspect of research though she was beginning to wonder whether Simon might suffer worse stage-fright than she did herself. The Cambridge conference would be a baptism of fire but they had time to hone his performance.

'We need to get together to tidy up some loose ends,' she said. 'How have you been getting on?'

'I was checking a few references this morning.'

'Good. Go and get your books and we'll do some work on it now.'

Simon drifted back to his office on a cloud of happy thoughts. His first serious research paper, on which his name would appear alongside that of H.P. Beaumont, was going to be presented at a prestigious conference within months. All his cares about the disagreement with his uncle and the disappointment of his mother were as nothing. In the world that mattered, his chosen world, he had arrived.

Chapter 11: Moments of Doubt

The phone was ringing as Simon struggled with the key of his office door. There was a knack to this particular lock which he had not mastered even after eight months in the job. When it gave in suddenly and he fell into the room, the ringing stopped. He looked at the last call display and, recognising the number, he dumped his knapsack and umbrella before locking the door again on his way out.

His knock at Dr Beaumont's door was answered immediately. 'Ah, Simon, good. I was just trying to ring you.'

'Sorry, I missed the call. Trouble with the key again.'

'I thought you were going to get Maintenance to have a look at that.'

He shrugged. A tricky lock was low on his list of priorities.

Hermione continued, 'Well, I thought you would like to know that the finds from the last season at Nagada have cleared Customs and should be arriving today. Dr Masterson has asked if you and Peter would like to help him check them in.'

'That's great. Is there anything in particular you want me to look out for?'

'I have glanced over Ian's notes and I think there are quite a few pieces that might be of interest to us; several samples of grain, for instance, from a variety of contexts, and a surprising number of fibre samples – basketwork mainly but also what might be fabric fragments.'

Simon's eyes lit up. 'That'd be fantastic. When can I see them?'

Hermione smiled at his enthusiasm. 'The boxes should be delivered to the Post Room by midday. I want you to find Peter and meet Dr Masterson there. But you must realise that you probably will not be able to do much more today than open one or two crates. The real work will begin tomorrow.'

Pete proved to be elusive. A glance through the porthole window showed that he was not in the laboratory, though Sally was so Simon ducked away before she saw him. The Ice Maiden had become even frostier with him since Uncle Eric's visit but he had no wish to find out why.

The only occupant of the post-graduate IT suite looked up from her monitor as Simon peered round the door. 'If you're looking for Pete, he's gone to the Library.'

Simon was somewhat in awe of Felicity-Anne Quinn She was Ian Masterson's post-doctoral student, a hands-on archaeologist specialising in pottery, and she had taken one of the much coveted student places on the very first season of the Nagada dig. A few years older than Simon she reminded him of his elder sister. Her long auburn hair was kept under control in a thick plait hanging almost to her waist, but a few wavy wisps escaped to soften her brow line. Her long fingers, currently resting on the keyboard, could move faster than the eye could follow. Her skill with computer imagery, reconstructing pots from the tiniest of shards, was remarkable and her knowledge of Egyptian ceramics in particular was encyclopaedic. Prof Jameson always referred to her as Dr Quinn and Dr Beaumont insisted on calling her Felicity, but she preferred to be known as Flick, though she also answered to her initials as she was Frequently Asked Questions.

While Simon had not had much contact with FAQ because of her absence in Egypt, he had heard enough about her to know that she was the sort of archaeologist he would dearly love to be. At this moment her grey-green eyes sparkled with a lively sense of humour which, on such short acquaintance, Simon was unable to judge.

'Do you know if he's got the message about the stuff arriving from Egypt?'

'Oh yes, he was here when Mac came to tell me about it. He got a bit excited.' Flick's eye's glittered with amusement.

'Well, it is rather like Christmas come again.'

'You're right,' she nodded, 'and even though I saw most of the finds when they first came out of the ground, I have to admit to feeling a bit excited myself. I'm looking forward to seeing whatever the Egyptian authorities have let us have.'

'Yeah, that's the downer, isn't it? Not knowing exactly what they decided to keep for themselves at the last minute.'

'I don't think it'll be too bad. There was no spectacular art work or significant historical material. The authorities have more than enough stuff from their own excavations piling up, waiting for scientific evaluation. They're only too glad to let other institutions bear the time and expense of doing it properly.'

'I know they don't let human remains out of the country. Is Pete going to be disappointed?'

'Possibly. But he knows the situation. Most of the graves we investigated had already been dug years ago so we found only a few small bones overlooked by the earlier teams. Other burials had been badly disturbed by animals, or treasure-seekers and I don't think we found enough bones all told to make one complete skeleton. But there were a few miscellaneous finds from other contexts, including a couple of long bones and a partial skull that Pete would find interesting. He'll just have to work from the photos and context records until he gets a chance to handle them for himself.'

Simon took in her unspoken message. 'He's got a place on the dig?'

'Pending the result of his MSc,' Flick grinned.

'The lucky sod! Does he know?'

'I would guess, yes. He was here a few minutes ago. He seemed about to burst with the news. You could try his mobile.'

'It's never switched on,' Simon sighed.

'Like most conscientious archaeologists, I suppose, can't afford a lapse in concentration.'

'Hah! More likely it's not charged or he's got no credit. Will you be going to the Post Room at noon?'

'Try and keep me away!'

Behind Simon the door opened and he had to jump out of the way to avoid being knocked over as Sally entered. He yelped as he barked his shin on the heavy waste bin and caught his hip on the corner of a desk. Sally glared at him then ignored him.

'Have you time for a coffee, Flick?' she asked

'For you, sweetie, of course,' FAQ's smile lit up the room. 'Let me just finish off here.' She saved her work to a memory stick before logging off the network. 'OK, she said, standing up. 'See you later,

Simon. Let's go, sweetie,' and, to Simon's astonishment, she gave Sally a peck on the cheek before the two left, hand in hand.

He was still pondering the implications of this vision when, crossing the atrium, he bumped into Professor Jameson.

'Ah, Goodhill,' the Professor said, 'I've been meaning to have a little chat.'

Simon surreptitiously rubbed his shin where a metal-clad corner of the Professor's sturdy briefcase had hit the same spot as the bin.

Jameson seemed not to have noticed. 'I meant to say, I hope there are no hard feelings over that business with your uncle. I'm hearing good things about you from several directions, from Dr Beaumont in particular. Keep up the good work.'

Simon managed to stammer something unmemorable as the Professor patted him on the shoulder and proceeded in the direction of his own office. This day was proving to be full of surprises and it was not yet half over.

Rain was still falling so he decided he would need his umbrella despite the necessity of another confrontation with the recalcitrant lock. The stubborn contraption gave way just as Pete appeared in the corridor. 'Still giving you bother?' he said.

Simon was cursing under his breath but not about the lock. He had rapped his shin against a chair. He pulled up the leg of his chinos to survey the damage.

'You've not become a Mason, have you?' Pete grinned, giving his friend a knowing nudge.

'No I bloody haven't!' Simon exploded.

'So-rry,' Pete said, 'What did I do?'

'You weren't where you were supposed to be and when I went looking for you I scraped this leg avoiding the Ice Maiden. Then Prof Jameson swiped me with his bag and now this chair seems to have it in for me.'

Pete adopted an aggrieved tone, 'I didn't know I was supposed to be anywhere in particular except at the Post Room by midday. That's why I came to collect you. Why so touchy?'

'I don't really know, apart from hurting. Look, there's blood.'

Pete peered at Simon's injury. 'Not very much blood,' he said.

'Did you know about Sally and FAQ?' Simon blurted out.

'What about them?'

'That they're – an item?'

'Oh that, of course. Everyone knows that.'

'I didn't. I've spent months avoiding the Ice Maiden because I thought, well, I…'

Pete's open-mouthed amazement gave way to laughter. 'You thought she was a man-eater with her sights set on you? The irony is beautiful!'

'Actually,' Simon tried to regain some dignity, 'I thought Theo was the object of her desires.'

'Oh that was just celebrity-worship. Flick and Sally have been together for years. I'd've put you out of your misery sooner if I'd realised.'

'What I don't understand is why she took such an instant dislike to me.'

'Have you looked at yourself in the mirror recently?'

'What's that supposed to mean?'

'You and FAQ could be brother and sister. When Sally first set eyes on you Flick was out of the country and she was probably feeling a bit lonely. Then you appear, looking like a masculine version of her lady-love and she's confused, and our Super-Sallius doesn't like being confused. It makes her feel out of control and that makes her snappy, with her snappiness aimed at the source of her confusion. In this case that's you.'

'Since when did you become a psychologist?'

'Aah, now there I have you. I did Psychology A-level.'

'And I'm supposed to be impressed by that?'

'Well...' Pete glanced at the clock on the office wall and groaned. 'Can we postpone this discussion 'til later. It's already five past twelve.' He turned and ran.

'Oh shit!' Simon grabbed his umbrella and slammed the door shut before haring after his friend.

Simon's garish gamp collapsed about his ears twice in the short gallop to the Post Room, which was situated at the rear of the 1960s extension to the St George's Building. Despite the umbrella's failure Simon was still drier than Pete when they came to shake themselves off in the entrance lobby. They found that their haste was unnecessary. Dr Masterson and Felicity Quinn were standing in front of the Post Desk and, from the way in which Ian was twisting his brown cap in his hands behind his back, their frustration was obvious.

'Has it arrived?' Pete asked, his voice breathy from the dash across the car park.

Ian threw him a glare over his shoulder.

FAQ said, 'We've been told that a lot of packages arrived this morning and they have to be dealt with in order.'

'But wasn't this a special delivery?' Simon asked.

'Of course it damn well is,' Masterson growled. 'It came by special courier and it should be smothered in Customs labels and accompanied by reams of paperwork. But that's not a good enough description, apparently.'

The Post Master appeared from the door behind the counter, consulting a closely printed list on his clipboard. He was a short, burly figure, whose height and bearing screamed 'military'. Simon recognised the type. Almost every member of the security staff of every university he had known had drifted into the job after a career in either the police or the armed forces. He put this particular example down as Sergeant Major. The man persisted in wearing his uniform cap indoors.

'We've found the consignment now,' the man said in a tone that invited congratulation. His reward was a steely silence which he seemed compelled to fill with the rustling of the sheets on his clipboard. 'We're just waiting for the float to get back. There was a big delivery for Chemistry this morning.' He was referring to the electric trolley used to transport heavy or unwieldy packages about the campus.

'If we could just take a couple of the boxes to be going on with...' Ian asked through gritted teeth.'

'Oh no, no, Dr Masterson, I couldn't let you do that. Health and Safety would be down on me like the proverbial. You have to be trained to handle crates that size. If you haven't had the training I can't risk you putting your back out and then suing the University. They'd probably have it out of my pay.' He laughed at his own joke, a bubbling, wheezing noise, more like a leaking boiler than an honest demonstration of amusement. 'Now, don't you worry. As soon as the float gets back I'll have the whole lot sent over to Garstang, asap.'

It was clear that no further progress would be made so, before he said something he would regret, Masterson turned on his heel and stomped out into the rain, followed by his acolytes. Simon offered the umbrella to FAQ who grinned and shook her head as she flipped up the hood of her sweatshirt. Ian pulled his cap down and turned up the collar of his leather jacket, saying, 'I need a drink but for now a decent coffee will have to do. Theatre A it is then.'

*

Hermione was waiting in the atrium of the Garstang Building. As they made their way up the steps they saw her look at her watch in a pointed manner that suggested it was not the first time she had done so. Nothing was said but her look was enough to make Pete hang his head and Simon felt his face warming. Ian, however, only had eyes for the polystyrene crates stacked at Hermione's feet.

'Five. I thought there were six!'

'Number six was too big to go on the cart,' Dr Beaumont said through straight lips. 'I was told to wait while they went back to fetch it.'

Even Masterson noticed her emphasis on *told*. He gave her what he hoped was a winning smile but her reaction was to say, 'I have better things to do than to stand guard over your boxes.' Then she turned on her heel and strode away in the direction of her office. They heard the door slam from around two turns in the corridor.

'Oh dear,' said FAQ.

'She'll be OK,' Masterson said, with doubt in his voice.

'Do all the Post Room guys have the same attitude as their boss?' Pete asked.

There was a moment's silence as they all imagined Dr Beaumont being patronised by a delivery man.

'I'd better go and talk to her,' Ian said as he started after Hermione, 'Get the boxes to the organics lab. I'll be there as soon as.'

Simon and Pete exchanged shrugs, and FAQ said, 'Well, you heard the man.'

'But we haven't been trained to carry boxes,' Pete whined.

'Don't push your luck, Frenchie,' Flick grinned. 'There should be a trolley in the cleaners' cupboard. Go and find it while I stay here in case number six turns up.'

Sally was waiting for them in the laboratory and by the time Dr Masterson arrived with Hermione the others were almost hopping up and down with impatience. They had checked Ian's inventory and each had made a case for which box should be opened first.

'Let's have a look at number two,' Ian said, after a quick glance at his lists.

Simon could not help sharing a smug smile with Sally. Box two held mainly botanical samples with some textiles and wood. Pete had had his eye on crate one which contained the few zoological finds the Egyptian authorities had allowed them to keep, and Flick was eager to get her hands on the pottery. But it seemed that Ian's mollification of HPB had included giving her the first choice of crate.

When the contents of the box had been matched to the inventory they were laid out on the bench and everyone stood back deferring to Dr Beaumont's expertise. She ran her hand over the finds, checking the reference numbers against the description on the manifest. When she picked up a plastic box about the size of a takeaway curry container the onlookers released a collective sigh of relief. As she broke the seal on the lid and removed the covering layer of tissue paper all heads craned forward to see what she had chosen.

'Oh, wow!' Simon breathed.

'What's that?' asked Pete, clearly unimpressed.

'Put it on Sally's viewer platform, and I'll show you,' Hermione said.

Once the picture on the viewer screen was tweaked into focus they could all see a lump of vegetable matter. A large part of the outer surface was blackened as if it had been burned and it retained the imprint of a covering of a woven material, a few fibres of which still clung to the pear-shaped mass.

'Is that linen?' Simon asked with awe in his voice.

'I believe so,' HPB's tone was almost reverent. 'I think it's a pouch or bag of some sort.' Turning the lump over on the viewing table revealed several square centimetres of fabric still adhering to the underside. 'See the thicker threads – they could be part of a string tie. And in the bag…' She used tweezers to separate out a tiny fragment of the dark brown mass.

'Grain!' Sally said with triumph, 'And beautifully preserved.'

'A good choice?' Hermione asked.

'Oh, yes!' Simon and Sally said together.

'Why all this fuss about a few manky seeds?' Pete moaned, 'I just don't get it.'

'That's because you're a bones man,' Simon laughed.

'Exactly,' Dr Beaumont smiled, 'and you still have your dissertation to finish, Peter, before we can let you be distracted by this new material.'

'It's OK, Pete,' Dr Masterson grinned, 'You'll get your chance, I promise. November will be along before you know it.'

'Oh, yeah,' Simon said, 'congrats on making the team.'

Pete shrugged feigned indifference but his broad grin spoke volumes.

'Come on, Frenchie,' Ian said, 'You can help me unpack some more stuff but you'll have to leave the real excitement for a while. You have much more important things to do.'

Pete's face twisted into a grimace and his shoulders slumped, his momentary triumph turned to abject misery. Simon laughed and FAQ, with a wry smile, patted Pete on the back, saying, 'There, there Frenchie. You'll get a go at the juicy stuff. Don't fret!'

Sally grunted without raising her eyes from the binocular microscope through which she was now viewing the contentious item. Hermione noticed Sally's air of concentration and turned her attention back to the screen. 'What have you seen?'

'I'm not sure,' Sally murmured, adjusting the magnification. 'You might see better through this,' and she moved aside to allow HPB to take her place.

'Oh, yes!' Hermione said. 'That is interesting.'

'That's it chaps,' Masterson said in a low, conspiratorial voice. 'They're occupied for the duration. The best we can do is find storage for all these finds before…' he gave Pete a meaningful look, '…we open another crate.'

FAQ said, 'I got the First Years to help clear out the finds cabinets at the end, there, and I've found some more space in the ceramics lab.'

'Well, let's call up the database and get on with it,' Ian said.

Simon was surprised at how long it had taken to inventory and cross-reference each item before finding it a secure home, but by the time Dr Masterson told them to call it a day and suggested a retreat to the Royal Oak, Hermione and Sally were still deep in their investigation of the mysterious grain find. The amorphous lump was being painstakingly broken up and seeds, chaff and fibres separated, photographs being taken at all stages of the proceedings.

'Coming for a drink?' Ian asked, but there was no response.

Flick chuckled. 'You go on with the boys. I'll get them out of their trance and follow you.'

An hour later, when there was still no sign of them, Masterson was becoming concerned. 'I think I'd better go and find them,' he said. 'You two don't need to stay.'

Simon looked at Pete who gave his usual shrug, and Ian left the bar without another word.

'D'you fancy a pizza?' Simon asked.

'Yeah, why not?'

*

The next morning, Pete had an appointment to see Prof Jameson to discuss some aspects of his dissertation. Since Masterson had not made any arrangement for them to unpack more of the finds, rather than sit alone in his pokey office, Simon retreated to the St George's Building, hoping to access some e-journals.

In the doorway of the library's computer room, he was confronted by the depressing sight of two rows of blue screens. Another student leaving the room said, 'Server's down. Big problems!'

Simon went to commiserate with Sylvia and found her looking uncharacteristically harassed, almost dishevelled. She glanced up, recognised him and snapped, 'All the Library systems are down. I can't find anything for you. I can't even issue books and I have to record returns by hand to put them on the computer later.'

'What did we do before computers?' Simon grinned, hoping to lighten her mood.

An IT technician, who had been rummaging around in a bundle of cables behind the desk, popped up with a crooked smile and said, 'I didn't have a job.'

'Any guess how long it will be?' Simon asked.

'How long's a piece of string?' the technician replied in a tone that was far too cheery for Sylvia's liking.

'Shorter than me but a bit longer than my patience,' she retorted.

'I think you need a coffee. My treat?' Simon offered.

Sylvia sighed then turned to her assistant. 'Can you cope for a while, Pam?'

The woman nodded and the Librarian bent to grab her bag. Simon fought back a chuckle as Pam raised her eyes heavenward and the IT technician put his thumbs up, both relieved to have Sylvia removed from the scene before her frustration turned to violence.

But Theatre A was more crowded than they had expected for the time of day. From animated conversations in the queue, some of them verging on the hysterical, they gathered that the computer problems were not confined to the Library.

'It's sunny out, for once,' Simon said. 'What say we take it outside?'

'Good idea,' Sylvia agreed, her tone somewhat calmer now she had a large coffee within her grasp.

They found a bench to one side of the lawn in front of the St George's Building, and indulged in a silent coffee moment while university life seemed to be falling apart all around them.

'No e-mail, no web chat, no internet shopping. It looks as if all network systems are off-line. Heaven forbid people might start talking to each other face to face,' Sylvia said at last.

'They look like ants when their nest's been disturbed,' Simon observed. 'This could become a spectator sport.'

'The best seat in the stadium would be somewhere nearer to Computer Services.'

'Sylvia! I'm shocked! You're suggesting that we seek entertainment in someone else's misery.'

'It's my misery too, and they caused it,' she waved her hands in the direction of the CS building.

'Come and see how we're getting on in the lab,' Simon offered.

After the mayhem of the outside world the organics lab was an oasis of calm. Simon blinked as his brain processed the scene. At first he thought he could have entered a time warp. Sally and Dr Beaumont were in the same positions at the viewing table as they had been when he had left for the pub the previous evening. Even the image on the laptop screen was the same. The he realised that Sally's hair was now in plaits and HPB was wearing trousers rather than the pencil skirt of yesterday. Both were so absorbed in their study that they did not notice his arrival with Sylvia. He coughed politely and, when Hermione looked up with a questioning quirk of an eyebrow, he said, 'You haven't got computer problems then?'

Sally growled without raising her gaze from the microscope.

'I think that means they have,' Sylvia said in a stage whisper.

'Yes, we are having to run our analysis on my laptop,' Dr Beaumont said, adding, 'It's nice to see you Sylvia, but why are you here?'

'I invited her. The computer glitches were driving her mad,' Simon explained.

'He's saving my sanity,' Sylvia agreed. 'Is there anything here to take my mind off those damned computers?'

'Well….'

Simon's ears twitched. He detected in HPB's voice a tone of suppressed excitement which he had never heard before. He took a closer look at the screen which was showing a looped sequence of images of the dissection of the mysterious grain find. Hermione moved towards the laptop, indicated to Sylvia to take a seat on one of the lab stools, then turned to Simon and said, 'I do not want to put any ideas into your head. Just watch these pictures and tell Sylvia what you see. Talk to her, not to me.' She pressed a key to return to the beginning of the loop.

Simon began, 'This is a sample of grain. It might appear quite small but, by the standards of finds from sites of comparable age this is something substantial. The grain seems to have been encased in a woven material of some kind. About half the fabric has either been burnt or decayed but what remains and the imprint it's left on the surface suggest quite a fine weave, and it's remarkably even too. The remaining threads have the appearance of vegetable rather than animal fibres, so probably linen, but I'd need a more powerful microscope to say for sure. There's no sign of stitching but there is a short length of a twisted cord of a similar fibre – could be the remains of a string or tie. The grain mass is basically pear-shaped. It looks to me as if it was in a simple pouch or possible just tied into a square of cloth.'

'Like an old-fashioned steamed pudding,' Sylvia said.

'Yes, exactly,' Simon smiled at her.

Hermione leaned forward to point at the screen. 'More looking, Simon,' she said, 'more about the grain.'

'But my area of expertise is fibres,' he moaned.

'You are supposed to be learning about grain too, so show me how much you have learned.'

Simon sighed and clicked back through a couple of images to replay them in sequence. 'You can see how well the grain is preserved, once Dr Beaumont had separated out some individual seeds from the mass.'

'I can see the imprint of the weave,' Sylvia said with a gasp of wonder.

'Yes, see how fine it is. That fabric could be equivalent to a modern cotton cheesecloth.'

'Is that unusual for its age?'

'We believe, from the context of the find, that this dates from the Egyptian Pre-dynastic, probably what is known as Nagada II,' Hermione explained. 'That makes it about five and a half to six thousand years old.'

'And fabric samples of similar fine weave have been found from that period,' Simon confirmed, 'though I'll admit from the imprint alone this looks better than anything I've seen of the type, and the remaining section of fabric is quite a lot bigger than most other early samples. Other finds were hardly more than tiny fragments.'

'The grain, Simon,' Hermione reminded him.

'Yes, well, we'd expect grain from this context to be either barley or emmer, that's a primitive form of wheat. This sample appears to have been partially carbonised, as if the outer layer at least had been subjected to heat, just like the fabric.'

'Burned?' Sylvia asked.

'Possibly, though sometimes burial in the hot sand can have a similar effect. Or it might have been stored in another container, like a pot, which was heated, perhaps in a house fire.'

'From the find record sheet and Ian's notes it seems that this was originally stored in a wooden box which was subject to burning in a domestic context. The remains of burned out buildings have been found in several Pre-dynastic sites; fire was a very real hazard in ancient times,' Dr Beaumont confirmed.

'Why is the carbonisation so important?' Sylvia queried. 'I know you talked about that when we were gathering resources against that man – sorry Simon..'

Simon grinned over his shoulder to show that he took no offence, and said, 'Because grain which has been rapidly carbonised before it had a chance to desiccate completely or, worse still, to rot, tends to retain its structure and is easier to identify.'

'Another way in which we get good preservation is if the site is waterlogged, as in a peat bog, for example,' Hermione added, 'but Egypt rarely has that sort of site.'

Sylvia chuckled at what she saw as Dr Beaumont's little joke, then fell silent as she realised that Hermione was not being funny.

Simon pressed on with his analysis. 'Anyway, this sample is particularly well preserved. Strictly speaking, most of these grains are spikelets. They're still in their glumes, the bracts or husks which have to be removed by milling. You can still see the point where the awn, the whisker has broken off. There are rachis fragments too, bits of the spines or stalks that attached the spikelets to the stem. Most grain in early times was stored in this form after threshing. The grains of these primitive cereals aren't so easily released from their ears. That's a feature of domestication. Wild plants shed their seeds readily as part of the natural reproductive cycle. When humans started exploiting such plants the ones which held on to their seeds when harvested were more useful than those which dropped their seed at the slightest touch. The inedible parts would be removed on processing.'

'So, can you say whether this is wheat or barley?' HPB asked.

'There are a few naked grains. My first impression is that it's emmer, but…' Simon paused as he leaned closer to the screen.

'Yes?' Dr Beaumont prompted.

'The shape isn't quite right,' Simon frowned. 'Can I have a look through the microscope?'

'Of course, help yourself,' Sally scowled, but gave up her seat without further comment.

Hermione said to Sylvia, 'I think you have lost your escort.'

'It's good to see him doing what he loves doing,' Sylvia said, then added quietly, 'I was worried that the trouble with his uncle might have dented his confidence.'

Dr Beaumont smiled, 'I think we have found just the thing to take his mind off that man. Shall we leave them to it?'

As Hermione and Sylvia made a discreet exit, Simon and Sally were deep in technical discussion with little sign of their customary animosity.

Simon had to admit that Sally knew her stuff. He looked at the sketches she had made by combining the evidence of her own eyes with the details revealed in the photographic images and was awe-stricken. Looking from microscope to computer screen to sketch pad and back he came to see why Hermione valued Sally's work so highly. She had the knack of highlighting just those features that were diagnostic while not missing out anything. Again and again he found himself referring to Sally's drawings as the definitive record of the find and as he did so he began to feel the hairs on the back of his neck bristling. There was something out of place, and he could not put his finger on it, but his instincts told him it was vitally important that he did so before Hermione returned.

'I'm relatively new to this but my first impression is that it isn't typical of the other Predynastic grain I've been working on with the Doc. We need to do some comparisons. Do you have access to the reference data base?' he asked Sally.

'Not with the computers down. We were using an international seed bank data base but Dr Beaumont only has a basic version on her laptop. We could use the photos and drawings from her publications, and many of the actual samples are available, though they might take some finding'

'Low-tech will have to do, then. I've got a couple of books in my office.'

On his way back to the lab Simon bumped into Pete.

'How'd it go with the Prof?' he asked his friend.

'Okay-ish,' Pete said. 'It was more about presentation than content – spelling, layout, labelling of tables, stuff like that. He seems quite pleased with what I've done so far. What've you been doing? More manky seeds?'

'Grain,' Simon answered shortly, suddenly feeling possessive of the find and reluctant to share his excitement with someone who could not appreciate the wonders of archaeobotany.

'Whatever. D'you want to go to the pub tonight?'

'Sorry. I've got a date. I'm going to the cinema,' Simon blushed as he remembered.

'A date!' Pete sounded incredulous. 'Who with?'

'Holly.'

'Who?'

'Holly Mitchell, you know, in the Arch Soc.'

'Wow!' was all Pete could say as they parted company.

Back in the laboratory Simon found Dr Beaumont peering through the microscope while Sally stood by. The Ice Maiden looked up and put a finger to her lips before he could say anything. The air of concentration was almost unbearable.

When Hermione at last lifted her head from the microscope her face bore a thoughtful, almost distant expression. 'Hmm,' she breathed, 'I think I need to arrange for some tests. I'll be in my office making a few calls.'

Simon could hardly contain himself but he managed to restrain his curiosity until Dr Beaumont had left the lab. Then he burst out, 'What is it? What have you found?'

For once, Sally looked uncertain. She was still diffident in her dealings with Simon.

'Go on,' he prompted, 'What is it about this sample that's got you and the Doc so worried?'

'We've been looking at the grain side by side with pictures of some emmer from the last season at Nagada. There's something about these, something I can't quite place…' She pointed to the computer screen which showed three individual grains in large magnification. 'They're not quite right.'

'I had the same feeling. Spooky or what?'

Sally gave him a pitying stare. 'Shall we try to be serious?'

'Sure,' Simon shuffled his feet as his cheeks began to burn. 'Tell me what you and the Doc have seen.'

Sally's frown softened. 'Well…' she hesitated for a fraction of a second before plunging on, 'If I hadn't checked against Dr Masterson's excavation notes and the sequence of photos taken at the time I would have sworn that this was a modern intrusion.'

'No!' Simon was horrified. It was an archaeologist's worst nightmare; that an apparently key piece of evidence should have to be dismissed because its authenticity was in doubt. 'It has to be right. I've seen Mac's notes too. The context record is immaculate.'

'That's what I thought, and that's what Dr Beaumont thought, but so far the best we can say from our observations is that it's confusing.'

'In what way confusing?' Simon sensed that Sally needed to talk things through.

'It's…well…,' the Ice Maiden was suddenly as close to thawing as Simon had ever seen her.

'Just tell me,' he said. 'Is it the shape of the grains? Because I think the ventral surface isn't flat enough for it to be regular emmer.'

'Yes, that's partly it,' Sally said.

'The dorsal face is also more ridged than rounded,' Simon went on.

'Yes, and there's more.'

'There is?' Simon was beginning to run out of ideas to demonstrate the usefulness of his recent intensive study of ancient grain.

'My feeling is that the grains are just a mite too big for what we would expect at this stage of domestication. The rachis scar is not quite the right shape, it looks too…too modern.'

Simon's eyes opened wide as he saw what she meant. 'I see. Everything about it is just that bit bigger and better than you'd expect.'

His heart sank as he realised what this could mean. The shadow of 'mummy wheat' flickered across his mind.

As if reading his thoughts, Sally said, 'No, it has to be right. The context is impeccable. But we have to check. That's one of the things Dr Beaumont is going to organise.'

Simon could sense there was something more. 'What else?'

'Something about the surface. It's only visible on some of the grains from inside the mass, the ones which haven't been so extensively carbonised. When you see the naked grains like this there's…Oh I can't quite explain…'

'I trust your instinct. What do you see?'

'A metallic sheen. It's not the silicaceous residue you might expect, it's definitely metallic. You can only see it when the light falls in a certain direction but it's there, and I can't explain it.'

Sally's response sparked in Simon's mind a flash of memory which fled as quickly as it had arrived. He shook his head in momentary bewilderment and brought his thoughts back to the matter in hand.

'If you didn't know where this grain had come from, what would your first impression be?'

Sally looked surprised at this intelligent question but she answered automatically, 'I'd say the grain had been deliberately and seriously hybridised…'

'You mean,' Simon paused, trying to absorb the implications of Sally's statement, 'you're suggesting something more than the natural hybridisation that led to the development of emmer from wild forms?'

'Yes, a lot more.'

'You're surely not talking genetic modification?' Simon felt a chill of apprehension.

'Of course not,' Sally's look was pitying, 'but this grain looks so much like modern wheat that I would have set it aside as an anachronistic anomaly…'

'…if not for the fact that it comes from a sealed context,' Simon finished.

'Yes,' Sally sighed.

'What does the Doc think?'

'She hasn't said much,' Sally admitted, 'I don't think she wants to cast doubt on Dr Masterson's work but she's been going over the record of the whole trench, again and again. She's worried.'

The image of HPB torn between academic rigour and loyalty to her colleague was not a pretty one.

'What will it take to ease her mind?' Simon asked.

'The first thing has to be to check the age of the sample, so carbon-14 dating must be a priority,' Sally said.

Simon nodded, 'I suppose the sample is big enough for carbon dating?' Radiocarbon dating of organic remains was a destructive process. There was always a fine line to be drawn between the sacrifice of part of a precious find and the knowledge that might be gained from its destruction. In this case, the little pouch contained sufficient grain for a dating sample to be taken without harming the value of the find.

'Oh yes,' Sally confirmed, 'and there's enough of it to allow for aDNA and other chemical analyses, but all these tests cost money and there are so many other finds from the site, we simply can't afford to test them all.'

Simon knew that, with Prof Jameson already paying for the Egyptian tests on the human remains and FAQ itching to have thermo-luminescence testing of the pottery, the budget was going to be stretched pretty thinly.

'I know I'm going to have to get in the queue to have the fabric tested,' he said with resignation, 'I'm well down on the priorities list.'

'Well those decisions aren't ours to make,' Sally said with her usual asperity.

'Exactly,' Simon said, 'so we'll have to do what we can while they sort it out between them.'

'Just what are you suggesting?' Sally bristled.

'Back to morphological analysis, the old compare, contrast and record routine and two pairs of eyes might be better than one. How about we take another look at the photos? Or better still, let's find some more actual samples.' Simon offered a cooperative olive branch.

'I suppose so,' Sally conceded with a faint smile.

Simon took care not to give voice to his exultant thought, 'The Ice Maiden thaws!'

*

Wsir was glad to have something to take his mind off what he thought of as his many failures. The grain stores had to be cleaned out ready for the new harvest. Even though none of his precious seed had been planted this season the yield promised to be good. This planet was again demonstrating the success of native breeds over the 'improved' varieties provided by the scientists on distant Perbau. 'How arrogant we were,' Wsir thought, watching the local farmers preparing the communal storage, 'to think that we knew better than these practical people with their generations of inherited wisdom and experience.' He felt like an apprentice learning from the master as he helped to set the fires which would burn out the grain pits and cleanse them of dirt, disease and pests. He followed the instructions of the senior farmer as they raked out the burnt debris of the reed-mat lining before scrubbing the remaining ash over the pressed mud surfaces. Moving on to the next pit the scientist in him wondered how the Kemites, who had been categorised by the Ba surveyors as level tawny primitives, had come to recognise the alkaline disinfectant properties of plant ash. How badly they had been underestimated and in so many ways!

His attention was so focused on the job in hand that he did not hear his attacker approach. The farmer facing him across the pit pointed at something and shouted an incoherent warning. As Wsir turned to see what had agitated the man, the blow aimed at his head instead connected with his shoulder, knocking him off balance. He tumbled into the grain pit where the cleansing ashes were still smoking. The pain was all the greater for being unexpected. Wsir's disorientation shocked him into sending a cry of alarm as his assailant jumped into the pit to continue his brutal attack.

Bau came running from all directions on hearing their leader's distress but by the time they arrived the farmers had already dragged Wsir's bloodied body from the pit and laid it gently on the ground. Ast pushed her way through the stunned crowd and fell to her knees beside her mate's prostrate form. He was still breathing, just, but one glance told her that he could not survive the horrendous head injuries. Her face glistening with tears she turned to the Kemites now huddled in a silent group, hardly able to believe what they had witnessed. Ast demanded, 'What happened? Who did this?'

Inbw appeared from the shade of a store hut where he had been observing the work. 'Do not blame them. This was the work of a Ba. It was Swty. Swty has killed Father.' Inbw's face, as always, was covered by the jackal mask but Ast knew from the catch in his voice that he too was crying.

Chapter 12: A Change of Minds

Nebt took control. She ordered the Bau to carry Wsir into the mansion. He should not draw his last breath lying in the dirt of a common farmyard. She ordered a reed hurdle to be pulled from the yard fence. She urged Ast to her feet and the two females walked beside the makeshift stretcher, all too aware that it might become a funeral bier before they reached the privacy of the Residence.

Though Wsir still breathed, Ast could not hear *him at all. There was a frightening empty space in her mind where she was accustomed to feeling her mate's comforting presence. She knew now something of what Imn had felt at his split from Min, or what Sakhmt had experienced when Pth died. The silence was black, claustrophobic but at the same time boundless. Surely he should still be there. Ast started to turn her own thoughts inwards, as if by searching the remotest corners of that void she could recover something of the Wsir she had lost. She knew the dangers of this sort of introspection. She knew that she could lose herself, that she could become locked in a cage of her own making, but what was there left outside for her to care about? Wsir was dead.*

A slap across her face brought her back to reality. 'He is not dead yet,' Nebt said, her voice harsh with fear.

Ast was suddenly aware of a buzz of voices outside the room and was overwhelmed by a cacophony of thoughts – angry, upset, bewildered, scared. She put her hands to her ears and sank to the ground curling into a foetal ball. 'Tell them to stop! I cannot hear *him! Tell them to stop!' she moaned.*

Nebt pulled Ast's hands away from her face. 'You cannot indulge your misery yet. You have decisions to make.'

'What?' Ast whispered.

'You can save something of him at least,' Nebt persisted, 'In your heart you know what you must do.'

Ast looked at Nebt in horror as the meaning of her words penetrated her grief-stricken mind. 'No! No! I cannot!'

'You must. You know that Swty's jealousy over Inbw is part of this. He has denied Wsir the chance of ever knowing his own offspring

but you can still give him a youngling. You must act now before Wsir's seed loses viability. Please Ast, you must empouch yourself.'

'But my cycle...'

'In these circumstances you have no choice. We can only hope that the empouchment takes. Ast, it is his and your last and only chance. Wsir deserves to have offspring. He is the best of us.'

Ast nodded. 'Of course. I will honour him as you suggest, if you will help me.'

'You know I will, my dearest sister.' She moved to slide the bolt on the door. 'We shall not be disturbed. Do you know what you have to do?'

Ast nodded again. 'I worked in a fertility clinic for one planetary cycle. I am ashamed to say I could not understand why some couples had to resort to such desperate measures.'

Nebt, flushing at the memory of her own breeding, said 'There are always difficulties, incompatibilities...'

'But we were never incompatible. There was no difficulty. It seems so remote, so calculated, so contrary to all we had planned.'

'That is the point. You must consider your plans changed. If you wait much longer there will be no hope at all of your conceiving – ever!'

Ast gasped at Nebt's directness but she knew she spoke the truth. Bau matings were for life and each partner remained committed to the union even after the death of the other. There were no second chances. The falling birth rate on Perbau was largely due to couples delaying breeding for so long that, when they finally decided to produce a youngling, artificial methods were their only resort. If Ast did not take the same path she would never know the joys of motherhood.

'I will do it,' she said, 'but you must be my witness. I will have no one say that I betrayed my mate.'

'Of course,' Nebt said, putting an arm about Ast's shoulder, 'but it must be now.' She tipped her head in the direction of the unconscious Wsir, whose breathing had become ragged and shallow.

'Yes,' Ast said with resolution in her voice in spite of the tears in her eyes.

'Can you remember the words?'

'They are etched forever in my mind,' Ast affirmed. She placed her hand on Wsir's chest and slid it under the waistband of his kilt to begin the massage of his seed sack. As the tears flowed freely down her cheeks she said, 'My dearest love, the time has come as we agreed for our union to be completed. Give me your seed so that our love may be consummated in the form of a child, flesh of our flesh, blood of our blood, bone of our bone.' Under Ast's gentle ministration the narrow slit, which humans would have mistaken for Wsir's navel, opened and a small, oval packet of sperm, enveloped in a creamy white membrane, slipped into her hand. She looked up at Nebt with an appeal in her eyes.

While Ast opened her own breeding pouch and as the sperm packet was secreted within, Nebt spoke the words of the male. 'My dearest love, the time has come to complete our union, as we agreed at our mating. Take my seed so that our love may be consummated in the form of a child, flesh of our flesh, blood of our blood, bone of our bone.'

The breeding pouch closed with an encouraging firmness. Nebt took both Ast's hands in hers and together they finished the ritual. 'May this new life prosper and be healthy! Love of our love, heart of our hearts, mind of our minds'. Ast and Nebt fell into each other's arms, sobs racking their bodies. They failed to notice the moment when Wsir gave up his last shuddering breath.

*

Sendings *between the dispersed groups revealed that a general state of confusion had permeated all the Bau settlements, leading to a major disruption of normal life. Every Ba sensed that community cohesion was breaking down and the chances of them surviving until the return of the scout ship were growing more remote with every passing day. The one Ba who had always seemed least affected by the environmental conditions which were at the root of the problem was Hwthr. On her arrival in Abdw, just two days after Wsir's death, she was confronted with scenes of such chaos that she hardly recognised the place. The leaderless Bau would have been in an even more parlous state had it not been for the loyal attentions of Wsir's human followers.*

The Bau were arguing amongst themselves as to how to deal with Swty. The natural Ba instinct for avoiding confrontation had been dulled by almost four years of isolation on Geb. The events in Sumer, the tragedies of Kem, had caused much heart-searching and the Golden Ones had to face some uncomfortable truths. To a greater or lesser degree, all the males and some of the females had experienced those raw emotions which, in the case of Swty, had spilt over into unthinkable violence. They had at least the glimmer of an understanding of what could make brother turn against brother and the fear that they too could be overtaken by such uncontrolled feelings made them hesitant in suggesting a remedy. Ndjty had flown into such a rage that others had had to restrain him from hunting Swty down. The more temperate females had exerted all their powers to keep him from encouraging others to join him in a raid on First. Only Hwthr's reasonable words had prevented her friend from compounding Swty's evil.

'Ndjty, think logically. Think like a Ba. He appeared out of nowhere and disappeared into nothing. You cannot be sure whether he has returned to First or whether he is out there, somewhere, simply waiting for the next attack. What would you feel if you were not here when that attack happened?'

Hwthr's first duty had been to observe the body to put the lie to the many rumours circulating. In the Bau *sendings* she had heard that Wsir had been burned to death, or that he had been decapitated, or that Swty had cut his brother's throat and drunk his blood. According to the most widely spread story, Wsir had been ripped apart by his brother's bare hands and Swty had then scattered the body parts in the desert to be consumed by animals. Inbw, the story went, was scouring the sandy wastes to recover his adoptive father's remains for preservation and repatriation to Perbau. Hwthr was relieved to find Ast and Nebt keeping vigil over the intact if battered body. They hugged their friend and shared a few more tears before she persuaded them to tell her what had happened. When she heard about Ast's self-empouchment she nodded, 'That was well done. Has it worked?'

'We believe so,' Nebt said. Ast gave a wan smile.

'Do you mind if I check?' Hwthr asked.

'Please do,' Ast agreed, 'I want to be sure.'

Hwthr's examination confirmed what her friends had told her, and more. 'If I did not know better I would say this incubation was some ten days more advanced than you say. The shape of the egg is already discernible. Can you not feel it?' She placed Ast's hand against her abdomen and watched the sense of wonder appear on her face.

'How can that be?' asked Nebt.

'I saw this sometimes at the clinic,' Ast remembered. 'When a couple were almost too late, or when they were beyond normal breeding age, it was as if the natural processes accelerated to give them more time with their youngling. And it was not only the gestation which was shorter. The offspring in such instances matured at a much faster rate. I saw one youngling who attained full adult capacity, both physical and mental, within one planetary cycle of his conception.'

'I have heard of such cases,' Hwthr confirmed, 'and amongst animals it is common for the offspring of prey species to be born ready to run with the herd. More species, especially in the insect world, reach sexual maturity extremely early. In fact, I know of certain uni-gender creatures being born pregnant with the next generation. I think we have less time than we thought to prepare for this birth.'

'But we must care for Wsir first,' Ast responded. 'I cannot think of anything else until we have made his body safe. I will send to Sakhmt for her advice.'

'I have done so already,' Hwthr said, 'but even I was not the first. Apparently Inbw contacted her on the day of the attack. Sakhmt has communicated with him and all is in hand. You have a remarkable youngling, Nebt.'

Nebt smiled at this compliment. 'That is his father's influence.'

Both Ast and Hwthr knew she meant Wsir.

*

Inbw planned to follow the same procedures that had been applied to the preservation of Ptah's body. He also insisted on a secret burial place as he explained to Hwthr. 'The sendings recently have been so random and careless that Swty would have no trouble discovering the location of the burial if anyone else knows of it. His rage will have been rekindled by the knowledge that Wsir lived long *enough for Ast to conceive. In his all-consuming, irrational jealousy he will seek to destroy the body. I will not let that happen because I have promised my mother and Ast that Wsir will go home. I shall bury father in a place known only to me. Our people and the humans will want to hold a funeral here but the tomb will be empty. Swty will not touch him.'*

'You are a credit to your parents, Inbw,' Hwthr smiled. 'What can I do to help.'

'I am worried about Ast. As soon as the funeral is over she must leave here. Without Wsir's body as a focus for his rage Swty will turn his anger against the youngling.'

'I agree,' Hwthr said, 'though getting her to accept that necessity will be hard.'

'But it must be done before the egg is birthed which means we have very little time.'

Hwthr tried to hide her surprise at Inbw's perception. 'So what you suggest?'

'First you must take the lenses from Wsir's eyes.'

'What?'

'The lenses. Wsir's eyes no longer require their protection but very soon my brother will have need of them. I would not wish him to be condemned to the half-light or to wear a mask like this.' Inbw's hands went to the muzzle of the jackal's-head mask.

Hwthr's astonishment at the young Ba's insight was only exceeded by her admiration for his unselfishness.

'You could take the lenses for yourself.'

'No, I do not think my eyes could adjust after all this time. It may be that my brother will find a similar difficulty but at least he must be given the chance.'

'Yes,' Hwthr said, 'we will not know unless we try.'

*

It was night time under a waning moon when Ast and Nebt set sail for the north. It had been announced that they were to consult with the physician Sakhmt. *Carefully controlled* sendings *had confirmed that they would be seeking shelter with Nyayt and Srkt who were already preparing a nest chamber for the birthing. Hwthr's main concern was whether Ast would reach her refuge in time. The incubation was progressing at an exponential rate. Even her fellow Bau were commenting on how big she was and, though no one voiced the suggestion, some began to doubt Ast's story of how she became pregnant. They speculated that she and Wsir might have foregone one of the guiding principles of the Experiment in gratifying their own desire for offspring. There were mutterings of betrayal and double standards with some arguments degenerating into scuffles of a most un-Ba-like nature. Hwthr found herself dealing with a worrying number of grazes, bruises and sprains. The length of time that such minor injuries would take to heal also concerned her. Khnsw broke several finger bones when he punched Mntjw in the face.*

'You will have to suffer,' Hwthr told him, as she bandaged his hand. 'I have no way of setting these bones and no topical remedy for the pain. It is lucky for you that we Bau are not well practised in physical violence or these injuries might have been more serious. In the meantime if you cannot keep the fingers immobilised that hand will be crippled for life.'

'For how long must I endure these crude bandages?' Khnsw asked, his voice sulky.

'For as long as it takes. There is no point in dreaming of plascasts and bone-grafters. Just consider how much Min endures and be thankful that your worst prognosis is a couple of bent fingers. And think twice before indulging in such ridiculous unseemly behaviour again. You know how our bone density has been compromised by the low gravity and our diet. I am only surprised that there have been no worse results of this spate of foolishness. I would never have believed that I would be treating injuries caused by Bau on Bau.'

Khnsw had the grace to look chastened. 'How is Mntjw?' he asked.

'His nose can never be straightened.'

'I am sorry.'

'Tell him, not me!'

In using her practical skills Hwthr had done all she could to repair the outward wounds of the Bau in Abdw but she felt the mending of their spirits was beyond her. There was no way in which she could imagine the unity of the settlement being restored. By the time she received the sending *from Ast to announce their safe arrival, Hwthr was feeling homesick for her own little house and the company of her beautiful beasts. Her leave-taking went unnoticed.*

*

Swty and his closest companions arrived in Abdw at dawn a few days after Hwthr's departure for her home at Iwnt. They marched to the Residence, brushing aside all attempts made by Bau and humans to stop them. In his hand Swty carried a mace, a fist-sized polished stone on a cubit-long wooden shaft. As he walked he slapped the macehead into the palm of his other hand again and again, with a force which must have caused him physical pain, but he gave no sign of this. Instead his face was contorted with an expression the Bau rarely observed in their own species, pure, unreasoning hatred

One of the farmers, who had witnessed the assault on Wsir, tried to catch Khnsw's attention. Though the man's words were garbled with anxiety Khnsw understood. He looked around and, catching Mntjw's eye he sent *the query, 'Murder weapon?'*

Mntjw turned his astonished gaze towards Swty but because of Khnsw's agitation his sending *had lacked tight focus. Swty, probably the most powerful telepath on Geb, turned on Khnsw, a broad smile spreading across his face. 'It is good to know who one's friends are. Seize that traitor and lock him up until I decide what to do with him.'*

Shzmw and Mafdt grabbed Khnsw by the arms and dragged him away, unresisting.

With their natural passivity none of the Bau made a move to help their friend. Swty's behaviour and attitude were so alien to Ba nature that they had no way of dealing with it. He scanned their startled faces and laughed. 'Spineless as ever!' he snorted. 'So, is there no greeting for your leader?'

That was the moment when the settlers realised why Swty had come back. He had been appointed as Wsir's Deputy and, by right of the Experiment Charter, if Wsir were to be incapacitated Swty would take over as Leader of the Kem settlement. There was nothing in the Charter to say that this right would be invalidated if Wsir's incapacity was the result of murder. There had been no civil war or family power struggle on Perbau for many generations. No one could have imagined circumstances in which Ba would turn against Ba, least of all the legists who had drawn up the Charter. Bau were happiest when their actions were guided by the rules and pronouncements of their superiors. There was almost a sigh of relief from some of Wsir's followers when they realised that Swty's invocation of the Charter could put an end to this period of uncertainty. In their few leaderless days since Wsir's death they had experienced such oscillating emotions, such a sense of loss and confusion, that anyone who could bring back calm and order would be welcomed. They began to understand how, after their initial horror, the Bau in Sumer had apparently accepted Mardk's leadership in spite of the manner of his taking it. For now it mattered little to most of them that Swty was Wsir's killer. Murder was so far beyond their understanding that, for many of Wsir's followers, the memory of the attack had already been relegated to the subconscious and they were ready to accept any solution which allowed the return of normality.

By contrast, the human inhabitants of Abdw could only look on in disbelief as their Golden Ones were seen to shift their allegiance to the very being who had murdered their beloved god, Wsir. They drew back from the scene, knowing that they had no place in this confrontation. There were fields to be tended and domestic chores to be done. When the Bau had settled their own differences they would still require sustenance and comfort. This was the role of the Great God's followers, to care for the Golden Ones as they believed Wsir was still caring for them from beyond the grave.

Swty's initial command was, 'Show me his body!'

Ndjty was the only Ba to react, 'We cannot.'

'You mean you will not. Perhaps you should join your friend in the lock-up.'

'No, I really mean we cannot. No one knows where Wsir is buried except Inbw.'

Swty looked around. He had noticed the absence of his son but put it down to the youngling keeping to the shadows as always. 'Bring Inbw here,' he commanded.

Ndjty was emboldened to reply. 'He is not here. No one has seen him for days.'

Swty's frown deepened, 'Are you not his keeper?' Ndjty made no response. Swty sent a ringing command to Inbw to make his appearance but felt his call fall into the deep silence of the desert wastes where no receptive mind heard it. He rolled the macehead in his cupped hand, considering the possibilities. Then he said, 'Of course, where is his mother? She will be sheltering him. Where is Nebt?'

'Gone,' Ndjty said.

'Gone? Where? Tell me!'

'North, and that is all I can say. Their boat went north.'

'They?'

'Ast went with her.'

Swty swung his mace at the nearest target and Ndjty fell, his skull crushed. For a brief moment there was complete silence. Then Swty kicked at the body and snarled, 'Take this carcase from my sight then search the place! Find anything belonging to my brother and his slut of a mate. Bring it all here! And as for the rest of you,' he waved his mace wildly in the direction of the Abdw settlers, 'you can get your own possessions together. You are all coming back with me to First.' In his head Swty screamed, 'And do not think you can escape me, Nebt, Ast!' His sending was so strong that it was heard by every Ba in Kem.

*

Inbw watched the boats leave, their sails raised to catch the northerly wind. When they were out of sight he returned to the Residence and the bereft humans gathered there. Having been deserted by their gods, bewilderment and fear were all they knew. They were relieved to see the Lad return from the River.

'I will not leave you,' Inbw declared, 'My father would not want me to. But I am still young. I need your help. First I must release Khnsw and then we will bury the Pathfinder.'

The humans nodded at the wisdom of the young god. They understood the importance of respect for one's elders. In due course the tomb prepared for Wsir was re-opened and Ndjty's body was placed inside with reverence. The jackal emblem adopted by Ndjty, the god who had died for his loyalty, was soon adopted as the settlement's mascot.

Khnsw was so demoralised by events at Abdw, and weakened by captivity, that he could not stay. For days after the burial he agonised over his choices. He wanted to be with his friends but not at the risk of once more inflaming Swty's wrath. At last he made the decision to join Djhwty and Imn. Inbw kept his promise and stayed in Abdw despite the appeal from his mother to join them in the northern marshes. He was aware of his brother's hatching and sent *his congratulations.*

At First, the youngling's triumphant cry of, 'I am Har!' was heard with mixed emotions. Swty cursed and raged, then called a community meeting to denounce Ast and her 'bastard spawn'. 'That abomination is no Ba. It has no father. It has no rights in our society. Any Ba who aids or supports it in any way will be ostracised. There will be no place on the scout ship for traitors.'

*

The lenses had taken well and Har appeared to be able to see normally. 'In fact', Sakhmt confirmed after her latest medical check, 'I think he sees better than any other Ba on this planet. I would not have believed it, given that we had no proper cleaning solution for them and they had already become attuned to Wsir's physiology.'

'That is, perhaps, further proof that he is his father's son,' Ast said, with pride.

In spite of the rumours circulated by Swty, no one who knew Har could believe that he was anything other than Wsir's child. As his accelerated growth took him to adult size in less than half a year, his resemblance to his father became apparent to all. Ast watched his development with pride and sorrow in equal measure. How cruel that Wsir should have been denied the opportunity of knowing this remarkable young Ba. Har learned quickly, too. Djhwty, Hwthr and Imn contributed to his education in visits to his secret home in the northernmost reaches of the River. He was in constant communication with his brother, Inbw, and with Khnm in the far south, proving that he was as powerful and controlled a telepath as Swty himself.

As the last year of the Experiment began, and the Bau started to plan for their departure, Ast noticed a subtle change in her son's attitude. He joined the group discussions about what they would take with them and what they would be glad to leave behind, but his contributions were non-committal, mere lip-service to the idea of leaving Geb. His mother confided her fears to her sister. 'He does not mean to go with us.'

Nebt was horrified, 'How can he possibly stay?'

'He is a child of Geb. He knows no other place. Perbau has no call on him.'

'Can you not make him see sense?'

'I would not try. Though he is young in terms of real time he is old in wisdom, old enough to make up his own mind. I am sure that, whatever he decides, he will do the right thing.'

'He is not taking any notice of the vile rumours being spread about him?'

Ast smiled a sad smile. 'He takes the denigration as a sign that he has right on his side, otherwise why would anyone bother to destroy the reputation of a Ba so soon after his hatching?'

'Then why does he want to stay? How can he stay? The Charter...'

'The Charter does not cover children born on Geb because there were not supposed to be any. Neither Har nor Inbw is bound by the agreement that all Bau should quit Geb after five planetary cycles. They will make their own choices.'

For the first time, Nebt realised that, if Har stayed, she was likely to lose her son too. 'How can you be so calm about it?' she asked Ast.

'I am only calm in appearance. Inside my heart is breaking,' Ast sighed.

*

Have you seen the Bulletin?' Pete asked, poking his head round the door.

Simon looked up from his desk. 'No, why?'

'Promotions announcements.'

'Anyone we know?'

'Mac and the Doc both made Reader.'

'Cause for celebration, I think.'

'Already sorted,' Pete grinned, 'Royal Oak seven o'clock.' He sidled into the room giving as wide a berth as possible to the filing cabinet with its precarious crown of papers and journals. 'How's the paper coming along?' he said, perching on the edge of Simon's desk.

'Difficult to keep my mind on it while we're still waiting for the results of those tests.'

After much discussion, some of it heated, between Mac and HPB, in which Prof Jameson acted as a not totally neutral referee, a selection of finds had been earmarked for laboratory tests. These included the ball of grain and its fragmentary fabric container. Despite Sally's misgivings, all agreed that it came from a sealed context within a properly recorded stratigraphy and its anomalous nature deserved further investigation.

As Head of Department, Prof Jameson had the final word on how the testing budget was allocated. 'Since this one find touches on several different areas of interest, I think we have to pursue it regardless of the expense. To double check, I would also like the remains of the wooden box in which it was found to be radiocarbon tested, and dendro-dated too if possible. The osteo tests are beyond our control so we must make the most of what we have.'

Hermione and Ian, surprised at the Professor's decision, were nevertheless happy to go along with it. The samples had been selected and dispatched to the appropriate laboratories within the week. An air of expectation hung over the Department only to be replaced, as weeks passed with no news, by a growing sense of doubt.

Pete was as worried as anyone. 'The Prof's getting twitchy about the bones results. He hates having no control over the tests. There's no way of speeding up things at the Egyptian lab. They'll see even the politest request as a criticism and they'll take the hump if they think we're challenging their expertise. We can only wait. I take it you've had no news either?'

'Yes and no,' Simon sighed, 'The lab's told us it needs to repeat a couple of tests so the whole lot's been delayed.'

'Have they said why?' Pete frowned.

'Something about contamination and software glitches.'

'Can it be both?'

'Haven't a clue. It's just so frustrating. We can't get on with anything until we've got some base-line data. Meanwhile, I'm having to find displacement activity. What's the news on your MSc?'

'Results should be posted tomorrow,' Pete grimaced, 'Talk about something else.'

'Come off it. You know you've passed. Didn't Prof Jameson give you a big enough hint about your dissertation?'

'Don't jinx it! Anyway, what's your difficulty with the paper? Isn't it a follow-up from that conference paper last month? I thought that went well.'

'It did, but this is a journal paper, peer-reviewed and everything. The Doc wants it absolutely watertight. I hadn't realised how much Uncle Eric's twisting of her words really affected her. Even after all this time she still feels that people will believe she's responsible for the crack-pot theories he built around her work. Every new publication she puts her name to has to be checked and checked again. There can't be the smallest doubt about its originality and authenticity. Of course, we had hoped to include something about the Nagada material but the Doc won't do that without the test results to back her up. Now it looks like the lab delay has put paid to that idea 'cos the deadline for submission is the end of this month.'

'Yeah,' Pete said with considerable feeling, 'and that's not the only deadline.'

'Of course, applications for the Prof's research assistant. D'you know how many people are interested?'

'Only one other internal applicant that I know of, and there's hints about someone from Cambridge and one from Durham. I think there'll probably be interest from Winchester and Bournemouth too.'

'Well that's it, then,' Simon said, in as cheery a voice as he could muster, 'Cantab and Durham won't want to descend from their dizzy academic heights. Winchester and Bournemouth won't have the right background. Who's the internal opposition?'

'Derek Oppenheim.'

'No problem, there. He's a prat!'

'But he knows the Prof well enough to hit the right buttons at interview.'

'So do you,' Simon saw that his friend was unconvinced. 'Do you want some help preparing for it?'

'Never thought you'd ask.'

Chapter 13: Questions of Integrity

Simon was regretting the third pint of cider, or was it the fourth? Pete had insisted on his matching him drink for drink and in spite of Holly's warnings Simon had considered it his duty to help his friend celebrate his double success – a distinction in his MSc and a new job. Now Simon was faced with packing while nursing a pounding headache and blurred vision. When he had volunteered to take part in the First Years' field trip he claimed it was to refresh his practical excavation skills but in truth it had seemed the ideal excuse for spending another three weeks away from home and the inevitable confrontation with Uncle Eric.

The weather had been so foul recently that he was unsure what to pack; wellies and waterproofs or shorts and sun-hat? It was also a long time since he had participated in a dig in a hands-on way. His hands, in hangover vision, looked even softer than he remembered. After two years or more of pure academic study the hard-won calluses of the real archaeologist had long ago faded. He could imagine, all too well, the blisters he would acquire after a couple of hours of manual labour. He was joining the dig part way through the six-week season so most of the tedious site clearance would have been done but it would be just his luck to arrive when a new trench was being opened. The physical effects of his rusty pickaxe and shovel techniques would not be pretty.

Simon had been feeling exceedingly sorry for himself, even before the celebration session in the Royal Oak. Holly, who had said a very terse goodbye to him in the pub, was leaving for a family gathering in Cornwall and Pete was off on a cycling holiday with his brothers before taking up his appointment in September. How Simon wished he had the sort of family with whom he would be happy to share his vacations. The best of the bunch was his sister. Simon was forever grateful that she had been born first since she had been given the name Erica. She too had found the Evers connection hard to live with and, at the age of sixteen, had announced that she would no longer answer to Erica but wanted to be known by her second name. Simon was the only member of the family who regularly called her Marion. This had brought them closer together in recent years, as Eric Evers' star was in the ascendant, but Marion was now married with two children and living in the north of England. A long weekend with them had been the best he could manage.

He stuffed three more scruffy teeshirts into corners of his rucksack and rummaged around for socks. At least the dig was fully catered even though he would be sharing a tent with two more post-grads, including the disappointed Derek Oppenheim. If the weather ever improved it could be a lot of fun but the prospect was one of persistent rain and the thought of ankle-deep mud was not inviting. More depressing was the news that the nearest pub was a mile and a half from the dig site. Simon hesitated over the towels. Should he take one or two? Shower facilities were available at a local youth hostel but experience told him that their towels were likely to be tiny and non-absorbent to the point of being waterproof. He had just decided to take two when his mobile phone quacked. Marion's son, Davey, had thought it great fun to set Uncle Simon's text alert to the sound of a duck. One glance caused him to drop everything, grab his keys and run.

HPB was pacing up and down the laboratory when Simon arrived, breathless. Her frown was not encouraging.

'Results?' was all he could say.

Hermione turned and threw a single sheet of paper on to the bench. 'Read that.'

Simon hoisted himself on to a stool and read the report. Reaching the end of the page he turned it over but the second side was blank, so he flipped it over again and reread the letter.

As he read he felt the last of the cider effects evaporate from his mind. 'This can't be right,' he said at last, 'There must be more. They've had the stuff for ages.'

'Exactly!' The single word was expelled through HPB's pursed lips with the force of an expletive.

'Have I missed something? I don't understand.'

'Neither do I. If I hadn't selected the samples myself I would be looking to blame someone here. Unfortunately we have no way of knowing how the finds were treated while they were in the hands of the Egyptian authorities but it's not as if they don't know what they're doing. Even allowing for less than perfect storage conditions while in transit, I cannot believe that the state of the samples was unacceptable.'

Simon scanned the letter again. 'But this doesn't suggest where the fault lies. What do they mean by "unexpected problems in analysis" and "unidentified contamination"?'

'Your guess is as good as mine,' Hermione sat down, her shoulders slumping.

'Is this really all they sent? No numerical data, not even a C^{14} estimate?'

'Nothing! I've tried telephoning but, of course, the lab is closed for the holidays and there's no one there to ask.'

'Has Mac seen this?'

'Dr Masterson is off on a cricket tour somewhere in the middle of nowhere,' Hermione's tone indicated clearly what she thought of cricket.

'I suppose there's still the tests on the human remains. They must have gone to a different lab.'

'I will not count chickens.'

Simon felt compelled to read the letter again. The words 'abnormal' and 'unusual' jumped off the page. The phrases 'atypical constitution' and 'anomalous formation' burned themselves into his retinas. He felt a rising resentment. 'Are they just covering themselves for their own incompetence? Is it possible that they lost or damaged the samples?'

'I wondered about that,' Hermione said, 'but it seems unlikely that they would have created such elaborate and peculiar excuses for their own failings. I get the impression that these samples have really upset them.'

'Yeah,' Simon mused, 'It's almost as if they're accusing us of perpetrating some kind of hoax.'

'That is the problem. If they really think that I would try anything so stupid as to falsify or invent data then this letter represents a challenge to my reputation and I have had quite enough of that sort of thing.'

Simon winced at the oblique reference to his uncle. 'What can we do?'

'Nothing, for now,' HPB took the letter from him and folded it in half. 'Our hands are tied until the laboratory reopens. Professor Jameson is equally frustrated. There is still no sign of the results of the human remains tests that were done in Egypt and the dating of the wooden chest won't be available for at least three weeks. When Ian has finished playing his silly games we will select more samples and then we will deliver them to the lab in person. Until then we must be content with observational analysis and recording and that will have to wait until Sally and Felicity come back from their holiday. So, Simon, go away and take your mind off things by digging up Romans.'

'And what will you do?' he felt emboldened to ask.

'My Greek grand-mother is celebrating her ninetieth birthday. I shall be going to Santorini.'

'Cool!'

'Hardly! It is August!' Hermione smiled.

*

It was raining again. More accurately, it was still raining. The persistent background noise of water slapping against tent canvas would forever be associated, in Simon's mind, with this particular dig; that and the inundated trenches, the glue-like mud and the smell of damp denim. Of course, the serious side of all these inconveniences was that the work had not progressed according to plan. In fact, there was a real likelihood that the dig would have to be closed down early. The University's site director, with members of the county's Archaeology Unit and a local authority Health and Safety official were currently inspecting the excavation. Through the gap in the tent flap Simon had seen them pass on their way to the main trench in the next field, their multi-coloured umbrellas bobbing about as they dodged puddles of indeterminate depth. He was all too aware of the depressing sight they were about to witness. He had cleaned up a carefully prepared section three times before the overnight rain had caused the side of the trench to collapse and all his hard work had been lost. Everyone else had suffered similar disasters and the morale of the excavation team was at a low ebb. In spite of feeling most sorry for the students who were experiencing their first serious dig, Simon would cry no tears if the inspectors declared the site to be unsafe. He longed to be dry and warm and not to smell like a wet dog.

Slouched in a folding garden chair, he was trying to take his mind off the miserable weather by reading a trashy novel from the dig library. Across the tent, Derek was frowning over a crossword puzzle.

'"*Propose account to the French*" ', Derek read, 'five letters, ending in E.'

'What?' Simon said, jolted out of his reverie.

'Five letters, last letter E. "*Propose account to the French*".'

Simon gave his tent-mate a pitying look. Derek had dismembered the newspaper to fold the puzzle page into a neat pad. The remainder was draped across the holdall which held such of his clothes as were relatively dry. Simon's eye was drawn to a photograph occupying almost half a page. From his point of view the caption was upside down but he could make out the words 'Family Celebration' and 'volcanic island'. The words came together in his head with a click of recognition. He lunged across the tent to grab the paper and took it into the better, if still gloomy daylight of the entrance canopy.

The photograph showed the guests at a birthday party on a Greek island. In the middle was seated an elderly woman beaming at the camera, basking in the adoration of her assembled family. Simon smiled too as he recognised several of the closest relatives. He read the short article below the picture.

'On the Greek island of Santorini this week a distinguished gathering celebrated the ninetieth birthday of Greek-born Theadora Crowther, widow of the British archaeologist Sir Martin Crowther. Lady Crowther was surrounded by her family; her daughter, the popular novelist, Xanthe Crowther, with her husband, eminent geophysicist Sir Anthony Beaumont, and their children, the television science presenter, Dr Theo Beaumont and his sister Hermione.'

'Hah!' Simon thought, 'Keeping a low profile, eh Doc? Well done!'

He looked at the other faces in the photograph, trying to match them to names in the article. The woman who looked like a shorter, plumper version of Xanthe Crowther must be her sister Aspasia. The handsome bearded man beside her was described as Lady Crowther's son-in-law Andreas, a local government official. Their four adult children were also present, three with partners, and an assortment of Lady Crowther's great-grandchildren. Grouped in a terraced garden surrounded by lemon trees, trellises laden with bougainvillea and terracotta pots containing rosemary bushes, it was the epitome of the family which Simon so envied, Then his eye was caught by another name in the text.

'Eric Evers, TV documentary-maker, who was filming on Santorini at the time, also took the opportunity to give Lady Crowther his best wishes.' And there he was, back row far right, the badger beard and the bow tie all too familiar. How typical of Uncle Eric to insinuate himself into this private, family occasion. How crass of him to see it as an opportunity for self-publicity. How dare he!

'Shit!' Simon exploded. 'Shit, shit, shit!'

'What's up?' Derek enquired from inside the tent.

Simon turned and advanced on his colleague in a manner which startled Derek into dropping his pen. Simon tossed the offending newspaper into Derek's lap, saying, 'Here! Look at that!'

Derek read the article as far as the description of HPB's family. 'Oh,' he said, 'Dr Beaumont won't like that. They've not given her title or anything.'

'That's not the problem. Look there!' Simon stabbed his finger at his uncle's smug smile.

'Oh! Is that...? Oh yes, I see,' said Derek, missing the point entirely. He handed back the paper. 'You can keep that if you like. I only want the crossword.'

Simon stared, open-mouthed in disbelief at Derek's uncomprehending innocence. He had come to realise that Oppenheim had no imagination and a literal outlook on life which would have been considered cute in a five-year-old but was annoying beyond belief in an adult. But there was nothing to be gained from giving way to that annoyance. Through gritted teeth, Simon said, 'Thank you. Oh, I think it's "table".'

'What?' Derek looked bemused.

'"Propose account to the French". Account is a tab, "the" in French is *le*. Put them together and you get T-A-B-L-E, as in to propose or table a motion. TABLE.'

'That's great. Thanks,' Derek enthused, retrieving his pen from under his camp bed. 'Do you want another clue?'

*

The field trip was not the only casualty of what was being called the worst summer on record. Holly's family had been flooded out of their holiday cottage and she had returned home to East Anglia until the start of term. Having encountered similar monsoon conditions in France, Pete and his brothers had taken refuge in an auberge and were sitting it out, sampling the local wines, until their scheduled return ferry. Ian's cricket tour had also been cut short by the weather but he had managed to get a last-minute flight enabling him to join Hermione in Greece for the final week of her holiday. Simon hoped that Mac had been able to take HPB's mind off her unfortunate encounter with Uncle Eric but he was still apprehensive of what she might have to say about the 'chance' meeting. He had known that his uncle was filming over the summer, having finally persuaded his production company that there was another series-worth of material in his latest theories, but Simon had taken little notice of the filming schedule, only too glad that the annual family gathering had been postponed.

Simon could not settle to his work, with all these anxieties preying on his mind, and the loneliness of his dreary office made things worse. Outside, the campus was swarming with conference delegates and summer school students who, in a fortnight or so, would be replaced by freshers, but a quick tour of the Garstang Building revealed its only other occupant to be Professor Jameson. The Prof spotted Simon in the stairwell and beckoned over the bannister, 'Goodhill? Have you got a moment?'

Simon sprinted up the stairs and found the Prof standing at his office window, looking out at the dripping hornbeam trees. 'Miserable weather,' Jameson muttered, 'Makes everyone so bad-tempered.'

'Yes,' Simon said, uncertain of what he was expected to say.

'Anyway,' the Prof turned and sat down at his desk, 'we must make the best of it. Have you heard anything from Doctor Beaumont?'

'Not for about three weeks. Should I have?'

'Well, I was wondering when she'd be ready to send off that second set of samples.'

Simon was surprised at the Prof's question. As Head of Department he would have known exactly when Mac and HPB were due back from their vacations and he would be among the first to know about the repeat tests since he would have to authorise the additional spending. There was something else on Jameson's mind.

'Have you still not heard anything from the dendro lab?' he asked.

'Hmm,' the Prof's brows furrowed. 'Sore point, there. The results are in but they don't make sense.'

Simon felt a tightening in the pit of his stomach at the thought of another expensive set of tests wasted. Was this dig cursed? 'In what way didn't they make sense?' he ventured.

'Sit down, sit down,' Jameson indicated a chair with a casual wave of his hand. 'There was not, apparently, a sufficient number of tree rings in the plank from the chest, to ascertain a date. At least that's what the technicians say but I've dealt with enough dendrochronology tests to know that the sample was more than adequate. The dating sequences from Egypt and the Near East are pretty well established and the context was secure. We should have had a result.' The Prof brought a clenched fist down on to his desk with a thump, such an uncharacteristic gesture making Simon sure that there was something very wrong.

'Any better news with the radio-carbon dating?' he dared ask.

'No!' the fist thumped the desk again, 'and that's even more annoying. The variety of samples they tested, all from the same trench, have produced a ridiculous range of dates. I've been told that they must have been seriously contaminated because there is no match with any calibrated sample. One suggestion is that the wood could have come from one of the Mediterranean islands because the offset is compatible with the effects of volcanic carbon dioxide. I know that the results from

Akrotiri on Thera have always been suspect. I must ask Dr Beaumont about that possibility…'

At the allusion to the Thera volcano, such a central theme of Uncle Eric's wild theories, Simon felt a flush rising up his neck, then he frowned before he realised that the Dr Beaumont that Jameson was referring to was Theo rather than his sister.

Prof Jameson was still talking, '…But then they say that the species of tree cannot be identified. They are adamant that it is not Lebanon cedar, which we had assumed, but they have no alternative identification to offer. It is really most vexing. I've never known such an unsatisfactory outcome.' Another thump of the fist followed, emphasising the Prof's frustration.

'I don't know what to say.' Simon said, 'except that Dr Beaumont was equally upset about the first set of results on the grain samples. I can't believe that separate labs could have made such a mess of everything.'

'I know,' Jameson said, 'and that's not the worst.'

Simon gulped. What more could have gone wrong? He raised his eyebrows in query.

Jameson went on, 'We've had the report on the osteo tests. Utter claptrap! The strontium isotope analysis makes no sense at all, the degree of osteoporosis is unbelievable, and as for the zinc…It all rather smacks of incompetence. If only we'd had some way of supervising the tests….If I didn't know where the samples came from I'd say we were being hoaxed but the laboratory director included a most insulting note implying that that's what his staff think we are doing to them! There is no way he will sanction a repeat series of tests and I fear we have burnt our boats there as far as any future testing is concerned. I don't know how I am going to tell Dr Masterson.'

'That was what Dr Beaumont said when she got the first report on the grain samples. Well, she saw it not so much a report as a stab at her integrity,' Simon said. He paused as a thought began to crystallise. He continued, almost talking to himself, 'It looks as if every lab has rubbished every sample we sent. If it was just one lab or just one type of test that had failed I might excuse it, but how likely is the failure of all the tests, of every sort, carried out in different labs, in different countries, at different times and by different people? Perhaps we should look at what links the failures, try to find the commonality…'

'You're right, Goodhill,' Prof Jameson leapt to his feet. 'I've been blinded by my aggravation. Of course there is a pattern here. The probability that all these tests should fail is so astronomically high that it is significant. We must go back to basics. Dr Quinn will have had the ceramic test results by now but I haven't spoken to her yet. If those results are equally flawed we will have to do some serious thinking. I want you to find her.'

'Yes, sir,' Simon stood up, resisting the temptation to salute. 'Er…where is she likely to be?'

'I have no idea. Just use your initiative.'

Simon took that as his dismissal.

His first plan was to speak to Sylvia who seemed to know everything about everyone, but she was not in the library. Her assistant, Pam, told him that Sylvia was involved with the learning resources conference which currently occupied a large part of the Arts Building. Theatre A was closed for refurbishment so Simon decided to brave the alien space that was the Oakapple Refectory. Since there were no undergraduates around, staff and postgrads, displaced from Theatre A, appeared to have taken root in the more Spartan, student environment and were defending their favourite tables from the invading hordes of summer-schoolers. Simon had not visited the refectory often enough to know where to start looking for FAQ so, for a moment, he stood in the doorway bewildered by the volume of chatter and clatter of crockery, overlaid with a loudness of music which made him feel old before his time.

'Are you in the queue?' a voice behind him asked.

'Erm…'

'Oh just get out of the way, will you?' The burly man pushed past followed by his mousey wife, who nodded an apology for her husband's rudeness. Knowing the summer school programme, Simon tabbed them as either local history buffs or amateur genealogists. He scanned the refectory horizon again and became aware of someone waving at him just as Flick put her fingers to her mouth and uttered a piercing whistle. The silence that followed was broken by Mr Burly saying, 'Bloody students!'

With everyone looking at him, Simon wove his way towards FAQ's table by the window, concentrating on avoiding treading on feet, tripping over bags and slipping in the puddles formed under dripping umbrellas. This reminded him of why Theatre A was so much more civilised. His face was burning so fiercely by the time he slumped into the chair Flick had cleared for him, that he welcomed the cool dampness left by her coat. As he shrugged off his own jacket he recognised Flick's companion. Miss Phillips was tucking into a bowl of pasta, a notepad and textbook at her side, while FAQ had set up her tablet with its keyboard and was monitoring her e-mails as she sipped an iced tea.

'Hello Miss Phillips. How are you?' Simon said, remembering his manners.

'Very well, dear, thank you for asking.'

'Adeline's here for the astronomy summer school,' Felicity explained, 'What brings you here?'

'Prof Jameson sent me to find you,' Simon said, reminded of his mission. 'He wants to know about the results of the ceramics testing.'

'Oh, what's so urgent? There's nothing spectacular in the report. They're pretty much what we anticipated, a good fit with finds from other Predynastic sites in the area.'

This was not what Simon had expected and his face gave away a disappointment which Miss Phillips recognised. 'What were you and the Professor hoping for?' she asked.

Simon began telling his story, sorting it out in his own mind as he did so. He wished Pete was there because they had become accustomed to bouncing ideas off each other, but Flick and Miss Phillips asked occasional searching questions or made sensible observations which helped to shape his thoughts into a coherent theory. He ground to a halt when the enormity of what that theory suggested finally hit him.

'I'll get you a coffee,' Miss Phillips said in a quiet motherly tone. As she patted his hand where it rested on the table he became aware that he was trembling.

FAQ moved to another seat, allowing Miss Phillips to make her way to the coffee queue. For a few moments Simon felt that they were enveloped in a bubble of silence and it was not a comfortable bubble. Then Sally's strident voice burst the illusion. 'What are you two moping about?'

Flick cleared a space on the table for Sally's tray and indicated the seat beside her but said nothing. Her lack of response caused a momentary frown to cross Sally's face but she knew her partner well enough to see that something serious was happening. She hooked her shoulder bag over the back of the chair and sat down, waiting for one of them to speak. After a full minute she could wait no longer.

'Will someone tell me what's going on?'

Simon shook his head then brushed his hair back from his forehead in a gesture guaranteed to make Sally even more annoyed. Flick placed a hand on Sally's arm and said, 'I think we've just had an unwelcome epiphany.' In a few spare sentences she conveyed the gist of their discussion.

Miss Phillips returned to the table as Simon gave in to the fear that he had kept hidden in the darkest recess of his mind but which had now pushed its way to the front of his thoughts, demanding to be voiced. 'What if Uncle Eric's basic premise is right?'

Sally snorted, 'Rubbish!' but her face belied a degree of uncertainty.

'No, sweetie, hear us out,' Flick said, 'You know you've been worried about those samples Hermione's had you working on. Just for a moment, allow the possibility that the grain was of alien origin…'

'You can't be serious!' Sally interjected.

Flick tightened her grip on Sally's arm, '…just for a moment. None of the test results make any sense. You've said yourself that, if you didn't know better, you'd think it was GM grain. What if it was genetically modified?'

'But the technology wasn't available thousands of years ago.'

'Not on this planet, no.' Flick let that thought hang in the subdued air between them.

Miss Phillips pushed a cup of coffee into Simon's hands. 'Drink up, dear. You look as if you need it. I bought doughnuts too.' She opened the cardboard box and almost as one they reached for the sugary offerings and munched in silent contemplation.

Sally broke first. 'It's too ridiculous. I haven't got time for this. I have students waiting.' She pushed back her chair, which gave a protesting screech across the floor, and flounced away leaving her salad bowl untouched.

Miss Phillips explained, 'Sally's running the botanical drawing course. The afternoon session will be starting soon.'

'And she's left her bag!' Flick grabbed the bag from the chair and hurried after Sally.

'She'll be back,' Miss Phillips reassured Simon, 'She's left her tablet here.'

'Does your class continue this afternoon?' he asked, grateful for her company but feeling guilty that he was keeping her from something more important.

'Yes, but I think I'm needed here. I heard about your Uncle turning up on Santorini uninvited.'

Simon groaned and lowered his head on to his folded arms on the table.

'It's not as bad as you might imagine,' Miss Phillips continued. 'I've been looking after Hermione's flat, watering plants and so on, and from her e-mails I'd say she sounds pretty positive about the experience.'

Simon looked up from his misery, 'Really?'

'Yes, really,' she smiled, 'I don't say she was ecstatic about him turning up out of the blue – such presumption!'

'That's Uncle Eric all over. Probably thought the family would welcome a surprise visit from a media star.'

Miss Phillips chuckled. 'As if they didn't have enough of those already.'

Simon's mouth twisted into the semblance of a smile, in spite of his dejection.

'That's better,' she said. 'In fact, I think you'll find Hermione rather less put out than you might imagine.'

He raised his eyebrows in query but she would not be drawn. Before he could press her further, Flick reappeared and flopped down into her chair. 'It's OK,' she said, 'I think she was already beginning to think the unthinkable. It was just a bit of a shock to hear someone else suggesting the same thing. She'll get over it.'

Simon suddenly remembered why he had come to the Oakapple, and slapped his palm to his brow. 'Shit!'

'Language, dear,' Miss Phillips warned, in a tone startlingly similar to HPB's.

'Sorry. I've just remembered. Prof Jameson cornered me for a moan about the results of the tests on the human remains. He's also confused by the tests on the wood. I could tell he was worried because he wouldn't normally confide in me but I was the only other person in the building at the time. I suggested that the probability of all the labs getting it wrong was remote to say the least and that seemed to cheer him up. That's when he asked me to find you, Flick. After his performance at Uncle Eric's talk, do you think we dare bring him in on our ideas?'

'I think we have to,' Flick said, 'and the sooner the better.' She looked at Miss Phillips.

'Oh, don't worry about me, dear,' the older woman said, 'I can still sneak in at the back of the class. But I'd like to know what Terence says.'

'I'll e-mail you,' FAQ said, as she packed her things into her canvas bag. 'Come on, Si, let's beard the dragon in his den.'

Simon was still processing Miss Phillips' use of the Prof's first name as they left the refectory. 'How does Miss Phillips know Prof Jameson?' he asked FAQ.

'Adeline? She's taken several of his evening classes in the past. She was one of the first to get the University's Certificate in

Archaeological Studies. Now she's close to finishing a Diploma. She's quite a girl, our Miss Phillips.'

'Apparently,' Simon mused. 'Why should she suggest that Dr Beaumont's attitude towards my uncle might have softened?'

FAQ stopped in her tracks, 'Did she? That's decidedly out of character. Strange that Adeline should say such a thing. I wonder what she's heard. She'll have been in regular contact with Hermione.'

'Yeah, she said she's been looking after the flat.'

'It's a bit more than that. Adeline was Xanthe's maths teacher and house mistress at her boarding school and they'd always kept in touch. When Hermione first got the job here Miss Phillips offered her a place to stay and that suited them both so well that it became permanent. Now Hermione is actually Adeline's landlady since she bought the house. Adeline's been a great support, almost like a second mother to her, and she's been adopted into the Beaumont clan as a sort of surrogate granny. She's more likely to know what's going on than any of us. Well, I suppose we'll just have to wait and see when HPB gets back from Greece.'

They continued on their way to the Garstang Building in silence, with Simon now mulling over these revelations and wondering how many more were waiting to ambush him.

*

Prof Jameson was speaking on the phone when Flick and Simon paused outside the open door. 'One moment, Doctor, they've just arrived. I'll put you on speaker,' he said, pressing a button on the receiver. 'It's Dr Beaumont,' he explained.

'Hi Hermione, how's it going?' Flick asked, sitting down in the one comfortable chair beside the Prof's desk. Simon helped himself to one of the stacking chairs from the corner.

'Hello Felicity,' HPB's voice sounded rather tinny. Jameson said, 'I was just telling Dr Beaumont about our musings earlier.'

Hermione chipped in, 'My call was coincidental. I wanted to let people know when we will be back. I want to set up another campaign meeting. Is Simon there?'

'Yes, Doc,' Simon started.

'Don't worry, Simon. I know you didn't tell him.'

Prof Jameson looked askance.

'Sorry anyway, Doc,' Simon reddened.

'I told you before. you can't be held responsible for your relatives. But as it happens, things have turned out for the best. I've been hearing from Terence how we all seem to be thinking along similar lines. Ian and I have been doing some research of our own and asking around some of our colleagues in other institutions. There are still a few leads we want to follow up. I have to go now, but before I do – Felicity?'

'Yes?' FAQ responded.

'Talk to Adeline. We're having the meeting at my house the weekend after next. See you there.'

The Prof returned the call to the handset and said, 'Thank you, Doctor. I will make sure all is prepared. I hope you have a good homeward journey.'

Simon let out a deep sigh of relief. HPB seemed positively cheerful about the encounter with Uncle Eric. He could hardly wait to hear about it.

FAQ brought him back to the moment. 'You wanted to see me, Professor?'

'Oh, yes, Dr Quinn, but Dr Beaumont's call has made what I was going to say somewhat redundant.'

'What can we do to prepare for Hermione's campaign meeting?' Flick asked.

'We need to gather together all the test results received so far…'

'For what they're worth,' Simon muttered.

The Prof frowned at him and continued, '…and set out any possible explanations, however outlandish, for the incongruities. I'm handing some of the osteo side of things over to French, who should be returning tomorrow, while I chase the various labs and follow up a few lines of enquiry of my own. As we concluded earlier, Goodhill, it is highly improbable that four or five different laboratories should all have had similar failures in very different types of test. I intend to make them aware of this strange occurrence and see if we can find any linking factors which might explain the anomalies. There is a rumour going around that another major British archaeological expedition has also had some disturbing results. I intend to chase up that rumour. If I find any truth in it we could have some interesting points of reference.'

'Which dig is that?' Simon could not resist asking.

'I won't reveal that until I have either confirmed or quashed the rumour. I don't want to cast doubt on the work of fellow professionals,' Jameson said, with a purse of his lips.

'I'll do a report on the ceramics results,' Flick said, 'but as I told Simon, there was nothing unusual there.'

'Much as I had expected,' the Prof said. He smiled at Simon's startled gasp. 'Think about it, Goodhill. What do all the other tested materials have in common?'

Simon's frown relaxed as he saw what Jameson meant. 'They all came from the same part of the site!'

'Exactly! Apart from the financial implications, there is little point in sending more samples for testing only to get the same results. So, firstly, we must thoroughly review the context of those finds to see if anything we did was at fault. We might have to resort to a review of the geological tests and soil sampling to identify possible contamination which might have skewed the analysis.'

Flick, the only one present who had taken part in the dig, said, 'So far, all the weirdness has centred on that burnt wooden chest and its contents. There are plenty of other finds from the site that we could test.'

'Of course, yes,' Jameson agreed, 'but the Department is not made of money and other projects have calls upon our budget for that sort of thing. That's why your ceramics are so important.'

'Oh, I see,' Simon said, 'the pots are a sort of control.'

'Yes,' the Prof said, 'but remember, however dubious we might be, we have had similar anomalous results from the human remains which were not from the chest.'

'No,' Flick stood up in her excitement, 'but they did come from the same trench. They were all in what was probably a storage pit for grain which had been filled with rubbish. The bones weren't part of a burial and we imagined they had migrated due to animal activity.'

'All the more reason to thoroughly check the context,' Jameson thumped his fist on the desk, 'So why are you still here?'

FAQ grabbed Simon's arm and pulled him to his feet. 'Come on. We have work to do and people to see.'

*

Flick, Sally and Simon were poring over the paperwork from the Box Trench, as they had taken to calling it, when Pete burst into the lab, shouting, 'Have you heard the news?'

'Welcome back, Peter. Nice to see you,' Sally said in her iciest tone.

'Yeah, thanks, but seriously…' Pete seemed flustered.

'What news is that?' Simon asked.

'The Nagada site has been vandalised!'

The three researchers sat back in horror. Pete threw the print-out of an e-mail on to the table in front of them. 'Prof Jameson just gave me this.'

The message was from Abdul el-Gubi, the Egyptian Inspector who had represented the Antiquities Authority at Nagada during the last season. The civil unrest in Egypt had led to a great deal of insecurity among government employees and, while people were concentrating on the politics of keeping their jobs, archaeological sites in remoter areas were left unsupervised. Throughout the country, dig houses and storage huts had been ransacked by thieves looking for artefacts they could sell on the black market. The more isolated sites had also been subjected to random digging by treasure hunters who cared nothing for the years of painstaking work they were destroying. The fact that very few items of any intrinsic value had ever been uncovered by such illegal digging did not deter the diggers. The more often they came up empty-handed, the more desperate and destructive their digging became.

El-Gubi reported that the University's storage magazine had been rifled. When the thieves had discovered no antiquities they could sell, they took out their frustration on whatever they found. Tents and other camping necessities had been damaged beyond repair. Tools and surveying equipment were stolen and remaining materials were emptied out of their containers, ripped up, trampled on and cast to the vagaries of wind and sand. Although they would be expensive to replace, these losses were not disastrous. From the archaeological perspective greater losses had been incurred when the store rooms containing crates of carefully packaged and labelled finds, including human remains, had been ransacked. Their contents, the results of five seasons of work on the site, having proved worthless to the thieves, were burned and scattered. The most upsetting news was that the robbers had then turned their attention to the dig site. Abdul described the whole area as being pock-marked with holes. The trenches, including the crucial Box Trench, which had been back-filled before Mac's team left Egypt, had been reopened and were now rendered useless for any future investigation. The worst damage had been done in the cemetery area. This was no Valley of the Kings. There were no elaborate stone tombs or mudbrick structures. The Predynastic burials of un-mummified bodies were made in simple pit graves. The only grave goods found were a variety of pottery vessels, mostly fragmentary, and the occasional broken slate palette or flint blade. The majority of the graves had been robbed in antiquity, as had been verified by British archaeologists in the late Nineteenth Century. In the last season Ian's team had re-examined a small group of burials on the edge of the cemetery and found only a few partial skeletons. The associated ceramics had confirmed the Predynastic date of the site. The main cemetery was to have been the focus for next season's work.

The final paragraph of Abdul's e-mail was the most depressing: 'My superiors have reviewed my report on the site and they say that the damage is so bad that nothing more can be learned from the excavation. They ask me to tell you that your concession has been revoked. You will receive official notification in due course.'

Pete's gaze moved from face to face taking in the stunned expressions. Simon felt really sorry for his friend. Pete had been due to join the dig in November specifically to study the skeletal remains which could not be removed from Egypt. The chance to work on real bones instead of photographs and written reports was now denied him. Simon dared not ask what would happen to the human remains now, assuming any had survived the depredations of the vandals and the treasure-seekers. Level-headed Flick was first to recover. 'Does Mac know?'

'He must do. He forwarded this to the Prof.'

'Well, Adeline says they're back after the weekend. The meeting is set for the Sunday afternoon following. We have a lot to do before then.'

*

With all the upheaval and trauma inflicted on the Kem settlement team, Djhwty had been hard pressed to keep an accurate record of the time elapsed since their arrival on Geb. Seeing the records of his observations over the first planetary cycle lost or irreparably damaged in the inundation was a demoralising experience from which he had never truly recovered. His observational skills had been honed on simulations based on maps and images of Geb's sky created from the original survey records. He had taken some while to become accustomed to a sky unobstructed by the great ecliptic arc of the Rings which provided a useful frame of reference for marking star positions on his home-world. Geb's exaggerated axial tilt also caused greater annual variation in the rising and setting of star groupings than he had experienced on Perbau so the sky he watched changed night by night and the recording of his observations had become ever more complicated. Many of the constellations he had learnt to recognise were obscured within the overall brightness of the millions of stars spanning the sky in a broad band, which mirrored the river below. Differences in colour, by which he had learned to identify individual stars, were dulled by the polarising lenses so that all stars appeared white. For a Ba normally sensitive to minute variations in spectral emissions this diminishment of his senses was a severe blow. Most perturbing was his inability to identify Perbau's home sun. He knew it was one of the small patch of stars which Ba astronomers had named the Eye, but of the twenty or more stars visible through even a simple telescope, only seven or eight could be distinguished by sight. Without the advantage of colour discrimination, Djhwty could not say which, if any of them, was the right one. He could not point to the Ba star and say, 'There is home.'

Only Geb's satellite, called Iah by the locals, provided Djhwty with a reliable means of marking the passage of time. By comparing its phases with his stellar observations and local knowledge of the river's rise and fall, over the second and third planetary cycles he had noted that thirteen of Iah's revolutions about Geb approximated to one revolution of the planet about its sun. This gave him the framework for a calendar of sorts which the next year's observations confirmed. But this approximation was not accurate enough to allow him to predict any particular day as precisely as the evacuation plan demanded. The fifth year was more than half gone, the latest inundation had reached its peak and the end of the Experiment was fast approaching. The remaining settlers were depending on Djhwty to give them the word to pack up and make their way to the rendezvous with the scout ship. What had seemed a reasonable window of opportunity when the recovery schedule had been planned was now an almost impossible target.

Chapter 14: The Beginning of the End

The native inhabitants of the little settlement of Khmnw were uneasy. Recently their Golden Ones had taken to distancing themselves from their human followers, holding earnest conversations in the language of the gods, and spending night after night watching the sky. There was a brooding atmosphere over the whole community, humans and Bau. The locals, fearing that they had done something to incur the gods' displeasure, made every effort to make the Bau comfortable and content, improving their accommodation, providing more lavish meals, inventing new entertainments. Still the feeling grew that a momentous change was coming.

Djhwty sat with Imn watching the sun set behind the western hills. 'Have you heard anything from any of the others?' Imn asked his friend.

Djhwty shook his head. He had maintained a tenuous telepathic contact with Nki, his counterpart in Sumer, but that settlement was still reeling from the chaotic aftermath of Tiamt's murder. Nki's response to the news of Wsir's death had been full more of self-pity than commiseration. 'There will be no help from that quarter,' Djhwty replied, 'Nki's sendings have become noticeably weaker. I can hear few coherent thoughts now and a proper exchange is impossible. The principal emotion I sense is despair. I fear the whole Sumer team may be lost.'

Imn bowed his head, remembering his own mental pain at the splitting from his double, Min . 'Before he became so despondent, did Nki have contact with any other settlement?' he enquired.

Djhwty said, 'He did mention a sending from Tmwz, but that was no more than a response to the tumult after Tiamt's death.' Imn nodded. The anguished telepathic shout of the horrified Bau in Sumer would have been loud enough to reach Astrt's zone.

'I wonder, though, that we heard nothing from any of the Middle Sea settlements after Wsir's death,' Imn mused. 'Surely our grief was as loud as Sumer's'

Djhwty had thought the same but in the days since that shattering event he had reached an uncomfortable explanation for the telepathic silence. 'Perhaps there is no one left to hear.'

That Imn did not immediately deny that possibility convinced Djhwty that he was right. 'We can do nothing for the others now,' he said. 'All we can do is to get as many of our own team as possible to the landing place and then home. If no one is there to meet the scout ship Perbau will never know why and how the Experiment failed.'

'Getting them there might be almost impossible with the team scattered so widely, and since Swty is in control of First I cannot see how we could assemble there in safety. At the very least he will try to prevent us reaching the landing site,' Imn said, 'and it is not certain that Swty will want to leave anyway, or allow any of his followers to go.'

'My best estimate of the landing time could be out by ten days or more either way,' Djhwty sighed. 'We would have to gather in the vicinity well before that.'

Imn sensed the self-guilt in his friend's voice and sought to console him, 'I am sure you will do the best you can. We must make the call. Everyone deserves the chance to go home.'

'And if Swty tries to deny us that chance?'

'We can do no more than warn people, and that includes everyone, Swty and his cronies too. We can only hope that he still considers himself bound by the Charter which he was so eager to invoke.'

'But when the authorities get to know of his behaviour...' Djhwty's voice faded.

Imn placed a long-fingered hand on his friend's shoulder. 'Yes, that assumes we survive to make our reports. Swty has shown what he is capable of and he has some devoted followers. I do not suggest that he would kill us all but forcibly keeping us from reaching the scout ship would have the same effect and save him a lot of awkward questions, should he decide to go home.'

'So what should we do?'

'Make your best guess. Pass on the news in time for each group to make the journey to First and then they can choose.'

'What about Swty? I could delay sending to him to allow our friends some hope of getting there without his knowledge.'

'He is such a strong telepath that I cannot see how he would not hear the message anyway but we must include him in the general call. We must do as Wsir would expect of us. Swty is still Ba.'

*

Knowing that there was safety in numbers, Ast and her companions had decided to travel to Skhmt's settlement of Rstaw before starting their journey upstream. There they hoped to meet the other Bau who had chosen to settle in the the river's delta region. They had acquired few personal possessions during their stay and so had little to pack. Whatever they left behind would be turned over to the local humans, along with the simple reed shelters they had come to call home.

'If we were to come back in a few years, I am sure we would find this had become a temple to our divinity,' Nyayt said, her voice tinged with sorrow.

'Your divinity,' Ast said with a smile. 'It was you they took to their hearts. It is you they will remember.'

'But I am no god!' Nyayt protested.

'Of course you are not,' Ast reassured her, 'but as I have told you before, it was easier to accept their homage than to try and explain the real nature of the Bau.'

'I will be sorry to leave,' Nyayt admitted. 'They have been so good to us.'

'Indeed,' Ast agreed, remembering a conversation she had had with Wsir, 'none of us would be here now except for the goodwill and charity of these humans. I would like to think that all our fellows found similar welcomes but I fear they did not.'

'We will find out soon enough,' Nyayt said.

Har appeared from one of the many paths that threaded the papyrus marshes surrounding their secluded settlement. He waved to his mother and held up a bundle of wildfowl.

'Your son has had good hunting,' Nyayt nodded.

Ast smiled, 'We shall eat well before we leave.'

Ast's love for her son was unconditional and he had endeared himself to all those who had known him since his hatching. But even his mother had to admit his strangeness. When he lost his hatchling hair one small dark patch remained on the right side of his scalp. Such birth marks were not unknown. They tended to occur in males who had been born into predominantly female families. Ast put this feature down to the overwhelming female influences that surrounded Har during his incubation. The egg had never been left alone for a moment, with Nebt, Nyayt and Srkt sharing duties with Ast as his guardians and protectors, and Hwthr and Skhmt had overseen his health and well-being. The pigmented patch had sprouted a tuft of thick blue-black hair which grew at the same accelerated rate as the youngling's body. There seemed little point in shaving it, as would have been the custom on Perbau, so Ast plaited it into a sidelock which hung behind his ear. His rapid physical growth was matched by his maturing intellect and he was accepted as adult by all who witnessed his development, but Ast knew he would not find such ready acceptance in other quarters. Despite his remarkable resemblance to his father, Har's manner, as much as his appearance, was not wholly Ba. Being born on Geb, like Inbw, he was untroubled by the planet's low gravity and the shorter day length, because he knew no different, and consequently the way he moved and his patterns of activity and rest were more human than Ba. Unlike his brother, his eyes were protected from the damaging light of Geb's star by his father's lenses and he was as comfortable in the full light of day as Inbw was uncomfortable.

Ast had found great difficulty in restraining Har's limitless curiosity and insatiable inquisitiveness. She had made him promise never to stray beyond her hearing *though, as his considerable telepathic ability blossomed, that restriction became meaningless. His ramblings had taken him north through the salty marshes to the sea coast, west into the desert wastes and south as far as Sbk's crocodile lake. At first Ast had been concerned that Har would succumb to one of the parasitic or bacterial infections which claimed the lives of so many of the native population, particularly their young. She, like all the Ba settlers, had been immunised against such diseases but she could not be sure if her immunity, or Wsir's had been passed on to their son. Reassured by both Skhmt and Hwthr, who had pronounced Har to be the healthiest Ba on the planet, she had abandoned her attempts to confine him, instead resigning herself to treating his scrapes and bruises and answering his* questions. She and Nebt had agreed that he should be told everything he wanted to know about the circumstances of his birth and they responded to every query honestly and fully. Har was left in no doubt about his Ba heritage. He had the mental and occasional physical companionship of Inbw, who had evaded Swty's spies as often as he could to meet his brother at Rstaw. Inbw told Har about Wsir, what sort of father he had been and how much he had believed in the Experiment, and Har had sought reinforcement of these ideas from every Ba he met.

*

When the visible lowering of the flood waters heralded the approaching completion of the fifth year of the Experiment, Djhwty's call had signalled the imminent end of their stay on Geb. All the Bau began to reminisce about what they had left on Perbau and to fantasise about what they would find on their return. If Har felt excluded from this nostalgia for a planet he had never seen, he showed no resentment. He seemed as eager as anyone to start the journey to First. The small reed skiffs carried them along the branch of the river furthest towards sunset to join the main channel just north of Rstaw. Passing between the towering walls of papyrus Ast and Nebt were lost in thought. Neither of their sons had yet expressed anything but excitement over the prospect of the return to Perbau, but the younglings had left much unsaid and both had become adept at shielding their thoughts even from their mothers. Har was standing at the prow of the lead boat pointing out one of the avian raptors which so fascinated him. To most of the party the bird was no more than a speck hovering high above but Har was describing details of its dappled breast feathers as if it were within arm's reach.

'Can he really see the bird at that distance?' Nebt asked, 'or is he describing what he remembers from seeing it before?'

Ast said, 'From what I can tell, he really can see that far. Skhmt has tested his sight as best she can with her limited resources and she is at a loss to explain it. Incredible as it seems, his range is unlimited.'

Nebt sighed, 'There are so many things about our younglings that are inexplicable. The doctors at home will be eager to study them.'

Ast leaned towards Nebt and whispered, 'Has Inbw said anything about staying?'

Nebt shuddered, 'No. What about Har?'

'Nothing. All I can hear from him is excitement but...'

'You feel it too, that uncertainty? We already know that they do not want to return with us to Perbau so what is it that they are not telling us?'

'I fear he means to challenge Swty.'

Nebt gasped then looked up at Har wondering if he had heard their exchange, but he was absorbed in his bird-watching.

Ast put a hand on her sister's arm, *'I will try to dissuade him but I will need help, all the help that you and our friends can give.'*

'Of course,' Nebt breathed, clasping her own hand over Ast's, *'of course!'*

The first to welcome them on their arrival at Rstaw was Skr, the avian specialist and oldest member of the Kem team. He opened his arms to embrace Ast and pressed his cheek to hers. In the last months she had relied on Skr's age and wisdom, pleased that Har had at least one senior male role model. Now she was shocked at the dryness of his skin and the frailty of his body, sensed in that briefest of contacts before Skr broke away to greet his young pupil. Har approached his teacher with due deference to his seniority but Skr swept all protocol aside. Reaching out to tug Har's braided sidelock, he said, 'You've grown taller, youngling, and so like your father.'

The bone-thinning experienced by all had had the greatest effect on the elderly Ba whose back was stooped enough for him to require the support of a wooden staff. Har, already a hand's breadth taller than his mother, now overtopped Skr's bent frame. To Ast's ears, even Skr's voice was weaker. She tried to study his face while he was engaged in animated conversation with her son. The irises of his eyes were obscured by his lenses but the whites were showing signs of discolouration possibly due to dietary deficiency. The back of his hand resting on Har's shoulder, was dappled with age pigmentation. The simple linen kilt he wore did nothing to hide his emaciated torso, across which deep amber shadows accentuated his distinctive Ba rib structure. Never, since their landing on Geb, had Ast been so conscious of being alien.

'Have you seen?' a quiet voice said at Ast's side.

Ast turned to embrace Skhmt, whispering, 'His decline is so marked.'

'From the moment he admitted to needing a staff,' Skhmt confirmed. 'It is as if he had exhausted his energy reserves.'

'Will he survive the journey home? Ast dared to ask.

'I am not sure he will survive the journey to First, was Skhmt's chilling reply.

The settlement of Rstaw was already looking neglected. The yards were unswept, the poultry pens vacant and the doors of the storage huts hung ajar revealing almost empty interiors. The substantial house, built from palm logs and mud-daubed wattle panels, had been stripped of its decorative reed matting and holes in the thatched roof remained unmended. Only in the kitchen area was there any sign of activity, though the humans gathered around the oven and hearth were talking in subdued tones, casting worried glances over their shoulders in the direction of their Golden Ones.

'The humans are preparing us a farewell feast,' Skhmt confirmed. 'They have just begun to accept that we are really going and they cannot hide their feelings. This could be a sad gathering.'

At that moment Har came to greet Skhmt with an exuberant hug that lifted her off her feet. Laughing, the two went to join Skr. Nebt came up to Ast's side, saying, 'Skhmt seems very cheerful. Has she mentioned the recovery of Pth's body?'

Ast flinched at the recollection that all the Bau settlers, living and dead, were expected to return to Perbau. She had put this to the back of her mind, not wanting to contemplate what she might feel at the sight of her mate's body. 'We have never spoken of it. I do not think that even now she knows where his body is and, after all this time, I am not sure that she wants to know. It would reopen too many wounds.'

'Are you suggesting that Pth's body should remain here on Geb?'

'Yes, just so,' Ast said, 'but whatever the decision, it is Skhmt's to make.'

'What about Ndjty? He had no partner.'

'I believe your son has already settled that question,' Ast smiled, attempting to take the sting out of the reminder.

'And Min?' Nebt asked.

'He is not yet dead, but he might decide that he does not want to risk a journey which, in all probability, will kill him.'

'So, what of Imn?'

'The double link is weakened but not destroyed. They will decide together.'

'How can you talk so calmly of the loss of our friends?'

'I remind myself that we all volunteered for the Experiment knowing there were likely to be losses. I strongly suspect that we have lost fewer than some of our other groups and for that we must be thankful.'

'And Wsir?'

'As his mate I will make that decision, but not yet.'

'Yours is not the only deferred decision,' Nebt tilted her head towards the mudbrick bench where Har and Skr were deep in discussion of the hawk. Har used his hands to illustrate wings in a hovering manoeuvre and then tipped his head back to imitate the high-pitched cry of the hunting bird.

'That is it, exactly,' Skr beamed at his pupil, *'the raptor to the life. I believe it is my favourite of all the avians here, so fast, so elegant, so efficient.'*

'You could take one home with you to Perbau,' Har said.

The silence which followed was uncomfortable, then Skr sighed and said, *'No, youngling. To remove it from this familiar place, to confine that free spirit in any sort of cage and then subject it to an alien environment. You do see how cruel that would be?'*

'Oh yes, Master, indeed I do,' Har said.

Ast suppressed a sob and accepted the comfort of Nebt's arms. *'It would be cruel to make them go, would it not?'* she thought to her sister.

'Yes, dearest,' Nebt replied, 'They must remain free, like the hawk.'

*

When the Bau assembled at the riverside for their departure, Ast was struck by their pitiful appearance. Some had tried to make a show by dressing in the garments in which they had arrived on the planet, clothes which were now, after five years on Geb, shabby at best. Most were dressed in the coarser but more durable linen shifts and kilts that they had assumed of necessity when their Ba-made clothing had worn out. The provisions for the journey took up more space than the simple draw-string sacks in which they had packed their personal possessions and a few mementoes of their stay. Ast watched Skhmt say her farewells to the humans of Rstaw. The physician had not mentioned her dead mate once and Ast had felt it was inappropriate to bring up the subject, so Pth would stay on Geb.

Their transport was the best that the local boat builders could provide. The hulls were made from sycamore planks stitched together with papyrus ropes. The large square sails were made from the flexible woven reed fabric which had so impressed Nyayt.

'That explains where all the wall-hangings from Rstaw went,' she commented, pointing to the canopies which had been provided to protect passengers from the sun.

Skhmt smiled, 'Our human friends have been very generous. Of course we will return the boats once we have finished with them, but it has been difficult to explain just how far we are going. Our crews are quite excited about this voyage, but they are unwilling to accept that we are not coming back.'

Nyayt looked surprised, 'Surely you did not try to tell them about Perbau?'

'No, no,' Skhmt laughed, 'that would be far beyond their comprehension. So few of them have travelled more than a few arur beyond their home, they do not have a means of measuring such distances. Even the traders who ply the river regularly describe their journeys by the number of days travelled and of course that varies depending on the vessel and whether they are moving up or downstream. These new boats are larger than any we have seen before so we have no way of gauging their speed.'

'Will we be in time?' Nyayt asked.

'We can only hope so. We will be at the mercy of wind and current.'

The journey started in an atmosphere of excitement and anticipation, but when they began to leave behind familiar landmarks this changed to a feeling of unease. The voyage seemed to be going much more slowly than expected and they could no longer predict, with any accuracy, whether or not they would achieve their window of opportunity for the scout ship rendezvous. Only Har and Skr seemed oblivious to the anxieties of their comrades, spending their days watching for birds. To Ast and Skhmt it was clear that Skr was now almost blind and equally obvious that Har recognised his teacher's incapacity. He had found a soft bundle to prop behind Skr's back and had wrapped a linen cloak around his shoulders. The aged Ba held himself upright with his hands clasped over the head of the stout wooden staff. Skr tilted his head to listen to Har describing avians in minute detail which only he could see while his master contributed information which he remembered from his previous studies.

'His mind is as sharp as ever, his memory is unimpaired, but his body is failing him,' Skhmt confided to Ast. 'You see how little movement he has in his legs now. He will not walk again.'

Their arrival at Khmnw was a great relief to all. Djhwty had been blaming himself for leaving his call too late. Only the increasing strength of sendings from the Rstaw group had reassured him that they were on their way.

'Sbk passed through here a few days ago,' Djhwty reported to Ast. 'He will meet us at Hwthr's settlement.'

'Har speaks with great animation of his visits to Sbk's lake, but I was always concerned that, once Hwthr returned to her cows, the isolation was not good for him. How did he seem?'

'He was very cheerful. He and Imn had a long conversation, well into the night.'

Ast sensed Djhwty's reticence, 'So, Sbk too?' she said with sadness.

Djhwty started, 'You know?'

'I guessed. They will not be alone. In a way I am glad that my son and Nebt's will have adult Ba company and that our dead will be remembered. You realise that Skhmt has left Pth behind?'

Djhwty nodded, 'Min's position was always going to be a consideration for Imn. Skhmt says she will assess him when we reach Qbt but Hwthr has monitored his situation so Skhmt knows what she will find. Min is dying.'

Ast bowed her head, 'It amazes me that he has survived this long. Of course Imn will not want to leave.'

'And what are Skr's chances?' Djhwty asked.

'He is determined to go home but you have seen how reduced he is. We do not expect him to live more than a few days,' Ast replied with honesty.

*

The little flotilla, augmented by boats from Khmnw, continued on its way upstream. The passage of time was marked by the rising and setting of the sun but the passing landscape gave no indication of how far they had travelled. The riverbanks were almost featureless, broken only by occasional groups of trees. The sporadic human settlements were marked by well-tended palm groves and the smoke from cooking fires and kilns, but the fields of black soil, newly irrigated by the miraculous inundation, were invisible beyond the endless stands of reeds and papyrus. In the hazy distance beyond the floodplain the desert hills were barely discernible, their pale heights blending seamlessly with the pearlescent sky. A few humans saw them pass – fishermen hunting from reed rafts, women washing clothes, children playing in the shallows. They waved and called others to come and watch the Golden Ones go by, but otherwise their passing went unnoticed.

Djhwty became ever more impatient with the slowness of their progress. Only when they had reached the familiar environs of Abdw did he begin to relax. By his calculations they would be cutting it fine but they would reach First in time, as long as they were not further delayed by farewells and partings at the other Bau settlements. He was encouraged by sendings that confirmed Khnm and his friends were well on their way.

They found a welcoming party on the landing place at Abdw where they planned their last overnight stay. Skr was carried into the shade of the old residence building where Inbw was waiting for them. Nebt hugged her son, holding him with an intensity that embarrassed him. When he drew his mother aside to a quiet corner, Ast knew that Inbw was about to confirm Nebt's worst fears. With a moment's panic she looked around for her own son but Har's place at Skr's side had been taken by Skhmt. Outside the mansion she was at once surrounded by a group of humans who had gathered to see for themselves that their Golden Ones had returned. Ast submitted to the tentative touch of many hands as well-wishers confirmed her physical presence. She tried to extricate herself from the friendly huddle but she was too grateful to these kindly people to treat them with disdain. When, at last, she was free she saw Inbw beckoning to her from the shaded doorway of the mansion. He pointed in the direction of a building which was new since their time at Abdw. 'He is there,' he sent.

The substantial building was of timber and mudbrick with a vaulted roof covered in reed thatch. It stood in a small enclosure marked by a low fence of stakes and reed hurdles. A standard pole at the entrance suggested that this was a shrine, the emblem it bore was a standing jackal. A human priest came out to challenge Ast's approach but when he recognised her he bowed deeply and stood aside. Sunlight spilled obliquely through the doorway of the windowless building catching one corner of a flat rectangular stone, an offering table, on which were the remains of a simple meal. Beyond, in the dark interior, Har was standing, head bowed, over a slight mound in the beaten earth floor. Without turning he said, 'It is the Pathfinder. Inbw served him well. The humans already revere him as you see.' He waved a hand behind his back indicating the primitive altar.

Ast approached and gently stretched her arm to encircle her son's waist, leaning her head into his shoulder. 'Inbw was right to honour Ndjty, who stood as his protector and guide for so long,' she said then, hesitating over the words she had been practising throughout the voyage from Rstaw, 'He did the same for your father?'

Har turned and took his mother in his arms as she cried the last tears she would shed for Wsir on this world. 'He did,' Har confirmed, 'and I have not asked where Father is buried.'

Through her sobs Ast understood him. Her reply was muffled by her face being pressed into her son's chest, 'And neither will I.'

*

In the pre-dawn light Inbw accompanied them to the riverside to watch the Bau take their leave of Abdw for the last time. Nebt, who had said her goodbyes the previous evening, gave her son one last embrace before taking her place in the lead boat. Ast knew better than to offer commiseration. Later there would be time for them to comfort each other but now Nebt had to be seen to be strong. She would need all her composure when she confronted Swty with the news that he would never see his son again. No one else seemed to notice when Inbw disappeared through the reeds ahead of the sunrise.

The start of the great bend in the river required the boat crews to put out oars to propel the vessels athwart the wind. In spite of Djhwty's anxieties, they made good time and reached Hwthr's settlement at Iwnt before midday. Hwthr and Sbk were waiting for them and wasted no time in boarding Imn's boat. Nebt commented to Ast, 'They have no luggage.'

'They need none,' Ast replied.

The sunrise part of the bend negotiated, they reached Qbt in good time. But this time no one waited at the water's edge. Imn leapt off the boat and turned to wave to his companions. 'Go with our blessings,' he cried, 'we cannot go with you.'

A chorus of voices reinforced by a frantic mental babble expressed the general dismay at Imn's statement. They knew he spoke for all the Bau at Qbt, not only himself and his dying double, but also the sociologist, Mwt, the physicist, Imnt, the chemist, Imsty, and several other scientists who had attached themselves to Min's research settlement. Ast was stunned into impotent silence by how many of her comrades were deserting them. To her surprise it was Har who broke the spell. The youngling stood up and waved his fellow Bau to silence.

'We understand, friend,' he shouted to Imn. 'Hold true and I will return to you.'

'What does he mean?' Nyayt whispered to Ast.

'What he says,' Ast sighed, 'Har will stay on Geb.'

*

They reached First under cover of darkness. All the travellers had been careful to shield their thoughts in an attempt to hide their arrival from Swty. They hoped to be able to circumvent the settlement and camp in the mouth of the wadi which led into the sunset desert towards the place where the scout ship was due to pick them up. Djhwty had given up all pretence at being able to predict the exact day of the landing. He could offer no better advice than to find the place and wait. But their plans were thrown into disarray even before they had reached land. Skr had been drifting in and out of sleep since they left Abdw. By the time they had reached Qbt he was all but comatose. As the boats nudged into the riverbank at First he suffered a fatal seizure, and his final mental agony was broadcast at such a level that it wakened even the weakest of telepaths. Within moments the place was swarming with Bau, some waving flaming torches, others brandishing clubs or spears. The new arrivals found themselves surrounded. Those still on the boats were forced to disembark, their few possessions were gathered together in a chaotic heap at the water's edge, and Shzmw slung Skr's body over his shoulder as if it were a spoil of the hunt. The human boat crews were ordered back on the river, powerless to intervene as their Golden Ones were herded towards the settlement like animals to slaughter.

*

The old residence building at First had become a prison. When Djhwty was pushed into the room he tripped over Mntjw's outstretched legs and was prevented from falling only by the quick thinking of Khnm. He thanked his friend and moved further into the room to allow those following him to find their own space. Murmured conversations in the dark confirmed that all the occupants of this cell were male. They knew that every thought would be overheard so they had to resort to the whispered spoken word which meant that they could not communicate with the females being held on the other side of the compound.

'How many are with Swty?' Djhwty asked Mntjw.

'Not as many as he would like but more than we could overcome without help. He has had us penned up here for days, ever since he heard that Khnm's party was approaching.'

'How has he treated you since Wsir....'

'With contempt, a sort of slavery. It is hard to believe that he is Ba.'

'And the females?'

'The same. It is only with the support of the humans that we have been able to do all that Swty demands of us. If not for them we would have suffered greatly.'

'Do you know what preparations he has made for departure?'

'No. Your call took him by surprise. We have been more closely confined since then.'

Khnm joined their conversation. 'When we arrived he had our possessions searched and anything non-Ba was tossed aside. He claimed that we would take away only that which we brought with us.'

'That suggests that he still intends to go home,' Djhwty mused. 'Has he said who will go with him?'

Mntjw lowered his voice to a whisper, 'Places on the scout ship are offered as rewards to the faithful few, as if he has the final say in the matter. He has completely abrogated the Charter.'

'Swty has proven himself to be capable of murder, what has he to lose?' Khnm said.

'His behaviour was always unpredictable but now he is almost totally irrational. You do not want to know what he threatens to do to the younglings, and Inbw is his own blood!' Mntjw said with evident distaste.

'At least Inbw is out of harm's way,' Djhwty said with feeling.

'But what of Har?' Khnm asked. 'Did he choose to stay with Inbw?'

'No, he came with us.' Djhwty peered around the crowded room lit only by moonlight filtering through window grilles high in the walls. He tried to locate Har then realised that he had not seen Wsir's son since they arrived at First. He tried to remember the order of events after Skr's death. Har had been at his master's side in those last moments but the youngling was not there when the body was taken ashore. Djhwty remembered a splash which at the time he had assumed was a dropped oar or perhaps a piece of cargo falling overboard. Now he knew that Har had evaded Swty and was at liberty. How long would it be before Swty discovered that his quarry had escaped? And what would Swty's reaction be when he found out?

*

Ast had known at once when Har had slipped over the side of the boat. It was all she could do to stop herself from crying out. She had guarded her thoughts as tightly as she knew how, and allowed herself to be led away without giving a backward look which might have alerted their captors to her son's absence. Swty had been so confident of meeting no resistance that he had yet to show his face. But now the dawn was fast approaching and if she knew anything at all about her mate's brother it was that he would want to make his first meeting with Har as dramatic as possible. Knowing her son, she was certain he would want the same. She almost wished that the sun would not rise.

*

When the door was thrown open by Mafdt the sky in the east was just beginning to show that greenish tinge which preceded the sun. 'Out!' the security guard shouted, gesturing over her shoulder, 'and don't try anything!'

Ast sat up, stretching muscles cramped after a night's confinement. She moved with deliberation as if it were her own choice to get up at that time.

'Move!' Mafdt growled.

'In our own time, Mafdt dear,' Ast said in her sweetest tone.

Nebt took the cue from her sister. 'Is it morning already?' she asked, yawning. 'Oh, hello Mafdt. How are things with you?'

'Leader wants you outside, now!' Mafdt almost shrieked.

Ast turned to help Skhmt to her feet while Nebt roused Nyayt and Srkt, who were still asleep, curled up in each other's arms. Hwthr was already standing, surrounded by a huddle of female Bau. They made a great fuss of smoothing their clothing, running fingers through their hair and finding sandals. By the time they indicated their readiness, Mafdt was trembling with frustration. She urged the female contingent outside into the area of beaten earth which served as a meeting space. Ast looked around discreetly trying to spot any sign of her son but in vain. In the dim pre-dawn light she could only just make out the outlines of the group of male captives standing in a dejected huddle on the opposite side of the congregation area, guarded by Shzmw and his security team, maces in hand. The guards were outnumbered by their charges but it was clear that no one had considered the possibility of overcoming them by force. That they should have descended so far from their civilized ways as to indulge in violent confrontation was still unthinkable but so was the idea that any Ba should feel intimidated by another. Ast wondered whether any of the guards was prepared to use his weapon in anger or whether they were constrained by the moral and psychological consequences of such action. Swty may be, so far, the only Ba of their group who had done so but the hero-worship demonstrated by Mafdt's calling him 'Leader' could so easily turn to emulation. Ast's deepest fear was that Har would be overwhelmed by the fanaticism of Swty's acolytes before he could achieve an honourable confrontation with his father's killer.

And there he was, striding out between his followers. 'Where is the brat?' Swty cried.

Before Ast could answer for her son, Hwthr had stepped out in front of her, saying, 'If you are talking about Wsir's son, we have not seen him since last night. You have nothing to fear from him. He will not be leaving this planet, and neither will I.'

Ast grabbed for Hwthr's hand but the veterinarian shrugged her off. 'Do not interfere, Ast,' she said, 'we know what we are doing.' Turning back to face Swty she continued, 'Apart from anything else, we do not want to face the shame of returning to Perbau. We would rather end our days – however few there may be left to us – here , among friends.'

Swty's face had drained of all colour at this unexpected rebellion. Hwthr's had always been the calm voice of reason and compromise, the least likely source of opposition, and as such seriously underestimated. For a short while complete silence hung over the little community. Then Nebt nudged Ast and pointed in the direction of the path from the river where a lone figure was silhouetted against the lightening sky.

Before Mafdt could react, Ast had broken free of the group and ran to embrace her son, hoping to keep him from that meeting which threatened so much pain and distress. But Har took his mother gently by the shoulders and whispered in her ear, 'I am staying, and I want him to stay too, but I wish him no harm.' Ast nodded and stood aside but, as Har walked on, her strength failed and she slumped to the ground.

Despite the reports of the youngling's rapid growth, Swty had never quite believed that Har was an adult. He was shocked by the appearance of this tall, powerfully built male, who looked so like his father that there could be no challenge to his legitimacy. Swty felt his tongue cleave to the roof of his dry mouth, every taunt and deprecation silenced. No words would come to express his fury, his disappointment and his fear.

Har walked into the centre of the clearing and slowly turned around, looking into the faces of all the assembled Bau, friends and foes. When he returned to face Swty, he said, 'I had meant to challenge you, to avenge my father, but I have learned from his friends as well as from my mother, that that is not the Ba way. You are not worth my anger. More, you are to be pitied because you have fallen so far short of the ideals by which he lived. If you return to Perbau you will not receive the triumphant reception that you hoped. There are too many witnesses here to your infamy. You cannot expect to silence them all and I think you are still Ba enough to allow those who wish to leave this planet to return home. There is really only one course open to you. Stay here with us and let everyone else go.'

Swty gulped, trying to moisten his mouth. Nyayt had slipped aside and was now comforting Ast who was sobbing with relief. Nebt stepped forward to comfort her erstwhile mate. 'Har is right,' she said, 'you have no prospects on Perbau apart from solitary exile. At least here there are some Bau to keep you company, your son amongst them.'

Swty swallowed again, then croaked, 'And you?'

'No,' Nebt said, 'you made my choice for me long ago.'

Hwthr took the initiative again, saying, 'The solution is clear. Stay here – with us or apart from us – it is for you to choose. Those who return to Perbau will simply report that we died. No one will contradict them.' She threw a challenging look around the assembly. There was a growing murmur of assent as the Bau recognised the simplicity and effectiveness of Hwthr's plan. They already knew, in their hearts, that many Bau had died in the failure of other Experimental groups. It would be so easy to convince their people back on the home-world that the Kem settlement had suffered similar losses.

Djhwty pushed his way to the front, brushing aside Shzmw's feeble threats. 'Whatever we decide, it must be soon. I cannot be certain of the exact time but...'

Sharp-eyed Har stopped him, shouting, 'Look!'

All eyes followed the direction of his pointing arm. A slow-moving object was just clearing the sunset horizon, sparkling like a star in the dawn light. The sight was quickly obliterated by the light of the rising sun but all had seen it and knew what it signified. The mother ship was entering Geb's orbit.

Sbk reacted first. 'There is no more time. Choose!' he shouted. 'All of you must choose now!'

*

'Engaged?' Simon almost screeched at Pete's news.

'Do you have to make that noise?' Sally snapped from her microscope.

'But the Doc and Mac are engaged! Aren't you just a little excited?' he rounded on her.

'I'm very pleased for them. But it's been on the cards a long time so I'm not going to act like an over-enthusiastic school kid.'

'Aw, lighten up, Sally,' Pete said, 'it's tremendous news.'

'But not unexpected,' Sally persisted, 'and we have a lot of work to do before this meeting on Sunday. Can we get on with it?'

Sally was comparing samples of emmer found at Nagada in earlier years with the contentious sample from the last season. Simon had teased a few small fragments of the fabric pouch apart from the ball of grain and had untangled the remnants of the twisted cord which had held the pouch closed. He was preparing them on microscope slides to study the structure of the fibres. Pete was frowning over the photographic record of the human remains, sighing with frustration that he would never get to handle the real thing. Looking from one picture to the next his eyes went momentarily out of focus and for a fleeting fraction of a second he thought he saw something. He blinked and repeated the scanning motion. 'Si,' he said, 'didn't you say something about a metallic sheen?'

Simon looked up from his slides. 'Yes, we thought the wheat grains had a bit of a lustre which we couldn't explain.' He was hit again by the nagging feeling that he had forgotten something relevant.

Sally tuned into their exchange, saying, 'Why do you ask, Peter?'

Still unsure of what he had seen, Pete reversed the slide show on his laptop to check.

'Don't keep us in suspense,' Simon urged.

'Come and look,' Pete said, his tone firm enough to make both his colleagues down their own tools to stand behind him, watching the laptop screen over his shoulder. He clicked back and forth between half a dozen images, views of the bone from the Box Trench which had been identified as a human femur. The pictures had been taken from the same angle but with different light sources placed in slightly different positions. Apart from the image reference numbers they all looked very much the same, but as Pete speeded up the transition between pictures, Simon said, 'Woah! Stop!'

'You saw it too?' Pete asked.

'I think so. Do it again.'

This time it was Sally who interrupted, 'Yes, I saw it. It's the same as the grain, only visible in certain light conditions and at a particular angle.'

'Well, now we're all agreed that it's there, all we have to work out is what the hell is it?' Pete exclaimed.

'You've never seen anything like this on bones before?' Sally asked.

'Never, and before you ask, I can't think of any explanation. This looks like something intrinsic to the bone. I mean, some prehistoric societies painted the defleshed bones of their ancestors with red ochre but this is deeper than a surface coating. Some soil conditions, peat bogs for example, can stain the bone almost black, but this is clearly metallic and there's nothing in the soil samples to account for it. I can't even think of any modern chemical contamination that would cause this effect.'

'It's the same with the wheat. There is nothing comparable showing up in the other samples,' Sally said.

Something clicked in Simon's memory. He had seen mention of a metallic sheen on organic remains from another dig, but which dig was it? It must have been quite recently, probably in one of the reference sources he had consulted for the Cambridge conference paper. Where did he find it?

Pete was speaking and jogged his arm. 'What about your fibres, Si?' he repeated. 'Anything there?'

'I've only just prepared the slides,' Simon grunted. The fleeting memory was gone again.

'Well get to it, pronto,' Pete said.

'Bring them over here to my microscope,' Sally ordered.

Twenty minutes later Simon broke the bemused silence. 'Let's recap,' he said. 'This is a pouch of grain which comes from an incontrovertible context. The excavation was properly recorded and each find appropriately documented by internationally recognised archaeologists. Are we all agreed?'

'Get on with it,' Sally said, sounding not nearly as self-assured as previously.

'I'll take that as a yes. We've already noted one common feature between the grain and the bones from the same context, to whit a certain metallic sheen. I can positively state that most of the fibres show the same modification, if that's what we're calling it, as the grain. There is a definite lustre about them, a shininess which I've never seen on flax fibres. There's also a distinct difference between the warp and the weft threads. The weft is linen, or something very similar to ancient Egyptian linen, but the warp is something else.'

'So what the hell is it?' Pete snarled.

'I don't know exactly...' Simon admitted. Sally and Pete snorted their disgust in unison but Simon continued, '...but I can tell you what it isn't.'

'Oh for pity's sake tell us!' Sally said.

'Well...' Simon paused once more for dramatic effect, looking smugly from one to the other, '...it's not natural. I'd call it manmade but I doubt that any human hand was involved in its manufacture. It has more the appearance of glass fibre than anything else but I'd need to have chemical analysis to confirm that. The shafts are smooth and the threads are of such consistent thickness and twist that no human being on Earth six thousand years ago could have made them.'

For the first time Pete and Sally were stunned into silence. Simon nodded, ''Fraid so. Looks like Uncle Eric might have been right all along.'

Chapter 15: Revelations

Simon had been grumbling ever since he had heard from FAQ that his uncle had been invited to the meeting. At first the grumblings were random and vituperative blaming Evers, once again, for blighting his life. Then he began to blame the Doc for allowing herself to be hoodwinked by Evers so far as to invite him into her own home. Next he turned the blame on Theo for allowing his sister to be manipulated. Finally, after one particularly venomous diatribe, Pete had taken his friend in hand. 'Look, Si, it's no good going on like this. You've got to see things from their point of view. Love him or loathe him, we need Evers on our side. If the Doc can bring herself to be in the same room with him then I think it's time you took a leaf out of her book.'

Simon, pulled up short by Pete's firmness, took a few moments to review his antipathy for his mother's brother. For as long as he could remember she had held up Uncle Eric as a real-life family hero. The young Simon had been overawed and then overwhelmed by his uncle's personality, but when he took stock of their relationship he realised that, whatever he might tell anyone to the contrary, it was Evers who had inspired him to go in for archaeology. For that reason alone Simon had to acknowledge a debt to his uncle but, as far as he could see, that debt had been cancelled the moment he had achieved his First Class degree on his own merits. Pete was right, it was high time he stood on his own two feet. There was no longer any cause for him to feel intimidated by his uncle, nor to allow him to interfere in his life. He was better qualified in his chosen discipline than Uncle Eric would ever be. Whatever opinion Evers might have formed of the Doc and her colleagues, he had no comprehension of the intellectual and scientific powers ranged against him. He might think he had the upper hand but by accepting the invitation to be included in this meeting at the Doc's house he was entering a hostile environment for which he was wholly unprepared. In fact, when Simon considered the situation, he had to feel sorry for his uncle. Evers was walking into an ambush.

Simon had the grace to apologise to Pete for his moodiness. 'You're right,' he said. 'I lost sight of the scientific imperative for a moment. The Doc has more reason to distrust Uncle Eric than I have so if she can set aside her doubts then so can I. It's no longer a matter of making money on the back of sensational speculation. He's got to be made to see that this is really important.'

'Yeah,' said Pete, slapping Simon on the shoulder, 'and we've got a lot to show him.'

*

Theo and Ian had man-handled Adeline's dining table up the stairs, risking skinned knuckles to get it through the sitting room door, only to find, when they pushed them together, that it was a good couple of centimetres higher than Hermione's kitchen table. 'We'll just have to be careful where we put the cups', Ian commented. 'I don't think Adeline will be too pleased with coffee stains.'

'True,' Theo agreed. 'So, what's next?'

'Chairs.'

'Did you see the size of Adeline's dining chairs? They must weigh a ton – each! Is there no alternative?'

Ian grinned, 'I asked the gang to pick up some stacking chairs from the Department. Flick's bringing them over in her van.'

'Good,' Theo sighed with relief. 'Time for tea then.'

In the kitchen they found Hermione entertaining Sylvia, Miss Phillips and Prof Jameson. 'Enough in the pot for us?' Theo asked.

'Of course,' Hermione smiled, reaching for more cups. She was pleased to see that her hand was hardly shaking when she poured.

Everyone's attention was drawn by the sound of Ian's mobile squawking a text alert. He thumbed the screen and muttered, 'He's on his way.'

Hermione hissed as tea slopped over the rim of a cup on to the draining board.

'Is there any chance he'll get lost?' Adeline asked sweetly.

'Not for a moment. He was very proud of telling me how good his sat-nav is,' Mac said.

'Well, I can't say I'm looking forward to meeting him if he is as obnoxious in ordinary company as he is in public,' Sylvia said.

'Nor me,' said Jameson, adding, 'I suppose we had to include him?'

Theo answered before his sister could stutter something rude. 'We're giving him the opportunity of a lifetime. He wants to become legit and even someone as egotistical as he is will recognise that this is his best bet for entering the scientific arena. Most importantly, he's media savvy. He can cope much better than H.P. or you, Terence, no offence meant.'

'None taken,' the Prof smiled, 'but I would have thought you were equally qualified to deal with the press and so forth.'

'It's a matter of testing the waters,' Theo explained. 'Evers has nothing to lose. Once he's made the initial revelations, if the reception for our findings is favourable then we can ease ourselves into the limelight. If not, we let Evers take all the flak.'

'He's got a thick enough skin,' Hermione said with feeling.

The doorbell rang. She looked out of the window and waved. 'It's Simon and Peter with a pile of box files. They came by taxi.'

'I'll get it,' said Ian. By the time he reached the front door, Flick and Sally had arrived with the chairs. It was fully ten minutes before Eric Evers' huge black vehicle turned into the quiet residential street. Sylvia and Adeline watched Evers search for a parking space, giggling like schoolgirls as they imagined the curses aimed at the battered VW camper van which had taken the prime spot. Before he stalked up the garden path, the laptops, files of context sheets and photographs, and other reference materials were all assembled. Simon volunteered to answer the door and escort his uncle upstairs where the others had already chosen their seats. Hermione welcomed him to her home with a polite but brief shake of the hand and offered him a cup of tea, which he declined. Shrugging off the rebuff to her hospitality she indicated that he should take the seat between Theo and Simon before sitting down herself, saying, 'Now we are all here, I think we should introduce ourselves so that Mr Evers can appreciate the breadth and depth of this investigation.' Turning to her right she gave Ian his cue. 'I'm Ian Masterson, Director of the University's Expedition to Nagada in Egypt.'

And so it began. Evers listened with growing annoyance to the introductions. He frowned at the inclusion of the black woman who said she was a librarian, and the old biddy who called herself Hermione's neighbour seemed to have no claim to academic authority. His nephew and his gangly friend were mere students. The ginger dyke and her blonde 'partner' he dismissed out of hand without listening to their qualifications. Only Theo Beaumont, the Egyptologist and the dapper Professor were worthy of his attention so they were subjected to his most charming smiles. The Beaumont woman still appeared to be the softest target. Their serendipitous meeting at the family party on Santorini had confirmed his opinion of her, formed all those years ago when he first found her thesis; she was a weak female who would know that tagging on to his coat tails would be good for her career. As always Evers underestimated the strength of support, both moral and academic that Hermione had attracted. He failed to notice the engagement cards on the mantelpiece. He overlooked the significance of the one empty chair at the table.

When the introductions were over, Evers fixed Hermione with his most ingratiating smile, saying, 'I have been looking forward to this meeting and I am so grateful to you, Ms Beaumont, for offering the hospitality of your charming home.'

Before HPB could respond to this condescension, Professor Jameson took the initiative. Stressing Hermione's title he said, 'Doctor Beaumont was good enough to offer her home as a venue because we wished to distance the University from any involvement in this preliminary discussion. We are all here as seriously interested parties but none of our deliberations will be minuted. Should anything of our discussions appear in the public domain without our authorisation we are all prepared to deny that this meeting ever took place.'

Evers blinked in surprise. Theo Beaumont continued the Prof's theme, 'I can speak for all of us here when I say that we have little respect for the garbled version of history that you promote and we are not prepared to see any more serious research perverted in the same way. We know how much of your success is built upon the hard work of others.'

'And how much money you've made in the process,' Sylvia added.

In his indignation Evers stood up, pushing his chair over backwards. He leant his hands on the table and snarled in Sylvia's face, 'I didn't come here to be insulted by…by a librarian. Do you know who I am?'

'I know what you are, Mr Evers,' Sylvia said calmly, holding his gaze.

'Sit down, Uncle Eric,' Simon said. 'If you want to continue making money on the back of other people's efforts, you need to listen to us.'

Evers turned his scowling face to his nephew but Simon had found his courage at last and was more than prepared to face down his uncle. 'If you can just keep quiet for a few minutes I think you're going to hear something to your advantage,' he said, 'but first you need to know where we're all coming from and how much this is costing us. So sit down and shut up.'

Pete had moved to pick up the chair just in time for Evers to slump back into his seat. The shock of Simon's treachery was enough to render him speechless. Jameson ignored the interruption. 'There is nothing to be gained by trading insults, Mr Evers, Sylvia,' he said, giving the librarian a meaningful look. 'We have arranged this meeting to discuss certain discoveries which might just enable you, Mr Evers, to keep making money for a very long time.'

Evers raised his eyebrows and opened his mouth to speak but before he could utter a word Simon said, 'I meant it, Uncle Eric. You've got to listen, and listen without interrupting. Hear the whole story before you say a single word. It's been a lot for us to take in, and it's been hard to make sense of it all. Our findings go against almost everything we thought we knew or understood but if we can change our way of thinking, so can you. If you approach this with an open mind, believe me, it'll open your eyes to a whole new world of possibilities. But we'll get nowhere if we start arguing every single point, so just keep quiet and listen.'

To Simon's amazement, Evers nodded his assent and sat back in his seat with his arms folded. To Hermione's amazement Simon had not blushed once during this confrontation.

Professor Jameson leaned forward slightly, folding his hands together on the table, and said, 'I shall start, Mr Evers, by giving a summary of the situation as we see it. Forgive me if I gloss over some aspects of your work but we must concentrate on those areas where we have common interests. I believe you will find this quite enlightening. Our understanding of your hypothesis is this: at some time in the prehistoric past Earth was visited by alien hominids who settled in several different areas of the world. These extra-terrestrials introduced new technologies and enhanced species of domesticated plants and animals which enabled human civilization to make a great leap forward. You suggest that the memory of this visitation is preserved in the mythologies of all the great cultures. You claim that humankind was also altered as the result of inter-breeding with these aliens. In the course of your research you have used a wide range of material to back up your theory, much of it the results of other people's hard work. The way in which you have edited, paraphrased and manipulated these sources could be seen, at best, as bowdlerisation, or at worst, plagiarism.'

Evers' sense of indignation overcame his confusion. 'I have never…' he began, but the Prof's imperiously raised hand reduced him to silence.

'I understand that you have no academic background and so you might be excused for not realising how many conventions of scientific research and intellectual property rights you have flouted. You are only redeemed by the fact that, for the most part, you have relied on out-of-date material and out-of-favour theories which you have repackaged as your own, knowing that no one will bother to challenge your ownership of them. However, you crossed a line when you chose to borrow, to put it politely, and then misuse the work of one of my colleagues. You can have no comprehension of how important Dr Beaumont's work is, to her, to the University and to the world. You cannot possibly understand how hurtful it has been for her to have her name associated with your brand of sensationalism.'

Evers, feeling he was on a surer footing, interrupted again, 'I have always been ready to debate my theories with Ms Beaumont...' He faltered at Sylvia's hiss of indignation at his repeated misuse of Hermione's title, then continued, '...but she has never responded to my approaches, even those made through my nephew.'

'That's because I never passed on your messages,' Simon retorted. 'I knew the Doc would have more sense than to engage in any debate with you, public or otherwise.'

Jameson called for order, 'Goodhill, we have limited time at our disposal. Please try to remain focused. Mr Evers, I don't think you appreciate just how much damage could have been done to Dr

Beaumont's career and her future research prospects, had she deigned to participate in a public slanging match. That she kept her counsel in spite of extreme provocation is very much to her credit. Now there will be no need for debate because the new information we are prepared to release to you supersedes those aspects of Dr Beaumont's work which you have previously misrepresented.'

Evers tried to catch Hermione's eye but she kept her gaze lowered, apparently scrutinising papers in front of her. He thought he discerned the slightest trace of a smile twitching at her lips. She looked altogether too relaxed for his liking.

'So, Mr Evers,' Theo rejoined the conversation, 'Now you know what we think of your exploitation of my sister's work you might be pleasantly surprised to hear that we're offering you the means to revive if not entirely reinvent your theories. We have come to the denouement. Why don't you go first H.P.?'

Hermione nodded to her brother and then looked to Ian for encouragement. He placed his hand over hers where it lay on the table. To the satisfaction of both there was not a hint of a tremble in her fingers. She cleared her throat and said, 'Mr Evers, I don't know how you got hold of my *first* doctoral thesis…'

Pete's whispered, 'Go Doc, rub it in!' was audible only to Simon.

'…but I am amazed at the inferences you have drawn from it. In fact I was so amazed that anyone would believe such a corruption of the truth that I felt it unnecessary to refute your theories. I will try to explain, in the simplest of terms why your theory about the origin of domesticated wheat in Egypt is utter nonsense. Simon, would you please show your uncle the images we prepared.'

Simon clicked the mouse to display the required pictures on his laptop and slid the machine sideways so that Evers could see. 'What you are looking at,' Hermione continued, 'is a reference photograph from a most reputable international seed bank. It shows grains of emmer wheat, the species you have been claiming to be of alien origin, together with grains from the wild parent species. Can you please tell me which is which?'

Surprised at being asked to contribute, Evers spluttered wordlessly.

'Perhaps the differences are more obvious in Miss Rowe's drawings.' Hermione signalled Sally to pass copies of her work around the table and Simon revealed them on the laptop.

As his gaze flitted between the screen and the paper copy which he had snatched from Theo's hand, Evers furrowed his brow. 'They're pretty much the same. Are you trying to trick me?' he snarled.

'That was unfair of me,' Hermione continued with a sad smile which could have been seen as condescending. 'Of course you cannot tell the grains apart because you have no botanical background, but I can assure you that to trained eyes there is a great deal of difference. Many scientists have produced vast studies on the origins of the domesticated crop species which account for sixty per cent of the world's edible plants. This work is absolutely vital to humankind. When we become too dependent on a single strain of a single species huge problems can occur. A new disease or a mutated fungus can devastate a crop – you only have to consider the consequences of potato blight in Ireland. But the domestication process breeds out diversity and the loss of diversity means that there is little scope for hybridisation or genetic modification to improve, for instance, immunity to pests or drought tolerance. That is why it is so important to refer to the source plants, the wild ancestors, and that means returning to their centres of origin. Taking coffee as an example, the most important commercial species derive from plants found in Ethiopia but all the plantations worldwide represent a tiny fraction of the diversity which is still to be found in the region where they originated. Studying the wild species allows us to assess the effects of climate change, soil condition, pests, and so on, and to select those traits which might improve or protect the domesticated varieties. But if the wild ancestors have become extinct, or the centre of origin cannot be identified, or the habitat has been destroyed, as with so much of the rainforest, we have to look to older sources. The plant hunters who contributed to botanical reference collections and seed banks are largely anonymous, their names known only to botanists and horticulturalists. I am not being melodramatic when I say that they are the unsung heroes whose dedication has contributed in no small measure to the continuation of our very existence. And the archaeologists who dared to spend time and money excavating and recording settlement sites rather than going after tomb treasures and works of art, they too have expanded the database of species back in time so that the stages in domestication can be recognised and understood. That is where archaeobotany is so important. It is not a dilettante subject. If we are to continue feeding the planet we need to understand where our food plants came from, and that, much as you would like us to believe, is not another world. However, in the light of our recent findings I will concede that there may have been an alien attempt to introduce an enhanced strain of emmer wheat in Egypt.'

Evers started and said, 'You have proof?'

'We think so, yes, but you will be disappointed to know that, as far as we can tell, the attempt failed.'

'But it really happened?' Evers' voice trembled.

'Yes,' Hermione said. 'Please show the next slide, Simon.'

The image on the screen changed to a set of comparative graphs. 'What am I looking at?' Evers asked.

'The graphs represent the chemical analysis of four samples of emmer from Dr Masterson's Nagada dig. What do you notice?'

Evers dug in the pocket of his safari waistcoat to find the glasses which he had never admitted he needed. He peered at the screen and then jabbed his finger at one of the diagrams, saying, 'The peaks on this one are different from the others.'

In spite of herself Hermione was impressed. 'You are right. That sample is higher in calcium and zinc as well as some trace elements like strontium and selenium. That particular combination is unknown in any other grain source on record. In fact, the chemical make-up of this grain is so different from anything we know that we were convinced the laboratory had made a mistake. Then we received the aDNA results from another lab. Next slide please, Simon.'

Hermione paused to allow Evers to study the new set of graphs, then said, 'Here the DNA sequencing also shows anomalies. Three of the samples are remarkably similar but there are significant differences in the fourth. The lab technicians who carried out the analysis actually accused us of presenting them with a sample of a GM crop as a test of their systems. Professor Jameson and I had to engage in very sensitive and diplomatic discussions to persuade them that we had done no such thing. When neither we nor the lab could find a match or even an approximation for this grain in any database, ancient or modern, we were forced to examine other possibilities, unpalatable as that might be. Meanwhile, Professor Jameson had had comparable experiences with the testing of organic remains so I will let him take up the story.'

Theo held up a hand and said, 'As that's quite a lot to take in at one go, I suggest that we break for refreshments and I think this calls for something stronger than tea.' On this cue, Adeline and Sally fetched bottles and glasses from the kitchen and poured wine for everyone regardless of protestations. Simon noticed with amusement that Mac and the Doc took their wine diluted with soda water whereas Uncle Eric downed two glasses of red in quick succession, hardly drawing breath between, and was the only person at the table to refuse the accompanying cheesy biscuits.

Everyone else sipped thoughtfully and in silence while Evers re-examined the images on the laptop and, to Sally's smug satisfaction, stared for a minute or more at her drawings. He pulled a small notebook and pen from another pocket of his capacious waistcoat and jotted down a few key notes. Simon tried to see what his uncle had written but for a big man Evers had minuscule handwriting and closed the notebook after each entry.

Taking a look around at the empty glasses, Professor Jameson cleared his throat and asked, 'Are we ready to proceed?' After a shuffling of chairs and riffling of papers he continued, 'I shall take up Dr Beaumont's trail of evidence. She consulted me over the results of the tests on her grain, particularly the aDNA analysis, because she knew that I had submitted other samples for testing at the same time. We could not understand why a lab which had proved to be reliable in all our other dealings should have suddenly produced nonsensical reports. I established that the scientists there were as troubled by the results as we were. So troubled, in fact, that they agreed to seek independent verification. They also agreed to a very much reduced fee which, since they are a commercial concern, indicated the depth of their bewilderment. While we were waiting for the new analysis I chased up the carbon-14 dating results. The date given for the grain matched those from similar grain samples tested in previous seasons. They all dated the site to somewhere in the fifth or fourth millennium BC, which was what we had predicted. These dates also agreed with the results of tests on the pottery from the same site. Dr Qinn, if you would.' The Prof turned to FAQ to confirm his statement.

'Yes, that's right, Professor,' Flick said. 'All the ceramics from the site over the last five seasons show consistency of fabric and form. The discovery of a kiln the year before last confirmed that pottery was being produced on site and not just being brought in from elsewhere. The dates given by archaeomagnetism were comfortably within the range 4500 to 3500 BC. We'd held off doing thermo-luminescence tests because of the cost but when Prof Jameson sanctioned the analysis as a form of control we got the same results. Most importantly, the pottery we sent for testing came from the same context as Dr Beaumont's grain. There's nothing in the ceramics results that came as a surprise.'

'Thank you, Dr Quinn,' the Prof smiled, 'and that statement in itself is highly significant. Pottery analysis is always considered to be a most useful diagnostic tool in the dating of contexts so we were confident in our understanding of the age of the site. Then I received a most upsetting result on the testing of the wooden box in which the grain was found. Before I go into that in detail I would like Dr Masterson to explain, for the benefit of Mr Evers, what we archaeologists mean by a context.'

Ian, who had been leaning back in a relaxed fashion in his chair, turned to Hermione and winked. Simon was sure they had been holding hands under the table. Maintaining the suspense, Mac opened a file box and made a performance of leafing through the contents to find the sheets he wanted, though Simon knew they were already at the front of the file because he had placed them there himself. 'OK Si, next slide please,' Masterson said.

The image was of a hand-drawn cross-section diagram of an excavated trench, layers and materials identified by a series of cross-hatchings and shadings. 'This is the context diagram of an imaginary trench which I use in my undergraduate introduction to archaeological record-keeping. The most easily recognised contexts are the individual layers, the strata. Since these build up over time the lowest layers are the oldest and finds within a single layer or context are taken to be contemporaneous. If you're lucky, you'll find a coin or some other item which can be dated absolutely to give a date post quam, meaning the earliest certain date possible for the rest of the context. The picture can become more complicated if, for instance, the walls or post holes of a later building cut through older layers, or when tree roots or animal activity disturb the stratigraphy. A rubbish pit is a classic example of how more recent material can come to be found at the same depth as much earlier stuff and so confuse the relative dating of the layers if the contexts have not been properly recorded. For this reason we have to be meticulous in drawing accurate plans and diagrams, numbering and labelling the sections, and completing context sheets.' To illustrate his point, Ian spread out the papers he had selected from the file box and Simon clicked on to the image of a cross-section diagram side by side with one of the associated context sheets that had been completed during the last season at Nagada.

Evers looked intently at the screen and asked, 'I see each context number has the prefix 5N. What's the significance?'

Simon was stunned. Uncle Eric seemed to have taken in everything that Mac had said and had asked a sensible question.

Smiling, Ian replied, 'This is a trench from last season, our fifth at Nagada. Contexts from the previous year are labelled 4N. We have been able to link contexts between seasons. You can see that this pit, 5N/1073, was cut into the occupation layer, 5N/1068, which has been shown to be continuous with context 4N/781, the layer in which we found the kiln mentioned by Dr Quinn. This enables us to date the digging of the pit to the same time as the kiln. Both contexts were sealed by the accumulation of wind-blown sand and natural debris represented by 5N/1065, and that has been carbon-dated, using charcoal inclusions, to the late fifth or early fourth millennium, about 4100 to 3800 BC. This means that the contents of the pit must be older than that.'

'And why are the contents of this pit so important?' Evers asked.

The Prof took up the tale again, 'It was in this pit that Dr Masterson found the wooden box and its contents, which have become the focus of interest.'

'Don't forget the bones,' Pete interjected.

Jameson flashed an indulgent smile at his favourite student. 'I hadn't forgotten, French. You will have your turn. Meanwhile, to return to the box. It's a plain rectangular structure which may have had a flat lid but only parts of the base and two sides remain since it, like much of the pit's contents, had been affected by burning. The small fabric-wrapped bundle of grain was wedged into the corner and stains on the floor of the box indicate that there had been several other similar bundles present when the box was burned. The thickness of the planks used to make the box promised good results from dendrochronology…'

'Tree-ring dating,' Evers interrupted, to show how much he thought he knew.

'Just so,' Jameson continued, unperturbed, 'however the results from the laboratory, a different institution this time, were baffling. They found no match with any of the established tree-ring sequences for that region. Then, when we received the results of the radiocarbon tests, we were even more confused. The date we were given was post-1950, that's AD.' The Prof paused to let that information sink in, then went on, 'The report suggested that the wood was either a modern intrusion, or had been somehow massively contaminated. Since we knew that neither explanation could be true we asked for further clarification. They said the level of radioactive carbon present was typical of a highly industrial, post-nuclear environment. The only ancient scenario that came anywhere close to accounting for the level of contamination was that of a massive volcanic eruption. Dr Beaumont, this is your area of expertise.'

Jameson turned to the vulcanologist but before Theo could speak, Evers turned to him, slapped the table triumphantly and said, 'Thera! I knew it, I was right!'

Theo's sad condescending smile was so much like his sister's that Evers' enthusiasm subsided. 'I'm sorry to disillusion you, Mr Evers,' he said, 'but there is no way that the Thera volcano can be held responsible. Even if the timing wasn't wrong, which it is, assuming the wood used for the box had grown locally, Nagada is much too far from Santorini for the native trees to have absorbed volcanic fall-out to such a dramatic effect. The lab's suggestion was a shot in the dark, they were just as befuddled as we were.'

'But what if the wood wasn't local?' Evers clutched at the one hope Theo had offered.

Prof Jameson replied, 'That was my first thought. The appearance of the wood's grain and the colour, what we could make out of it, at first suggested Lebanon cedar. This was quite exciting as it would have been one of the earliest examples in Egypt of timber being imported from the Levant. But after the dendro results we took a very careful look at the cell structure and we found no match, ancient or modern. This wood is of a tree species unknown to science, one that was grown in an atmosphere very alien to that of ancient Egypt or any other place on Earth. We have come to accept that it is not of this planet.'

'Another glass of wine, Mr Evers?' Adeline enquired.

During the ensuing discussion Sally fetched another bottle and refilled Evers' glass twice. Simon thanked her on his uncle's behalf and was rewarded with an almost friendly smile. Sylvia, sitting to his left, leaned towards him and murmured, 'It seems to be going well so far, don't you think?'

She was overheard by the Prof, returning from a comfort break. He stopped, resting one hand on each of their chairs, and said, 'We've certainly given him a lot to mull over. Do you think your uncle will accept our version of events?'

Though Evers was sitting less than two feet away he heard nothing of this exchange, so engrossed was he in examining a heap of photos, drawings and record sheets. His notebook lay unnoticed on the floor beneath his chair. Simon turned to the Prof and said, 'He looks pretty much convinced already. Is Sylvia going to have her say next?'

Jameson nodded and moved to resume his place on the opposite side of the table. Once seated, he tapped a glass with his pen and said, 'Time is pressing, ladies and gentlemen. We must push on. The finer details of our discussion can be thrashed out at a later date. For now we have a few more strands of investigation to bring together. Dr Perraud, if you would.'

This was the first Simon knew of Sylvia's doctorate. He twisted in his seat to find her grinning from ear to ear. 'You kept that quiet,' he said.

'Not really,' she said, 'you never thought to ask.'

'Dr Perraud?' Jameson repeated.

'I'm sorry, Professor,' Sylvia said. 'Where would you like me to start?'

'Wherever you please.'

'Well, Mr Evers is correct in saying that, throughout history, there have been tales of supernatural beings – we generally call them gods – having appeared on Earth. Many myths relate how these gods shared their knowledge with humankind and bestowed on them all sorts of gifts before returning to their home in the sky. It's not surprising that in our space age some people should identify these superior beings as coming from another planet. Belief that such creatures exist has fuelled the modern imagination – from Jules Verne and H.G. Wells to the new wave of science fiction screen-writers. But when you examine those stories closely you find that most of them can be traced back to some common source and those sources are remarkably similar no matter where or when they originated. The relevant story for us is the Osiris myth cycle, which Mr Evers has applied selectively to justify his claims of alien influence. But like so many myths which have been edited, adjusted and revised, deliberately or otherwise, in the course of word-of-mouth transmission over the millennia, the original source material has become totally obscured. To use the Osiris myths, as retold by Plutarch, to describe the Egypt of the Predynastic era, five thousand or more years earlier, is to fundamentally misunderstand the nature of myth. It would be akin to using the works of Mallory as a guide to finding the Holy Grail – not that this prevents all too many treasure-hunters from trying. However, the persistence of the myths and the fact that certain stories resonate throughout many very different cultures, seems to confirm the existence of a common source. The description of the gods descending from and returning to their heavenly home in pillars of flame or chariots of fire suggests a folk memory of some sort of visitation from the stars. The myths portray the gods, for the most part, in hominid form, but then man in his supreme arrogance has always created his deities in his own image.

'The Egyptians believed their deities generally took human form with flesh of gold, bones of silver and hair of pure lapis lazuli. But unlike many other civilizations, the Greeks for example, they did not have a tradition of god-human liaisons producing semi-divine offspring. Nor did they have the uneasy relationship with their gods shown in other cultures. The gods were not feared but loved as the most honoured members of Egyptian society. They didn't require huge human sacrifices. They demanded no slavish obedience to an arbitrary set of rules. Pharaoh was the earthly successor to a line of kings who claimed their authority as the appointed heirs of Horus and so, ultimately, of

Osiris, the ancient god of agriculture. If such a being ever existed it would have been at a time well before writing had been developed so any 'memory' of him would've survived through oral transmission from generation to generation, like Chinese whispers, and we all know how reliable that form of communication is. But, though the very persistence of the basic story over such a vast timescale argues for there being something in it, that something is likely to be far less than you would have us believe, Mr Evers. Like so many theorists of your sort you haven't allowed for the intelligence of humankind. Why should it have taken outside interference for our ancestors to come up with ingenious solutions to tricky problems? Just because we can't imagine building a pyramid without modern lifting gear and power tools doesn't mean that the ancient Egyptians couldn't have done so. Where there's a will there's a way, as the Giza Pyramids prove. So, if the myths suggest that there were alien visitors and yet the adoption of agriculture and other skills were simply the natural products of the ingenuity and adaptability of our species, where does that leave us?'

'Thank you, Sylvia,' Prof Jameson said with quiet respect. 'As you can see, Mr Evers, we have come around to your way of thinking in as far as being willing to accept that aliens have visited Earth. What we cannot accept is that every advance, every sophistication, every success in human prehistory must be accredited to these aliens. Goodhill, would you like to take up this theme?'

Simon took a deep breath, ignoring his uncle's snort of contempt, and said, 'There's a popular belief, fostered by science fiction, that all the most important extra-terrestrials must be physically very much like us and that they'll have the same needs and imperatives as humans. In terms of how they interact with us, either they'll be so much more advanced than humankind that we're beneath their notice, or they'll see us as vermin to be exterminated. The picture we've built up is one of benevolent, well-meaning beings whose attempt to live on this planet in harmony with humans failed. There must have been some sort of exploratory mission that discovered our planet and took samples of flora and fauna for scientific study. Back on their home-world they used genetic manipulation to make certain food species compatible with their physiology in preparation for a serious colonisation mission. But their society was already so far ahead of Earth's that they were unprepared for life on a primitive planet. In spite of a superficial physical resemblance to humans, the aliens never really fitted in. It's highly likely that they weren't able to fully adjust to Earth's environment. Most of them probably died before a rescue mission could be mounted. All that's left of them is memories and a few archaeological enigmas.'

Evers folded his arms. 'Simon, I'm very disappointed. You are asking me to accept this so-called theory of yours with hardly more supporting evidence than I could have got from one of your trashy Sci-Fi novels. I'll need a lot more convincing before I put my reputation on the line by leaping into publication with this,' he said, his voice oozing contempt.

Before Simon could rise to his own defence, support was offered from a most unlikely direction. 'Well really, Mr Evers,' Sally said in the tone by which her friends knew she was about to deliver a controlled but devastating put-down, 'you are hardly in a position to complain about lack of evidence. Your whole career has been built on fudging facts and pulling the wool over people's eyes. If you had the least bit of understanding of what you've been told today you'd see how much evidence you've already been given. I'm sorry that you don't seem to have the intellectual capacity to deal with it but that doesn't give you the right to dismiss the ideas of others who do. And it's unfair to treat Simon like a schoolchild.'

Pete could not resist punching the air and shouting, 'Yay! Go for it, Sally!' as Flick took Sally's face in her hands and gave her a resounding kiss. Adeline and Sylvia were clapping. Simon sneaked a sideways glance at his uncle who seemed to be paralysed with the shock of this verbal attack. No one at the table heard the front door opening or the footsteps on the stair. No one noticed the figure standing in the doorway waiting for the appropriate moment to make her entrance.

As the applause subsided a distinctive voice said, 'What a jolly meeting this is. Are you having fun? What have I missed?'

Theo stood up to greet his mother with a hug. 'We just got to the good part. We saved you a seat.'

Xanthe Crowther moved around the table to kiss Adeline and her daughter and, to his obvious consternation, her future son-in-law, before taking her place next to Ian, with Eric Evers looking on in speechless horror. Professor Jameson nodded a welcome and said, 'So good to meet you again, Dr Beaumont.'

Evers found his voice, 'Ye gods! Another one!'

'Continue, please, Goodhill,' Jameson said, with an encouraging smile.

'Yes, well, where was I?' Simon mumbled.

'Tell him about the linen,' Sally reminded him.

'Oh, yes. As you may not know, Uncle Eric, my speciality is fibres of vegetable origin. I've been looking at the fabric in which the grain sample was enclosed.' Simon clicked on to a new image on the laptop. 'On the left is a magnified image of the weave, on the right are SEM images of fibres from the two sorts of thread it contains, warp at the top, weft below.'

'SEM?' Evers enquired in spite of himself.

'Scanning Electron Microscope. We managed to get some time on a machine in the Medical School. Anyway, the results are pretty spectacular as you can see.'

'Explain,' Evers grunted.

'Well,' Simon continued, 'the weft has the appearance of flax fibres, with clearly defined horizontal bands, but the warp fibres are absolutely smooth and incredibly regular. At first I thought they might be silk but when I saw the SEM images I knew they were artificial, perhaps extruded like polyester. In cross-section you can see they're perfectly cylindrical which doesn't occur in nature, and there was no way that the Egyptians at Nagada would have had the means of making them. The chemical analysis confirmed my suspicions.' He loaded another image. 'These graphs compare the Nagada samples with modern examples of man-made fibres. The opinion of the lab was that the Nagada threads don't match anything on file but the closest they could get was to describe the material as silicaceous glass fibres. The carbon-14 tests on the vegetable fibres gave the same results as Professor Jameson described for the wood, post-1950. For a moment it looked as if we had a possible hoax on our hands, a modern mixed-fibre material like a poly-cotton being passed off as ancient cloth. But then we tested the threads of the cord tying the pouch.' Simon pulled up a photo of the thicker string twisted from several threads. 'From the very first images this looked different. It's indisputably linen and the C-14 test confirmed a date of between 4400 and 3750 BC, much the same as the grain inside the pouch. The only explanation we have for this anomaly is that, for whatever reason, a sample of grain grown at Nagada from seed genetically modified on and imported from an alien world was put into a pouch made from cloth of extra-terrestrial origin, then tied with a cord made from locally-grown linen. I'm not willing to speculate as to why this was done. Making up stories around the facts, that's your area of expertise, Uncle Eric.'

Before Evers could come up with a riposte, Professor Jameson stepped in, 'Time is now against us. I think we must give French his moment.' He gave Pete the nod.

Pete shuffled a few papers and then launched into his presentation, 'The Prof asked me to look at the human remains tests, such as they were, while he was chasing up the other results. You may not be aware that the Egyptian Antiquities Authorities don't allow archaeologists to remove finds of human remains from the country so any tests have to be first approved by them and then carried out in Egyptian facilities, which are nowhere near as reliable or as efficient as ours. By themselves the results from the tests on a thigh bone found in the same trench as the box were inconclusive to the point of being nonsense but in the light of all the other tests we've just heard about, a pattern was emerging. By comparison with other skeletal remains found at Nagada the bone's more robust than a normal human femur. This might be expected of a being from a planet with a gravity higher than Earth's. It shows signs of osteoporosis, which is a feature of long exposure to reduced gravity, as experienced by astronauts who spend months at a time on the ISS. Photos taken with a variety of light sources reveal a silvery sheen on the bone's surface, a feature which Sally spotted on the grain and Si has seen on the vegetable fibres of his cloth. Chemical analysis shows the calcium-zinc balance is very different from human bone and the levels of metallic trace elements are all higher than we'd expect. The oxygen and strontium isotope tests were inconclusive but then I'm not sure they were done properly if at all, so I can't even give a suggested place of origin, though, of course, if that's extra-terrestrial the strontium levels wouldn't match any location on Earth. I took as close a look as I could, using the photos, at the end of the bone to study its articulatory surfaces. Superficially it is a hominid but I'm pretty certain this bone is not human.'

Hearing this fact voiced for the first time in front of an outsider brought home to Simon just how momentous their discoveries were. Now Uncle Eric had access to this information the world of archaeology would never be the same again. Professor Jameson cleared his throat and said, 'I must say that I can confirm French's opinion. I was, at first, understandably sceptical, but rumours of such anomalies have been circulating for many years. I started to chase up some of those rumours, discreetly of course, and I have been astounded at how much more evidence there is already in support of our theories.'

'I think this is where I can add my contribution,' Xanthe Crowther interjected smoothly. Jameson beamed with relief that he was not yet expected to reveal his sources.

Xanthe continued, 'I was brought up within an elite circle of distinguished classicists and archaeologists, my father's colleagues and professional contemporaries. I acted as my father's amanuensis in his later years, putting his papers in order and transcribing his diaries. Consequently I have access to all his archaeological findings including some of the anomalous material which the Professor has got wind of. These were discoveries which did not make sense at the time of excavation and so were never published but virtually every archaeologist had stories to tell and since archaeologists are a gossipy lot these things became the stuff of legend. They were explained away with all manner of excuses – modern intrusions, contamination, bad record-keeping, deliberate hoax – but they were talked about in whispers around expedition camp-fires and at conferences, in the evenings, when alcohol had loosened tongues. It's only when you examine all such evidence from the sources over a considerable period that patterns begin to emerge. Even I didn't see them while Dad was still alive. It was only when Professor Jameson called that I began to put two and two together.'

Xanthe nodded at Jameson, who said, 'Yes, that's right. Everything began to fall into place when we started thinking, as the modern phrase has it, outside the box.'

'Well?' Evers snapped with exasperation. 'Are you going to get to the point any time soon?'

Sensing that they were losing Evers' goodwill, the Prof said, 'Perhaps we should summarise to speed things along. I've prepared an outline list. Next slide please, Goodhill.'

Simon knocked his elbow on the table as he grabbed for the mouse. He had not yet seen this evidence. While Evers peered at the screen, Jameson circulated paper copies of the list which everyone submitted to intense scrutiny. The silence was punctuated by gasps and sighs and a soft, 'Holy shit!' from Pete.

Masterson was the first to break the spell. 'We've identified eight sites where some of our anomalies are also present and two or three more where there's sufficient doubt to justify further investigation. And the archaeology in every case is pretty reliable, given the age of some of these cases. There's even the possibility of retesting some of the finds using modern techniques, assuming they've been stored properly. There's massive scope here for further study if we can get the original excavators on side.'

Simon recognised a name on the list with a surprised squeak. 'Lamoine!'

'I'm afraid Pierre Lamoine is beyond our reach,' Xanthe said. 'He died last year.'

'Yes, sorry,' Simon blushed. 'I've just remembered something. I came across a footnote in one of his last reports on the Iraq dig. Something about a metallic sheen he'd noticed on textile fragments. He tried to identify it as silk but he wasn't happy about it because he couldn't reconcile the early date. I wonder if his original notes are still available.'

'Lamoine's work is being carried on by his daughter, Aure, though the dig you're talking about was more than 25 years ago. I'm sure we can pick her brains,' Ian confirmed.

'Sounds like something worth following up, Pete said. 'Would they have been allowed to bring out bones?'

'Later,' Jameson chided. 'We are confusing our guest with too much detail.'

Evers looked more than confused. He was not sufficiently familiar with archaeological etiquette to be able to join up the dots suggested by the exchange. For the first time, Simon felt sorry for his uncle. Presented with the biggest discovery of his career, Evers had no idea how he could use it.

Theo seemed sympathetic to Evers' situation. 'I know it's a lot to take in,' he said. 'I'm not an archaeologist and I can't see the full picture but these people are offering you the chance of a lifetime. If you'll accept their help and guidance you could be the one to bring this to the world. But without their support and cooperation you will be a laughing stock. It's up to you.'

'But I still don't see…' Evers stammered.

'Will you explain, Mother?' Theo sighed.

'Mr Evers,' Xanthe crooned, 'the examples before you are all genuine, verifiable archaeological discoveries by well-respected scholars and scientists. Their material has far more authority than any you have used in your previous works, except perhaps my daughter's. They range from my father's work on an early agrarian site in southern Italy, just after World War II, through a proto-city site in Iraq, excavated by Lamoine's team before the Gulf War, to more recent work on a Neolithic tell on the Danube floodplain in Bulgaria, a lakeside settlement in Switzerland and one of the first rice-growing communities on the Yangtse River. You will need our help with the appropriate contacts to access this material and bring it all together, because none of the archaeologists concerned will talk to you directly.'

'Why not?' Evers bridled.

'To be blunt, because they have no respect for you.'

'But I've written best-selling books which have made a hell of a lot of money.'

'So have I,' Xanthe reminded him, 'but monetary gain will cut no ice with true scientists. Your form of writing has almost the same amount of factual content as my novels which, if we are keeping score, have sold considerably more copies than yours. You need the backing of legitimate scholarship and you will have to acknowledge the contributions of others if you are to restore those flagging sales. You need us more than we need you.'

Professor Jameson allowed that message to sink in before saying, 'There is much for us all to absorb from this afternoon's revelations. I think we should adjourn for now. Whether we meet again is up to you, Mr Evers. You know where we are. But I advise you to make a decision quickly. By asking around my colleagues I have raised a lot of interest in this matter and there's nothing to stop any one of them going into print before you.'

*

Watching the flame put to the fire, Ast finally let the tears fall. She had been surprised to find Wsir's koram-wood box in the hut where her male friends had been incarcerated overnight. It had been amongst the possessions swept up by Swty when he ordered the evacuation of Abdw. The contents had been rifled and anything of practical use had been removed. All that remained of her mate's personal effects were the grain sample pouches and they were not worth keeping now. Ast had agreed with Djhwty that there was no point in taking much away with them if they were to persuade the Experiment Directors that a return visit to Geb was out of the question.

'I appreciate all Wsir tried to do,' the archivist had said, 'but if we are to keep our story simple we must leave such evidence behind us. I destroyed my calendar notes and star maps before we came here. Khnm has burned his records of the river's height, and Skhmt has destroyed her medical journal.'

'I know it makes sense,' Ast had admitted, 'it's just so hard to let him go.'

'You have better memories than this.'

Djhwty had removed the wooden labels from the grain pouches and thrown them into the river. The box was tossed into an abandoned grain storage pit along with other unwanted belongings and accumulated rubbish including broken pots, straw hats and fans, linen rags and cordage. The remnants of the pit's reed matting lining were scraped out and piled over the remaining evidence of the Bau's presence at First and a burning torch applied. This simple act of finality brought tears to many Ba eyes.

Har came to stand by his mother's side. 'This is a good thing,' he said, 'Father would understand.'

Ast turned to her son, 'What about Skr?'

Har's hesitation was enough to make Ast gasp. 'What has he done?' She had no need to explain which 'he' she meant.

'Swty ordered the body buried last night while you were locked up.'

'With respect?'

'Skr's body has been buried. That is all you need to know.'

She knew he was right. The truth would only add more pain to their parting.

The bonfire collapsed in a cloud of sparks which drifted in the light morning breeze. The on-looking humans started to throw sand and earth into the pit to smother the embers before the fire could spread.

'Time to go,' Har said softly.

Chapter 16: Loose Ends

Ast beckoned to Nebt to follow her to their cabin. 'Close the door,' she murmured.

Nebt checked that no one had followed them from the assembly area then palmed the plate to shut and lock the door. Ast waved her hand over the desk to activate the computer before dropping the data crystal into the reader. 'The Commander slipped this to me in passing. It is the initial report which has been forwarded to the Directors. She thought we ought to know what has been said about us. Do you want to hear it or shall we just read it from the screen?'

'Let us read it,' Nebt said. 'I would not want it to be overheard.'

Ast thumbed her identity into the computer pad and the text of the report appeared on the optisonic screen.

Initial report of the survey ship *Star Searcher* to the Directors of the New Home Experiment on the recovery of Experiment personnel from the planet hereafter referred to as Geb.

White settlement areas in the lower hemisphere had been marked with short-range location beacons which were to be automatically activated at the end of the Experiment period. On making planetary orbit a general sweep scan was initiated and amethyst beacon signals were detected. Plans were made for energy and life-sign scans of all zones and landings at each site, if possible, to recover survivors and remove the beacons. Repeated aerial passes by a scout ship were to be carried out if landing was deemed too dangerous. The findings of the recovery party are given below in the order of inspection.

Site crimson: Riverine site with substantial communities supported by primitive crop-growing and herding of small mammals. No Ba life-signs were registered in the vicinity and the message capsule in the beacon was blank. The reaction of the Geb natives indicated their recognition of and antipathy towards Bau. This settlement must be assumed to have failed with the loss of the whole team. Ba losses: yellow-by-white.

Ast paused the playback and sighed, *'That was Ywti's zone.'*

'And we will never know what happened or even how long they held out,' Nebt added.

'I fear they did not last long,' Ast said. *'If they had survived for even a short time, no matter what the opposition, surely they would have been able to record a message on the beacon.'*

'Perhaps they had so much to think about that they forgot it. We did,' Nebt reminded her.

Ast thumbed the computer pad to resume the reading of the report.

Site red: Riverine/estuarial site with well-established urban settlements supported by relatively sophisticated agriculture. A hierarchical social structure is already apparent in some nascent cities. The message capsule was recovered from the beacon and awaits decryption. A single Ba survivor, Nki, was found in extremely poor physical and mental condition and unable to communicate anything relating to the fate of the rest of his team. Nki died shortly after return to the *Star Searcher*. An autopsy revealed severe malnutrition, muscle wasting and osteoporosis as well as early-stage skin cancer. Ba losses: blue-on-tawny-by-white.

A tear trickled down Nebt's cheek. Ast sniffed and wiped her nose, saying, *'Poor Nki. I think he could not bring himself to remember let alone tell of Tiamt's murder. He recognised me when I visited him in the sick bay and he clasped my hand so tightly. I tried to reassure him but there was little I could say with medical staff all around. I sent him a promise that I would say nothing if that was what he wanted and he nodded. I asked who had recorded the message and if there was anything on it that I needed to worry about. He put a finger to his chest and sent the single word "no". I think the Directors are going to be very disappointed when that message is decrypted.'*

Nebt brushed away her tears and said, *'It is better that way, for all of us.'*

They turned their attention back to the screen.

Site tawny: Riverine/coastal site with hilltop settlements supported by hunting and primitive mixed agriculture. Early signs of substantial defensive structures suggest serious inter-community rivalries. Natives are likely to have been wary if not actively confrontational to the arrival of our settlers. The message capsule was recovered from the beacon and awaits decryption. A ground scan revealed a burial site from which green Ba bodies were recovered but there was no indication of who was responsible for the burials. A wider scan was initiated but no further evidence of Ba presence in this zone was found. The bodies were subsequently identified by comparison with genetic samples on record. The deaths were estimated to have occurred at least three Geb-years ago. The degree of decomposition of soft tissues has not allowed cause of death to be established but skeletal changes are in keeping with those exhibited by Nki. The dead Bau were: Astrt, team leader; Tmwz, agriculturalist and Astrt's mate; Baal, team hunter; Nnrta, team physician; Qdsh, security team member. Ba losses: crimson-on-yellow-by-white.

'No wonder we never heard from Astrt,' Nebt sighed. 'It is so sad not to know what happened to them.'

'The message capsule may reveal more about their deaths,' Ast warned. 'We have to assume that others of their team saw to their burial and those Bau would also have left a message at the beacon. We will not know until we get home.'

'Whatever the message reveals it is not likely to tell the Directors anything about us because Astrt and her companions died before the news of Wsir's death could have reached them.'

'Let us hope the Bau who left the message were as circumspect as Nki,' Ast said, tapping the computer pad to advance the report.

Site yellow: Large island site in the central sea with coastal settlements dependent on the herding of small mammals and simple arable agriculture. The beacon had been removed from its original position and crude attempts had been made to destroy it. The housing had been repeatedly hammered by or against a heavy object, traces of its heat-resistant surface being found on stones nearby. As a result of the broken antenna the signal emitted by the beacon had been weakened and the power source compromised. Consequently it is not expected that anything useful will be recovered from the message capsule. Ba losses: green-on-tawny-by white.

'This is so depressing,' Nebt said. *'Rhia, Minws, Gya, all gone.'*

'Remember,' Ast advised, *'there is the possibility that some survived even though the scout ship's scans found no trace of them. They could have moved away from their original site as we did. Perhaps they do not want to be found.'*

'You do not believe that, do you?' Nebt asked in a sad, quiet voice.

'No.'

Site green: Riverine site with open village communities supported by the cultivation of cereal crops and animal husbandry. The initial scan of the beacon detected several Ba life-signs in the vicinity. On landing, yellow-on-crimson-by-white Bau were found waiting for recovery. Medical scans have shown that the survivors are suffering in various degrees from malnutrition, muscle weakness, especially in the lower limbs, and osteoporosis. Most survivors present with skin lesions and parasitic infestation and some show evidence of healed or partly healed minor injuries. Treatments for these physical conditions have been started and the patients are responding well but all the survivors are mentally fragile and will require specialist counselling which the *Star Searcher's* medical crew are not qualified to give. Interrogation is deemed inappropriate at this time and the survivors have not volunteered any information about the fate of their missing team members who include the leader, Wsir, and his brother and Deputy, Swty. The remaining settlers, who have become firmly bonded by their shared experiences, are being allowed time to recuperate in an area apart from the ship's crew. Ba losses: cobalt-on-red-by-white.

'Well,' Ast sighed again, *'it appears we have been given time to collect our thoughts...'*

'*...and consolidate our story,*' Nebt finished.

'*Yes, there are bound to be many questions about how we managed to come through this experience alive when so many others did not. We cannot betray our friends by admitting that more of us survived but that some chose not to return. What concerns me most is that no one must mention our sons. I am unfamiliar with counselling practices and I cannot say how intrusive the questioning will be, nor how much of it will be telepathic.*'

'*Skhmt would know,*' Nebt suggested. '*We should ask her to prepare us.*'

'*That is a good idea. At least our medical examination will not have revealed that we have had children.*'

'*I do not think the medics will have considered that possibility. They cannot imagine any Ba going against the spirit of the Experiment's Charter so the question will probably never arise.*'

'*Let us hope so.*'

Site blue: River plain site with timber and mudbrick settlements supported by stock-breeding and some crop-growing. The distribution of stone tools and pottery provided strong evidence for trade links along the rivers so it was expected that the settlers could have dispersed in different directions away from the original landing site. The beacon had activated but no message had been recorded and there were no detectable Ba life-signs within green-by-white arur of the beacon's location. Ba losses: purple-on-tawny-by-white.

'*Jwmla and Twni are resourceful. I hope they and some of their friends have made new lives for themselves on Geb.*' But even as she said this Nebt knew that all her colleagues had perished.

'*So do I,*' Ast said with little certainty in her voice.

Site cobalt: Inland plateau site at the extremity of a broad peninsula extending into the middle sea. The natives live in ditched homesteads and some cave dwellings. These communities are supported by mixed farming. The beacon had not been not activated because its automatic function had been disabled. This must have been by the action of Bau. No Ba life-signs were detected in the vicinity but buried next to the beacon was a pottery sherd on which a message in Ba characters and a crude map had been scratched. Message reads: 'Survivors seeking sanctuary on sacred isle.' It was signed by the team leader Krns. On his own initiative the scout ship's captain made a sweep of the area where several large islands extend in a rough chain from the peninsula to the opposite coast. He was able to identify the island mentioned by comparing the rudimentary map with survey images and charts. Scanners registered no Ba life-signs but indicated several subterranean complexes cut into the bedrock with megalithic superstructures. It is possible that Bau were hidden there, shielded by the solid rock, but landing was considered too hazardous. There is no way of saying how many of the settlement team may still be alive. None was recovered. Ba losses: amethyst-on-tawny-by-white.

'Is it possible, could Dna have survived?' Ast asked, remembering their training days when Dna was still expecting to be Wsir's Deputy.

'Anything is possible. Dna is strong and Krns is a capable leader. If he got them away to a place of safety there is every chance that they too will live out their days on Geb. Let us hope that they can make contact with our friends in Kem.'

'If they made their escape across the sea that means they have access to transport which could take them to the far continent. They could be within sending *range of Geb even now.'*

'Oh I do so hope that is true!'

Site amethyst: A lakeside settlement supported by hunting, some herding and foraging of wild plants. The beacon had not been activated. When investigated it was found to have been deliberately smashed with stone implements. Traces of Ba blood were found on the beacon housing. The sample taken for genetic comparison was identified as that of team Deputy Dgda. No Ba life-signs were detected and no message of any sort was found. Ba losses: yellow-by-white.

'The story is becoming sadly repetitive,' Nebt observed. 'How is it that we were so fortunate?'

'The people of Kem are clearly exceptional. It was purely the luck of the draw that sent us to their zone.'

Site purple: Riverine site with communal housing built largely of wood and other plant materials. Society supported by semi-nomadic herding and primitive crop-growing in cleared forest areas. A message capsule was recovered but proved to be blank. No Ba life-signs were detected. Ba losses: cobalt-on-tawny-by-white.

'Is that all?' Nebt asked with amazement.

'Wsir told me that this particular site was almost left off the list of Experimental settlements. But with other zones already abandoned the Directors could not afford to lose another. Too many people would have been disappointed,' Ast said.

'So instead they died.' The sadness in Nebt's tone was overlain with anger. *'So many Bau were set an impossible task by others who completely underestimated the difficulties and dangers of the mission. What lesson will the Directors learn from this report?'*

'They will learn nothing that we do not tell them. The consequences of their failure to recognise those dangers are written on our bodies. We will have to insist on making our own reports so that the truth of the depth of that failure is known.'

'Yes,' Nebt sighed, *'we cannot allow others to throw away their lives in such a useless manner.'*

Site white: Coastal site with communal wooden housing and some megalithic structures. Society supported by maritime activities, notably fishing, stock-breeding and simple agriculture. The beacon had not been activated. When investigated there was no sign of the beacon and no message of any sort. A wider scan revealed blue Ba life-signs scattered over a wide area but all were extremely weak. By the time a repeat scan was instigated no Ba life-signs registered. Examination of the life-sign energy signatures suggests that team leader Wdin was among the last survivors. Ba losses: blue-on-tawny-by-white.

'Fish!' Ast spluttered. 'I smell that horrible odour at the very mention of the word. How could they be expected to survive in a fishing community?'

'The surveyors did a very poor job of the aquatics. We nutritionists discussed this in depth and Tiamt was particularly forthright in her warnings. It seems that, having found a sentient species so similar in appearance to the Bau, the Directors made too many assumptions about the similarities between human and Ba metabolism.'

'And put too much faith in our ability to provide for ourselves in such a short time,' Ast continued. 'For all his ambitious plans, in his heart Wsir knew that there was never any prospect of his attempts at viticulture succeeding but he would have stood a chance with the cereal crops if only he had been given the right information. So much time wasted, so many hopes dashed.'

'How sad that Wdin survived so long only to fade at the moment of his rescue,' Nebt wiped a tear on the sleeve of her shipsuit. 'So many lives lost. So many friends left behind.'

Ast reached out a hand and Nebt clasped it with a fierceness that surprised both of them. They would never be able to put into words their deep sense of loss and they knew they could never have open conversations about their experiences but they could share their thoughts and memories and so keep alive those colleagues, friends, lovers and children lost forever. Ast brushed her own tears away with the back of her hand. 'They cannot be allowed to put Bau in such jeopardy ever again.'

'You think they would try to repeat the Experiment?' Nebt gasped.

'I believe they would. I have been considering their motives and I think their main objective was to find a cheap way to provide colonies. Terraforming is far too expensive and takes too long, so they tried using a planet which is an approximate analogue of Perbau. But the match was nowhere near good enough and I doubt that any better match will ever be found. We must convince them that the Experiment was ill-conceived from the start.'

'But what is the alternative? There is already severe overcrowding in our cities.'

'They will have to accept that the domed communities of our first colonies are the only way to go if Ba civilization is to survive. That is the message we must spread when we return to Perbau. When we get home we must see to it that no Ba ever sets foot on that planet again.'

Nebt looked up and gazed intently into Ast's eyes. The amber irises, free at last of the black lenses, seemed to glow, lighting up her pale face from sockets deepened and darkened by deprivation and sadness. Nebt read her own recent history in her sister's sunken cheeks and dull, brittle hair and every livid sun-blemish on her dry skin. Geb had left its mark on their bodies as well as in their hearts. Were they still Bau?

'When we get home,' she repeated, *'but where is home?'*

*

Simon raised his head from the desk as Pete's hefty push against the troublesome catch caused the door to slam back into the filing cabinet. 'Come in!' he said, with less sarcasm than he intended, before lowering his head on to his arms again.

'It's my office too, remember,' Pete moaned, dropping his jacket over the waste bin. He pulled up a chair and took his place at the second desk placed back-to-back with Simon's to save space in the miniscule room. Then he, too, dropped his head on to his folded arms muttering, 'Boy, can those cricketers drink!'

'Tell me about it,' Simon's muffled voice was full of self-pity.

Several minutes passed before they sat up together saying, 'Coffee?'

It was more than a year since Theatre A had been revamped and renamed Acorns. The seats were more comfortable, though there were fewer of them, and the décor less stark, and despite price rises in keeping with the improvements, it was still their refuge of choice. Sylvia had anticipated their arrival and had saved places for them at their favourite corner table. 'Oh dear, boys,' she laughed, 'did you have a busy weekend?'

Neither Simon nor Pete felt capable of a coherent response until at least half a mug of black coffee had been consumed. Sylvia watched with amusement until she could wait no longer, 'Well, how did the stag do go?'

'Bloody cricketers!' Pete groaned.

Simon said, 'That Jamie chap, Mac's Best Man, he must have a bladder the size of a space hopper.'

'Have you seen Hermione this morning?' Sylvia asked. 'She was expecting a report.'

'Oh no,' Simon said, wincing at the loudness of his own voice, 'that's not part of the deal. We made sure Ian didn't get hijacked and sent off to Iceland or somewhere.'

'And we stopped them tying him to a lamppost in the nuddy,' Pete added.

'Yes, and we made sure he got home. We went in the taxi with him and saw him safely inside.'

'Tucked him up with his teddy bear,' Pete confirmed.

Simon chuckled, 'But what happened before that is boys' business and the Doc doesn't need to know.'

'I think she was more worried about who might have gate-crashed the party,' Sylvia said primly.

'Well she needn't worry,' Simon sighed. 'Apparently we threw Uncle Eric a googlie, to use a phrase I learned last night but still don't understand.'

'Think it's the cricketing equivalent of the off-side rule,' Pete added.

'So, what happened?' Sylvia's patience was wearing thin.

'Yeah, well,' Pete went on, 'he was led to believe that Mac was a Yorkshire supporter so we think he went to Leeds.'

'Uncle Eric was last seen heading for Headingley,' Simon began to giggle and Pete joined in until their laughter was too much for their aching heads and they had to pause for more coffee.

'That man hasn't changed as much as we might have hoped,' Sylvia observed. 'He's still trying to find ways of wheedling himself into our company. When will he realise that he's not welcome?'

'Ever since the TV company insisted that he shared screen time with his collaborators he's had no option,' Simon hiccupped. 'He didn't expect Ian and the Doc to steal the show.'

'But at least he knows which side his bread's buttered,' Sylvia smiled. 'He would never have got the two films on the screen in such a short time if it hadn't been for all their support and their contacts. The fact that all the academics took nominal fees for their appearances also made it a relatively cheap documentary to make. For once he had to publicly acknowledge his sources and he couldn't be seen to be making a profit out of them so his income from the programmes is much less than he's used to. Now he's got to keep in with them for the sake of the book because that's where the real money will be. He can't afford to annoy any of them. He'd never have been offered a follow-up series if it hadn't been for them. It's only a shame his people skills haven't been improved by all the exposure to normal human beings. I'm just glad he hasn't realised that he's indirectly responsible for bringing together one of the greatest collections of archaeological expertise ever.'

'And don't forget Theo and Aure,' Pete smirked.

'Oh yes,' Sylvia beamed, 'none of us saw that coming!'

'She's great,' Simon said, 'she's given us access to some fantastic stuff from her father's digs. The fabrics are amazing.'

'And the bones,' Pete was almost drooling. 'Aure's given us enough material to keep Prof Jameson going well into retirement. Theo'll have to watch out that the Prof doesn't monopolise Aure's time. I'd never have guessed the old guy was a sucker for a pretty face.'

'Don't be so disrespectful,' Sylvia gave his cheek a meaningful pinch.

'Ow!'

Simon nearly choked on his coffee and had to wipe his face on a napkin before pointing at the librarian, saying, 'And what about you? I've heard about your so-called editorial meetings with Uncle Eric and his publisher.'

For the first time ever, Sylvia was lost for words and Simon could swear her skin darkened with the glow of embarrassment. 'Ha!' he said in triumph, 'I was right!'

Pete looked shocked, 'Please tell me Sylvia is not going to become your auntie.'

'Oh, for heaven's sake!' Sylvia snapped. 'Give me credit for a little more sense.'

'No,' Simon ignored Sylvia's retort, 'it's Alex, Uncle Eric's literary agent. I met him last week and I think he's smitten. Sylvia was all he wanted to talk about.'

'A man of immaculate taste,' Pete said with a straight face.

Sylvia reached over and patted the cheek she had so recently abused. 'There's a nice boy,' she purred. 'For that you deserve another coffee and a bun.'

Simon and Pete watched in awe as Sylvia marched to the head of the queue at the servery, senior academics ceding their places with cheerful smiles and polite greetings.

'That's celebrity for you,' Pete said. 'We'd never've been allowed to jump the queue like that.'

Simon nodded, 'The University's done well out of the TV exposure and Sylvia ticks a lot of boxes as far as equality and diversity are concerned. That's one of the reasons the producers were so glad to have her on screen.'

'Cynic! Don't let her hear that!'

'Wouldn't dream of it.'

Sylvia returned with the coffees and a plate of iced buns and custard tarts.

'Thanks, Sylv, you're a real star,' Simon said, planting a kiss on the librarian's cheek.

Having made substantial inroads into the sticky treats, Pete asked, 'Anyway, when's the book launch?'

'In a couple of weeks, if all goes to plan.'

'A best-seller would be a great wedding present,' Simon commented. 'Is that possible?'

'I don't think there's any doubt, going by the pre-orders and, considering the number of contributors, it's gone smoothly so far. I'm keeping fingers crossed that there's no last minute hitch. The audience's appetite has been whetted by the films and the production company have already drawn up a schedule of promotional events including radio and TV interviews so they can't afford to miss the publication date. They also have an eye on the Christmas market.'

'Uncle Eric's a bit put out. The publisher's had loads of requests for interviews but they all want one of the professionals,' Simon said, 'and all the publisher can offer is Eric Evers. Ian and the Doc could make their fortune on the chat show circuit, if they wanted to.'

'Well, that's not going to happen,' Sylvia said, 'not with the wedding and everything.'

'No, but it's surprising how many of the specialists are queuing up for their moment in the spotlight. I'd never have believed it if I hadn't seen and heard it for myself. The list of collaborators reads like a *Who's Who?* of archaeological nobility, and all brought together through Xanthe. She's been terrific.'

'Certainly a force of nature,' Sylvia chuckled.

'She seems to have an eidetic memory,' Pete enthused. 'She made the Maltese connection and knew exactly where to find the info in her father's papers. Reopening the mystery of the missing Hal Saflieni skeletons has the archaeological fraternity buzzing again. Archaeologists are falling over each other to get involved.'

'And not just archaeologists,' Sylvia added. 'Adeline's been in contact with some astronomers who want to identify the alien home-world.'

'Miss Phillips?' Simon was amazed.

'Yes, she's thrilled to be involved, even if it means having to act as a go-between for that man. Did you know he's actually had tea with her twice?'

'Wow!' Pete was impressed. 'Does he realise how honoured he is?'

'Not if I know my Uncle Eric,' Simon laughed.

*

Hermione lifted the satin-lined lid from the box and unfolded the silk. Nestling in the shimmering white fabric was a coronet of delicate gold filigree work representing vine leaves and tendrils threading through ears of wheat. 'Oh, Mum, it's beautiful, thank you.' she breathed, and with tears welling in both their eyes, she hugged Xanthe. Then she turned to Sally, whose eyes were also shining, and hugged her too. 'Thank you, thank you!'

'So, we did justice to Sally's design?' her mother asked.

'It's perfect.'

'Good. I was almost expecting you to complain about the expense.'

'I would never be so churlish,' Hermione sniffed. 'Besides, it covers the something gold and something new all in one spectacular item.'

'Ah, I'm glad you reminded me.' Xanthe took a second jeweller's box from her bag, 'Here's something blue and borrowed. Nonna asked me to give it to you.'

The box was old, its maroon leather cover slightly battered. Inside Hermione found a simple gold chain from which was suspended a small oval pendant of lapis lazuli, the rich blue stone sparkling with golden flecks. 'Grandpa gave this to Nonna on their wedding day,' Hermione said as tears spilled down her cheeks.

'Yes. Nonna lent it to me and Aspasia on our wedding days, and your cousin Melina wore it too when she was married. Grandpa found it on one of his first digs, in the days when archaeologists were allowed to keep some of their finds. The stone is Roman, probably a ring bezel, but the gold setting and chain are modern, well 1930s anyway, but that's modern in archaeological terms. Will it do?' Xanthe asked.

'Oh yes, of course it will,' and Hermione hugged her mother again.

Sally cleared her throat, not wanting to admit to uncharacteristic sentimentality, and said, 'I'll make the tea.'

Just then Miss Phillips appeared in the sitting room doorway. 'Look who I found at the front door.' She stepped aside to let in FAQ and Sylvia.

Flick held up two bottles of champagne, saying, 'We can do better than tea. Let's get the party started before this warms up. Where are the glasses?'

Sylvia put down a tray of food and said, 'There's more downstairs in Adeline's kitchen.'

The first bottle was emptied by the time Hermione had modelled her wedding jewellery to be admired by all. The second was somewhat soaked up by the crudités, canapés and quiches. Xanthe found two more in the fridge to accompany the strawberries and rum-and-raisin ice-cream.

'This is very civilised for a hen party,' Miss Phillips observed from the comfortable armchair where she was still nursing her first glass of champagne.

Xanthe, sharing the sofa with Sylvia, said, 'You've got the right idea, Adeline. Champagne of this quality is not for getting drunk. It needs to be savoured.'

Sylvia agreed, saying, 'It is very good with the strawberries,' before hiccupping.

'Bubbles!' Sally giggled from her position on the hearth rug, leaning against Flick.

'I hope it's true about champagne not leaving one hung over,' Sylvia said. 'I wouldn't want to wake up tomorrow like the boys did after Ian's stag weekend.'

'Oh, do tell,' Xanthe grinned. 'Did my future son-in-law disgrace himself?'

'No, Mother, he didn't,' Hermione defended her fiancé. 'In fact, he was back at work on the Monday afternoon and perfectly coherent when the news came through from Egypt.'

'What news?' Xanthe asked.

'You can tell her, Felicity,' Hermione's expression was smugness personified.

FAQ shifted her position to lean against the sofa allowing Sally's head to slide into her lap. 'We heard from Abdul. The Egyptian authorities were quite unprepared for the publicity generated by the TV series. Now they see the opportunities it's opened up for archaeology in other countries they're bitterly regretting refusing to cooperate with the producers. They've asked if the University would reconsider the abandonment of the Nagada concession.'

'That's rich,' Sylvia snapped, 'when they withdrew it in the first place.'

'Whatever the wording, the message is the same. Ian's team has been invited back and there's a promise of much better security and access to all sorts of expertise in terms of conservation and analysis. They've even offered to replace the equipment that was stolen and rebuild the dig house.'

'Has he accepted the invitation?' Miss Phillips asked.

'In principle, but he's holding out for a properly drawn-up and legally binding agreement, particularly as far as publication rights are concerned. He's also hoping to get it made a joint expedition with Aure's institution. Of course, there's no way of knowing what state the site is in after two years. There may be nothing left worth digging, so Ian's asked for an alternative site in case Nagada's out of the question. He's got his eyes on a Predynastic settlement at Abydos but the Egyptian authorities were never known for their sense of urgency. There's no way we'll be back in Egypt before the New Year at the very earliest and who knows how the political situation might change before then. Meanwhile we just have to get on with what we've got.'

'Tell them about what you've found, Flick,' Sally said, her voice drowsy with champagne.

'Have you found something new?' Adeline asked.

'Possibly,' FAQ drawled. 'I was studying a pottery storage vessel from the box trench. It's nothing spectacular, it's not even very well made, but although it had been smashed, most of the shards were recovered so I was using it as a demonstration of reconstruction.'

'Don't tease them,' Sally admonished her partner.

'OK. I found finger prints,' Flick said.

Her statement was met by puzzled silence then Sylvia said, 'You mean the potter's finger prints?'

Felicity smiled, 'Yes, though that's not unusual. I almost ignored them but something made me have a closer look with a magnifier and that's when I realised how clear they were and how different they were.'

'You mean, alien finger prints? Ooh, how exciting!' Xanthe crooned.

'I've had them studied by forensic experts and police specialists. They all say they've never seen anything like them.'

'It's a good job you made this discovery after the great reveal. They wouldn't have given you the time of day before we went public,' Sally muttered.

'I think this calls for another drink,' Xanthe announced.

'It had better be coffee,' Hermione said, 'We have the lunch with Ian's parents tomorrow, remember.'

*

Hermione turned slowly in front of the mirrored wardrobe door. The soft drapes of the chiton-inspired dress shimmered, the warm ivory colour of the silk high-lighted by the glint of gold from the bee-shaped sleeve fastenings. The cord gathering the fullness at her waist was the same antique golden tone as the bride's simple sandals. She twitched the gold-embroidered stola on her shoulder being careful not to dislodge the filigree coronet which, set against her dark hair, completed the Greek look. As the final touch, Xanthe fastened the lapis pendant at Hermione's throat and stood back to take a long look at her daughter. 'There. You look lovely. Nonna and Grandpa would be so pleased.'

Hermione gazed at her reflection as if seeing herself for the first time. She had never taken much interest in fashion. To her mind clothes had to be practical, wearable and durable. But even she had to admit that the feel of the silken fabric against her skin was almost sensuous, a thought which, to her surprise, did not cause her a moment's embarrassment. She assessed her appearance with critical approval. The change to rimless spectacles had been her first concession to vanity, though she could still not bring herself to try contact lenses. Allowing her hair to grow longer had enhanced its natural wave. The make-up artist who had prepared her for her first publicity shoot had given her the confidence to experiment with foundation, blusher and eye shadow, but only for special occasions, like today.

There was a knock at the door and Adeline asked, 'Can I come in?'

'Of course,' Xanthe and Hermione responded in unison.

'Anthony says the car is just …..' Miss Phillips paused as she saw Hermione in her wedding finery, then fumbled in her handbag for a tissue and discreetly wiped away a tear, saying, 'How silly of me.'

Xanthe reached out to take Adeline's hand. 'Not at all, dear. Have you got a spare tissue for me?' she sniffed.

'Oh for goodness' sake, Mother, you'll get me crying too and I haven't got time to redo the make-up,' Hermione teased.

'She's so beautiful,' Adeline observed.

'Yes, isn't she?' Xanthe agreed. 'I'm terribly proud.'

'Well,' Adeline continued, 'I've brought something else for you both to be proud of,' and she took a newspaper Arts supplement from under her arm. It was already folded back to show the literary section. Miss Phillips pointed to the Best-Sellers chart at the bottom of the page, 'See the double entry?'

The first position in the Fiction category read, '*Island of Darkness*: the final volume in the *Thera Trilogy*, by Xanthe Crowther'. Heading the General list was, '*Seeking Osiris*: where archaeology meets science fiction, by Eric Evers, H.P. Beaumont and Ian Masterson'. Both books were labelled as having gone straight to number one in the first week of their publication.

'Congratulations, Mother,' Hermione smiled.

'And to you, though I never thought to see the names Beaumont and Evers on the same by-line,' Xanthe said.

'I see you're still trying to maintain your anonymity, hiding behind your initials,' Miss Phillips remarked.

Xanthe looked surprised, 'For some reason she's always been a bit sensitive about her name,'

'And you wonder why?' Adeline laughed, patting Hermione's cheek, 'Poor darling!'

'It's all right,' Hermione assured her, 'having lived with it for thirty-six years now, I'm sort of used to it.'

'She does seem to be remarkably composed considering she's just about to have her name announced to the world by the registrar,' Xanthe mused. 'You should have seen her before her graduation, a bag of nerves at the very thought of having to own up to her name. And always insisting on using her initials so no one knows if she's male or female. But look at her now, as cool as a cucumber. Not the typical nervous bride.'

'I am still here, you know,' Hermione said. 'Listen, Mother, I've had plenty of time to get used to the idea and if I can stand up to Eric Evers then I can face anything. What's in a name, after all?'

Afterword

My two passions are Egyptology and science fiction. I have wallowed in both from time to time and finding a way to combine the two has been immensely satisfying. In recent years, a lot has been written about the origins of the Egyptian civilization, much of it sensational and highly imaginative. It seems that everyone has a theory about how or why the Pyramids were built, and by whom. Why is it that the ancient Egyptians cannot be given credit for their own ingenuity? And why is it that all alien visitors are assumed to be superior beings bent on the domination if not the total annihilation of the human race?

One science fiction device that has always worried me, when I stop to think about it, is that all aliens are essentially humanoid and virtually indistinguishable in their habits and biological make-up from human beings. As a mathematician, I know how improbable this idea is but, like all science fiction fans, I'm willing to suspend that disbelief for the sake of a good story. It is also extremely unlikely that any other planet in the galaxy has the same length of day or year as Earth, and yet I am expected to believe that all space travellers, humans and aliens, reckon time in hours and talk of distances in light-years, a measure based on the period of rotation of our insignificant planet about the Sun. My premise is that when extra-terrestrials visited us in the distant past they found the differences between Earth and their home-world overwhelming and they were forced to admit that humans were better suited to Earth's environment than they could ever be.

Archaeologists are always turning up bewildering artefacts which may never be properly understood but technological developments have enabled much more information to be extracted from some of the most mundane discoveries. The methods involved in analysing these finds have led archaeologists to embrace new scientific disciplines so that the subject is now so much more than the treasure hunting activity pursued by the likes of Lara Croft and Indiana Jones. I may have somewhat simplified the science and contracted the timeline in terms of achieving publication but this is fiction so I invoke author's artistic license.

This is the story I didn't know I wanted to write. I do not apologise for leaving some things unsaid and some puzzles unresolved. That is the joy of the written word – readers are left to create their own images and to fill in the gaps between the lines. Please feel free to do so.

Printed in Great Britain
by Amazon.co.uk, Ltd.,
Marston Gate.